Praise for

Wicked Fantasy

"If you need a good laugh, then gra[b] ... filled with surprise twists and turns a ... forward to finding out what trouble the ... next."

—*... Eternal Night*

"A sensational read full of humor and romance. You'll be burning through the pages while you follow . . . all the hijinx and scorching sex. *Wicked Fantasy* is a great read, and I enjoyed every minute of it. Nina Bangs has created a story with outrageous and hilarious characters and a romance that will make you wish for your own fantasy at the Castle. It goes on my bookshelf as a keeper. Enjoy!" —*Night Owl Reviews*

Wicked Pleasure

"Wicked fun from start to finish . . . [A] side-splitting, sexy tale that dazzles and delights." —*The Best Reviews*

"Another terrific Nina Bangs humorous action-packed paranormal romance . . . Readers will enjoy this wicked tale."

—*Midwest Book Review*

"A delightful comedy." —*The Eternal Night*

Wicked Nights

"Paranormal romance filled with humor and sex . . . and with the right touch of suspense . . . Action-packed. Readers will enjoy this wicked tale and look forward to novels starring Eric's siblings, a demon and an immortal warrior, that will surely sparkle with fun." —*Midwest Book Review*

"Intriguing." —*The Eternal Night*

continued . . .

. . . and the novels of
Nina Bangs

"Sinfully delicious." —Christina Dodd

"The key to Ms. Bangs's clever . . . novels is the cast never does what the reader expects. [She] combines vampires, time travel, and . . . amusing romance that will lead the audience to read it in one enchanting bite."
—*Midwest Book Review*

"Bangs puts a . . . darkly brooding hero together with a stubborn heroine; adds an amusing cast of secondary characters . . . and then mixes in several different paranormal elements and equal measures of passion and humor to create . . . [a] wonderfully creative, utterly unique romance." —*Booklist*

"A witty, charming, sexy read." —Christine Feehan

"Sensuous and funny . . . [A] true winner." —*RT Book Reviews*

"A sizzling story . . . With steamy love scenes and touching characters, Ms. Bangs brings readers into her world and sends them away well satisfied with the power of love." —Karen Steele

"I know I can always count on Nina Bangs for an exceptional read! A pure stroke of genius." —*The Best Reviews*

Berkley Sensation titles by Nina Bangs

WICKED NIGHTS
WICKED PLEASURE
WICKED FANTASY
WICKED EDGE
WICKED WHISPERS

Anthologies

MEN AT WORK
(with Janelle Denison and MaryJanice Davidson)
SURF'S UP
(with Janelle Denison and MaryJanice Davidson)

eSpecials

"Color Me Wicked" from MEN AT WORK
"Hot Summer Bites" from SURF'S UP

Wicked Whispers

Nina Bangs

BERKLEY SENSATION, NEW YORK

THE BERKLEY PUBLISHING GROUP
Published by the Penguin Group
Penguin Group (USA) Inc.
375 Hudson Street, New York, New York 10014, USA

Penguin Group (Canada), 90 Eglinton Avenue East, Suite 700, Toronto, Ontario M4P 2Y3, Canada
(a division of Pearson Penguin Canada Inc.) • Penguin Books Ltd., 80 Strand, London WC2R 0RL,
England • Penguin Group Ireland, 25 St. Stephen's Green, Dublin 2, Ireland (a division of Penguin
Books Ltd.) • Penguin Group (Australia), 250 Camberwell Road, Camberwell, Victoria 3124, Australia
(a division of Pearson Australia Group Pty. Ltd.) • Penguin Books India Pvt. Ltd., 11 Community
Centre, Panchsheel Park, New Delhi—110 017, India • Penguin Group (NZ), 67 Apollo Drive,
Rosedale, Auckland 0632, New Zealand (a division of Pearson New Zealand Ltd.) • Penguin Books
(South Africa) (Pty.) Ltd., 24 Sturdee Avenue, Rosebank, Johannesburg 2196, South Africa

Penguin Books Ltd., Registered Offices: 80 Strand, London WC2R 0RL, England

This book is an original publication of The Berkley Publishing Group.

PUBLISHING HISTORY
Berkley Sensation trade paperback edition / October 2012

Library of Congress Cataloging-in-Publication Data

Bangs, Nina.
Wicked whispers / Nina Bangs.—Berkley Sensation trade paperback ed.
p. cm.
ISBN 978-0-425-25313-7
1. Demonology—Fiction. 2. Fairies—Fiction. 3. Imaginary places—Fiction. 4. Imaginary wars
and battles—Fiction. 5. Immortality—Fiction. I. Title.
PS3602.A636W55 2012   2012025601
813'.6—dc22

PRINTED IN THE UNITED STATES OF AMERICA

10 9 8 7 6 5 4 3 2 1

To Dianne Byrd.
Thanks for suggesting such a wonderful title.
Love it!

1

The music pressed against the inside of his skull, a melodic migraine pounding out a deadly rhythm in his head. Murmur resisted the urge to just let go, to free his songs, to stop their ice-pick notes from jabbing at him. Pain-free seemed like a good place to be.

He clenched his teeth against the agony. "I need to do a pressure release before my head explodes. I don't think vacuuming up demon brains is part of the maid's job description." Even pacing this hotel room would work off some of the tension buzzing in his brain, but moving hurt too much, so he simply sat as still as he could in the chair facing Bain.

"Control it. If not, they'll kick you out of the castle, and I need your help." Bain leaned back in his chair and watched his friend from hooded eyes.

Murmur took a deep breath. "I *never* lose control. So to keep my record intact, I'll have to take my show on the road. Where can I go to defuse?" The castle/hotel might specialize in fantasy role-playing, but Murmur didn't think they were ready for what he'd deliver.

Music was his power, but it was also his weakness. If he kept it captive for too long, the pain crippled him. And at some point it might even drive him crazy. What the world did *not* need was a mad music demon.

Bain shrugged. "It's late, so I'd try the beach. No one there to hear you. But if some of your music does creep back into the castle, no big deal. Remember, I saw you in action here a few weeks ago. You pissed me off with that compulsion you laid on everyone, but we all danced and had a good time. No harm." He shrugged. "And sure, you were a little scary in the final showdown with Ted, but all demons ramp up the terror." His grin promised he could take scary to a whole new level. "It's what makes us beloved by all."

No harm because I stopped the dance in time. But I didn't want to stop it. I wanted it to go on and on and on . . . Murmur knew his smile was bitter. He winced. Damn, even that small use of facial muscles upped the agony. "Don't be an ass, Bain. You know what would happen if I lost control, so don't act as if it's nothing." He stood and walked slowly to the door, each tortured step sending new vibrations rattling around inside his aching head.

"Fine. Do your thing." Bain's tone said he still didn't get it. He glanced at Murmur's music system. "This is a pretty fancy setup for just a hotel stay. Maybe you should turn it on and relax with some mellow tunes instead of dragging yourself to the beach."

"I have a 'fancy setup' because I *need* the music." He and the other demon had been friends for millennia, but that didn't mean they knew squat about each other. Demons weren't social creatures, and being friends simply meant they didn't try to tear each other apart when they met. All right, so Bain and he were a little closer than that, but Bain had only experienced Murmur's music on a small scale. He'd never really seen what happened when Murmur got serious.

Bain heaved an exaggerated sigh and rose to follow him. "Then

I'll leave you to your midnight concert. I'm due for my last fantasy performance of the night in about ten minutes. Give a shout if you need me." He paused before heading for the winding stairs leading down to the great hall. "And thanks for sticking around. I appreciate it." Then he was gone.

Coming from a demon, Bain's words were the same as a big hug and a sloppy kiss from a human. Demons didn't display emotions. Most of the time, they didn't have any to display. Okay, so maybe there were occasional outbursts of rage leading to mass destruction. But that was about the limit to their softer feelings.

Murmur took the elevator. No way would he survive the explosion of pain as each foot landed on those stone steps. From there he staggered out of the castle, his hands over his ears, trying to block all those human voices adding to the din in his head.

He stumbled across Seawall Boulevard and down the steps leading to the beach. This was all Bain's fault. The other demon had asked Murmur to help with some as-yet-to-be-explained plot. That had been a few weeks ago. Since then Murmur had been stuck on Galveston Island, unable to find a place far enough away from people to free his music.

Sure, he could've abandoned Bain. But Bain was a friend. His *only* friend. And wasn't it pathetic that Murmur actually cared? Not a positive demonic character trait. He'd have to shore up his I-don't-give-a-damn wall of indifference.

Right now, though, he needed to stop the pain. When he'd put some distance between himself and the Castle of Dark Dreams, he glanced around. Not far enough away from humanity to cut loose completely, but he could at least siphon off some of his music and relieve the agony for a while.

A moonless night, but there was some light filtering down from the streetlights across the road. No one on the beach. That's all he had to know. The pain was almost to the point of exploding from him. That would be a bad thing for everyone in Galveston *and* for him. He wasn't ready to leave the castle yet.

Drawing in a deep breath, he allowed his music to escape in a slow, controlled flow of sound. It mirrored his mood of the moment— dissatisfied, confused, and even a little sad. Murmur let the intertwined melodies build to a crescendo of angry frustration. Why the hell was he feeling these emotions now after so many thousands of years?

He closed his eyes at the remembered bliss of times long past. Times when he released the fury of his songs on entire villages, watching as everyone within the sound of his music died screaming. Or, if he was in a more playful mood, they'd die dancing, unable to stop until their puny human hearts gave out.

Murmur hadn't done that in a long time. He wasn't ready to examine the reason why.

Ivy stepped onto the beach and wandered toward the waterline, where gentle waves lapped at the sand. The Gulf was quiet tonight. The lights from the street didn't do much to help her see where she was going. Symbolic? Maybe. Because three days ago she'd made the first impulsive decision of her adult life.

She'd taken a job at Live the Fantasy, an adult theme park where people could unpack their dreams of being more than they were, dust them off, and play the part for a half hour. Tomorrow she'd meet her boss for the first time. Ivy glanced back at the castle. Still time to run.

Before she could begin to obsess about the insanity of accepting a job as the personal assistant to someone named Sparkle Stardust, she heard the music.

It came from everywhere and nowhere. The melody wrapped

around her, tendrils of compulsion that seeped into her soul and made her—she widened her eyes—want to dance.

Ivy didn't dance. Ever. She had no rhythm. But she was okay with that. Dancing didn't further her life's goal—a solid, well-paying job so she could build her own white picket fence around a home in suburbia. She'd never depend on a man to do her picket-fence building.

But suddenly, for no apparent reason, she wanted to dance, *had* to dance. Without her permission, her feet began to move with the throbbing beat. Closing her eyes, she let it happen. If she really concentrated, she could almost hear words—of futility, frustration, *need*.

Ivy realized she was dancing farther and farther away from the castle, but she didn't seem to care. All that mattered was the music. Its bass pounded out an ever-more-frenetic message of anger and so much need that brought tears to her eyes. She swirled and leaped on waves of emotion, even as the Gulf's waves curled around her ankles before retreating.

The person she'd always been—logical, grounded in reality—screamed, "What the hell are you doing?" But nothing mattered. Everything she was floated away on the compulsive rhythm urging her to dance and dance and dance . . .

And then she saw him. He stood in the darkness, waiting as she danced closer and closer. At first he was only a shadow among many shadows. But as she drew nearer she saw him more clearly. Tall, elegant, with broad shoulders and a body that she imagined would be powerful and lean-muscled beneath his black boots, black pants, and what looked like a black silk shirt, open at the throat. All that unrelieved black only served to lead her gaze upward to . . .

Her heart was a frantic drumbeat, her breathing a harsh rasp in her throat, and it had nothing to do with exertion.

His face. She gathered all of her willpower and forced her body to still while she studied him from only a few feet away, too close for safety.

Shining blond hair fell in a smooth curtain to halfway down his back. He watched her from eyes framed by thick lashes. She couldn't see the color of those eyes in the darkness. The angles and planes of his face cast shadows highlighting male beauty that seemed impossible, but obviously wasn't. Her gaze drifted to his lips, full and so tempting that . . .

He smiled. Ivy felt that smile as an ache that started in her chest but moved rapidly south. This was *not* good. She glanced away and tried to recapture her sanity along with her breath. "I wonder where that music is coming from."

He ignored her comment. "Dance with me." His voice—husky, compelling, but with a harsh rasp of some emotion she couldn't identify—hinted that unspeakable pleasures awaited anyone who danced with him.

No. She didn't dance with strangers she met on the beach. It absolutely wasn't going to happen. "Sure."

And so they danced. Together. Touching. Not what she thought she'd ever enjoy, because with his arms around her she'd have to follow his lead. Ivy knew from experience that she couldn't match her steps with a partner, not in any aspect of her life. But she did.

It was like floating. She swayed in time with her silent partner as he swept her into the dance. Everything seemed more intense, more . . . everything. The sand felt deliciously cool beneath her bare feet. When had she kicked off her shoes? The water sparkled. There was no moon, so how could it sparkle? When she tipped her head back to allow her hair to float in the sudden breeze, she saw a sky filled with millions of glittering stars. Not real, *couldn't* be real. But the impossibility of all those stars didn't bother her. Only the man and the dance mattered.

He'd pulled her close, and she felt the realness of him as surely as if he wore nothing—the hard planes of his body, the pounding of his heart where her head rested against his chest. And when he cupped her bottom to tuck her between his thighs, she had proof that the dance was affecting him in the same way it was her.

Desire clenched low in her stomach. Shock made her miss a step. She drew in a deep, calming breath and tried to recapture the magic of the dance. But she couldn't. This wasn't her. Ivy didn't go around wanting to throw men to the ground and then ride them until a screaming orgasm shattered her. She pulled away, and it was the hardest thing she'd ever done.

The music stopped. Ivy just stood there breathing hard. Exertion or hyperventilating? Didn't matter, the result was the same. She felt lightheaded.

"Thank you." His words were cool, his tone distant. He turned and disappeared into the darkness.

Ivy stood staring at the water that no longer sparkled. When her dizziness finally passed, she found her shoes, and then walked slowly back to the Castle of Dark Dreams. Aptly named, as it turned out. If anyone qualified as a dark dream, her unknown dance partner did.

She felt strange, all shiny and new, *younger*. But that was impossible. Ivy was twenty-seven, and a brief dance with a stranger shouldn't make her feel nineteen again. Go figure.

She decided to wait until she got back to her room before thinking about what had just happened. There was always a logical explanation for everything. *Except when there wasn't.* Ivy pressed her lips together. Of course there was an explanation. She just had to find it.

Ivy paused before entering the castle. For a moment, she thought about going around to the great hall entrance and taking a look at the ongoing fantasy. No, she didn't need another shot of make-believe after what she'd experienced on the beach.

Was he staying at the castle? Would she run into him again? Ivy narrowed her eyes as she strode through the door leading into the hotel lobby. He didn't matter. What did matter was her new job. She needed to concentrate on that.

She stepped into the elevator still wrapped in thoughts of what tomorrow's meeting with Sparkle Stardust would bring. Someone stepped in with her. Ivy dragged her thoughts away from her new job long enough to notice the man sharing the elevator.

She blinked. He was short and squat with dark hair that stuck out everywhere and looked like steel wool. He had a nose that seemed to swallow his face, and his wrinkled skin was the color and texture of a walnut shell. He stared at her from beneath bushy brows the same color as his eyes. Black. Did anyone really have shiny black eyes? He didn't look friendly. She prayed the elevator door would open and spit her out onto her floor.

"You took my job, human." His voice was a dark, threatening rumble.

Human? Ivy stared gape-mouthed at him. "Your job?"

The elevator door slid open. But shock rooted Ivy in place.

"I would have made a better assistant than you. What do you know about the needs of a person of power?" On that contemptuous snarl, he stepped from the car and the doors silently closed behind him.

Okay, that was just bizarre. Ivy took a deep fortifying breath before pressing the button to open the door again. She stepped out. Thank God, the strange—and yes, disturbing—man was gone. He must have a room on her floor, though. That made her uneasy.

Trying to shake off the encounter, she unlocked her door and stepped inside. She sighed her relief as she turned on the light. And froze.

Her room was crawling with spiders. Thousands of them. Big, fat, ugly spiders. They crawled over her bed, up her walls, and across the ceiling. They watched her from gleaming eyes that oozed malice.

Another woman might have screamed and run. Ivy just muttered a few curses as she strode to the phone on her night table. She didn't see any black widows or brown recluses, so nothing too dangerous. What truly scared her was the thought that someone had purposely done this. She swept spiders from the receiver before making her call, even as she mentally chanted her personal mantra: *no fear, no fear, no fear.* Then she went back to stand at the open door and wait.

She tried not to think, to conjecture, to *panic*. Ivy had built her entire life on the premise that any problem could be solved if approached in a calm and rational way. There was always a logical explanation for things. Okay, so the man on the beach was an anomaly.

At least she didn't have long to wait and stew. She heard steps behind her and turned.

A wizard? Would the weirdness never end? He was about the same height as her, and she wasn't tall. Thin, gray-haired with a matching long, pointed beard, his narrowed gray eyes promised that she'd be sorry if she'd brought him here on a fool's errand.

She scoped him out from head to toe and thought of the spiders to keep from chuckling. He was a walking stereotype. His gold-trimmed blue robe was decorated with glittering suns, moons, and stars. He wore a matching tall conical hat. It added almost a foot to his height. And he carried a strange-looking staff.

"Holgarth, I presume?" It had better be, since that's who she'd demanded to see when she'd called the desk. Ivy moved aside so he could step into the room. "Unless you intend to beat them to death with your staff, I'd suggest you call in the exterminators."

He pursed his thin lips, his cold stare saying that she wasn't amusing him. Ivy decided that not much *would* amuse this guy.

"How unfortunate." He sounded as though a plague of spiders was nothing more than a minor irritation. "I'll get rid of them, and then you can—"

"Uh, no, to the rest of what you were going to say. I mean, you can certainly get rid of them, but I won't be here to see the miraculous event. I want another room and . . ." She thought about the man in the elevator. "And I want one on a different floor."

Holgarth sniffed. "Hired help used to know their places."

Ivy widened her eyes. "Oh, I absolutely know my place. It's in a new room not infested with spiders." Was she trying to get fired? Maybe. All the weirdness that had happened so far didn't bode well for her new job. "*You're* the one who hired me. I'd think you'd want me to be happy."

"I did *not* hire you." He seemed bitter about that. "I wanted someone more tractable, but Sparkle insisted that you were right for the job."

"Tractable? Does anyone even use that word in everyday speech? Well, if wanting a room where I won't wake up every ten minutes imagining spiders two-stepping across my face makes me intractable, then so be it. I want out of here."

He pressed his lips into a thin line of disapproval. "Come with me."

She frowned as another thought surfaced. "I never spoke with Ms. Stardust, so how did she know I was right for the job?"

For the first time he looked as though he approved of something she'd said. "Exactly the point I tried to make." He glanced at his watch. "Enough useless chatter. My time is valuable."

"What about my things?" She moved into the hall and stopped to wait for him.

"Someone will bring them to you." He lingered in the doorway, mumbling something to himself.

And just before he joined her, closing the door behind him, Ivy got a peek into the room. The spiders were gone. She blocked the sight from her mind. The unexplainable was piling up at an alarming rate, and her brain couldn't handle it all at once.

Holgarth led her down the winding stone steps. "I prefer to avoid the elevator. It performs in an erratic manner when I use it."

Hey, Ivy understood completely. She'd probably perform in an erratic manner too if she spent much time around him.

He didn't stop when they reached the great hall, but took another flight of stairs down. Pulling out a bunch of keys on a large ring, he used one to open a door. "Your new room, madam." He didn't try to hide his sneer.

Ivy had a few questions. "There aren't any windows on this level. And the sign over that door across from me says Dungeon. Why am I on the dungeon level?"

Holgarth raised one brow. "You're not on the dungeon level. You're on the vampire level. The dungeon just happens to be here. We use it in our fantasies." He paused for effect. "Except when we're using it to hold a recalcitrant creature."

She glared at him. "Now you're just being annoying. Fairy tales don't scare me. You didn't answer my question. Why am I here?"

His lips twitched. She had a feeling this was Holgarth's version of a belly laugh.

"A fairy tale? Yes, the fae sometimes visit us. But we haven't had to incarcerate one yet." He looked thoughtful. "They would present some unique difficulties." Then he widened his eyes. "Oh, but you asked about this room. The hotel is full right now. You could, of course, return to your old room." He looked hopeful.

He'd like that. Ivy prided herself on being even-tempered, but Holgarth totally ticked her off. "Fine. I'll stay here." Not waiting for his reply, she walked into the room and shut the door in his face. Then she leaned against it and closed her eyes.

Finally, she sighed and walked over to one of the chairs in the small sitting area. The big four-poster bed called to her, but if she gave in she'd be out as soon as her head hit the pillow. She had to stay awake until someone delivered her clothes.

She tried not to think. Attempting to figure things out when she was so tired wouldn't work. Tomorrow morning, when her mind wasn't a mushy banana, would be time enough to think about the weirdness.

Instead, she studied the room—dark period furniture, a stone floor covered with what looked like oriental rugs, and jewel-toned tapestries on the wall. Hello, Texas gothic. The only thing missing was an open window with sheer curtains blowing gently in the night breeze and the scent of honeysuckle. Okay, so maybe that was southern gothic.

The knock interrupted her thoughts. She pried herself from the chair and opened the door. Holgarth stood there beside a man loaded down with her things. The wizard watched as the man dumped her clothes on the bed, her shoes on the floor, and everything else on the coffee table in the sitting area.

Love the five-star treatment here. But Ivy didn't voice her thoughts, because she wanted Holgarth to answer a question for her. She waited until the man left.

"I was on the beach tonight, and I heard music. I don't know where it was coming from, but it seemed . . ." What? Tempting, arousing, compelling? "Strange. Then I met a man—tall, long blond hair—and he asked me to dance with him." This was dumb. Holgarth would just make fun of her. "I danced."

She watched Holgarth's face, expecting to see his usual disdainful expression. "Do you know if he's staying in the castle?" Not that Ivy really cared. Okay, maybe she *did* care. A little.

The wizard stared back at her from eyes that gave nothing away. "If you hear the music again, cover your ears. And *never* agree to dance with him." He sounded completely serious.

"Why?" *There's always a rational reason for everything.*

Holgarth's gaze speared her. "Explanations would be useless.

Remember, you don't believe in fairy tales." He turned and walked away.

Well, that was totally unsatisfying. She closed the door and got ready for bed. After searching under her pillow for spiders, she relaxed enough to fall asleep.

And dreamed of the man, the music, and the dance.

2

Murmur knocked on Bain's door. He had to know why Bain wanted him here, and he had to know now. No more bullshit about not having time to explain, that it was a complicated story.

Last night had been a wakeup call. Murmur had thought he was in control, but when he'd flung out the net of his melody and pulled her in—that had been a hell of a surprise—he'd kept her. If the woman's will had been even a little weaker, he would have danced on and on until he'd held only a corpse in his arms.

He paused to think about her. There was something . . . Murmur shook his head. Whatever he sensed about her wasn't important now.

He was glad she still lived, though. The fact he even cared at all was a warning. Time to move on. So either Bain gave Murmur a good reason to stay, or he was out of here tonight.

Bain opened his door. "I have a meeting. Can't talk now."

Murmur raised one brow.

"What?"

"I'm going to this meeting with you, and when you leave the meeting I'll be right there."

Bain raked his fingers through his hair. "Now isn't a good time."

Murmur lost his temper. "I've hung around for weeks. I have places to go, music to play, people to kill." Not really. The longer he spent away from the Underworld, the less compulsion he felt to kill. He used to go back at regular intervals to ramp up the old murderous urges, but as long as he had his music he was okay. "You owe me an explanation. If I don't get it within the next few hours, you'll have to find someone else."

Bain's muttered curse told Murmur what he thought of his friend's ultimatum. "Tag along if you want, but Sparkle probably won't let you in. She's only invited a few of us to meet her new assistant."

Murmur smiled, not one of his nicer smiles. "Then I'll meet her with you." He pointed at Bain and then back at himself. "Attached at the hip, brother."

Bain scowled, but didn't say anything else as they walked to the small conference room beside the castle's restaurant. Murmur could hear voices, so he knew the meeting had started without Bain. Good. Murmur loved making an entrance.

Bain flung the door open and strode to an empty seat at the table without looking at anyone. He pointed over his shoulder at Murmur. "Didn't invite him."

Sparkle's frown eased into a cat-eyeing-canary smile. Not a good sign.

"Murmur, you're always welcome. We think of you as almost . . . family." She didn't even blink as she said it.

Bad, really bad. Murmur thought about backing out of the room, but that would make Bain happy. Right now, Murmur wanted him miserable.

"Thanks. It feels good to have family. Dysfunctional, yes, but still family." He tried to look suitably grateful.

Ganymede's snort said what he thought of the new family member. The cat sat atop a pile of pillows on the chair next to Sparkle.

Murmur scanned the rest of the "family." Holgarth, Edge, Passion, and . . .

Crap. His dancing partner from the night before stared back at him. Her eyes widened. She recognized him. He frowned. This must be Sparkle's new assistant.

"I was just about to introduce Ivy to everyone. Now that I'm taking over a few of the Big Boss's duties, I'll need someone reliable to do the little day-to-day things that I'd normally do." Sparkle studied her nails before raising her gaze to her assistant. She smiled.

Murmur couldn't believe the woman didn't knock over her chair in her rush for the door. That particular smile had made strong men weep and weak men flee. How could the new assistant miss the avid hunter's gleam in Sparkle's eyes? He almost shook his head. She wouldn't last a week. That was good for him.

"This is Ivy Lowe, everyone. Starting a new job is always difficult."

"Some more difficult than others." Murmur thought no one had heard him, but Sparkle cast him a warning glance.

"So I hope you'll all make her feel welcome." Sparkle's expression said that if they didn't, their deaths would be slow and painful. "And I've changed my mind. I think you can each introduce yourself. The personal touch is always better, don't you think?"

Her glance flicked to Murmur and then away. Every hair on Murmur's arms rose. Sparkle had something planned, and that never boded well for anyone. Then his attention switched to Ivy.

Murmur watched her watch the others. Medium-length dark hair. Ordinary style. Brown eyes. Ordinary shade. Good lips. Not spectacular. The usual makeup. Nothing edgy about her. This woman didn't look like a risk-taker, didn't seem like someone who could accept the truth about the castle. He felt a moment of sympathy. Only a moment. Murmur wasn't kind. The kind died young in his reality.

"Murmur, it's your turn." Sparkle leaned forward, anticipation alive in the tapping of one bloodred nail on the table.

He started. What had everyone else said? They damn well hadn't told the truth or else Ivy wouldn't still be sitting there, her unblinking gaze fixed on him. She offered him a tentative smile, and he made a decision.

He'd do her a favor worth more than she'd ever realize. He'd tell her the truth. The sooner she left the Castle of Dark Dreams, the faster she could return to the ordinary world where she so obviously belonged.

He smiled, the smile he saved for special occasions, meant to terrify and intimidate. "I'm a demon of music, Ivy. I kill with my tunes." He stopped smiling. "Meet me on the beach tonight and we'll dance some more."

"Delightful." Holgarth sniffed. "Now we'll be subjected to a fit of hysteria."

"Oh, shit."

Ganymede's voice in Murmur's head wasn't unexpected. A glance at Ivy assured him that the cat spoke only to him.

"Gotta give it to you, demon: you have balls. Sparkle will eat you alive for spoiling her plans." Ganymede raised one gray paw to wash his face. *"Thought about leaving you guys to watch* Top Chef, *but this'll be more fun. Cooked goose tops chicken marsala every time."*

Ivy paled. "Demon?"

Sparkle reached over to pat her hand. "Murmur's always joking. Ignore him." Her expression said he was a dead demon.

Murmur shrugged. "Believe what you want to believe." He glanced at Bain. "You've met her, now it's time for us to talk."

Bain stood. "Right. Let's get this over with." He glanced at Ivy. "Enjoyed meeting you, Ivy. Don't let Murmur scare you away." He walked from the room.

Murmur followed him. His last view of Ivy was of her shocked expression as Sparkle worked on damage control. It didn't matter what Sparkle said; Ivy would run. The word "demon" had that effect on humans.

He was glad she was leaving. Of course, demons lied, even to themselves. You always had to take that into consideration.

Murmur didn't say anything as he followed the other demon up the winding stone steps, then down the hall to an unfamiliar door. "We're not going back to your room?"

"No." Bain didn't offer any explanation. He knocked.

The man who answered was fae. No faery creatures in the universe were more beautiful or more dangerous than the Sidhe. Long silvery hair, pale blue eyes with a metallic sheen, perfect face, and a heart so cold it would shatter like ice if you tapped it with a fingernail. That about described every one of the Sidhe he'd ever met.

"This is Tirron. Seelie Court." Bain stepped past the faery, and Murmur followed him. "I've already told Tirron about you."

The Seelie Court? Was that supposed to convince Murmur that Tirron was more trustworthy than his evil twins in the Unseelie Court? He'd have to explain to Bain that courts didn't matter to him. He didn't trust any of the Sidhe.

Murmur gave Tirron a noncommittal nod as he chose a chair in the small sitting area. While he waited for Bain and the faery to settle, he hummed. Tirron looked interested. Bain shot Murmur a warning glance. He shut up. No music around the faeries. They enjoyed it too much.

Bain leaned back in his chair. He seemed relaxed, but that didn't fool Murmur. Tension stretched between them.

Murmur decided that Bain must really need him. Interesting. "Whatever it is, let's hear it. I'll either help or I won't. Putting off the telling won't make it easier."

"I lost someone important to me a long time ago." Bain stared straight ahead. "The Sluagh Sidhe took her. Now the faery host is about to enter the mortal plane again. I want her back." He stopped talking.

Murmur frowned. The Sluagh Sidhe. He'd only met them once. They'd impressed the hell out of him—a dark cloud sweeping across the night sky. Close up, he'd seen hundreds of the Sidhe along with countless other fae creatures and the humans they'd taken. They'd steered clear of him that night. Even the Sidhe thought twice about messing with him. He was tempted to ask for details about the person the Sluagh Sidhe had taken, but maybe now wasn't the time. He'd find out more later. "So what's my part in this?"

Tirron answered him. "We need a way to draw the faery host to this place. No faery can resist your music." His expression said: "Even you can figure out the rest, stupid."

Murmur nodded. "Okay, I get it. You need my music as the carrot. So how're you involved?"

"The hunters are all Unseelie. They sweep up everyone in their path." Malice filled Tirron's smile. "Bain wants to retrieve his human toy. And I want the destruction of certain members of the Unseelie badly enough to join forces with two demons. I'll track them and be here to help fight. That is all you need to know." His expression said they could leave now.

Murmur rose and walked to the door. His smile was no smile at all. "Arrogant, aren't you? Perhaps you'd like to dance to my music for a while."

Tirron's already pale face grew a little paler as he quickly closed the door behind them.

Murmur didn't say anything more until they returned to Bain's room. He didn't sit down as Bain sank onto the nearest chair. "Your human toy?"

Bain shrugged. "Tirron is a faery. To him, humans are all playthings—use them and then toss them in the trash when they break. Cold son of a bitch."

Mumur didn't point out that demons weren't known for their warmth and caring either. "I need more details before I commit." A lie. The thought of a good, old-fashioned bloodbath energized him. He needed to wield his music as he once did, with joy and savage glee.

Bain stared past him, and Murmur got the feeling he was somewhere else right now. "I loved a human woman. The Sluagh Sidhe took her on a clear winter's night hundreds of years ago. It was my fault. I left her unprotected." His eyes darkened. Loss and fury along with immense power filled the room, pushing at Murmur.

"You *loved* her?" The Bain he knew didn't love anyone.

Bain met his gaze. "I've only experienced love that once. It will never happen again." His expression hardened. "It hurt. I'm not into pain."

"Do you still love her?" Murmur congratulated himself on never having loved.

"It was a long time ago. Who knows? But even if I don't, the responsibility is mine. I'll free her."

Intriguing. Demons didn't have a strong sense of responsibility. He'd like to meet this woman. "What makes you so sure she'll still be with the hunt?"

"They returned to Faery afterward. Time passes differently there, so she'll still be alive." Bain looked thoughtful. "The Sluagh Sidhe keeps everyone they capture. She'll be with them."

Murmur did some mental number crunching. "Wait, that's impossible. Every hunt gathers up hundreds of victims." He thought about the horde descending on Galveston. Crap. This would be ugly. Then he smiled. He couldn't wait.

But his smile faded. "Why did you wait so long to tell me about this?"

Bain met his gaze. "We have one thing in common with the

Sidhe: favors aren't free. I'll owe you. I was trying to decide if your help was worth it."

His friend's expression signaled an end to the questions. But Murmur asked one more. "Anything else important I need to know?"

Bain started to glance away.

"Amducious."

Bain's attention returned to him. Anger filled his eyes. "Don't use that name here."

Murmur shrugged. "I don't like being ignored, and if using your true name, O mighty Destroyer, gets your attention . . ." He left the rest unsaid.

Bain looked impatient. "Okay, maybe you should also know that I can't just yank someone away from the Sluagh Sidhe without offering up a replacement."

"You're the Destroyer. So why play their game? Just crush the damn faeries."

"Unlike Tirron, I'm not anxious to start a war with Mab. If Tirron wants to take a shot at batting faeries out of the sky, that's his business. I'll cheer him on. But I won't help."

Murmur thought about that. As much as he'd enjoy a battle, he didn't want the queen of the Unseelie Court as an enemy. "Got it. You have someone in mind?"

He nodded. "Ivy. Young, pretty, human, and clueless to the wicked ways of the Sidhe." Bain frowned. "That's if you haven't scared her away."

The thought hit before Murmur could stop it. *He hoped to hell he had.*

Ivy walked down the castle stairs in a daze. When she got to her door, she stopped to lean her forehead against the cool wood. Bizarre was the new black. She'd barely had a chance to absorb Murmur's stunning announcement before Sparkle had handed her a key and her first assignment. Ivy had just finished emptying every freaking complaint box in the castle, and she'd swear there were dozens of them stuffed to overflowing. Sparkle wanted her to read them, put them into some kind of order, and then make a report on her findings. She now clutched the garbage bag filled with small papers while she tried to come to terms with what had happened during the short time she'd been here.

She'd danced with an insane man last night. Sparkle might believe he was only joking about being a demon, but Ivy didn't. She'd sensed that he was deadly serious. The frightening part was that, even though she knew he was crazy, he still took her breath away. What did that say about her?

And her boss was . . . Ivy didn't know how to describe Sparkle Stardust. She was every man's sexual fantasy—tall, beautiful, with long dark red hair, amber eyes, and a full, sensual mouth. Ivy frowned. She had the same amber eyes as her cat. That was just weird.

But there was something beyond Sparkle's beauty and obsession with her nails that bothered Ivy. If she listened to her instincts, she'd go into her room, pack, and leave right now.

That's what Dad would do. He'd bailed on every job he'd ever had. Mom had held the family together for as long as Ivy could remember. And as quickly as that, Ivy made her decision. She lifted her head and rooted around in her pocket for her room key. She would stay. Because she would *never* be her father.

"Why are you still here, human?"

She turned slowly, knowing who she'd see. "Why would I *not* be here?" The man was still squat, and his attitude still needed adjusting. His bushy brows were drawn into a straight line over black eyes filled with rage.

"I sent the spiders."

The weirdness had reached epic proportions and didn't seem about to let up. She could either run screaming from the castle or stay and fight back. If she left now, she'd have to go home and admit she'd quit without working even one day. Mom would look at her with sad eyes that said, "Just like your father."

No. Fear might eventually drive her from the castle, but not at this exact moment, and not because of this creepy guy. "It's never safe to make assumptions. Spiders don't bother me." She shrugged. "Better luck next time." Perhaps goading him wasn't the best approach, but she was too ticked off to care. "By the way, what's your name? I'll need it when I report you to the hotel management."

"As if I would give the power of my name to a mere mortal." He was almost sputtering as he paused for a moment to stare intently at her door before turning and disappearing up the stairs.

Ivy rubbed the spot between her eyes where a headache was forming. Did she believe in magic? Not before arriving at the Castle of Dark Dreams. But she'd seen the spiders, and she'd seen Holgarth make them disappear. If she accepted that as magic, then she had to believe another nasty surprise waited inside for her. All she had to do was climb the stairs to the great hall, find Holgarth, and ask him to go into her room first.

Pride was a terrible thing. She pulled the key from her pocket and opened the door. She held her breath. Nothing.

Limp with relief, she walked in, closed the door, and slumped onto the nearest chair. She dropped the bag of complaints beside her.

Then she saw them. Rats. Lots of them. They scampered from under her bed, sniffing and watching her from beady black eyes.

The little jerk expected *this* to make her quit? There was something he didn't know about her. She was here at this castle of nightmares because she'd lost her pet shop to the crappy economy. She'd worked with rats on a regular basis, and she'd handled more than one tarantula. Rats were intelligent animals. Unlike Mr. Obnoxious and Creepy. If he'd really wanted to terrorize her, all he had to do was wave last month's credit card bill in front of her face.

She didn't move except to pull out her cell phone and call the front desk. Someone had better hurry because she had plans to make.

A few minutes later, the door swung open.

Ivy closed her eyes and then opened them. Yep, Murmur was still there. She sighed. She didn't need the emotional storm he brought with him. Demon or not, he was a scary man. *And sexy. Don't forget sexy.*

"What's the problem?" He scanned the room, his gaze stopping when he reached the rats. "Never mind. I'll get rid of them for you, and then we'll talk about who put them here."

She had no words. What did you say to someone who thought he was a demon? And what did it say about her mental health that the longer she stayed in the castle the more reasonable his claim seemed? Ivy shook her head. No, that was nonsense. He was delusional, and she was . . . She slid her gaze over the long amazing length of him. She was attracted. Horrified, Ivy found her lost voice.

"Don't kill them."

He raised one expressive brow. "Not an expected request from a guest who finds rats in her room."

She met his gaze. "Maybe I'm not your usual guest."

Then he smiled. A real smile. And Ivy forgot all about Creepy Guy and his rat attack.

"Now there's something we can agree on." Then he shifted his attention to the rats.

Ivy was thinking about the power of that smile as he turned to the still-open door, walked across the hallway to the dungeon door and opened it as well. Then he returned to stand beside her chair.

She was picking through her tangled web of confused thoughts when the music began. It was a single finger of haunting melody that circled the room—searching, beckoning. Startled, she realized she wanted to trail after it, discover where it would take her, because she knew that place would be exactly where she'd always wanted to be. Ivy fought the need to stand, to follow.

Murmur placed his hand on her shoulder and she froze. The weight of his hand wasn't a compulsion, but it was heat and pleasure and a suggestion that she'd be more comfortable right here with him touching her.

Then she looked at the rats and forgot about his hand for the moment. They emerged from all the places they'd been hiding in her room—damn, there must be hundreds—and streamed toward the open door. The musical lure drew them across the hall and into the dungeon. When the last one was inside, the dungeon door closed. The music stopped.

"You're the Pied Piper of the Castle of Dark Dreams." Ivy knew she sounded calm, but the words didn't even begin to describe the chaos churning her stomach into nauseating waves and scattering all her preconceived notions of how the world worked.

She might not know if he was a demon, but she was certain now that his music was magic. And that thought segued right into . . . "Last night. The dance. You used magic."

He didn't bother to deny it. "I'll get a wizard down here to send them home."

One word of snark from Holgarth and she'd go ballistic. She'd flatten his pointed hat with her fist.

"Not Holgarth. But it'd be fun to watch you flatten his hat." Murmur's sensual lips lifted, and his eyes gleamed with wicked anticipation.

She didn't keep him waiting long. "How did you know I was thinking . . . ? Wait, were you in my head?"

He shrugged. "I'm a demon. I can be anywhere." He paused for effect. "Even in your bed, if that's what I want."

He was baiting her. And he probably thought she'd rant and deny and then pack and leave. It seemed that's what everyone wanted except for Sparkle. He'd have to live with disappointment, though, because it wasn't happening. She didn't like people pushing or manipulating her. That's about all she'd gotten since she'd arrived at the castle. "I want to talk to this wizard after he's finished with the rats."

She didn't miss the flash of surprise in his eyes. Good. She lived to crush expectations.

He didn't have time to respond before a man came down the stairs and stopped in the doorway. Tall, intense, with ice-blue eyes and dark, tousled hair, he didn't fit the wizard image. Not old enough. No wand, no staff, no wizardy clothes. Just jeans and a T-shirt.

"You interrupted lunch. Where are they?" His voice was heat, smoke, and simmering bad temper.

Murmur ignored him and spoke to Ivy. "This is Zane. Best rat removal service in Galveston. Too bad it comes with a giant helping of surliness."

Okay, she'd try on a big, fake smile and lots of syrupy gratitude for her beautiful but cranky exterminator. "I'm Ivy, and you're a huge improvement over the sarcastic old grouch with the pointy hat." The lie almost embarrassed her. Almost.

"You mean my father?"

Oops. "Umm, I'm sure he isn't always sarcastic and grouchy."

"Trust me, he is."

Murmur nodded at the closed dungeon door. "In there."

Zane moved closer to the dungeon, but he didn't open the door. He just stared the way Creepy Guy had. Thirty seconds later he joined them in Ivy's room. "Gone."

Ivy didn't trust anyone in this place. She stood. "I'll check." She walked past Zane, ignoring his scowl, and peeked into the dungeon. Chains, whips, iron maiden, but no rats. She returned to her seat. No way would she remain standing, an open admission that all their looming was intimidating her.

"Good. Now I have a favor to ask." After seeing his jolly good humor, she didn't hold out much hope that Zane would do anything for her. But at least Murmur would know that his rooting around in her brain had really ticked her off.

"I'm Ivy, Sparkle's new assistant." She cast Murmur a quick glare. He hadn't bothered to even introduce her. "And if I'm going to work here, I'll have to learn how to keep busybodies who need to get a life out of my head." She smiled at Zane and hoped it didn't look as plastic as it felt.

She felt Murmur tense beside her. Zane narrowed his eyes, but at least he didn't reject her outright. Finally, he smiled. And the sun rose over Texas. Wow. There were no halfway measures in the Castle of Dark Dreams. The men were either butt-ugly or gorgeous. She mentally wrote Zane's name in the gorgeous column. She could feel Murmur leaning closer, but she kept her gaze fixed on the smiling wizard.

Zane glanced at Murmur, and his smile widened. "I think I can help you with that. I'll give you a call when I'm free, and we'll see what we can do to slam the door on demons with too much time on their hands." His soft laughter trailed him as he turned and left the room. He closed the door, and they were alone.

Murmur allowed the silence to gather, and Ivy forced herself to remain quiet, to not fidget. Now that Zane had gone, she could feel Murmur's presence filling the room, pressing against her from every side. She was just about to say something, anything, when he spoke.

"I'll find out who put the rats in your room, and then take care of them." He started toward the door.

"I already know who did it." Was that wispy voice hers?

He paused with his hand on the knob, turned, and walked back to stand in front of her. "Who?"

To hell with not admitting she was intimidated. She stood. Gee, that was so much better. Now she was at eye level with his chest. "I don't know, but he wants my job. He thinks if I'm gone he'll have a shot."

No emotion crept into his expression, but Ivy sensed building anger. It was aimed at her. Maybe she shouldn't have spoken to Zane in front of him. She took a deep breath and stiffened her rubbery spine. Too bad if she'd embarrassed him, although his anger didn't feel like embarrassment. He deserved a put-down for creeping into her mind without her permission.

"He wouldn't tell me his name."

Murmur nodded as though that made sense. "What does he look like?" Each word was clipped, cut short by his obvious rage.

She resisted the urge to step back. "Shorter than me, dark hair that sticks out everywhere, huge nose, black eyes, and really wrinkled skin. Oh, and he keeps calling me 'human.'"

"Got it." He headed for the door again.

"Wait. I'll go with you."

Ignoring her, he pulled open the door and strode into the hallway.

Jerk. She followed him.

He didn't look at her once as he climbed the three flights of stairs.

"Why didn't you take the elevator?" She was sucking air by the time he stopped in front of a door.

The glance he shot her gleamed with malice. "The stairs don't bother me."

He allowed his gaze to slide over her—slowly, suggesting that stairs would soon be the least of her problems. "*Humans* don't have the stamina for them." He made sure she understood he was distancing himself from those out-of-shape humans.

While she was composing a reply that would be as insulting as possible, he pushed on the door. It opened.

"Wasn't the door locked?"

"Locked doors won't stop me." His tone dismissed her question as foolish.

"Who has dared enter my room without—?" Creepy Guy rushed toward the door and then came to a sliding stop.

"Troll." Murmur spoke quietly, but menace lived in his voice.

Murmur said only the one word, but Ivy swore the walls actually vibrated and the air thickened with the threat of it.

"You!" Creepy Guy backed slowly away. He stuck his fingers in his ears. "Don't."

He didn't specify what he didn't want Murmur to do, but the fingers in his ears gave Ivy a pretty big clue.

"Leave." Murmur didn't bother shouting. He simply pointed to the door.

Creepy Guy nodded, took his fingers from his ears, and rushed past them.

"If you ever threaten the human again, I'll find you." Murmur's smile was terrifying. "And you'll dance. Forever."

"Won't threaten human, won't come back." And then he was gone.

Amazed, Ivy stood frozen while her brain processed everything. Creepy Guy was a troll? What was with the dancing thing? Then it hit her.

"If I hadn't pulled away from you last night, how long would you have danced with me?"

"Until you died." He turned and walked away.

3

Murmur was freaking furious. Sure, he'd been in her mind. And sure he'd done a little taunting. But that was no reason to run to Zane for help. And she'd done it right in front of him.

A melody line wound through his head, one full of thorns tipped with poison. He controlled his need to send it Zane's way. That would indicate emotional weakness, *jealousy*. Demons weren't emotional beings. *Then what do you call all this anger?* Even though he recognized the dangerous path his thoughts were taking, he couldn't stop them.

He wondered how she'd feel when he told her that behind Zane's big, smarmy smile lurked a sorcerer. Murmur might have called Zane a wizard, but he knew the truth. *Holgarth* was a wizard—annoying as hell, but with no dark magic in his bag of tricks. Zane was a sorcerer—malicious intent lurked in the heart of his magic.

Murmur paused at Bain's door. He took a deep breath, trying to deny the anger any power over him. He pictured a blank, white screen and shoved his feelings behind it. Ivy could do whatever she wanted with Zane behind that damn screen. She was merely a placeholder for the woman Bain would snatch from the faery host.

He wrapped himself in his customary persona, honed over millennia—someone who observed, who took advantage of the foolishness in others, and who never, ever allowed strong feelings about anything except his music to infect him.

Once again secure with his personal identity, Murmur raised his fist to knock. He did have to take back one of his earlier assessments, though. She had the most sensual lips he'd ever seen. Murmur had no idea how he'd ever thought they were just ordinary.

Bain opened his door on the third knock. He was holding a burger. He frowned at Murmur. "I don't work during lunch. Tell Holgarth to deal with it himself."

"This isn't about the castle." He walked past Bain and sat on the couch. "I need a few more details about how you intend to pull off stealing from the faeries."

Bain followed him and sat in the one chair. He dropped the half-eaten burger on the coffee table next to his drink and fries. "So what do you want to know?"

His friend looked open, but Murmur had learned long ago not to trust anyone, even Bain. "What's the woman's name?"

"Elizabeth."

Bain wasn't into elaborating on his answers today.

"I don't think we should use Ivy." Murmur tried not to wince. Had he really said that? "Sparkle will go crazy when she finds out that we traded her shiny new assistant to the Sluagh Sidhe." Murmur breathed easier. See, he had a perfectly logical reason for his suggestion.

Bain shrugged and picked up his drink.

Guess he'd have to spell it out. "Let's follow your plan to its logical conclusion. You trade Ivy for Elizabeth. Sparkle goes ballistic and runs to Ganymede. The chaos bringer will do anything for her, so he comes out blasting. Are you ready to match your power with his?"

Bain narrowed his eyes. "We command legions of demons."

"And he has the Big Boss behind him. What would a war between legions of demons and the Big Boss's cosmic troublemakers do to earth? I, for one, would miss humans. Who would be left for us to tempt and destroy? All because you were too stubborn to choose another woman. Our master won't be happy." Actually, Murmur hadn't cared much about making the big guy down under happy for quite a while. He probably did need that trip back to the Underworld to get his head straight.

Bain looked thoughtful before slowly smiling. "Are you asking for a favor? If so, it would cancel out the one I owe you."

Fury punched a hole in Murmur's imaginary screen. Friendship should mean more than trading favors. *Demons weren't meant to have friends, stupid.* Bain was just being true to his nature. So why was Murmur pissed at the other demon?

Disappointment made him reckless. "Look, I don't care who you use. Take Ivy. You're not doing me a favor. I'll just walk away when the Big Boss comes calling. Elizabeth doesn't mean a thing to me." He waited to see if Bain would call his bluff.

After Murmur met Bain's glare with what he hoped looked like disinterest, the other demon put his drink down a little too hard and some of it splashed onto the coffee table. "You win. Find me another woman to hand over, and I'll forget about Ivy. But it has to be someone who's working at the castle, because I can't take the chance of her checking out unexpectedly."

Murmur nodded. What the hell had he gotten himself into? Now he had to find a victim for Bain. He strung a few dozen silent curses together but refused to examine why he'd agreed to the whole thing. Why should he care what happened to Ivy or, for that matter, to Bain? His redundancy wasn't lost on him. He'd asked the same question several times already without getting an answer. The next time he considered growing his friends list, he'd have to remember what a pain in the ass they were.

Bain didn't have a chance to comment on Murmur's agreement. The door suddenly swung open, and Tirron strode into the room.

"Knocking is an accepted preliminary to entering."

The faery ignored Murmur's mumbled complaint. He sat on the other end of the couch and leaned forward. "The Sluagh Sidhe has crossed over from Faery. They're gathering humans in California now. They hunt by night, and since they always travel from west to east, they should be here in about two weeks." He looked at Murmur expectantly. "That's if you can make sure their flight to the East Coast swings through Galveston." His pale cheeks flushed with excitement.

Murmur smiled. The ice king was actually showing signs of thawing. Too bad. He would enjoy putting a few cracks in Tirron's anticipation. He made no excuses for his need to be mean. It was a demon thing. "Think of my power as a musical tsunami. The wave travels across the country, picking up strength and intensity as it goes." He paused.

Bain speared him with a hard stare. "Why do I sense a 'but' coming?"

Murmur's smile widened. Bain knew him too well. "No weapon is perfect. Any fae caught in that wave, even if they're not connected with the hunt, will also be drawn here." He held up his hands, palms up in a hey-it's-not-my-fault gesture. "So you might want to prepare for random faery visits before the Sluagh Sidhe arrives."

"Shit. How will I explain that to Ganymede?" Bain raked his fingers through his hair.

"You? It won't take long for Ganymede to realize my music is drawing them to the castle. My ass will be on the line." Would Bain even care about collateral damage? Murmur admitted to cynicism. Yes, he had trust issues.

Bain looked distracted. "You'll be fine. You saved the Big Boss along with the whole castle a few weeks ago. They owe you. Just call in the favors."

Tirron seemed oblivious to minor problems like staying alive once the cosmic troublemakers realized what was going on. "When will you start drawing them to us?"

"I'll go to my room now. I need to concentrate." Not true, but he was having difficulty keeping his annoyance safely behind that white screen. A show of temper would damage his legendary reputation as the ultimate cool guy.

On the way out, he realized that Bain still hadn't given him any solid information about how everything would go down. But he didn't feel like continuing the discussion with Tirron in the room. Something about the faery felt wrong. Murmur left Bain and Tirron discussing whatever they were discussing and headed toward his room. Once there, he'd send out his call to the faery host and then . . . Maybe he'd check to see if Ivy had left yet.

Murmur didn't have to do any checking, because as he reached his tower floor, he saw Ivy pounding on his door. She turned as he approached.

He didn't know what expression he'd expected, but it hadn't been grim determination. "You have to add the I'll-huff-and-I'll-puff line if you want me to answer."

She didn't look amused. "Can we go inside?"

The best thing he could do for both of them was to send her away. Murmur knew he wouldn't. He didn't answer her, just unlocked his door and stood aside for her to enter. And then watched her flinch as she heard the door click shut behind her.

He waved at the couch. "Sit."

Ivy hesitated but finally perched on the edge of the cushion. "I decided to quit after your full-disclosure moment."

"Smart decision." He was thrilled. Really. Thrilled.

She took a deep breath and met his gaze. "Were you telling the truth?"

He didn't have to think about his answer. "Yes."

She nodded, and he watched her repress a shudder. For whatever reason, her response triggered his anger. He couldn't remember his emotions ever being this close to the surface.

A melody began building in his head, one with minor chords and major warnings. He walked over to the narrow window, putting some distance between them.

"I called my mother after the meeting. I wanted to tell her I was coming home."

"And?"

She stared at him. "I'm staying."

"Dumb decision." But no matter what he *said*, a part of him celebrated. Not the smart part.

"She said that Dad lost his latest job."

"I'm sorry to hear that." He didn't give a damn about her father's job, but since it obviously had something to do with her staying, he'd hear her out.

"Don't be sorry. He loses a job every week. Mom has always supported us." She folded her hands in her lap and stared at the closed door. "I've never wanted to be like him. I went to college. Got a business degree. Worked until I had a down payment and then bought my pet store. None of it mattered. I still lost the store to the bad economy. Sparkle's offer was a godsend. It pays good money with great benefits."

And some not-so-great ones. "You'll find another job." Damn, the melody was gaining volume, but he forced himself not to listen, not to think about where it would take him.

"No one will offer the kind of paycheck Sparkle is giving me."

"And the big paycheck is important because . . . ?"

"Dad bails on every job he gets, so that's no big deal. But when I called, Mom said she got notice that her company is downsizing, and she'll have to take a job that pays less. My brother is still in high school. I have to help."

"Money." Of course it was money. With humans it was always about money. If he couldn't find someone else in the castle to offer up to Bain, he could pay Ivy to leave before the faery host arrived. Humans all had their price. "You could always bring your brother here. It would be one less mouth for your mother to feed."

Ivy shook her head. "Not with a demon in residence." She speared him with a hard stare. "If you touched him, I'd have to kill you." Her expression said she meant it.

Under ordinary circumstances, her threat would amuse him. But there was nothing ordinary about how he was feeling right now. Her answer just made him angrier. *And he couldn't turn off the damn music in his head.*

Murmur nodded even though he didn't understood human love of family. It was tough to empathize with something you'd never experienced. "So you didn't mention wanting to quit and come home?"

"No." Now for the hard part. Ivy needed information. "Since I'm staying, I want you to tell me the truth about the people in this place."

He raised one brow. "Why come to me? Sparkle could've told you. Besides, I only tell the truth on Tuesdays. Well, most Tuesdays. If Tuesday falls on a full moon, all bets are off." He smiled. "Demon, remember?"

She huffed her irritation. "Why you? Because you scare me. And if I'm going to work here, I have to face my fears." She thought about the total weirdness of the whole castle. She could handle the rest of the strangeness, but only he truly frightened her. On a whole bunch of levels. Some of which she wasn't ready to examine yet.

His smile was slow and wicked. "Sweetheart, you have no idea what true terror is. But thanks for the compliment just the same."

What a bizarre reaction. Ivy thought about bolting from the room, but forced herself to stay seated by thinking about how much she needed this job. She'd lost her sense of self along with her pet shop. She damn well wasn't going to lose this chance. She would *not* fear him.

He reached out and opened the window. She thought she could hear faint music coming from somewhere. Probably from outside.

"I'll give you a quick rundown. Holgarth is a wizard, and his son Zane is a sorcerer. Bain is a demon. You haven't met Dacian yet, but he's a vampire. Sparkle, Ganymede, and Edge are cosmic troublemakers, and Passion is . . ." He shrugged. "I'm not sure if she has an official title yet. Oh, and Dacian's wife, Cinn, is a demigoddess or something. I guess that's it."

He looked as though he were checking a list in his head to make sure he hadn't missed anyone. "You won't see much of Edge and Passion for a few weeks. He's the troublemaker in charge of political chaos. He'll be spending some quality time in Washington encouraging incendiary speeches and discouraging bipartisanship. Got to keep those politicians at each other's throats."

Ivy could actually feel the blood draining from her face with each word he said. She gripped the arm of the couch to keep herself from toppling over onto her face. "I don't believe you."

"Feel free to disbelieve all you want. You came to me. Remember that." His eyes gleamed with malicious satisfaction. He was enjoying every second of her horrified reaction.

She swallowed hard, trying to dislodge the boulder stuck in her throat. "Cosmic troublemakers? Ganymede?"

"I'll let them explain. And Ganymede is the fat gray cat."

"The cat. Of course." She would *not* vomit. "Thanks for clearing things up. I think I'll leave now." Ivy doubted she could stand let alone walk from the room.

"There's no rush. I'll get you something to drink and you can watch me do something demonic. How does that sound?"

He's trying to scare me. Knowing that didn't help much. *Stay grounded.* Sparkle had given her a job. She would do the job. And if that meant she had to deal with Murmur and the others, she'd deal. Besides, her mind still refused to accept what he said as truth no matter what she'd seen. "Water would be great." Where was that music coming from?

She hoped he didn't notice her shaking hand when she took the glass.

He smiled at her, not a kind smile. "I'm sending a music-gram to some very special people." That's all he said before turning to face the window.

Suddenly, music filled the room. Music that felt soft and gooey, as if it would stick to her if it brushed against her. It dipped and swirled and she swore she could see it flowing out the open window. Just as on the beach, the melody wasn't familiar. It didn't seem like music at all. It had heat and texture. She almost believed that if she reached out she could grab the notes from the air. A crazy thought, but Ivy kept her hands at her sides.

A primitive fear tapped out its own rhythm along her spine with icy fingers. Ivy didn't understand what Murmur was doing, but she *did* know that she didn't want this particular tune seeking her out. "Why isn't your music affecting me the way it did on the beach?"

The music stopped and he calmly closed the window before returning to stand in front of her. "If I don't use my music, it builds up in my mind and gives me the mother of all migraines. I was just releasing the pressure when you wandered onto the beach. By the time I realized I wasn't alone, it was too late to aim it away from you."

He smiled, and as she forced herself to meet his gaze, she finally believed he was what he claimed. Her fear almost suffocated her. Thank heaven for her terror, because without it she would have a tough time keeping him at a distance. Even now, she felt the pull that had nothing to do with his music.

She blurted out the first thing that came to mind. "You don't look like a demon."

He raised one brow. "And how should a demon look?"

Ivy shrugged. "I don't know. Big, red, tail, horns . . ." This was a stupid conversation.

"Stereotypes, always stereotypes." His sexy lips tipped up in a mocking smile. "Cosmetic surgery took care of the tail. It gave my Armani suits an unacceptable bulge." His smile eased into something achingly sensual, suggesting that not all bulges were unacceptable. "Sure, I was a little flushed when I first reached the mortal plane, but excessive heat—I come from an overly warm climate—will do that. I cooled down in a few days."

Ivy doubted he'd cooled down even one degree.

"And the horns are just ridiculous. Who has horns?" He shrugged away that part of demon mythology.

She'd had enough of his derision. "I think it's time to go." Ivy forced herself to stand. Good, she was only swaying a little. She tottered toward the door. *What happened to all your big talk about facing your fears?* An honest mistake. She'd underestimated his scary factor and overestimated her courage.

Between one breath and the next he was in front of her. He leaned forward and she forced herself not to shrink away in response. This close he was overwhelming. She was sure those green eyes saw to the heart of her terror.

But the pounding of her heart and the catch in her breath wasn't all fright. She only wished it were. No one had told her demons could be beautiful, and funny, and smell like wild nights and mornings filled with regrets. He obviously had a two-pronged attack. She balanced on the edge of either racing from the room or reaching out to touch that hard chest just a few inches away.

She opted for running. Yanking open the door, she stumbled into the hallway.

As he closed his door softly behind her, she caught his final comment.

"Coward." He sounded disappointed.

All she could think about was reaching her room. She would calm herself and then get on her computer and start searching for another job. She stared at the floor as she concentrated on putting one foot in front of the other. A sudden noise made her look up.

And up, and up, and up. Ohmigod! Whatever it was, this thing was enormous. It had to lower its head so it wouldn't scrape the ceiling. Its arms hung almost to the floor and were thick with muscle. And its head was colossal with beady eyes and . . . She swallowed hard. *Breathe. You can't run without oxygen.* She stared at its face, at the two six-inch long tusks framing a mouthful of pointed teeth. She forced her gaze to its eyes. It was staring at her.

It smiled, baring every one of its teeth. "Eat girl later. Find music maker now. Dance." It demonstrated how ready it was for *So You Think You Can Dance* by doing a clumsy pirouette.

Ivy now understood what it meant to be frozen in fear. She'd always felt a certain contempt for anyone who couldn't act in an emergency. Payback was a bitch.

"An ogre. Large but not overly intelligent. Perhaps you should warn Murmur that his dance student has arrived."

Not even the snooty female voice in her head could force her to look away from the . . . ogre? No, ogres were misunderstood and lovable and green. Ogres were . . . Shrek.

"Oh, for crying out loud, stop ogling the ogre and move. Death by ogre is not a pleasant way to go. Get Murmur."

This time Ivy did look down for just a second. A Siamese cat sat staring up at her from brilliant blue eyes. Its diamond-studded collar sparkled in the dim light coming from the fake wall sconces. Not real diamonds. Couldn't be. But why the hell was she thinking about the cat's collar when . . . ? She returned her attention to the ogre. She opened her mouth to scream.

"*Stop. People coming to investigate equals angry ogre. Do you really want all those deaths on your conscience? Now, let me keep this simple: Ogre. Run.*"

Ogre! Run! Finally, her brain had decided to send the message to flee to the rest of her body. Ivy turned and raced back to Murmur's room. She didn't have much trouble staying ahead of the shambling ogre because it was busy doing a rhythmic bob and shuffle as it worked its way toward her. She pounded on his door while she tried to suck in enough breath to talk when he answered. Not that he'd need her to explain what was happening. The ogre attempted a graceful leap. Epic fail. The whole castle shook as it landed.

Murmur flung open the door. "What the hell is . . . ?" He spotted the ogre. "Not possible. Not this fast. Give me a freaking break." He moved to her side. "I will *never* have another friend."

Ivy didn't have a clue what he was talking about. "Do something."

Murmur paused to study the dancing ogre. "Not bad form. For an ogre. He at least has a sense of rhythm."

"Do. Something. Now." Her voice rose to a screech. She couldn't control it.

"Consider it done." He took a step toward the ogre, and his voice fell into a hypnotic cadence. "Hear no more, yearn no more, dance no more. Return from whence you came."

Suddenly, the hall was empty. Silence filled the space where the ogre had stood.

"Where'd he go?" Not that she cared. All that mattered was that he'd disappeared.

"I sent him home." He stepped back into his room, then paused to stare at her. "Interesting. You saw past his glamour." His expression hardened. "You won't tell anyone what you just saw. If you attempt to tattle, the words will freeze in your mouth."

She narrowed her eyes and glared. "Is that a threat? Because I intend to go right to Sparkle and tell her . . ." Nothing. She couldn't finish the sentence. Ivy tried rearranging the words in her mind, but she couldn't push them past her lips.

"You did this." *State the obvious, why don't you?* She wanted to hurl every curse she'd ever heard at his manipulative head—he'd crept into her mind and taken away her free will—but she couldn't concentrate because what sounded like some sort of Gregorian chant was playing over the words she wanted to scream at him.

"It could be worse. I could've taken the memory from you completely." His frown said he was wondering why he hadn't.

Fury, panic, and terror jockeyed for position as she numbly turned from his door. She didn't even glance back when she heard it shut. How did he think he could keep this secret? Like everyone hadn't felt the castle shake?

Then she remembered the Siamese cat. What was it about cats and this castle? A quick glance assured her it was gone. She closed her eyes for a moment and rubbed her forehead. Maybe there'd never been a cat. Maybe this whole thing was one giant hallucination.

Ivy made it back to her room without encountering any more creatures. She sighed her relief as she closed her door and locked it. Then she turned around.

The Siamese cat lay on her bed, its tail twitching and its collar gleaming. *"You took long enough to get back. You can order lunch from room service for both of us."*

Ivy blinked. "Room service?"

The cat's sigh was a cool shiver in her mind. *"Perhaps you've* noticed my lack of opposable thumbs? And hotel minions rarely respond to meows, even imperious ones. So you'll have to order."

It said a lot about how Ivy's day had gone so far that she didn't even question the cat's presence. She ordered a sandwich and salad that she probably wouldn't be able to choke down, and then she glanced at the cat. "What do you want?"

"A tender lamb chop and a bowl of milk would be nice."

Ivy repeated the order and hung up. She sat down on the chair farthest away from the cat. "Okay, who are you? What are you?" Her body felt heavy with fatigue, pulled down by a vague sadness. She'd really needed this job to work. "And are you real?"

"Of course I'm real. I don't think you're a stupid woman, so don't act like one. Now, since Sparkle allowed her hatred of me to get in the way of common sense—because I was absolutely the best choice for her assistant—I've decided instead to help you survive the job."

"Survive the job?"

"First, introductions. I'm Asima, messenger of the goddess Bast. I've spent time at the castle helping where I can. Sadly, only a few perceptive people appreciate my value." She raised her elegant nose, a haughty gesture that crossed species lines. *"I was away for a short time and came back to find that Sparkle had hired you. Truly shortsighted of her."* She seemed to think about that for a moment. *"Although I'm sure you're a perfectly nice person. I simply meant that you're unprepared for the . . . unique demands of this job."*

Ivy didn't want to think about the "unique demands" of her new job. She was too busy dealing with the earthquake happening in her head, obviously caused by the massive shift in reality taking place there. Her last bastion of belief in a sane world was, well . . . insanity. At least if she was certifiable she could get help from her local mental health facility.

The delivery of their lunches shut the cat up for a little while. Too little. It made short work of the lamb and milk with delicate bites and refined laps. Ivy sat and stared at her lunch. She might never eat again. Okay, so that was stupid. *Don't implode. Stay grounded.*

Once finished, the cat . . . No, Asima—Ivy decided to assume she was still sane—stared at her with unblinking intensity.

"The first thing you need to know is how to dress for your job. I took the liberty of dropping a few things off in your closet while you were in your meeting. Sparkle will love your professional look."

For just a moment, something sly moved in the cat's eyes. Ivy studied Asima, but before she could do any analysis, the expression was gone. "Thanks. I think." So many questions to ask, but Ivy's thoughts still staggered in shocked circles.

"You're welcome." Asima leaped from the bed and padded to the door. It swung open. *"I'll get back to you later with some guaranteed ways to impress Sparkle."*

"Wait." Ivy might not know or trust Asima, but the cat was her only weapon against Murmur now. "You saw the . . . You were there in the hall. Please, go with me to Ganymede or Holgarth if you don't want to deal with Sparkle, and explain what you saw."

"Why would I do that?" Asima seemed genuinely perplexed.

Ivy took a deep breath before blurting the truth. "I can't say the word . . ." She flung her arms up in frustration. "You know, the thing we saw? Murmur messed with my mind. He wants to keep it secret, but I think someone needs to be told. It could've injured guests. Sparkle's my boss. I have a duty to inform her." Okay, the truth? She was furious at Murmur. He'd dared to manipulate her mind without her permission. Ivy hated her feeling of helplessness. And yes, she wanted to make him pay. If that made her a vengeful bitch, then so be it.

Surprise widened Asima's eyes. *"Can you text it?"*

Ivy pulled out her phone and tried. Damn, she couldn't even write the word. "Nope."

Asima's expression turned calculating. "*You can't say or write the word 'ogre.' How interesting. I'll need time to consider your request.*"

"But—"

"*I'm afraid I have to go now.*" Asima paused before leaving. "*By the way, you might want to ask yourself how you were able to see the ogre's true form. A normal human would have seen an old man. We'll explore the intriguing possibilities at another time.*" She left the room, her waving tail an arrogant question mark over her back. Fitting. The door clicked shut behind her.

A normal human? Ivy knew soul-deep that she'd never be normal again. Once seen, an ogre couldn't be unseen. She stared at the indentation in her comforter where Asima had lain. Real; it was *all* real. And she didn't have a clue how she'd been able to see the ogre as he really was. Murmur and Asima had to be mistaken. There was nothing special about her. The ogre must've been so wrapped up in his dancing that he'd forgotten about his glamour.

Her heart was racing. *Calm. Stay calm.* She needed something to take her mind off Murmur, Asima, and random . . . whatevers dancing throught the castle's hallways. It was time for her to start doing her job. Ivy dragged the bag of complaints from her closet and dumped what must be thousands of folded papers onto her coffee table. Then she began to read them.

"Holgarth told me I had the acting ability of a cactus." Ivy set the paper on a designated spot on the table for all wizard complaints. She picked up the next paper. "Your chef sucks. Tell him I've eaten tastier shoe leather than that steak from last night." Restaurant pile. "Holgarth refused to make me the handsome prince. He said I'd have to lose a hundred pounds and get a new face to qualify." Wizard pile. "I found dust above the door to my room." Who the heck checked for dust above the door? Guest room pile. "Holgarth wouldn't let me be in the fantasies. He said he'd call me when they began doing nightmares." Wizard pile.

Ivy frowned. She was beginning to see a pattern. Her cell phone shattered Ivy's silent contemplation of the pile of complaints still to be read. She almost ignored the call. Then she sighed. Life had to go on. She pulled the phone from her pocket and put on her fake perky voice. "Hello?"

A few minutes later, she shoved the phone back into her pocket. Part of the giant boulder resting on her chest lifted. One of the other job applications she'd put in had come through. Sort of. She wouldn't start work for three weeks, and she'd have to move to Denver. The money wasn't as good as here, but if the workplace was demon-free, hey, she'd make do with less. She could work here for two more weeks and then tell Sparkle she was quitting. After all, Sparkle had misrepresented the job description. Nowhere had it mentioned dancing with demons and facing down ogres. Definitely a deal breaker.

But as she sat trying to work up the energy to read more complaints, the boulder settled back onto her chest.

She was a coward. Sure, no one else would call her that. No one would blame her for walking away from this nightmare. But Ivy would know. She would be quitting after just a few weeks. *Just like Dad.* If she called home and told Mom she was quitting because the castle had a sexy demon along with assorted other nonhuman entities, Ivy knew what her mother would say.

First, Mom would sigh wearily. Then she'd say she understood. Mom always said that to Dad when he quit a job. Each time he used the same excuse. He couldn't concentrate on his work because he could hear voices when no one was there. He claimed the voices followed him wherever he went.

Ivy had wanted Mom to lose her temper just once, to scream at Dad that she was tired of supporting the family, tired of his weak-ass excuses. But Mom never yelled, never threatened to leave him, just looked sad.

Ivy loved her father, but she'd never for a minute believed his story. Mom should've gotten help for him years ago. Ivy had even believed he was faking the voices so he wouldn't have to work.

But now? Ivy knew her smile was bitter. *What goes around comes around.*

She stood and headed for the door. If she had to work two weeks here, she'd give Sparkle her money's worth. Her boss would probably be at Sweet Indulgence now. There was something weird about Sparkle owning a candy store. Images of Hansel and Gretel came to mind.

And if she thought just a little about never seeing Murmur again after she left the castle, she would concentrate on his mind manipulation and allow her anger to smother any regrets.

4

Earbuds in, Murmur lay on his bed listening to the latest pop pap. It helped to neutralize the music in his head so that he could think. Guilt? He almost didn't recognize the feeling. Demons didn't do guilt. But there it was, buzzing around his head like a demented fly. And all because of the accusation in Ivy's eyes—betrayal. A scary revelation, because he'd betrayed and been betrayed so many times over the centuries that there should be no emotion connected to it. Why now? Why her?

He folded his hands behind his head and contemplated the ceiling. She wouldn't sympathize with his reason for sealing her lips. The longer they could keep Ganymede and Sparkle in the dark about the fae visits, the better chance they had of being here when the faery host arrived. Sure, they could probably move their operation to another place, but no other hotel would offer a built-in army. No matter how ticked Ganymede would be at them, when the time came he'd defend his home against the Sluagh Sidhe.

At some point, Murmur realized he was dozing off. Unusual for him to feel sleepy. Demons didn't need much down time. His last waking thought was that he'd have to face Ivy with the implication of her ability to see through glamours.

When he opened his eyes he was somewhere else. *What the . . . ?* He was lying in the grass on a hill overlooking a village. Murmur glanced around. Centuries old from the looks of the buildings and the people's clothing. He watched as they scurried about doing the useless things humans did. A dream?

"Today is a good day for them to die."

Murmur turned his head. He recognized Klepoth's voice before he saw him sitting on a nearby tree stump. Today Klepoth looked about sixteen with spiked blue hair and bright red eyes. His appearance changed with his mood. It had been a long time, but Murmur still remembered that a visit from the demon who dealt in illusions was never a happy event.

"What do you want?" Murmur didn't feel like pretending he was glad to see Klepoth.

The other demon tried to look wounded by Murmur's tone, but his sly anticipation leaked through. "I thought we might experience one of your happier memories today. From what I've seen, you've forgotten how to have real fun."

Murmur glanced back at the village. Did he remember this? There'd been so many villages, so many slaughters. He looked away. "Do I have a choice?"

"Not really." Klepoth grinned. "The Master just wanted to remind you what a good time felt like."

"Is that all?"

Klepoth shrugged, but his red eyes were slits of malevolent pleasure. "For now."

Murmur stood. The need to destroy seeped through him—familiar, comfortable. That's how he'd felt back then, and it seemed as though Klepoth meant for him to experience the same emotions with the same results now. He should relax into it, enjoy the moment. This was just a realistic simulation. Klepoth was good at what he did.

Then why did he feel reluctant about the coming slaughter? *You're becoming like them, the humans down there—too fragile, too soft.* The very idea outraged him. He was what he'd always been, and "soft" was never a word that anyone would say to his face and survive the saying. "Let's go and end some lives."

Klepoth whooped his agreement. "Now you're talking."

Together they swooped down on the village. Klepoth patrolled the perimeter, herding anyone trying to escape back toward the town center. The Master must have ordered Klepoth to let Murmur do the killing, because he watched Murmur from hungry eyes filled with barely controlled bloodlust. The other demon might specialize in illusions, but he liked to bloody his hands as much as any of them.

Murmur stood surrounded by terrified villagers, who trampled each other in their panicked need to get away from him. *Too late. Much too late.* He grinned.

Then he composed a special melody just for them. It was filled with jagged edges and deadly needles of sound. He drew the notes from the power curled in layers deep within him and then gave it form. The music spiraled out from him—seeking, destroying.

A razor-sharp chorus stabbed a fleeing man over and over until he lay dead in a growing pool of blood. Murmur hummed the harmony as he killed.

The melody line wrapped around the wrinkled throat of an old woman and tightened.

He didn't wait to see her face darken before he targeted a huge man trying to hide behind one of the hovels. Murmur trapped the man between the notes of his crescendo, slamming them against his body, battering him with the swelling climax to his musical masterpiece. The man's agonized screams made Murmur wince. The guy's shrieks were so off-key that they hurt. When the music ended, the man lay dead.

Murmur spun in a slow circle. They all were dead. Wait for it, wait for it . . . *It came.* The unbelievable euphoria that mindless killing had always brought him. It was a power surge he never grew tired of. Why had he ever stopped? This was what he'd been created for.

"Remember that, Murmur." Klepoth's whisper came from right behind him.

Murmur turned, his mind still soaring on his killing high. "What does the Master want?"

Klepoth smiled. "He wants you to remember. To reclaim the savagery and cruelty you once had." Then he was gone. The village with its dead went with him.

Murmur opened his eyes. His euphoria had disappeared, and he was soaked with sweat. The feeling churning in his stomach was so unexpected that he almost didn't make it to the bathroom. He emptied his stomach and then dry heaved until his abs ached. When he finally struggled to his feet, he felt almost weak. He stumbled into the shower and scrubbed the memory of the dream—the torn flesh, the blood, the shrieks, the ease with which humans died—from his body.

Once out of the bathroom, he dressed again and headed for the door. He needed out of here. The reaction to his dream had struck a chord of fear he couldn't face right now. The demon he'd once been and still should be would *never* puke his brains out over a few human deaths.

And in a place he kept hidden even from himself, he suspected his nausea had nothing to do with the blood and gore, the human deaths. He was . . . Murmur closed his eyes for a moment. When he opened them again, his white screen was once again in place and all temptation to take a peek into his psyche was tucked neatly behind it.

Rather than sit staring at the screen, he decided to search out someone who'd irritate him so much that he'd forget about the dream.

Ivy stared at the stone steps as she walked down to the great hall. No way would she take the chance of trapping herself in an elevator where scary nonhumans could join her at any moment. The winding stairway might be narrow, but at least she had somewhere to run if she needed to escape. And as long as she watched where she put her feet, she wouldn't slip and take a header.

She heard the sound of footsteps coming up the stairs at the same moment he spoke.

"You must be Ivy." His voice was smooth and cool.

Startled, she glanced up. He was tall enough that even though he was standing a step below her, they were still at eye level.

"Yes. And you are?" She knew her words sounded a little breathless, but who could blame her?

"Tirron. I'm staying here for a few weeks."

In some ways, he looked like Murmur. Both were tall with long hair—his almost silver instead of blond—and beautiful faces, but their similarity had nothing to do with the physical stuff. His power pushed at her. She could *feel* it. It felt like Murmur's power and yet different—harder with no flexibility to it, brittle. *When did you begin to feel power?*

He had cold eyes. Murmur's eyes could grow just as cold, but he had a sense of humor that softened them a little. Caustic, mocking, but still humorous. Ivy sensed no humor in this man.

"Wait? How do you know me?" She would have remembered meeting him.

He smiled, but it never reached his icy blue eyes. "I'm a friend of Murmur's. He described you."

He leaned closer and, no matter how gorgeous he was, she had the urge to move back. "Why would he describe me?" Something about this man's interest made her want to turn and run back up the steps.

He raised one brow. "You're a very attractive woman. Why wouldn't he notice and comment on it to a friend?"

She controlled the urge to squirm, to look away from his stare. And yet . . . There was something about his beauty that drew her. How could she feel attracted and repelled at the same time?

"You're perfect, just perfect."

"Yes, well . . ." Perfect for what? She wasn't sure she wanted to know. Because something more than sexual interest lived in his eyes for a moment and then was gone.

"Perhaps we'll hunt the night skies together." His comment was almost a whisper.

She smiled, because he was kidding, right? Ivy took a deep breath. If she were a braver person, she would have asked if he was a demon too. Time to get out of here. He was making her way too nervous. "I guess I'd better stop blocking the steps. Nice meeting you." She flattened herself against the wall so that he could pass.

After one more long, searching look, he eased past her and was gone. She exhaled the breath she hadn't realized she was holding.

For the rest of the walk to Sparkle's shop, she pushed the thought that Murmur had spoken to Tirron about her around in her head. She wasn't sure how she felt about it.

But thoughts of Murmur turned to annoyance as Ivy waited impatiently for Sparkle to dole out a bag of candy to a woman who seemed to want one of everything. She sighed. All she wanted from her boss was a list of routine jobs she was expected to complete each day, things that a normal personal assistant would do. Not that "normal" was in Sparkle's vocabulary. Ivy thought about the mountain of complaints. Fine, so she shouldn't be asking for more duties on top of the sorting job still waiting for her. But Ivy needed to lose herself in her job.

Finally the woman left and Sparkle perched on a stool behind her counter. She folded her hands with their perfect nails on the glass top. "Have you calmed down?"

"Yes." Translation: not even a little. "I need a list of things you want done each day."

Sparkle crossed her long legs and dangled one metallic stiletto from her toe. "You're still upset. Did anything happen after our meeting that I should know about?"

"You could say that." Did she sound bitter? Ivy hoped so.

"Tell me." Sparkle's gaze sharpened.

"I . . . can't tell you." Damn, damn, damn.

Sparkle frowned. "Of course you can. I'm your trusted confidant, your best friend, your . . ."

"*You don't understand, babe. She* really *can't tell you, like in 'can't tell you because someone laid a compulsion on her.' Interesting.*"

Who . . . ? An unfamiliar male voice in her head. And how did he pick up on Murmur's compulsion? Ivy stepped up to the counter and leaned over to take a look. A chubby gray cat stared up at her from big amber eyes. This must be the Ganymede that Murmur mentioned. "There're too many cats in my head."

Ivy was sure her visions of an ordinary secure job and a house with a white picket fence were morphing into something dark and unrecognizable the longer she spent in this cursed place.

Sparkle was instantly alert. "What do you mean?"

"I just met a Siamese cat named Asima. She thinks she could do a better job as your assistant."

Sparkle's eyes were amber slits of fury. "The bitch is back."

That didn't sound good. Ivy thought about backing out of the store and putting some distance between her and her boss. But she discarded the idea before it could get any traction. Two weeks. That's how long she had to stick it out.

"Do you have a problem with Asima?" An obvious yes, but Ivy wanted a few details.

"*A little misunderstanding. Girl stuff. Nothing important.*" Ganymede's gaze shifted away from Ivy.

Furry little liar. "I know what you guys are." Sort of. "So don't try to hide things from me."

They both ignored her.

The gray cat leaped onto the counter to rub his head against Sparkle's arm. "*Calm down, sugarhoney. You know that you do things you regret when you lose your temper.*"

Sparkle turned her outraged gaze on the cat. "She told Isis where to find Holgarth. He was devastated. Not just a bitch, but a traitorous bitch."

Ivy stood staring. She didn't understand any of this. It seemed that everyone here had shared histories. She'd always be on the outside looking in. And for the few weeks she'd be here, that's exactly where she wanted to stay.

"I want her out of my castle." Sparkle's long red hair was starting to lift from her shoulders as though blown by a phantom breeze, and her eyes were glowing amber.

"*Will the drama never end?*" Asima suddenly appeared next to Ivy. She sat and curled her tail around herself.

Ivy gasped. Where had Asima come from? Not that it really mattered. From the look in Sparkle's eyes, it might be wise to move away from her target of choice. Ivy backed toward the door, only to make contact with a hard body.

"This is just the distraction I needed."

Ivy didn't have any problem identifying the husky voice so close to her ear. Murmur. She hadn't heard him come into the store. He put his hand on her shoulder and leaned close.

"You can't leave now. This is entertainment at its best."

Ivy was torn between her need to escape whatever was about to happen and her desire to turn around and punch Murmur in his perfect face. She tried to ignore the warmth from his hand. She didn't want any part of him touching her.

She wasn't sure what she would have said to him, because Sparkle interrupted.

"Get her out of my castle. *Now.*" Sparkle stared at Ganymede. "I'd do it myself, but then she'd say something snotty and I'd have to tear her head off."

Ganymede's fuzzy face wore a hunted expression as he glanced at Murmur. *"Do something, demon. Let's hear some music. I don't give a damn what it is as long as it calms my sweetie. Even 'Dirge for a Dead Donut' would sound great right now."*

"Sorry, but I don't interfere in private disagreements." Murmur didn't look sorry.

Asima yawned, showing every one of her sharp little teeth. *"You can't order me out of your castle, slut queen. You and Ganymede said I could stay here."* Her elegant cat face wore a smug expression. *"Perhaps it was after I convinced Bast to save you, or it might have been any number of times I came to the rescue of you and your tubby sidekick."*

"Tubby sidekick?" Ganymede was doing a lot of mental sputtering.

Not only was Sparkle's hair now floating in an invisible breeze, but she was levitating off her stool. "I take back my permission. Now get your ass out of here."

Undaunted, Asima lifted one paw, licked it, and calmly washed her face. *"I'm afraid that would be impossible. Cats take promises seri-*

ously. Once you give a cat permission to stay somewhere, it's binding. Tell her, Ganymede."

Ganymede hissed at Asima before leaping from the counter and joining Ivy and Murmur by the door. "*Hate to say this, cupcake, but I'm afraid she's right. Cats honor their promises to other cats.*"

"I guess it's lucky then that I'm not a cat." Sparkle actually growled. "Honor this, bitch." And she leaped over the counter at Asima.

Murmur grabbed Ivy's hand and pulled her from the store. Ganymede rammed into the back of her legs in his need to escape. Murmur slammed the door shut behind them.

"*Run.*" Ganymede bounded away, his ears pinned flat against his head and his tail puffed up to twice its size.

Murmur dragged Ivy along with him as he hurried her back to the castle. Ganymede had already disappeared from sight. As she ran, she heard the sounds of shrieks, feline howls, and things breaking. The whole store shook.

"Shouldn't we try to stop them?" *Please say no.* All Ivy wanted to do was run to her room and bury her head under the covers.

"Are you crazy?"

Despite everything, she sensed laughter in Murmur's words.

"You don't step between two powerhouses like Sparkle and Asima without waving good-bye to your ass beforehand." He glanced at Ivy. "Don't worry, they won't destroy each other. This is just a claws and hair-pulling event. If they were out for a kill, half of Galveston would be gone by now."

Gee, that was comforting. She glanced around at people still walking nearby. "Why isn't anyone noticing the noise? I mean, you can see the store *moving.*"

"Ganymede glamoured the place before he ran."

Glamoured? The word triggered her memory of the ogre and what Murmur had done to her. She yanked her hand from his. "I want your compulsion gone. The whole thing will come out anyway. Asima saw . . ." She ground her teeth in frustration as once again her lips refused to form the words. "Anyway, Asima will tell everyone what she saw, so you may as well let me tell it first."

Asima knew? Murmur had to rethink his plan. He couldn't stop the cat from talking if she decided to blab. But he could negotiate for her silence. Asima was as manipulative as anyone in the castle. She'd have a price.

"I don't think so. I need your silence for a little longer." Say about two weeks.

He studied Ivy. Now that he'd spent some time with her, he realized that not only did she have a great mouth, but her eyes weren't an ordinary brown. They were deep, rich chocolate framed by long dark lashes. Strange how he hadn't noticed that before.

"You are such an ass."

Of course, that beautiful mouth didn't always form beautiful words.

"Why should it matter if I saw . . . ?" Her lips clamped shut while her eyes promised him a slow painful death as soon as she figured out how to do it.

He smiled. "I love a woman with a healthy temper. It's a sign of passion."

She paused as though she couldn't think of anything insulting enough to toss at him. Not surprising. People who'd lived a lot longer and knew a lot more than she did usually had trouble too. Of course, they were usually dying at the time. Tough to concentrate under those circumstances.

Ivy finally settled on "Go to hell."

"Been there, given guided tours." He shrugged it off. She'd have to do a lot better than that. "It doesn't look as though you'll have a chance to talk to Sparkle for the rest of the day, so what will you do?"

She pushed her hair away from her face. Beautiful dark hair—

shiny and smooth with red highlights when the sunlight touched it. Not ordinary at all. Where had his mind been that first time?

She shrugged. "Go back to my room and hope nothing unexpected pops in." She shot him a pointed stare. "Oh, and read complaints."

Complaints? He didn't need to know. "Since Sparkle won't be available, I can fill in some of the blanks for you." That was a dumb offer. Instead of wasting time with her, he should be scouting out an acceptable substitute to offer to the Sluagh Sidhe. But since she was still pissed at him for compelling her silence, she'd probably turn him down anyway.

"Fine. I need information, and if you're the only one who'll give it to me . . ."

She left the rest unsaid. The part where she swore she'd rather kiss the ogre than spend time with him. Too bad. He smiled.

"But you're not setting one foot in my room. And I don't want to go to your room either."

"Afraid to be alone with me?"

"Afraid of being trapped with you."

Murmur nodded. "Fair enough. I have a place we can talk without interruptions." He wouldn't shatter her illusion. She couldn't run fast enough or far enough to escape his music if he wanted her. Okay, maybe a good set of earplugs might help.

But as she followed him through the great hall, she spotted Holgarth. He was busy harassing the castle employees who were helping to set the room up for tonight's fantasies. She headed toward him. Damn.

She stopped in front of the wizard. "I want to talk to you for a few minutes."

Holgarth stared pointedly at his watch. "I suppose a few minutes spent in meaningless chatter won't unduly upset my schedule."

"I don't give a damn about your schedule."

The wizard blinked and glanced at Murmur.

Murmur shrugged and hummed quietly to himself. He turned his head to stare at the workers so Holgarth wouldn't see his smile.

"If I'm going to work here, I want to know about everything that could impact my job. Sparkle and Asima are over in the candy store right now giving new meaning to the term cat fight."

"Really? I don't know quite how to respond to that." The wizard had lost his supercilious sneer.

"You don't need to respond. Sparkle said something that made me think you were involved, and since she's my boss and Asima made it a point to visit me, I want to know the story."

For a moment, Murmur thought Holgarth wouldn't answer her. Then he simply nodded.

"The goddess Isis and I spent a brief time together. Since I knew she would never choose to stay with me, I left her first. For centuries I kept my whereabouts hidden from her." His gaze turned distant. "I don't know why. Fear of her wrath because I deserted her? Fear that my feelings for her would make me do something foolish? It's quite amazing how much of what we do or don't do in life is driven by fear."

He seemed to shrug off thoughts of the past as he focused on Ivy once again. "Asima met Isis and told her where to find me. The goddess showed up here and told me that I had a son. Zane." His expression softened. Once again, Holgarth seemed lost in his own thoughts. "All those wasted years when I could have known him. I was so utterly stupid. So you see, I don't know how I feel about Asima. She betrayed my whereabouts to Isis, but without her I might never have realized that Zane was mine."

The story wasn't quite that simple, but Murmur wanted to get Ivy to himself, so he allowed the telling to stand. "Now that you know, we need to let Holgarth do his job."

Ivy seemed thoughtful as she followed Murmur from the great

hall and down a long hallway lit by sconces with fake flickering candlelight.

When they entered the small chapel, Ivy looked shocked. "A church? You can really be on consecrated ground without going *poof?*"

"*Poof?*" He couldn't help it; he threw back his head and laughed. Murmur couldn't remember the last time he'd allowed himself that much positive emotion. A sinister laugh was fine, and a wow-look-they're-all-dead laugh even better. But this was neither. He hoped his master was listening. *And when did you start developing self-destructive tendencies?* "Yes, I can stay here all day if I want."

He slid into one of the pews, hooked his feet over the top of the one in front of him, and flung his head back so his hair trailed almost to the kneeler behind him. Ivy slid in beside him.

"So what would you like to know? And, no, I can't explain why I don't want anyone to find out about the ogre. And, no, I won't believe you if you promise not to tell anyone."

She watched him from eyes that measured, judged, and found him wanting. But that was okay because something else flared in those big brown eyes—sexual attraction. He could work with that.

"When will you free me?"

He could see how much she hated to ask that. "When it doesn't matter anymore if everyone knows, or if I can't keep Asima quiet."

She took a deep breath. Probably trying to control her temper now that he'd said he liked it.

"What're cosmic troublemakers?"

"Exactly what they sound like. They're supernatural beings who spread their own brand of chaos throughout the universe. For example: you met Edge back in the conference room. He was the cosmic troublemaker in charge of death."

She paled. "Then he was like you."

Evil incarnate. "Not exactly. He worked under a different

management system. The Big Boss keeps a tight rein on the trouble-makers. My master encourages every kind of excess as long as the end results are deaths or damned souls."

He saw the questions lining up in her mind. Why did he use the past tense with Edge? Why did he refer to the big guy down under as Master? All things she didn't need to know now.

"So you're the ultimate rotten apple." She sounded serious.

He sighed. "The clichés keep coming. Humans don't believe in gray areas unless it pertains to them. Demons aren't a uniform army marching to the same wicked beat. Some are the ravenous monsters humans picture when they say the word. Others are varying shades of gray."

"I don't believe you."

"I didn't expect you to." There was nothing more he could or would say to convince her. Not after experiencing Klepoth's fun-filled trip into the past. There was nothing gray about that.

She remained still for a moment. He liked that about her, that she didn't have to fill every second with talk to keep her fear at bay. And she *was* afraid. He was an expert at sensing terror in his prey.

"I was just thinking about what Holgarth said. He's right. Fear *has* driven me most of my life. Fear that I'd be like Dad—drifting from job to job, ending up a burden to my family. Fear that I'd grow weak and fall in love with a man just like Dad. Don't they say that women end up marrying men like their fathers? Now fear of this place. Fear of *you*."

Ivy took a deep breath. "And I don't have a clue why I'm telling you this."

"So what are you going to do with all this fear?" The music was beginning again in his mind. Something liquid and lyrical, filled with joy and mystery. He allowed the melody to take form and breathe. When it was ready, he might play it for her.

She met his gaze. "I'll deal with it one monster at a time." She met his gaze. "And I'll never respect a man who steals my words from me."

He didn't know what that had to do with fear. Why should he care if she respected him? For just a moment, he felt like telling her about the bargain he'd made with Bain. See if she'd respect the demon who was trying to save her butt. He resisted the urge. It was immature. And one thing he'd never been was immature.

Ivy stood. "I think I'm through with my questions for now." She bit her lip as she looked away from him.

Something mean in him—yes, he was a demon, so meanness was a given—made him want to get in one last jab at her. If she thought he was a monster, then he'd say something monstrous for her to remember him by.

"By the way, you might want to talk to your parents."

She glanced back at him. "Why?"

"You were able to see through the ogre's glamour. A one-hundred-percent-certified human being wouldn't be able to do that."

Her eyes widened.

"Exactly. I'd say you have your own little bit of monster in you."

5

Ivy thought she could handle the fear, the panic. She had so far. Sort of. But this terror was different, *personal*. She could leave the castle behind her, forget about Murmur with his beautiful everything. But she couldn't forget his words: *You have your own little bit of monster in you.* A rotten, lousy lie. Except that it didn't feel like a lie.

She needed to think, but not inside the castle. It felt like a living thing, gleefully watching as she drowned in her own uncertainties. Escaping through the great hall door, she paused in the courtyard to look around. Ivy shivered. Galveston didn't get really cold in winter, but in February, when the wind was blowing off the Gulf, it was way too cool to sit outside.

Then she spotted the small greenhouse tucked off to the side of the castle. Wrapping her arms around herself, she walked toward it. At least it should be warm for the plants and hopefully empty. She stepped inside. Finally, alone.

"Hi, there. Can I help you?"

Or not. Ivy sighed. She glanced at the woman standing among the plants at the back of the greenhouse. About Ivy's age. Pretty. The woman had warm brown hair with blond highlights and big hazel eyes. "I'm sorry. I didn't know anyone was in here." She turned to leave.

"No, wait." The woman stepped toward her. "Don't let me scare you away." She smiled, and it reached her eyes.

Kind eyes. Ivy didn't sense any scary things lurking beneath the surface. "That's okay, I was just looking for a quiet place where I could sit and think."

The woman pointed toward one of two folding chairs near the door. "Feel free to sit and think all you want. It's just me and the plants. We don't waste a lot of time chatting." Her smile was warm and her voice friendly.

Ivy dropped onto one of the chairs. "I'm Ivy, Sparkle's new assistant."

The woman laughed. It made Ivy want to join her.

"If this is your first exposure to Sparkle, I'm not surprised you're sneaking off to the greenhouse. You're safe from her here, though. Sparkle is *not* one with nature." She moved back to her plants. "I'm Cinn, Dacian's mate."

"The vampire?" Funny what a difference a few days could make. Meeting a vampire's wife didn't even quicken her heartbeat.

"Yes, the vampire." Cinn didn't look at Ivy as she examined a delicate fernlike plant. "I see someone has told you about the . . . specialness of the castle."

"If you mean did I dance with a demon on the beach, have a troll threaten me, chat with a couple of cats, and . . ." She still couldn't talk about the freaking ogre. "I'd say, yes, I know about the castle's *specialness*."

Cinn abandoned her plants and walked over to sit beside Ivy. She looked worried. "Which demon?"

"Murmur."

Cinn nodded. "Of course, Murmur. He's a spectacular man, and I understand his lure, but—"

"I know. I should never dance with him. Holgarth warned me. But I didn't die. I danced with him, and I'm still here." Ivy didn't understand how she could be so furious with Murmur for what he'd done to her and still jump to his defense.

Cinn looked sympathetic. "You like him."

Ivy widened her eyes. *Like him?* Well, maybe. The same way she'd "like" a tiger. She could admire its beauty and power, but she'd never invite it to dinner.

Ivy shrugged. "I suppose so. That doesn't mean I don't recognize how dangerous he is."

"I try not to judge him." Cinn's expression turned thoughtful. "I mean, what would it be like to have no free will, to never love anyone or anything except your music? And that one thing you love is tied to evil." She glanced at her plants. "I can't imagine giving up my plants. But if Murmur tried to walk away from his master, he'd probably lose it all—his music, his power, and probably his life. Well, maybe not his life. His corporeal body would die, and his essence would end up back in the Underworld."

Put that way . . . Ivy shuddered. "His music. He has no power over how he uses it?"

"I'm not sure. That's something you'd have to ask him."

Wasn't going to happen anytime soon. Time to change the subject. "What does it mean if you can see through glamours?"

Ivy hadn't meant to blurt that out, but since it balanced on the very top of her pile of terrors, she had to know. And who else could she ask? None of the others she'd met here. They all made her uncomfortable. Besides, there was something about Cinn that said she could be trusted.

"You?"

Ivy nodded.

"Surprising." Cinn frowned. "I'd bet Sparkle knew this when she hired you. Sparkle plays all the angles."

"I doubt it. There was nothing strange in my life until I got here."

"Yes, well, Sparkle has ways of *knowing* things." Cinn looked as though she had personal experience with Sparkle's "knowing."

"So, what does it *mean?*" Before she left here in two weeks, Ivy was going to have a heart-to-heart with Sparkle Stardust. Sparkle might not have exactly misrepresented the job, but she'd left out a lot of important details.

"I'm not sure. It does mean that someone on your family tree was more than human." Cinn bit her lip as she thought. "Not vampire or shape-shifter. Probably not demon, or else you'd have definite personality symptoms. Maybe angel." She met Ivy's gaze. "But my best guess would be that you have Sidhe blood somewhere."

When she saw Ivy's blank expression, she explained. "Faery blood. The Sidhe are the beautiful ones." She smiled. "Unfortunately, they're also scheming, manipulative, and not too loveable. But they're powerful. Very powerful."

Ivy's heartbeat pounded a frantic accompaniment to her inner wails of *no, no, no.* All Murmur had to do was add a melody line and they'd have a hit. "How do you know all this?" *What are you?*

"Because I'm married to a vampire, and he made sure to fill me in." Cinn reached out to pat her hand. "I understand what you're going through, Ivy. I was like you. I'll tell you my story someday when I have more time." She glanced at her watch. "But Dacian will be waking in a few minutes, and I want to be with him when he does." Her smile said exactly why she wanted to be there when he woke.

"Oh, sorry. It was great meeting you. I'll—"

"Wait." Cinn stood and went over to the small fernlike plant. She picked it up and brought it back to where Ivy still sat. "Take Whimsy. She'll make things a little better."

Ivy blinked as she took the plant. "Uh, thanks, but I'm not very good with plants." It would take more than a plant to right her personal ship.

"Don't worry, Whimsy is low maintenance. Put her on your nightstand." Her voice softened. "And talk to your parents."

Ivy didn't even remember stumbling back to her room. She placed Whimsy on the nightstand and then flopped onto the bed. She wrapped the comforter around her, but it didn't help. The cold was on the inside. Taking a deep, calming breath, she pulled her cell phone from her pocket and called home.

Dad answered. Of course. Mom would still be working. But that was okay, because Dad was the one she wanted anyway. "Do you have a minute, Dad?"

"I have an hour if you need it, honey. Time is the one thing I have plenty of."

She heard an underlying sadness in her father's reply. Had it always been there? Why hadn't she recognized it before this? Maybe because she'd been too busy feeling resentful toward him and his "voices," blaming him for Mom having to work so hard to support them.

"Dad . . ." What should she say? But she had to tell him, had to find out if she was like him. And he was the only one in her family who wouldn't call her crazy for what she was about to say. "These voices you hear . . ."

She could sense his sudden tension.

"Yes?"

"Do you just hear them, or do you . . . see things too?"

The silence dragged on so long that Ivy thought he wasn't going to answer.

When he spoke, it was barely a whisper. "I see things too."

"Why didn't you ever tell us?" She closed her eyes.

His bark of laughter held so much bitterness that tears prickled behind her closed lids.

"Everyone already thought I was crazy with a side helping of lazy. If I started seeing things too . . ."

She heard the shrug in his voice.

"It didn't matter. No one would believe that I saw things any more than they believed I heard voices."

"So why are you admitting it to me?"

His laughter gentled. Once again he was the man she might not have respected but always loved.

"Because I think the same thing is happening to you, or else you wouldn't have bothered to call me. I might not know how to make them go away, honey, but I'll do my damn best to make sure they don't hurt you." He sounded fiercely protective. "Tell me about them."

She nodded even though he couldn't see her. Tears slipped down her face. "It's my new job. Dad, there really are trolls, demons, and other things. They *exist*. I've seen them and talked to them." She paused to grab a tissue so she could head off a runny nose.

"Why now, Ivy? Why are you seeing them *now*?" He didn't sound shocked or disbelieving, just worried.

"I don't know. Maybe because there're so many of them here, and they have so much power that they jump-started something in my head."

She thought back to the story Dad had told about when his voices started. He hadn't mentioned the beginning for a lot of years. But who would keep telling a story when not even his family believed him? *I'm so sorry, Dad.* "You touched a live wire, didn't you? After that, you could hear them." *See them.*

"Maybe that's it. Both of us took a huge power hit, even if the jolts came from different sources." He sounded excited.

Now for the tough part. "Dad, was there anyone in your family who was . . . different? I mean, someone who never felt right." She wasn't handling this well. May as well come right out and say it. "Was there anyone who might not have been human?"

Ivy heard him suck in his breath before speaking. "No one. I can't believe you're even . . ." Then, silence. Finally, he sighed. And when he spoke again there was wonder and something else in his voice. "My grandfather on my father's side. I never knew him. He disappeared from my grandmother's life before my father was even born."

"Any pictures?"

"None. I suppose he never seemed real to me. My grandmother didn't tell any of the family much about him other than that he was a beautiful, cold bastard and that she was glad he'd left. Dad told me he thought she still loved him no matter what she said." Her father sounded distracted. "Dad never admitted hearing voices or seeing things, but he might've been smart enough to keep it to himself. I need to do some research."

Ivy's grandfather had died years ago, so there would be no questioning him.

"Yes, well, I just wanted to let you know there are now officially two crazies in the family." She widened her eyes. "Please, don't tell Mom."

"I won't. She'd never understand." His resignation sounded years old. "Your mother is a wonderful woman, but staying grounded is her obsession." The silence built. "And I'm sorry I never handled things better, sweetheart. I pushed everyone out of my life except for the voices and the . . . things I saw. You, your mom, and your brother deserved better."

Ivy swiped at her tears and focused on not sniffling. "At least you're not alone anymore, Dad."

He sighed. "I'd rather stay alone forever if it meant you'd be spared this—a lifetime of pretending you didn't see them standing right next to you, pretending you didn't hear them talking to each other."

She wondered if he was wiping away his own tears.

Then he was all worried-Dad again. "Do you want to come home? I don't think you should stay in that place. I have a final check coming from the job I just quit. I can send you a plane ticket tomorrow and—"

"No, I'm fine here." Maybe. "I'll stay for a few weeks and then if things don't work out I'll find another job."

"If you're sure that's what you want."

"I'm sure." She stared out the narrow window. Darkness was falling. She would meet her first vampire tonight.

"Then stay safe. I love you."

"Love you too, Dad." She listened as he hung up.

Ivy lay there a while trying to think things through. Maybe it was her imagination, but it felt as though curls of comfort were unwinding in her mind, pushing away the bad stuff, warming her from the inside out.

Take Whimsy. She'll make things a little better. Ivy glanced at the plant. *Nah.* She swung her feet to the floor.

Just in time to answer the knock on her door. She paused with her hand on the knob. What might be on the other side of that door? She dismissed her fears. Any of the scary things in the castle wouldn't have to knock if they wanted in. Ivy pulled the door open.

Murmur stood smiling at her.

How did he *do* that? The pure impact of him, from his shining fall of blond hair to the almost-imagined music in her mind, drove every thought from her head—what he was, what *she* was, what he'd already done to her, and what he could still do to her if he chose. All gone.

"Sparkle wants us in her office."

She blinked, and it all came flooding back. She wanted her glare to freeze him into a solid block of ice, but she doubted it would work. He was way too hot to ever freeze into a solid anything. "Us?"

He motioned her from the room. "Us."

Ivy knew she could refuse to go with him, but that would give him further proof that he bothered her. He'd enjoy it too much. She went back to the nightstand to retrieve her room key, and then followed him into the hall. "Stairs." She might never get into an elevator again.

He followed her down the steps, and she could feel his glance skimming her back and coming to rest on her butt. It wasn't a bad feeling. "Why does she need *you*? I assume she just wants to go over my duties." With the sound and fury she'd heard coming from the candy store, Ivy was surprised that Sparkle was in any condition to meet them at all.

Murmur's laughter was soft and cynical. "Sparkle is the cosmic troublemaker in charge of sexual chaos. She's decided that we're absolutely not right for each other, but the sexual vibes feel good, so she'll play with us for a while."

Ivy didn't like the sound of that. There were *no* sexual vibes. Not many anyway. Okay, so maybe there were a few. "How do you know what she's planning? Besides, she can't force us to do anything we don't want to do." She wished she felt as positive as she sounded.

"I've been here a little longer than you. I've seen her in action." She sensed his smile.

"I wouldn't mess with Sparkle. Ganymede can end your life in a moment, but Sparkle can make you wish for death for a thousand years."

Ivy almost smiled. "You're exaggerating."

"No, really."

She turned her head in time to see him widen his eyes in mock sincerity.

They reached the office tucked around the corner from the conference room. Murmur held the door open for her. Ivy took a deep breath and then stepped into the room.

Sparkle sat behind a massive desk. An empty desk. She watched them from across its wide expanse of richly polished wood, her expression that of a cat with a particularly tasty mouse. "Come in and sit." She gestured at the two chairs facing her.

Ivy obeyed, aware of Murmur taking the seat beside her. She scanned the room, her gaze stopping as she realized who sat in a shadowed corner of the office.

Zane slouched in a chair watching her. He looked annoyed, dangerous, and beautiful all at the same time. He offered her a brief smile.

"Who won?" Murmur sounded amused.

Sparkle sniffed. "The bitch is lucky I didn't unload all my power onto her furry ass." She glanced at her nails. "Broken. Three of them. I've already made an appointment at the salon. And I snapped the heel off one of my favorite stilettos trying to drill a hole in her ungrateful head."

Ivy caught herself staring. Livid scratches and what looked like bite marks marched up Sparkle's arms. Her hair sort of stuck out all over. Sparkle saw the direction of Ivy's stare and reached into her desk. She pulled out a mirror, comb, brush, and hair spray. They all waited while Sparkle whipped her hair into its usual tumbled glory. Murmur coughed at the cloud of hair spray.

"Now, where were we? Oh, I wanted to talk to both of you before I had to leave. Ivy, I want you to answer my e-mails. I've let them pile up while I took care of some of the Big Boss's business." She waved at the work station against the far wall.

"Answer them?" Panic. "How can I answer them? I don't know what you want me to say."

Sparkle looked unconcerned. "Be creative. Murmur will stay to help you. He knows me well enough to figure out how I'd probably respond. Oh, and my password is 'sexyforever.'"

"Why is *he* here?" Murmur nodded toward Zane.

Ivy didn't miss the animosity in his voice. But she couldn't worry about Murmur's attitude. She was too busy hyperventilating.

Sparkle didn't even glance at the sorcerer. "Zane and I were discussing a few minor details about the castle."

"*Minor* details?" Zane snorted his opinion of Sparkle's description.

Sparkle didn't get a chance to respond because a woman walked into the office. She was petite with short black hair and wide blue eyes. She wore a gray business suit, sensible shoes, and a disapproving expression. She paused, hesitant, when she realized Sparkle wasn't alone.

"I'm sorry. I didn't realize . . . You said you wanted to see me." The woman glanced at each of them before focusing on Sparkle.

Sparkle sighed. "This is Ella. She's one of the cosmic do-gooders we liberated from Ted, the fake angel." She glanced at Ivy. "Ted had raised an army of powerful nonhumans like me—not nearly as interesting, though, because they're disgustingly righteous and nauseatingly kind, merciful, and all that other crap. He told them they were angels, and they believed him. Long story short, they attacked the castle trying to overthrow the Big Boss. Edge got rid of Ted for us. Unfortunately, he left Ella and the others here."

"Edge? But I thought he was in charge of political chaos. How did he—?"

"He was in charge of death back then. He has a new job description now. His work doesn't take him away from the castle much, though. The politicians usually create their own chaos."

"I see." Not. Ivy thought her head would explode.

Ella's smile looked ragged around the edges. "Since we lived our whole lives following Ted's rules, we have no idea how to interact with humans on the mortal plane. The Big Boss assigned Sparkle as my mentor." She didn't seem totally down with that arrangement.

"Interesting." Murmur cast a speculative glance Ella's way. "And what is your particular talent, Ella?"

Ivy wanted to draw the conversation back to the e-mails. How could she possibly answer—?

"I encourage loving committed relationships between couples. I help them see the advantage of practicing purity, sexual control, and modest dress." Ella didn't look at her mentor.

Sparkle's eyes narrowed to dangerous slits. "I will personally kill the Big Boss and take over his stupid empire for this." Then she stood. "I'm taking Ella with me. After I get my nails done, we're going shopping for some more stylish clothes."

"But they must be modest," Ella reminded her.

"Of course." Sparkle's smile was a brief lifting of her lips to expose perfect white teeth.

Ivy wondered why Ella didn't see the cunning anticipation in that smile.

Sparkle walked around the desk and headed for the door.

"Wait." Zane finally spoke. "We didn't finish our discussion."

Sparkle paused to cast him an impatient stare. "We don't need increased security, Zane. The gargoyles protect everything in the park."

The sorcerer stood and reached her in two strides. "They're not enough. Ted was able to shut them down. Any powerful entity could do the same."

Sparkle edged closer to the door. "The Castle of Dark Dreams has three cosmic troublemakers, a vampire, a wizard, a sorcerer, and two demons in residence. I believe that's sufficient security."

Without giving Zane time to mount an argument, she hustled Ella out the door.

Zane stared at the closed door before turning his frustrated gaze on them. "She refuses to listen." He threw up his hands in disgust. "An attack by a powerful force could destroy the gargoyles and take the castle down stone by stone. The castle needs more powerful wards."

Murmur shrugged. "So why don't you take care of that?"

"She won't let me. Sparkle and Ganymede don't trust me enough."

"You worked for their enemy, so, yeah, I can understand their distrust." Murmur didn't try to hide his dislike.

"That has nothing to do with the castle's safety." Zane's expression said he wasn't a fan of Murmur either.

"Maybe Holgarth can—"

Zane didn't give Ivy a chance to finish. "My father is a powerful wizard, but he isn't strong enough to create the wards the castle needs."

She didn't have any other ideas to offer, so she walked over to the computer and sat down. Zane and Murmur positioned their chairs on either side of her. "Let's take a look at these e-mails." It shouldn't take too long to answer them. How many could there be? She just hoped she could get away with general answers. And if she messed up, it was Sparkle's fault for not giving her some directions.

She put in Sparkle's password, clicked enter, and waited for the e-mail list to appear. It appeared. She stared. "Crap. Is this even possible? She has two thousand unanswered messages? How am I supposed to answer all these?"

"One message at a time." Murmur reached over to open the first one.

Hi Sparkle,

I was so happy when you hooked me up with Sidney. You can see from my photo that I created a new me. Everything was perfect. The sex was incredible. I fell in love with him. But then I found out he hunted defenseless animals so he could put their heads on his wall. I told him I couldn't live in a house filled with dead animals. He broke up with me. Sparkle, he loved his ten-point buck more than me. Now I'm so sad. What should I do?

Totally depressed,
Sally

Zane muffled his laughter. She suspected Murmur was doing the same. Jerks.

Ivy stared at Sally's photo—really short body-hugging dress that gave new meaning to cleavage, and stilettos with heels high enough to give Sally a nosebleed. Sidney never had a chance.

"What am I supposed to tell her?" Ivy had no desire to mess around with someone's broken heart. "I can answer business mail. I can't answer this." Ivy looked at Murmur.

Murmur smiled. "I can channel Sparkle as well as anyone. I'll take care of this one."

Ivy changed places with him and then watched him type his answer to Sally.

Sally,

Accept my deepest sympathy, and now suck it up. Sidney was a loser. He didn't deserve you. Forget him.

Concentrate on the positive. You look hot, lady. Think of Sidney as a practice game. You know the rules now, so go out and get another man. Just make sure you vet the next guy a little better.

Stay sensual,
Sparkle Stardust

"That is so cold." Ivy was horrified.

"That is so Sparkle." Murmur didn't sound too concerned. "If you intend to work for her, you have to think like her."

"I'll never do that. I want my seat back."

Murmur moved without commenting.

She opened a few more e-mails. "I've changed my mind. I'll answer these if it saves one person from the kind of answer Sparkle would give. It'll take a long time, though. I'll have to think about my answers, make sure I'm giving people the right advice for their situations. But it'll be *my* advice, not Sparkle's."

Ivy frowned. This would be a monumental job. "I'll print out twenty of these and take them back to my room so that I can really get a feel for their problems." She waited as the printer did its thing.

"Oh, good grief." Zane shook his head. "This isn't that deep."

She glared at him.

"Okay, here's what I'll do to help you. I have some free time. I'll go through these and answer only the ones thanking Sparkle for her awesome advice. Will you trust me to do that much for you?"

Ivy glanced at Murmur. His narrowed-eyed expression said he wouldn't trust Zane to take out the trash. For a moment, she wondered why he seemed to dislike Zane so much. Then she allowed the thought to slip away. It wasn't any of her business.

She bit her lip. Could she trust Zane? It wouldn't be as though he was doing the tough part of her job, and it would give her more time to spend on answering the people who really needed her.

She nodded. "Okay. But make sure you don't touch any of the ones from people who need serious help."

Zane grinned. "Wouldn't think of it."

Murmur stood and strode to the door. "Let's go." He looked disgusted.

Ivy joined him. She ignored his expression. He could just get over himself.

Zane stopped her as she was about to leave. "By the way, let me know when you want those tips on how to keep people out of your mind."

Murmur sent him a murderous stare.

"I won't forget."

Ivy didn't elaborate. No use in putting Murmur in a worse mood by bringing the whole rat scene up again. She left the office. Murmur followed her and closed the door behind him.

She stopped. Ivy now had two unfinished job assignments. "I should go to my room and start working. Or maybe I should just pack. She won't be happy when she sees how I answer her e-mails. Sparkle doesn't strike me as a patient woman."

Murmur laughed, a soft husky sound. It was so sensual that it made her stomach clench.

"She won't fire you. If she wants to make us her latest sex tag team, she has to keep you around." He sounded calmly certain.

"That doesn't make sense. Why us? You're a powerful demon and I'm . . . nobody." Okay, that sounded pitiful, even to her own ears. She needed to work on her self-image.

Murmur looked sincerely surprised. "Nobody? Not true. You were courageous in the face of spiders and rats. You didn't run from the castle after seeing your first ogre. I'd say you were brave for not panicking after dancing with your first demon, but I'm sure my natural charm convinced you that danger can be fun. You are an amazing *somebody*." His smile challenged her to deny it.

Ivy couldn't help it; she laughed. And that was exactly what he'd wanted her to do. She hated being predictable. She stopped laughing as she thought of the ogre. "Cinn said she thought I might have Sidhe blood in me." Now why had she blurted that out?

He didn't say anything for a moment, and then he nodded. "Why don't we sit in the lobby for a while? I need to people-watch."

Ivy blinked. That was a strange reaction to her revelation. Did she want to be with him? He was a demon, and he was manipulating her mind. So, no. Her mind didn't hesitate. But she realized there were other parts of her chiming in with their opinions. The part of her that was shallow and unhealthily focused on his total hotness thought spending a little time with him wouldn't be a bad thing.

After all, what could he do in a crowded lobby? It would be a lot more interesting than sitting alone in her room reading e-mails and sorting through complaints.

She nodded. It was only a few steps to the lobby, and they found a small table tucked into the corner of the room. Ivy allowed him to buy her a drink. "I still can't talk about the . . ." Nope, guess not.

He leaned back in his chair and stared at her. "Did you find out anything about your family?"

Evidently he didn't intend to ignore her earlier comment about the Sidhe after all. "I talked to my father. He said our . . ." Damn, she didn't know what to call it. Gift? Ivy didn't think so. More like a curse. She didn't want to see things like the ogre. "Our ability might come from his grandfather. No one knows much about him though."

Murmur's gaze followed a passing woman in medieval costume who was headed for the great hall. "I suppose she'd do. She's young. She's beautiful." He sounded as though he was talking to himself.

"What?" Was he scoping out women while he was sitting with her? "Maybe you'd like me to leave so you could get to know her better." She sounded as bitchy as she felt, and she didn't give a damn.

He looked startled for a moment, and then he smiled. It was slow, and knowing, and filled with the promise of every forbidden pleasure she could imagine, and some she probably couldn't. "Are you jealous?"

Ivy could feel heat flooding her face. She glanced down. She couldn't believe she'd said something so stupid. "Absolutely not. I just don't want to hold you up if you have something else you want to do." No matter how professional and detached she sounded now, she didn't think her explanation would fool him. "Besides, how can I be jealous of someone I only met yesterday?" She was beginning to think there was a stranger hiding inside her, one who said stupid things and felt dangerous emotions.

"You're jealous." He practically glowed with the joy of knowing. Stupid man. No, stupid *demon.* She had to keep remembering what he was.

And just in case she might forget, a soft melody began to play a background to her thoughts. She opened her mouth to tell him to shut off the music, but it was so beautiful that she decided to let it stay. "Why are you playing music in my mind?"

He shrugged. "No reason. I just like it. It reminds me of you, all soft and sensual." He didn't look down as he reached over and put his hand over hers where it rested on the table.

Her hand evidently thought this should be a shared experience, because it felt as though he'd cupped her entire body. His fingers were warm and smooth against her skin, and she'd never known that one small touch could scatter her thoughts and send her heart into hyper-drive.

Control. She took a deep breath. "Oh." She didn't want to be pleased by his answer. She really didn't. But she was. Although she didn't agree with the soft part. She'd spent years practicing to be hard and focused on her life goals. *Don't just touch my hand. Touch my body, my hear*— No. Where had those thoughts come from? She shoved them away.

"And I wasn't checking out that woman for me."

He met her gaze directly, but then Ivy figured that all demons would be qualifiers for the Liars' Olympics. Murmur probably had the medals to prove it.

His hand. She couldn't concentrate with him touching her. But she also couldn't summon the will to pull her hand away. Maybe his music wasn't the only addictive part of him.

"I need a woman for a particular job. She has to be young, beautiful, and enjoy traveling to unusual places." Something about what he'd just said seemed to amuse him, because he smiled.

Ivy waited for him to tell her more, but after a few seconds of silence, she decided that's all he intended to say. "Now that we're just chatting, I have a few questions for you."

He looked wary. The music stopped.

"Do you have to use your music for evil? I mean, what would've happened if you hadn't just shut off the music in my head?" She couldn't believe she was actually giving a demon the chance to assure her he wasn't all evil. *Shades of gray.*

"The music is insidious and addictive. If you listened to it for long periods of time, you'd crave it more than any human drug." His voice was hard. He made no excuses, didn't try to sugarcoat the effects of his music. He removed his hand.

Ivy mourned its loss, but at least she could think straight once again.

She couldn't help but respect him even as what he said horrified her. "How do you feel about that?" Jeez, she sounded like a shrink.

Murmur's stare was cold, expressionless. "I'm allowed to feel rage, anger, hate, and any other negative emotion you can name. Positive emotions aren't covered in the demon's handbook."

"But you do feel positive emotions. I've seen you smile, laugh."

"Lapses. Nothing but unfortunate lapses."

Ivy searched for sarcasm or humor in his eyes and found none. She sighed. "Well, that just sucks."

He smiled. "See, another lapse. I seem to be having a lot of them around you. Don't feel sorry for me. I get my kicks in strange and unusual ways." He glanced across the table. "And here comes the strange and unusual now."

Ivy followed his gaze.

Asima appeared sitting on the chair across from them. Only her head showed above the top of the table. One ear looked a little ragged, and Ivy could see a few suspicious bald spots. Sparkle had done some damage.

"Ohmigod. Someone will see you." Ivy's gaze skipped around the lobby. No one was staring.

The back of the chair hides most of me. And anyone who does see me won't care. Humans rarely care about things that don't impact them. The cat seemed unconcerned.

"Why are you still here? Didn't Sparkle make you leave?" Ivy scanned the room, certain that at any moment someone from management would bear down on them, lift Asima by the scruff of her neck, and deposit her outside.

"I'm still here because I'm the messenger of Bast, the Egyptian cat goddess. She who is the goddess of sensual pleasure, protector of the household, bringer of health, and guardian of firefighters would be insulted if her messenger was tossed out of a castle she helped save at one time. Sparkle knows this." And if a cat could smile, Asima was smiling.

"Why are you here?" Murmur didn't sound friendly.

Asima yawned. *"I saw the ogre, and I know that you compelled Ivy's silence."* She fixed her gaze on Murmur.

"And?" He seemed more relaxed now, as though he knew what Asima would say next.

"Isn't it obvious?" The cat sniffed her disdain. *"I'm here to make a deal."*

6

"Wait. You're here to make a deal with *him?*" Ivy sounded outraged.

Asima managed a cat shrug. *"It's nothing personal. You'd be much more entertaining. I could help you survive the slut queen's tyranny. But I'm afraid you have nothing to bargain with."*

"Bargain with?"

Asima yawned. *"As in, you have nothing that I want, so why would I do a favor for you?"*

"Because it's the right thing to do?" Ivy's voice rose.

Asima looked puzzled. *"What a quaint concept."*

"I don't believe you." But Ivy's expression said she did and that Asima had better guard her tail when Ivy was in the room.

Asima shifted her attention to Murmur. *"Now, my gorgeous music demon, we'll negotiate. Which means that I'll state my terms for silence, and you'll agree to them."*

Murmur smiled. He'd just gotten a crazy idea. Asima could solve his problem with Bain. If things worked out the way he planned, the bitch cat would earn an added bonus in this deal, one that might *not* entertain her. "Let's hear them."

He could see that Ivy wanted to yell at them and walk away, but he could also see the curiosity in her eyes. She'd stay.

"First, I want you to escort me to operas, ballets, plays, and other cultural events of my choice." The cat glanced at Ivy. *"There are so few in the castle who have any appreciation of the arts."*

Ivy crossed her arms over her chest and glared at the cat. "Don't expect any sympathy from me."

"How many 'cultural events' and for how long?" Asima would find that he'd done some horse trading in his day.

"Twelve and for a year." The cat's eyes gleamed with excitement.

"Wait. If that's all you want, I can go with you." Ivy looked hopeful.

Asima gave the cat equivalent of a sigh before glancing at her. *"Of course that's not all I want. My silence comes with an expensive price tag."*

"Six and for six months." Murmur countered. He was enjoying this. "And you're in human form when we go. I assume you can take human form." He tried to look concerned. "You're not ugly, are you? An ugly woman would damage my cool cred with other demons."

"Shallow jerk." Ivy.

"That offer doesn't sound as though you care if I mention the ogre to Ganymede." Asima's blue eyes narrowed to calculating slits. *"And I'm not only dazzlingly beautiful, I also know how to look glamorous without resorting to butt cheeks and nipple displays."*

Murmur tried not to look disappointed. Butt cheeks and nipple displays would impress the hell out of the faery host. "I'm keeping the ogre's presence from Sparkle and Ganymede to protect someone else. Demons have no true loyalty, so if you get greedy, I'll simply pack and leave. It's always about protecting my own ass. I'm selfish and self-serving. Deal with it." He forced himself to ignore the contempt in Ivy's eyes. "It's your choice."

His loyalty comment bothered Murmur, because loyalty to Bain *had* brought him to the castle. He could understand why the Master wanted him back for a total refurbishing.

Asima hissed. "*Fine. Six glorious events within six months. Now, for my second demand. I want you to play my favorite musical pieces in my head when I command you to. Six months will have to do. I miss my music when I'm away from home, but a cat wearing ear buds makes humans act foolishly.*"

"I'm curious. If you can take human form, why don't you do it more often? It would make life a lot easier."

Her hiss sounded impatient. "*I have several reasons. The only one you need to know is that Bast is a cat goddess, and she wishes her messengers to remain in feline form except for emergencies.*"

Murmur grinned. "Do you have a lot of emergenices?"

She sniffed. "*Perhaps I stretch the rules more than I should, but I always make sure that only those who are deserving see me in all my amazing mortal beauty.*"

He nodded as he bit his lip to keep from laughing. "So, any last-minute demands?"

Her expression turned sly. "*You also must agree to stop at my command. I'm aware of how dangerous listening to your music for too long can be.*"

"Command, demand, you obviously like to be in charge." He'd allow her that illusion.

She widened her eyes. "*Of course. Who wouldn't if they found themselves in a position of power?*"

"I'll play the music, but you can't interfere with my sleep."

Asima flattened her ears and whipped her tail back and forth. "*Fine.*" She didn't sound as though it was fine.

"Now, I have a demand of my own." Murmur tried to look as

though what he was about to say wasn't important. He hoped the cat bought it.

"I don't think you understand. I'm in control." Asima purred her satisfaction with her on-top position.

"I know. You've made that clear. But what if you could get the full year that you originally wanted just for doing one small thing for me?" He watched greed war with suspicion in her eyes.

Greed won. *"Explain."*

Careful, careful. "You'd have to attend one function with me. My choice. Nothing dangerous, just a friendly gathering." He made sure his mental shields were up for that lie. If she got a glimpse into his mind now, everything would be over. "You'd have to be in human form and look as beautiful as possible."

She frowned. It looked strange on her elegant Siamese face.

"Not that you'd ever be less than spectacular." He glanced at Ivy. Her expression said that he was such a slime lord.

Asima twitched her tail and glanced away. *"I don't know . . ."*

"What possible problem could there be? You're more powerful than most nonhumans"—she'd have to be if she'd survived a fight with Sparkle—"and humans don't pose any threat."

She met his gaze. *"Why?"*

He took a deep breath. "I need to impress my master. And having goddess connections opens all kinds of doors."

Asima nodded as though she understood that reasoning. *"I agree. The deal is done. You can begin the music as soon as I leave. I've left a playlist in my mind."* Then she was gone.

Murmur leaned back in his chair and waited for Ivy's anger to explode. He'd ride it out. Too bad he couldn't tell her how his little deal with Asima had probably saved her life, or at least her existence as she knew it.

She remained silent, staring at Asima's empty chair for a few moments, and then shifted her gaze to him. "Is this how you do

everything—with force or coercion or making deals? Why don't
you ever just ask someone to do something for you?"

What? Was she joking? "Were you even listening to Asima? No
one does anything for me without wanting something in return.
That's the way things work in my life."

A frown line formed between her eyes. "Don't you have friends
that will help you when you need it?"

"No." He thought about Bain for a moment. Even Bain thought
in terms of favors given and owed. "People don't do favors for demons."

"When was the last time you asked?"

He'd asked Bain to use someone other than Ivy to trade to the
Sluagh Sidhe. Bain had only agreed after Murmur pointed out the
flaws in his plans. "That's not important."

"Maybe you should ask sometime, trust someone."

Her voice was so low he wondered if she'd even meant him to
hear. Murmur wished she'd let it go. "My life, my terms."

Bain had trusted him enough to tell Murmur his plans. In his
place, would Murmur do the same? Probably not. It was dangerous
to ask for or give trust in his world. "Look, I don't want to talk about
this anymore."

But she didn't seem ready to drop it. "But everyone has someone
they—"

He knew how to stop this. "Come to my room right now and
we'll discuss all your concerns. Just you and me."

Her eyes widened. "I don't think . . . I mean, I have to—"

"Exactly. No one trusts demons, so we get things in other ways."
Suddenly, he didn't want to spend any more time with her, with
anyone. "I'll probably see you tomorrow. Sparkle will find a way to
make that happen." He pushed his chair back and stood.

"I'll go to your room." She got up, prepared to follow him.

What the hell? She'd officially surprised him, not an easy thing
to do. "Great. Let's go." And maybe on the way he'd figure out

something to say. Unfortunately, talking wasn't high on his wish list of things he wanted to do with Ivy.

By the time they reached his room, he'd decided that this whole thing was a bad idea. He had nothing to say to her that she would want to hear. It shouldn't take much effort to convince her to leave without actually ordering her from the room. He could get rid of her with his music, but somehow the thought felt wrong.

Stripping off his shirt, he flung it onto the floor and then sat on his bed. After taking off his boots, he laid back on the bed with his hands folded behind his head. "Just getting comfortable for our nice long talk." He looked at her from beneath lowered lids and then slid his tongue across his lower lip. "Feel free to make yourself just as comfortable." The foolish part of him hoped she'd take up his challenge.

She hadn't moved, hadn't blinked the whole time he'd been going through his act. Her expression said a silent war was raging somewhere behind those big brown eyes. Finally, she moved.

Ivy looked regretful as she glanced at the nearest chair before sighing and walking over to his bed. She kicked off her shoes and propped herself up against the pillow beside him. "Your game, your choice of a playing field. Now, what else can you do with your magic besides compel people to dance until they die?"

Murmur bit his lip to keep from smiling. None of this should amuse him in any way, but it did. *She* did. "I can make you feel any emotion I want with my music."

She shrugged. "Nothing special about that. Lots of songs can make me feel happy or sad."

"Not like mine. *Never* like mine." His voice was soft, a whispered promise.

Ivy hoped she was pulling off her laying-in-bed-with-you-is-no-biggie act. And it *was* an act. Her heart pounded as she forced herself to breathe in and out, in and out without gasping for air, without reacting to his scent—heated temptation and dangerous male. From the corners of her eyes, she could see every inch of his amazing chest—smooth, golden skin over hard muscle. All she had to do was reach over and slide her fingers across his ridged stomach. His flesh would feel warm, inviting her to move . . . higher. Danger lay in even thinking about going in the opposite direction. She'd place her hand over his heart and feel it beating, beating, beating . . . Did demons even have hearts?

"You *can* touch me, you know."

His smile dripped with so much rich, sweet sensuality that it made her teeth hurt.

She had no answer for that smile, so she pulled the first thought she came to from her jumbled mind. "Do demons have hearts?"

"Yes."

Well, that didn't generate much conversation. She'd try again. "Give me a sample of how your music affects emotions." There, that should keep things going for a few minutes while she thought of other things to ask him.

His glance told her what a complete coward she was. "Tell me when to stop."

"Bring it." She tried for lightness, but it fell as flat as her deflated self-image. She'd always thought she was brave. But he'd unraveled her courage just by lying next to her with his shirt off.

Suddenly, his music was in her head, music that was quiet, sad. It filled her mind with thoughts of things she'd believed long forgotten. She shut her eyes. The music swelled, the notes crying bitter tears behind her closed lids.

Ivy had been five years old when her kitten died. The music became the slow strokes of her fingers across kitty's fur, the confusion when kitty didn't wake up, the way she'd cried all day because Mommy said kitty wouldn't be coming back. *Gone forever.* Just like Grandma when Ivy was seven. She remembered holding her mother's hand, not believing, certain that Grandma would be there to give her a big hug the next time Ivy visited her house. She wasn't. *Gone forever.*

Tears leaked from under Ivy's closed lids. She refused to wipe them away at the same time she tried to deny the music. The melody hurt her heart, made it ache so badly that she wanted to roll into a ball and rock to ease the pain. Loss, so much loss.

Voices joined the song in her head. She couldn't quite understand what they were saying, but each voice clawed at her emotions, forced her to remember. Harry. Ivy had thought she loved him when she was seventeen. She felt once again the soul-deep agony when he said he didn't want her anymore, would never hold her again. *Gone forever.*

Every single memory crowded around her, slashing at her, opening wounds in the exact same way they had on the days they'd happened. She bled sorrow.

"Please." She could barely get the words past her lips. "Enough." The music stopped.

She opened her eyes and reached for the tissue box on the nightstand. It was a few minutes before she could speak. Murmur said nothing.

When she finally felt in control again, she asked the question she already knew the answer to. But she wanted to hear him say it. "What would happen to someone if you decided not to stop?"

He didn't turn his head to look at her. "What would *you* do if the feelings I gave you went on forever?"

Ivy felt ice filling her veins, freezing her from the inside out. She'd do anything to stop the grief—go mad or die.

"You had your choice of emotions. Why didn't you choose a sexual one?" Maybe she should screen her questions before they popped out of her mouth.

"Because it would've been too easy." He looked at her then. "When it happens, I want it to be honest, something we both want."

When? His homeland would become a giant ice rink before that happened. Was the word "honesty" even in a demonic dictionary? "How do you use emotional attacks?" She tried to hide the coldness in her voice that matched the coldness inside her. After all, she'd asked for the demonstration.

"Evil draws demons. I particularly enjoy claiming humans who've committed unspeakable crimes, who think they're powerful because they've ended lives, who think no one can touch them. Then I scare them to death with my music."

He smiled. She shuddered.

"So you become their judge, jury, and executioner." She didn't know why she was pushing so hard. Did she want him to tell her to leave? Did she want to sever the tentative connection she'd begun to feel? Yes. No. Damn, she didn't know.

He looked at her, surprised. "It's never that. Demons don't care about justice. Life is never fair, and most evil goes unpunished. Each of us chooses our victims. Some target the innocent. I get my thrills by targeting the most vicious among you. I love to see their expressions when they're faced with the impossible—something more evil than they are."

Something. That's the word he used to describe himself. She studied the painting on the wall across from her without even seeing it. He thought of himself as a thing. How could she feel any sympathy for a demon, for heaven's sake? But she did. And felt the world as she'd always believed it to be tilt.

"Next question, and then it's my turn." He turned on his side to face her.

Ivy yawned. This day seemed never-ending, and she hadn't even met the vampire yet. She slid down until she was laying flat. She bunched two pillows beneath her head and then stared up at the ceiling. There, that was better. Her lids started to close. "Can you ever escape? Assuming you want to, of course." Soft music played in the background of her mind as she let her tension go.

And just before sleep claimed her, she thought she heard his whispered answer.

"No."

Ivy woke to darkness and someone's hand over her mouth. Terror widened her eyes as she stared into the darkness. Where? Not her room, not her bed. She started to struggle.

"Shh, don't move, don't say anything." Murmur's whisper in her ear.

She subsided, sure that guests throughout the castle would hear her thudding heartbeat.

"We have visitors. They're not dangerous, but they're shy. If we make a sudden move, we'll scare them away. But then they'll be ticked off and get back at us in small, unpleasant ways." His breath was warm against the side of her neck.

What? Now that her eyes had adjusted to the darkness, she glanced around . . . and saw at least a dozen small figures with human shapes. Not more than a foot high, they danced as they scampered everywhere—on top of the furniture, in the closet, over the foot of the bed. She controlled the instinct to jerk her feet away. And they were . . . She peered closer. They were *cleaning*. She watched as one dragged Murmur's discarded shirt over to the closet and disappeared inside. Ivy could hear scrubbing noises in the bathroom. Why were they dancing? She didn't hear any music. And what *were* they?

"Brownies." He answered her unspoken question. "Just stay quiet until they're finished. They won't take long."

He'd moved close to whisper in her ear, and for the next ten minutes she suffered through his closeness. Okay, so "suffered" wasn't quite the right word. Her body soaked up his heat while her mind played with possibilities. What if she wiggled back just a little? Would he wrap his body around her? Would he touch her?

The brownies disappeared. Too soon, much too soon. At least that's what her body was telling her. Her mind thought they'd left just in time.

Murmur reached out to turn on his bedside lamp. He sat up and raked his fingers through his hair. "I don't need this. I'm tired of wondering which freaking faery will turn up next."

Right now, she didn't much care what he did or didn't need. "Why didn't you wake me?"

"I didn't want to. I liked how you looked sleeping in my bed."

She didn't know what to say to that. Avoiding his gaze, she swung her feet to the floor and stood. He must have covered her sometime during the night, but at least she still wore all her clothes. She glanced at the narrow window where the pale morning light was growing brighter. "Why were they dancing? I couldn't hear any music."

"Remember when you came to my room and demanded a run-down of all the nonhumans in the castle? Afterward you sipped a glass of water and watched while I sent out my music-gram. It was a request aimed at a particular group of faeries. Unfortunately, any random members of the fae who were in the path of my musical summoning will also follow it back to me. The brownies weren't invited to the party. Neither was the ogre." He shrugged. "Unfortunately for them, my music plays on."

"But won't they die if they keep dancing?"

"It's not a death summoning. They'll be able to rest, but the music will keep drawing them back until I end it."

She should ask him what was going on. Something obviously was. Maybe she didn't want to know, because it seemed that in the Castle of Dark Dreams ignorance truly was bliss.

Right now, though, she was feeling totally selfish. It really was all about her. "If I had Sidhe blood in me, wouldn't I be spending all my time dancing in your room too?"

He didn't seem surprised by her question. "The thought intrigues." His smile said it did a lot more. "I don't know, because I made sure the music didn't actually touch you. You only heard it."

She remembered the stickiness of the melody, the feeling that she didn't want it near her. She shivered. "I have to go. I still have to talk to Sparkle."

He stilled. She sensed danger in that stillness and remembered. "Oh, that's right. I saw the brownies, and I now know that you've invited some of the fae to the castle for a communal dance. Which will it be: memory loss or a can't-say-the-word-'brownie' compulsion? Probably memory loss would be the most efficient. Then I'll only be mad at you because I still can't say the freaking word—" Arrgh! She was mad all over again.

Murmur still didn't move, didn't speak. And that was just plain scary.

No one does anything for me without wanting something in return. Murmur's words. He didn't trust, and if she'd lived his life, she probably wouldn't either. Ivy had no illusions that he'd suddenly trust *her*, but what did she have to lose? Only her memories.

"I won't tell anyone about the brownies or your music-gram." She held his gaze.

"What will *your* silence cost me?" His voice filled with bitter scorn.

"Your trust."

"Demons don't trust."

"So you've said. Maybe you should this time."

The silence went on forever as he watched her, and she resisted the urge to glance away. Any minute now she'd find that she couldn't say "brownies."

Finally, he nodded. "Go."

She just managed to control her gasp of surprise. Ivy sensed this wasn't the moment to dissect his decision. He'd decided to trust her, and she swore she wouldn't betray him, even if Sparkle yanked her fingernails out by the roots.

Ivy usually controlled her impulses because they could be costly. But she couldn't resist this one. Walking around to his side of the bed, she leaned down and kissed him. It was supposed to be a light thank-you.

He thought it should be more. Reaching up, he tangled his fingers in her hair and deepened the kiss. For just a moment she savored the firm pressure of his lips, the texture and taste of him. *And knew that something amazing had happened.*

Murmur released her, and she backed away from his bed. His gaze followed her, filled with heated promises.

Wow, just wow. "Well, I'll umm . . . I guess I'll see you later." She turned and made her escape.

He'd kissed her. As she closed the door quietly behind her, she put her hand over her mouth to muffle a hoot of triumph. She wasn't worried about torture. Her nails were safe. Sparkle had an unhealthy reverence for them. For whatever reason, Ivy felt suddenly . . . happy. He'd trusted her. He'd really *trusted* her. *And he'd kissed her.* "Brownies, brownies, brownies." She said the word all the way to her room.

She stopped in front of her door. How *much* had he trusted her? Should she try? She took a deep breath and said . . . "Ogre." She almost did a happy dance before remembering. No, definitely no dancing. But ohmigod, she could say it. "Ogre, brownies, ogre, brownies." She continued her litany of freedom as she unlocked her door.

Once inside, she shut the door, and then laughed as she twirled in the middle of the room. Ivy wished she had someone to share this with. Cinn's plant would have to do. "He trusted me, Whimsy. And he kissed me. What do you think of that?"

If Whimsy thought anything, she wasn't saying.

Ivy showered, dressed, and then headed down to the castle's restaurant. She needed a good breakfast to prepare her for Sparkle.

She'd finished her second cup of coffee and was on her way out of the restaurant when her cell rang. She glanced at the screen. *Mom? This early?* She stepped out into the lobby. "Hi."

"Kellen is gone." Panic lived in her mother's voice.

"What? When?" Fear for her brother choked her.

"I got home late from work. Your father had gone to bed early. I thought Kellen was asleep too. But when your dad got up this morning, he found a note."

"Where did he go? Why?" Ivy's head was whirling with thoughts of where to start looking for her brother.

"He said he knew we didn't have a lot of money now that I had to take a pay cut."

Ivy could hear the tears in her mother's voice.

"He said he had a plan, somewhere he could go so I wouldn't have to support him too. He said not to worry." Her voice rose, hysteria close to the surface. "We're his parents. How would we not worry?"

Ivy collapsed onto the nearest chair and closed her eyes. "Did he give a city, any hint at all?"

"No. But he took his phone, and he said he'd call as soon as he reached where he was going. I tried calling him, but he didn't answer."

Where would he go? Ivy wanted to shake Kellen for doing this and then hug him to her so she could keep him safe forever.

"We're trying to find out if he bought plane tickets or . . ." Her voice died out for a moment. "Lord, he wouldn't try to catch a ride with a stranger, would he? He's only sixteen and . . ."

Ivy understood her mother's unspoken fears. Kellen was special. He'd not only gotten all the looks in their family, he'd stolen a bunch from at least fifty other families. Her little brother was beautiful, like people-on-the-street-turning-around-to-look-at-him beautiful. She didn't even want to think about him on the streets alone. Any predator out there would . . . No, she wouldn't go there.

"What's Dad doing?"

"He's contacting Kellen's friends to see if they know anything. When I let you go, I'm calling the police. Kellen and you were always so close. Maybe he'll get in touch with you."

Ivy spent a few more minutes trying to soothe her mother before shoving her phone into her pocket. The huge breakfast she'd eaten churned in her stomach. She stood, not sure what to do next.

"What's wrong?"

Startled, she jumped even as she recognized his voice. Murmur. "How did you know?"

"I have a vested interest in you now, so I've tuned in to your emotions."

Tuned in to my emotions, my foot. He'd probably been in her head to make sure she wasn't running to Sparkle babbling about ogres and brownies. At another time, she would've told him what she thought of that, but not now. She needed someone. She needed *him.* Ivy didn't question her reasoning. Maybe later, but for now it was enough that he was here.

"My brother ran away. My parents don't know where he is, and I don't know where to start looking for him." She blinked fast. She would *not* cry in front of Murmur.

He didn't bombard her with questions. "Come with me." He led her into Sparkle's office. "Sparkle's a late riser. She won't be up for a while. We'll use her computer."

She didn't question him. If he could help find Kellen, she could keep her mouth shut. Ivy sat beside him at the computer.

"Brother's full name?"

"Kellen Patrick Lowe." Ivy didn't even try to figure out what he was doing. While she was at it, she gave Murmur her parents' address.

"Would he have plane fare?"

She nodded. "He worked after school. I don't know if he kept what he didn't give to Mom in an account or not."

A short time later, Murmur leaned back in his chair. He looked at her. He didn't look happy. "Your brother took a late-night flight to Houston's Hobby Airport."

"That means?" She knew what it meant.

Murmur glanced at his watch. "It means that—"

The door swung open. Sparkle stood there with Ganymede beside her. Someone else waited behind them.

"You have a visitor, Ivy." Her smile said that Santa Claus had left her a late Christmas present.

Sparkle stepped aside so the person behind her could move forward.

Ivy's world tilted ten more degrees off its axis.

She jumped to her feet.

"Hi, Sis." Kellen smiled at her.

7

As he watched Ivy's expression change, Murmur beat himself up over not compelling her silence. He'd allowed his emotions to rule. *His emotions.* That was something humans did, not demons. He'd have to make sure it didn't happen again, or else his master would resort to more than visits from Klepoth.

First she closed her eyes, and when she opened them, relief shone there, followed quickly by love. He'd never say it out loud, but he sometimes wondered what it might have felt like to have a family, people who would look at him like that no matter what he'd done. He took a deep breath. What was he thinking? Demons never craved love. It was a sticky rope of emotional taffy that eventually strangled you. *Remember that.*

Murmur returned his attention to Ivy. Now she wore what he assumed was her angry-sister expression.

He tried not to grin—demons stayed cool and detached in the face of human emotions—as she rushed past Sparkle and wrapped her arms around her brother.

"I'm going to kill you, Kellen." Tears slid down her face. "Never scare me that way again."

"I love you too, Sis." Kellen hugged her back.

Finally, Murmur dragged his gaze away from Ivy long enough to really look at her brother.

Oh, crap. Kellen's face had Sidhe stamped over every inch of it. Worse, he had a particular faery's features, only it was a masculine version. Mab, the queen of the Unseelie Court, had no sons left, but obviously one had planted his seed in the mortal world before his destruction. He must have looked like his mother.

Often unpredictable and always deadly, the Queen of Air and Darkness would want this boy to replace those sons. If Kellen was too human, she would quickly discard him once the novelty wore off. If he had enough of her blood in him, she'd keep him in Faery forever, molding him to serve her. Either way, things would end badly for Kellen and the sister who loved him.

Ivy. Murmur studied her closely. Yes, he could see the resemblance now that he looked for it, though it wasn't as obvious as Kellen's. He should probably mind his own business and ignore his discovery. Warning Ivy would be considered a good deed. And bad things happened to demons who weren't . . . well, bad.

Pushing aside thoughts of Mab and what she'd do if she saw Kellen, he focused his attention on what was happening in the room. He allowed the music that always played quietly in the background of his thoughts to grow louder. Right now, he didn't want to think too hard about things.

Ivy stepped back from her brother. "You're going to call—"

"I already called Mom." Kellen's expression turned rebellious. "I want to stay here."

His sister's expression softened. "I know why you left home, Kellen. Mom told me when she called. But you belong there. I can help with the money."

Kellen looked away from Ivy. "You don't want me here. Hey, that's cool. I understand. I'll go somewhere else and—"

"Of course I want you." She reached out to touch him and looked hurt when he shifted away. "But what would you do here? You'd need someplace to stay. You still have to go to school. And you'd have to make new friends. Besides, Mom and Dad would worry about you."

Murmur could sense the tension in her. She wouldn't want her brother exposed to *demonic* influences along with all the other crazy stuff going on at the castle. He understood that. Yes, he was taking her tension personally. And yes, again, that was bitterness he felt.

Kellen glanced back at her, hope beginning to shine in those faery eyes. "I could work at the park after school, do odd jobs, help clean up. I could go to high school here in Galveston and not lose any time. Besides . . ." Whatever he'd intended to say died unsaid. He stared at his shoes. "Please let me stay."

Murmur didn't know what Ivy would have said, because Sparkle took charge.

"There's no reason he can't stay, Ivy. We can always use extra help. He can even have the room next to yours."

Ivy looked puzzled. "But Holgarth said the hotel was full and—"

Sparkle narrowed her eyes. "I'm sure that Holgarth was mistaken. February is a slow month for us, so we always have some vacancies."

He could see Ivy's determination hardening. "No, I really don't think he should stay."

"*Yo, Ivy, we have a situation here.*" Ganymede leaped onto Sparkle's desk. "*As soon as I got a look at him, I knew you needed us.*"

Kellen didn't react, so Murmur knew Ganymede was only broadcasting to the adults in the room.

Ivy narrowed her eyes at Ganymede, but Murmur could see the uncertainty in them.

"Let the kid stay at least until you hear what we have to say and until he tells you the rest of his story. Because he hasn't told you everything."

"You were in his head." Ivy clenched her hands into fists. "I hate that about all of you. You have no right—"

Kellen looked startled by her words, but he didn't comment.

"Look, it's not about having a right. It's about doing what I want to do when I want to do it. That's me. I have a high guilt threshold." Ganymede leaned over the edge of the desk and poked at a closed drawer with one gray paw. *"Still got that Snickers bar in here, babe?"*

Sparkle took advantage of Ivy's momentary distraction. "Kellen, go with Holgarth and he'll show you to your room. Unpack and relax. Your sister will be along in a little while."

Holgarth seemed to appear out of nowhere to stand behind Kellen. The boy turned and gulped. He glanced back at his sister. "You're joking, right?"

The wizard whipped his robe around him and glared at Kellen. "Just what the castle needs, a teenager—rowdy, loud, and given to undisciplined outbursts fueled by an overabundance of testosterone." He beckoned imperiously. "Come. I hoped to avoid ever having one living here, but I suppose no one really values the opinion of a wise and powerful wizard."

Kellen hesitated as he scanned the room, obviously looking for someone to save him. No one offered, so he followed Holgarth.

Sparkle closed the door behind them before strolling to her desk. She sat on it and crossed her long legs. Then she stared at Ivy.

"What?" Ivy looked as though all her thoughts were still on Kellen.

"Sit."

"I have to go to Kellen and—"

"Sit." Sparkle infused a little more command into the word this time. "He'll be fine for a few minutes."

Ivy drew in a deep breath. Murmur could almost see her trying to collect her scattered thoughts and then herd them into a mental corral.

She nodded. "I guess a few minutes won't hurt."

Ivy sat in one of the seats across from Sparkle. She *didn't* cross her legs. Instead, she tapped out a nervous rhythm with one foot. He controlled the urge to supply a few stringed instruments to accompany her.

Sparkle glanced at him. "You should stay, Murmur. I think Ivy will need you."

Murmur took the seat beside Ivy, but he held Sparkle's gaze. He hoped she understood that he knew exactly why she thought Ivy needed him, and it had nothing to do with her brother. Sparkle's lips lifted in a sly smile. Ivy didn't seem to notice.

Sparkle reached out to slide her fingers over Ganymede's back but didn't interfere as he continued to try to pry open the drawer. *"I need help here. No opposable thumbs."*

"I ate the Snickers bar." She didn't look at him.

"That's just mean." Ganymede flopped onto the desk, somehow twisting his cat face into a sulky pout.

"I suppose you've wondered why I chose you, Ivy." Sparkle didn't wait for Ivy to answer. "I like to surround myself with unique people."

Ganymede snorted. *"Surround yourself with unique people? That's one way of putting it."* He looked at Ivy. *"What my fluffy bunny means is that she wants to be around sexy people."*

Murmur laughed. Ganymede was the cosmic chaos bringer, and he called Sparkle a fluffy bunny? He hoped someone would kill him before he ever called any woman something like that. Love made fools of even the most powerful males.

Ivy huffed her impatience. "What does that have to do with Kellen?" She started to get up.

"Stay there." Sparkle didn't sound like the queen of sex and sin right now. Power infused her voice. "I have a point to make."

"Well, make it fast."

Ivy was saying the tough words, but Murmur could feel her unease with all of them.

Ganymede rolled over. *"Rub my tummy to make up for eating my candy."*

Sparkle scratched his stomach as she met Ivy's gaze. "I chose you before I even saw you because Holgarth said you had faery blood."

"How did he know?" Ivy sank back in her seat, her body language saying loud and clear that she wished she were somewhere else right now, wished she knew what the hell was going on.

Sparkle waved her question away. "Holgarth has his own methods for background searches. What's important is that I love to help ordinary people maximize their sexual potential. Of course, you weren't exactly ordinary, but I decided you were close enough. In fact, your Sidhe blood made you a sensual powder keg." She looked as though she were contemplating the joy of holding a match to that keg.

Ivy seemed to sink deeper into her seat with every one of Sparkle's words. "I still don't see what that has to do with Kellen."

Sparkle looked at Murmur. "I know you saw the same thing we did. Why don't you explain everything to Ivy while I get Mede some candy? I'll be back in a few minutes."

At the word "candy," Ganymede leaped from the desk, padded to the door, and stared at it until it swung open. He stepped into the lobby and waited for Sparkle. Then he shut the door.

"How does he do that?"

Ivy sounded as though she didn't really care how he did it, so Murmur ignored the question. Sparkle always played angles. She must think they'd bond if he was the one to lay the cold hard facts on Ivy. *Way to miscalculate, Sparkle.* In the unlikely event they actually did bond, Murmur felt pretty sure it wouldn't be a good thing. His coldly analytical mind demanded that he back off. His body had a whole set of other demands. He turned his mental music up another decibel.

"You already knew about your Sidhe blood, but did you ever think beyond yourself?" Murmur moved his chair a little closer to her.

He didn't try to touch her, though, and he kept his music to himself. It wouldn't take much to send her running from the room. She'd collect her brother, and he'd never see her again. That wasn't an acceptable conclusion for him anymore.

She frowned.

He didn't wait for her to comment. "Kellen has a true Sidhe face. You look human, but any nonhuman who saw your brother would know what he was."

"But he *is* human. I've lived with him my whole life. Don't you think I'd know if he wasn't?" Her voice rose and she clutched the arms of her chair in a white-knuckled grip.

"He has the blood of both races, but from his looks I'd say his faery blood is predominant." He held up his hand to keep her from interrupting. "Think about it. He's lived in a house where his mother and sister held his father in contempt because of the voices he heard."

"I didn't hold Dad in contempt." She glanced away, then sighed. "Yes, I'll admit that the respect wasn't always there, but I never stopped loving him."

Murmur nodded. "So why would Kellen allow either of you to

suspect that he was like his dad in any way?" He thought for a moment. "He could be like you were—unawakened—but I doubt it. From appearances, I'd say his fae blood flows strongly. And right now he's at the prime age for a power surge. I bet he's one confused kid."

"Ohmigod." She dropped her head into her hands. "Poor Kellen."

Now came the toughest part. "Ganymede had a reason for suggesting that Kellen stay here. Your brother could be in danger."

"Why?" She straightened, her expression distressed, protective.

"Kellen doesn't just have the face of any ordinary Sidhe. Looking at him is like looking at the male version of Mab, queen of the Unseelie Court."

"What does that even mean?"

He hated the way every word he said was overwhelming her, turning her safe world into a savage jungle. But she needed to understand.

"Mab's blood runs in your brother's veins, in yours as well. But you've inherited the face of your human relations. I assume your father did too, or else he wouldn't have escaped the Sidhe's notice for so long.

"Mab has no living sons, and if she finds out about Kellen, she'll try to take him." *She* would *take him*. Not much could stop the Winter Queen. But no need to tell Ivy that right now.

He could almost see her gathering her strength. She would try to keep her brother out of Mab's hands if it came to that. Murmur refused to look beyond that statement, to what *he'd* do if that happened. He didn't know, and it wouldn't do any good to speculate.

"Shouldn't I take Kellen somewhere away from this place? There are too many nonhumans here who might recognize his face the same way you guys did."

"The fae are everywhere, Ivy. Humans just can't see them the way you can now. Your brother has flown under Mab's radar so far, but his luck won't last forever. One of them might recognize Kellen even on that desert island you're probably thinking about."

"So what should I do?" She dropped her hands to her lap, clenching and unclenching them.

"Stay here with Kellen while Ganymede and Sparkle think of some way to protect your brother for the long haul, so that, some night years from now, the queen's forces don't come for him."

"Just Ganymede and Sparkle?"

"We'll *all* work on it." He'd been a demon too long to feel comfortable offering aid to anyone, but if he was part of a mob helping Ivy then it wasn't really personal. He almost laughed. Was he trying to lose himself in the crowd? Who was he kidding? Certainly not his master. Murmur was planning to do a freaking good deed. He could expect another visit from Klepoth soon.

Klepoth dealt in illusions, though, not reality. Could he make them bad enough to drive Murmur back to the Underworld? There was a time when that would have been a definite yes. But Murmur had grown more powerful through the centuries. Powerful enough to defy the Master? Something to think about.

Ivy nodded, shell-shocked. "I need to talk to Kellen." Without looking at Murmur again, she stood and left the room. She didn't bother shutting the door behind her.

And as much as he wanted to go after her, he realized she probably needed time alone with her brother. Besides, if someone wasn't here when Sparkle came back, she would just come looking for them. At least he could occupy the queen of sex and sin long enough to give Ivy the time she needed.

While he waited for Sparkle to return, he tried to untangle all the plot threads in his life. He had to sell Bain on the idea of giving Asima to the Sluagh Sidhe. He had to keep his master off his back. He had to get rid of Klepoth. He had to help deal with Mab along with the faery host.

Asima's musical request pinged in his mind. He winced as she chose some opera featuring a man and woman with really big voices. Damn, he wouldn't last through six months of this crap. *Relax, all you have to do is last two weeks until the Sluagh Sidhe claims her.*

Sparkle entered her office with a much happier Ganymede in tow. She looked around. "Just you?"

"Ivy needs time to talk to her brother."

Sparkle nodded as she once again took a seat behind her desk.

Ganymede leaped onto the chair beside Murmur. *"I've had my sugar fix. I'm good for another half hour."*

Sparkle steepled her hands beneath her chin and studied Murmur. "Maybe it's better to have you alone right now. Ivy wouldn't be in any mood to listen to me anyway."

Murmur thought about excusing himself before Sparkle had time to roll out her sexual agenda. He didn't. He hated to admit it, but he was curious. "So talk."

"I want you and Ivy to hook up."

Sparkle was nothing if not direct.

"Got it. And I should do this why?" Murmur knew a hypocrite when he heard one. And this one was speaking with his voice. He didn't need a reason to want to spend a night or two or three with Ivy.

"Because it's what you want." She didn't make it a question.

"Maybe. But I have a well-developed survival instinct. Things are about to get ugly with Mab, and Ivy will be right in the middle of it. Maybe I should just pack up and leave." He knew that wasn't going to happen. "Besides, I have a few issues of my own that I need to take care of before I worry about anyone else."

"Murmur, my beautiful demon, I don't give a damn about your personal problems. You should know by now that it's always about me." She smiled at him. The smile promised good things if he pleased her and an eternally limp dick if he ticked her off. "Besides,

I'm not asking you to stand by Ivy's side forever. I just think you'd both enjoy some touching time. You're a sensual creature, Murmur. Use it for a good cause. If you need any pointers I—"

"I don't need any damn pointers." It was puzzling how angry he was with Sparkle for suggesting he do exactly what he really wanted to do. He amazed even himself sometimes. "I know you're the cosmic troublemaker in charge of sex, but this direct approach doesn't seem your style. You're usually sneaky and manipulative. What's up?"

Sparkle sighed and leaned back in her chair. "The Big Boss chose me as his successor in case he ever bit the big one. He's been training me. But I still have to keep up standards with my regular work. The problem is my numbers are down. I need a shining success so that the Big Boss continues to believe he chose the right person for his job. A powerful demon and a human with faery blood would definitely impress."

She made a sweeping gesture. "You're wrong for each other on so many levels, and yet, the sexual chemistry practically bleeds from you." She narrowed her eyes to slits, obviously contemplating experimenting with all that sexual chemistry in her personal lab.

"And if I decide I don't want any part of your plan?"

She stared at him.

"I know, I know. A limp dick forever. But what else?"

"Ever thought about being free of your master, demon?"

Ganymede had evidently gotten over his sugar-induced coma and was ready to participate.

"Before you say no and tell me a bunch of crap about how much job satisfaction you get from doing the dirty work for the jerk down under, know that I've seen Klepoth here. I had a talk with him over a few drinks." He thought about that. *"Okay, over a lot of drinks. Demons can't hold their liquor. Anyway, I know why he's here."*

Murmur figured this was where the coercion would come in.

Sparkle and Ganymede would help Klepoth unless Murmur helped them. That was fair. Coercion was an accepted business practice in demon circles. "And?"

Ganymede licked one paw. *"I'm happy when my cupcake is happy. She wants you and Ivy to hook up. Make it happen, and we'll talk to the Big Boss, see what we can work out."*

"Nice try, Ganymede, but my master isn't going to give a rat's ass about your Big Boss."

Ganymede fixed him with one of those unblinking cat stares. *"I assume your master is an arch demon. I don't need a name because they all think the same. Besides, saying a demon's true name gets his attention. No one wants that."*

Murmur nodded. He hadn't said his master's true name in centuries. That would be like waving a red flag and shouting into a megaphone, "Here I am, your disobedient subject, waiting to be punished."

Ganymede continued, *"You give an arch demon a hard time, and he doesn't pass your name on to his boss, because the Big Bad doesn't want to be bothered punishing demon insubordination. He has other fun stuff going on down under. So your arch demon gets to punish you."*

"Right." What did the cat have in mind?

"Now, he'd like to destroy you outright, but my guess is you're too powerful for that. So he'll do the next best thing and try to strip you of all your power."

Murmur didn't answer. He'd never stopped to think things through, but Ganymede was right. "Go on." He'd hate to lose his power, but he was more afraid that his master would take his music from him. Murmur didn't think he could exist without his music. It had always defined him; it *was* him.

"The Big Boss has enough power to talk mano a mano to your master. He can work a deal, favors and items of interest will change hands,

and you will then be working for the Big Boss." Ganymede began to purr.

"So it's like going to work for a new crime boss instead of sleeping with the fishes."

"You got it. But the Big Boss is more of a freethinker; there's a little give in him."

Mumur didn't believe a word the cat said. Ganymede was running a con, and Murmur wasn't about to be his clueless mark. The Big Boss had no incentive to make an enemy of an arch demon. Why would he bother? But since Murmur really wanted to spend quality time with Ivy, he'd agree. Allow Ganymede his small triumph. "You have a deal."

Sparkle clapped her hands. "Oh, good. I can't wait to begin."

Murmur allowed himself to relax for a few moments. "Hey, where's Zane? I thought he'd still be hanging around bugging you about castle security." He didn't give a damn what the sorcerer was doing, but he wanted to keep track of the competition. Not that Zane *was* competition. Oh, what the hell, who was he trying to kid? He hated every time the sorcerer even glanced at Ivy.

Sparkle frowned. "I banned him from my office. He answered all two thousand of my e-mails."

Uh-oh. Ivy would be ticked at Zane. Murmur lowered his head so Sparkle wouldn't see his smile.

"He told all two thousand women to stay pure and virginal, not to wear revealing clothing, and never to think sensual thoughts." Sparkle actually growled. "If he weren't Holgarth's son, I'd toss him out on his virginal ass."

"My honeybun has no sense of humor when it comes to sex." Ganymede allowed himself a cat chuckle. Sparkle glared at him, and he stopped.

Sparkle threw her arms wide. "Now go forth, Murmur, and seduce the hell out of Ivy." She smiled benevolently at him.

"Sure. Getting right on that." He stood and headed for the door. He'd had about as much of the two troublemakers as he could take.

Deep in thought, he stepped into the lobby and slammed into someone. He looked up.

Tirron smiled coldly at him. "Hi, partner."

Hell. He'd forgotten about the faery.

8

Kellen slouched in the chair with one leg flung over the arm. He wouldn't meet her gaze. "If you send me back, I'll just leave again."

Ivy sat on the end of his bed. She loved Kellen, but now she wondered if she'd ever really known him. Thinking back, she remembered the years spent listening to Mom complain about Dad and his voices. When had Kellen started disappearing whenever the conversation turned to Dad?

"Kellen, do you hear voices like Dad does? Do you see things others can't see?" She had to ask. There was no way to avoid it.

He looked up. His eyes widened. "What do you mean?"

She took a deep breath. He was going to make her spell it out. For a moment, she wished Murmur were here. He'd be able to speak to her brother without emotion getting in the way. No, this wasn't Murmur's job. Her brother, her responsibility.

"Since I've been here, I've suddenly started seeing . . ." *Say it. Just say it.* "Monsters. Or maybe not monsters, but beings who aren't human. Ordinary people don't see them as they really are. But they're real. They're *all* real."

She watched her brother's face crumple. He blinked, trying to hold back tears that would embarrass him.

"There are people here who can explain what's happening to you." Ivy didn't care if she mortified the hell out of his teenage psyche; she crossed the space between them and hugged him tightly. He leaned into her.

Finally releasing him, Ivy sat cross-legged on the floor in front of his chair.

He scrubbed at his eyes and turned his head away. "I thought I was crazy. I started seeing them when I was twelve. I didn't tell anyone."

"Because of Dad?"

"Yeah."

"Why didn't you talk to him? He would've understood what you were going through. It would've made him realize he wasn't crazy if you were hearing and seeing the same things." Why hadn't she noticed that her brother was suffering? *Maybe you were too busy staying grounded.*

"Dad *sees* things too?"

Ivy nodded.

Kellen shrugged. "I figured if I was seeing things, that made me twice as wacko as Dad. Then Mom would start in on *me.* I thought maybe insanity ran in families."

"Is that why you left home?" Guilt poked at her, whispering that if she'd been closer to her brother he would have shared his fears. What kind of sister did that make her?

And how could she explain this to her mother? Mom, who thought shows like *Ghost Hunters* were giant cons, that things that went bump in the night didn't exist.

"That was part of it." He swung his leg off the arm of the chair and sat up straight. "The money was part of it too. Mom's thinking of taking a second job to help pay for everything." He stared down at his hands clenched in his lap. "Things aren't great between Mom and Dad either. Mom wants him to get help. He won't go to a shrink. I think she might finally walk away. I guess I can't blame her."

Oh, boy. "How do you feel about Dad?"

Even though she'd always believed it might happen, the thought of her mother and father splitting shook Ivy more than she'd expected. But right now was Kellen's time. She'd worry about her parents later.

Kellen took a deep breath. "I think Dad needs to suck it up. No matter what I can see and hear, it's not going to keep me from going to college and getting a great job."

"Good." *Thank God.* "All those people you saw in the room with me were nonhumans. I'll ask one of them to explain what you've been seeing." She'd do it herself, but Ivy was still almost as confused as he was.

"Really? None of them are human?"

"None of them."

"So can I stay?" He made the question sound casual, but there was nothing casual about the fear in his eyes.

Ivy didn't know what to say. Finally, she came down on the side of keeping her brother close so she could help protect him—from whatever was out there as well as from her parents' turmoil. "You can stay for now." She only hoped she could convince her parents.

Ivy watched the tension drain from him. "Thanks, Sis."

She stood. "Let's find someone who can set you straight on things."

Murmur would do the best job. *Wouldn't he?* Or was he just the one she trusted most right now? Or maybe this was only an excuse to spend more time with him. She dismissed the thought. No way was she going there.

"I'll get you something to eat first."

She stood and walked to the door with Kellen trailing behind her. A few minutes later, they were in the hotel lobby headed for the restaurant.

Ivy was reaching for the restaurant's door when she saw Murmur. He was standing in the lobby talking to someone whose back was to her, but she didn't bother looking at anyone except the music demon. She'd interrupt him for just a second to ask if he could speak to her brother later.

Suddenly, he turned toward her. But instead of a welcoming smile, he glared at her. *What the . . . ?* Ivy didn't have a chance to wonder what was going on before music—something tuneless and discordant—blasted in her head with enough power to shove her backward. Sound beat at her mind, a shrill demand that she turn and run. Instinctively, she clapped her hands over her ears. No use when the music was already inside her head. She tried to force it from her mind. Didn't work. She was helpless against its command. She grabbed Kellen's hand and started to drag him backward.

He resisted. "What's wrong?"

Before Kellen could say anything more, the man talking to Murmur turned toward her. It was Tirron, the guy who'd passed her on the stairs, the one who'd said he was Murmur's friend.

He smiled when he saw her, and then his gaze shifted to Kellen. Shock wiped the smile from his face. And before Ivy could decide what to do, Tirron was walking toward her. Murmur strode beside him, his expression thunderous.

Ivy gasped as the music stopped. She hadn't realized she was holding her breath. It was too late to run without looking silly, and besides, she wanted to know what the hell was going on with Murmur's musical attack, because it definitely *was* an attack.

Tirron stopped in front of her, but his attention never left Kellen. "We meet again, Ivy. Who's your friend?"

She'd forgotten how uneasy he made her feel. "This is my brother, Kellen."

"Hello, Kellen. I'm Tirron. Will you be staying here?" He held out his hand.

She didn't like the way he stared at her brother. Questions tripped over each other. Was he human? Probably not if he was Murmur's friend. Was he a demon too? Murmur looked furious as he stood a little behind Tirron.

Then she put it together—Tirron, the musical attack. Murmur had been trying to drive her away before Tirron saw them. Why? Did Tirron see Kellen's resemblance to Mab? Fear pushed at her. There was so much she didn't know. And ignorance was dangerous in this new world she'd fallen into. Whatever happened, she had to protect her brother.

Kellen shook Tirron's hand, but he looked puzzled. "Hi. Yeah, I'll be staying for a while." He glanced at Murmur uncertainly.

"Good. Very good." Tirron looked away. "As much as I'd like to stay, I have somewhere I have to be. I'll see all of you again." He speared Kellen with a hard stare before walking away.

Ivy looked at Murmur. "What was that about?"

Murmur raked his fingers through his hair. "That was an unfortunate meeting. Where were you headed?"

"The restaurant. Kellen needs to eat." She glanced at her brother. "Kellen, this is Murmur." Ivy started to add "a friend" but stopped herself. Right now, she wasn't sure who her friends were. She thought about packing and leaving, but then decided she was overreacting. At least here there were people powerful enough to protect her brother. Besides, if she was going to support Kellen, she needed the money from this job until the new one kicked in.

She turned to her brother. "Kellen, why don't you head back to your room? Order whatever you want from room service. I'll be along in a few minutes. I have to talk with Murmur about something." Ivy had to find out what was going on with Tirron.

Kellen shot her a frustrated glance. He wouldn't be held at bay much longer. "Sure."

She watched him walk away before turning to Murmur. "Now, why the flexing of your musical muscles?"

He hesitated and looked past her. She turned to follow his gaze. Holgarth was bearing down on them, robe swirling and pointed hat swaying. The wizard stopped in front of them and glared.

"I hate playing messenger boy. It's demeaning for someone of my stature. But I suppose this time it's necessary." Huge dramatic sigh. "We have a situation in the great hall that Ganymede feels you should address, Murmur." Holgarth shifted his attention briefly to her. "And Sparkle wants to see you. She's not available at this very moment, but she will be. Eventually." He turned, his blue robe whipping around him, and strode away.

Murmur strung together his favorite curses and put them on repeat as he followed the wizard. He glanced at Ivy. Her expression said she'd talk to Sparkle and then she'd talk to him. No escaping.

He followed Holgarth through the door separating the hotel lobby from the great hall. Music swirled around him. *His* music. The music he'd sent winging its way to the faery host. It was playing to human and nonhuman ears alike. Not good. And there was a crowd of women surrounding someone in the middle of the room. What the hell was going on?

Ivy moved closer to him. He didn't think she realized it. Murmur allowed himself a moment to feel satisfaction. Instinctively, she trusted him to protect her. He listened to his music that was *not* coming through any speakers. Okay, moment over.

"That music. I remember hearing it in your room. You said you were sending someone a music-gram. Did that someone answer it?" She leaned forward, trying to peer around the seething mob of women.

"No."

"*Yo, demon. Someone just showed up, and he brought your music with him. Said he had an invite. Explain.*"

He glanced down. Ganymede glared up at him, eyes narrowed to amber slits. Murmur tried to ignore the cat as he strode toward the women. Ivy kept pace with him.

"*My honey-tart is in there somewhere. I think you need to trim the deadwood from your list of visitors. I don't like any guy who makes Sparkle get that look in her eyes.*"

"Right. Got it." Murmur pushed his way through the growing crowd of women. He finally was able to see who was at the center. "Oh, crap."

"Who is it?" Ivy stood on her toes trying to look over the head of a tall woman in front of her.

He heard Ivy gasp. Yeah, she'd seen him.

"Who is *he?*" The word "he" was drawn out on a breathy sigh.

"*He* is a faery, a Gancanagh. Unseelie Court. Now what the hell am I supposed to do with him?" Murmur knew he was muttering, but things were getting out of control. He'd have a long talk with Bain. This plot was his baby, so he needed to do some of the policing. Murmur had agreed to do a favor for his friend, not run around corralling random members of the fae.

"Is he bad?" She sounded fascinated.

He hated the faery already. "He's rare. Thank the gods. Bad? He is if your woman is in that mob."

She looked puzzled even as she edged forward.

Murmur grabbed Ivy's hand to stop her. He watched Sparkle plant herself beside the dark faery and then glare at the other women. Sparkle had some dangerous vibes going on because, despite the faery's lure, they backed up.

"He's irresistible to the women he seduces. Some think there's an addictive substance in his skin. Maybe he just has overactive phero-mones. Who knows? But he's deadly. Women he targets die from the withdrawal when he leaves." Murmur had to get rid of him fast.

Ivy studied the faery. "I don't think he'd need anything addictive to seduce women. That pale skin, black hair, and wow face are winners."

"*He's going down*"—Ganymede pressed against Murmur's leg to keep from being trampled by the women—"*as soon as I can get the bastard somewhere away from Sparkle. Don't want her mad at me.*"

Murmur was deciding how to reply when the faery saw him. His eyes lit as he walked toward Murmur. Too late to get Ivy away. He held her hand more tightly as the faery stopped in front of them.

"Your name?" Murmur wouldn't get his true name, but he didn't need it right now.

"Braeden." The faery shifted his gaze to Ivy.

Instinct kicked in. Murmur released only one strand of his music. It was wire-sharp, meant to cut.

Startled, Braeden stared at the thin line of blood that had sud-denly appeared on his hand. Then he looked at Murmur. A chal-lenge stretched between them.

Finally, the faery nodded and turned to watch Sparkle join them. Murmur's tension eased as Braeden and Sparkle locked gazes. *Lots* of interest there. Ganymede's growl vibrated, low and menacing. Time to defuse the situation.

"Turn off my music, Braeden. It wasn't meant for you." He glanced around at the sea of female faces edging closer. "Send the women away before they touch you."

Braeden raised one dark brow. "Not exactly welcoming, demon. Your music slammed into *me*. I didn't go searching for *it*. The message just said to come to the Castle of Dark Dreams for a good time. Well, I'm here." He glanced around. "When do the good times begin?"

Sparkle ran her fingers under the cuff of the faery's jacket to touch his wrist. "Good times are always happening at the castle. Why don't you send those other women away?"

Braeden looked intrigued. He nodded, and the crowd of women turned and went back to whatever they'd been doing. He'd made his choice. "I'll go ahead and register, and then we can—"

"You can leave, you thieving bastard."

Ganymede's voice was a roar in Murmur's head. He winced. Ivy did the same. The cat had lost his cool, and he wasn't being careful. Some of the nearby humans looked shocked.

"Calm down. Everyone can hear you." Murmur nodded toward the humans who were now looking around.

Ganymede had puffed himself up to twice his normal size. His ears lay flat against his head and his tail was a bottlebrush of feline aggression. Suddenly, all the humans in the room simply left.

Murmur started to pull Ivy away from the cat. If Ganymede was getting rid of witnesses, then bad things were about to happen.

Sparkle glared at Ganymede. "What was that all about?"

The door leading to the courtyard slammed open. Ganymede's yowl of outrage rose from deep in his throat, and as it grew louder and louder, the walls of the great hall began to vibrate.

"Stop it. Right now."

But Ganymede's tantrum was flying free, and nothing Sparkle could say would stop it. Murmur's music cut off as Braeden started to back away. Smart faery.

"Maybe we should get out of here."

Ivy had barely finished speaking when some unseen force picked Braeden up and flung him through the open door. The door slammed shut behind him.

"*I know trash pickup isn't until tomorrow, but that piece of shit was stinking up the place.*" Ganymede looked smugly satisfied. Until he looked at Sparkle.

Sparkle hissed her fury as she rose into the air. She hovered three feet off the floor, her hair floating around her on a nonexistent breeze, and her amber eyes glowing. "Who gave you permission to throw a guest out of my castle? Remember? This. Is. My. Castle. And you can sleep in your litter box for the rest of your miserable existence for all I care, because one place you won't be sleeping is in my bed."

She drifted back to the floor, turned her back on Ganymede, and tapped an angry beat with her sky-high heels as she followed Braeden out the door. Murmur composed a bass and drum rhythm to accompany her exit.

"It's all about subtlety, cat. Jealousy made you stupid." Murmur couldn't empathize. He'd never experienced the emotion. He dropped Ivy's hand. No, he had *not* been trying to keep her from the faery. Absolutely not.

Ganymede sat down and stared at the door. "*Did I just fuck up? And is my honeybun as mad as she sounded?*"

Ivy sighed. "I hope your litter box is clean."

The cat glared at her. "*That's just insulting. The cosmic chaos-bringer doesn't use a litter box.*" He turned his attention to Murmur. "*This is all your fault. Why the hell did you send out your music?*" Ganymede looked as though he was ready for another eviction.

The cat was out of the bag, or in the litter box, depending on how you looked at it. "This isn't my story to tell. Let's meet tonight in my room and get things straightened out." Murmur wouldn't be surprised if Bain, Tirron, and he were sitting out on the curb with Braeden by morning. Asima's music played in his head, something dark and ominous. Perfect.

Ganymede looked thoughtful. "*Okay, I'll give you till tonight. Your room at seven. Have any music to soothe Sparkle's temper?*"

Murmur decided now wasn't the time to turn the cat down. "Maybe."

"*Yeah, well, maybe it might soothe my temper a little if you could do that.*" The threat was implicit.

Murmur watched the cat pad toward where Holgarth lurked in the shadows. "Damn." He mentally scanned his playlist. Nope, nothing *that* soothing.

"I'd like to be at the meeting."

"What?" Murmur dragged his thoughts from the mess he'd created. "No, you need to stay as far away as possible from everyone involved in this."

Ivy's stare was lethal. "I was involved from the moment I saw the ogre. I'm coming."

He recognized stubbornness when he saw it. If he said no, she might follow the cat right now to tell him her tale of ogres and brownies. And with Ganymede's crappy mood, the cat would probably kick him out without giving him a chance to warn the others. Murmur took a deep breath. No big deal. So he'd leave the castle and never have to see her again. Why did that thought make him angry?

"It's your decision." He couldn't help the coldness that crept into his voice.

He hated feeling as though she'd backed him into a corner. Yes, he could still compel her silence, but he didn't *want* to do it. The fact that he couldn't name a reason for why he felt that way annoyed him even more.

If she went to the meeting and discovered what Bain and Tirron had planned for her, so be it. At least then he wouldn't have to worry about his attraction to her. She'd grab her brother and put as many miles as possible between them.

"Good." She looked away from him. "Okay, I know you don't want me to be there, but this isn't just about me. I need to make sure that none of what's happening will put Kellen in danger."

"I understand." And he did, even though her presence would make things a lot tougher. *For him.* Not that it mattered. Not that *she* mattered.

He must have been scowling, because when she finally glanced back at him she looked uncertain.

"You say you understand, so why all the glaring?"

He wouldn't lie. "I understand, but that doesn't mean I have to like it."

"If you're so against me going, why didn't you fight harder to keep me away?"

He shrugged. "If I said no, you could just chase after Ganymede and tell him what you saw."

She looked as though he'd struck her. "You honestly think I'd do something like that?"

The hurt in her eyes bothered him. But he was getting used to her affecting him in ways no one else had before now. "A demon wouldn't hesitate."

Ivy didn't say anything for a moment, and he could almost see her testing different responses, searching for exactly the right one to blow him out of the water with. But when she finally spoke, there was no anger, only sadness.

"I'm sorry. It must be hard to trust so little." She stood a little straighter and met his gaze. "I don't break promises."

"I know." And strangely, he did.

He sensed that she wanted to ask something, but was hesitating. He waited quietly for her to decide what she would say.

"Would you talk to Kellen about what he's seeing? I don't know enough to help him."

"Now would be best." Before he hunted down Bain to break the bad news.

Ivy looked relieved. "Thanks." She ventured another question. "Why didn't you send Braeden away like you did the ogre?"

"Ogres are big and dangerous, but not too smart. And they don't have the magical power of the Sidhe. Braeden wouldn't leave without a fight." Besides, Ganymede and Sparkle had already seen him, so there wasn't much to hide.

They'd reached Kellen's door. Ivy's brother let them in and then returned to his seat at a small desk where he'd been finishing his meal. His netbook was open in front of him. Murmur pulled up a chair while Ivy sat on the end of Kellen's bed. Kellen pushed the remains of his meal aside and stared at Murmur. He swallowed hard.

"Tell me."

So Murmur told him: of the fae, of vampires, of demons and fallen angels, of werewolves and others that could change their shapes, and of all the assorted beings that were not human but shared his plane of existence. When he was finished speaking, silence filled the room. Had he said too much?

Ivy leaned forward, her expression a mixture of shock—after all, she was hearing most of this for the first time too—and worry for her brother.

Kellen finally took a deep breath and nodded. "Cool. I'm not crazy, and the world's a lot more interesting than I thought it was. So what're you?" He stared at Murmur.

"I'm the demon of music." And Murmur waited—for the horror, the fear, the rejection.

"Explain demons—not what everyone thinks they are, but what's real." Kellen looked tense, but he didn't bolt.

I wish your sister had been the one to ask. The thought struck before he could block it. Murmur glanced at Ivy. Her eyes were wide with . . . fear—of what he would say, of knowing things she didn't want to know. It hurt, and that scared the hell out of him. Her fear shouldn't surprise him, though. She barely knew him, and demons didn't get much positive press. It was no big deal if she was afraid to face what he was. She didn't matter. Really. She didn't. *Then why are you so upset?*

Murmur took a few moments to collect his thoughts. No one had ever asked him to explain what he was. *You wanted her to be the first.* Angrily, he shoved the thought aside. He clicked off Asima's music and replaced it with something quiet and calming. Sure, it would tick the messenger of Bast off. Who cared? Not him. By the end of the night, Asima's secret wouldn't be worth much anyway.

He met Kellen's gaze without even glancing at Ivy. "All demons are born to evil." No use sugarcoating it. "When we're released onto the mortal plane, all we care about is raining as much death and destruction on humanity as possible." He shrugged. "It's our nature." Not that Ivy would think it was much of an excuse.

"Then?" Nothing in her voice gave away what she was thinking.

He kept his attention on her brother. "Contrary to popular belief, demons are bent and shaped by their time on earth, just as every other being is. There are those who grow indifferent to humanity, those who grow more vicious as the centuries pass, and the vast majority that are somewhere in between."

"So you have free will?" Kellen looked puzzled.

This was the tough part. "Not really. A demon that remains too long on the mortal plane and loses his zest for evil is called home." He attempted a smile, but it didn't feel right. "It's sort of a reeducate-a-demon-gone-good thing. Once the demon has finished his refresher course—this involves lots of pain—he's turned loose on humanity again."

"What if he refuses to return home?" Ivy sounded as though she really cared.

Forgetting that he *didn't* care, he glanced at her. Ivy's expression made him frown. Sympathy? He didn't want her pity. "I don't need a refresher course. I remember my roots." Not as well as he had a few centuries ago. He hoped she didn't notice that he hadn't answered her question.

"If you're a music demon, does that mean you only use your music for evil?"

Damn, the kid had a lot of questions. "That's the plan. It's my first instinct." Maybe he should remind Ivy in case she'd forgotten. "My music is a weapon—to kill, to tempt, to control."

"Wow." Kellen sounded impressed, if not particularly scared.

The fear would eventually come. It always did. Kellen opened his mouth to ask his next question. Murmur sensed he'd want to know about his blood heritage. He glanced at Ivy. Kellen should find out about his Sidhe blood from family. She nodded her understanding.

"I think I've covered the main points." He stood. "I have things I have to do." Murmur wanted out of there—away from Kellen's questions and Ivy's presence. Because now that he wasn't concentrating on her brother, he couldn't stop thinking about her.

"Sure. Thanks." Kellen was already turning back to his computer.

Murmur figured the kid would be doing lots of research during the next few days. He headed for the door and forced himself not to look at Ivy.

"Would you wait outside for me, Murmur? I'd like to talk to Kellen for a few minutes."

He met her gaze and nodded. He wanted to say no, but that would be admitting cowardice. "Oh, I almost forgot to tell you. Don't worry about answering Sparkle's e-mails. Zane answered all two thousand of them. He told everyone to stay pure and virginal. Sparkle banned him from her office."

Murmur left the room and closed the door behind him, but not before hearing Ivy's muttered, "I'll kill him."

Once in the hallway, he lowered himself to the floor and leaned back against the stone wall. It was dark here. This was the vampire floor. No natural light filtered in, and the lights in the hall were kept to a minimum. Sleeping vampires didn't need well-lit hallways, and the dungeon was only used during the evening fantasies.

Still, he closed his eyes, a symbolic shutting out of the unease that had grown too real back in Kellen's room. The things he'd told Ivy's brother had forced him to face truths he'd been trying to avoid for a long time.

He'd stayed too long on the mortal plane. He wasn't just indifferent to humanity; it was much worse. He actually cared. When had he slipped beyond his nature? Why had he finally realized it now? Not only realized it, but was willing to admit it?

Murmur opened his eyes to the darkened hallway. The truth was there in the shadows that mocked him, that jeered at what he'd become, at how far he'd fallen. Or risen, he wasn't sure which. He'd lost himself, and he wouldn't be checking in the demonic lost-and-found department anytime soon.

He stood and headed for the stairs. Now wasn't a good time for him to speak with Ivy. He'd promised to wait for her, but, hey, demons didn't keep promises. See, he was on the way to recovery already.

A few minutes later, he was pounding on Bain's door. The other demon opened the door and Murmur strode into the room. Tirron sat watching him from the chair. Good. Both of them needed to hear this.

Murmur sat on the couch. He smiled. Being the bearer of bad news could be fun. He'd give it to them in one power-packed sentence. "Ganymede's down in the great hall hacking up a virtual hairball of pissed-off cat because a Gancanagh named Braeden followed my musical weave to the castle and stole Sparkle's heart." He leaned back and relaxed. "Do you want a tune to accompany that bit of bad news?"

9

Tirron's fae eyes were the color of chipped ice, and that was the warmest part of his expression. "Why didn't you take care of it?"

"Take care of it?" Murmur raised one brow. "Was that my responsibility? Sorry, I must have misread my contract. I would've sworn that Bain only wanted me to draw the faery host here with my music. I did that." He was out of patience with the Sidhe today. "And what have you done to further the cause?"

Tirron looked affronted that Murmur would dare question him. "I will not answer to a demon." He said "demon" in the same tone of voice he'd say "pig shit."

Murmur narrowed his eyes. "I don't like you, Tirron of the Seelie Court." Demons had evil down to an art, but at least they were straightforward. If you saw a demon, you knew one of two things was going to happen: either you were going to die, or the demon was going to lay a supersized temptation on you. The Sidhe destroyed you with half truths and deception. He would take straightforward every time.

Something flickered in the faery's eyes and was gone. Interesting. Murmur would pursue that flicker later, but now he had something to say that needed saying. He and Tirron had to understand each other.

"My directness is probably horrifying your Sidhe soul. Too bad. I'll work with you because of Bain, but never think you can play the arrogant jerk with me." He met Tirron's gaze, injecting all the contempt he felt for the faery into his stare before looking at Bain. "Ganymede wants to meet with us tonight at seven in my room. We need a plan or else he's going to toss us out on our asses."

Bain paced the room, his gaze fixed on the floor. Finally, he stopped and sank onto the other end of the couch from Murmur. "Sparkle is Ganymede's only weak link. How can we use her?"

"His only weak link?" Murmur stretched his legs out in front of him and tapped a rhythm with one foot to Asima's music playing in his head. Thank the gods she had a few songs on her playlist that weren't depressing dirges. "His love of ice cream, candy, popcorn, and chips is legendary. You might explore that avenue if the Sparkle one fizzles."

Bain cast him an exasperated glare. "Not funny. Get serious."

Murmur widened his eyes. "I'm completely serious."

Tirron ignored Murmur. "Can we threaten Sparkle to force him to allow us to stay?"

He couldn't help it, Murmur laughed. "Only if you want each of your severed limbs to land in a different state and your head to end up as a paperweight on his desk."

Bain nodded his agreement. "Ganymede is one of the most powerful beings I've ever met. We definitely don't want him to think she's in danger from us."

"Braeden interested Sparkle, but I don't think it'll be anything more than a brief flirtation. Besides, Gancanaghs never stick around long. Ganymede is too caught up in his jealous rage to realize that.

I think what really ticked Sparkle off was Ganymede's interference."
Murmur considered the possibilities. "We could offer to sabotage
the budding romance in return for being allowed to stay here."

Tirron watched him with unblinking intensity. "That's not much
to offer in exchange for bringing the faery host down on his head."

Murmur knew his smile was insincere. Tirron knew it too. That
was the beauty of insincerity: it was so easy to express. "Bain and I
are demons. We understand the nuances of temptation. Ganymede
is a chaos bringer. He was meant to create planet-changing events,
but his Big Boss has reined him in. He can only do minor stuff now.
I bet Ganymede would give anything to be able to explore his wild
side again. If the Sluagh Sidhe endanger the castle, Ganymede would
feel justified in defending it. A built-in excuse if the Big Boss gave
him static about the death and destruction." Of course, Ganymede
couldn't blame *them* if the big fight never happened.

Bain nodded. "I bet Ganymede would jump at the chance to
kick some major butt without the Big Boss punishing him."

Tirron looked thoughtful. "It could work."

"I hate to point out the obvious, but this whole confronting-the-
faery-host thing has some dangers, Bain. If the exchange doesn't go
as planned, it could get ugly. The humans will notice a war going on
around them, and there're just so many minds we can wipe. We don't
want to go viral on YouTube."

"It won't come to that." Bain stood again to pace some more.
"It'll be a simple exchange, and then—"

Tirron interrupted. "It will *not* be a simple exchange. I agreed
to help so that I could destroy the Unseelie. You will not deny me
that pleasure."

Murmur held on to his temper. "Sure. Destroy all you want, but
do it after the exchange." And after Bain and he drew up a disclaimer
stating that Tirron was waging war on his own. Although . . . Damn,
he'd love a good fight right now. Battles were great stress relievers.

"We have to make sure Ivy is with us for the trade. Will you be able to control her, demon?" The faery's stare challenged him. "You seem to be friendly with her. I hope emotion won't interfere with your commitment."

Murmur resisted the urge to rearrange Tirron's perfect face. "I'll do what needs doing." But maybe not exactly in the way the faery hoped.

Bain stopped pacing. "That's all, I guess. We'll meet with Ganymede at seven and—"

"Ivy was there when Ganymede said he'd meet with us. She wants to be at the meeting." Murmur waited for the blowback from that announcement.

Tirron's expression grew even colder, if colder was possible. "No."

"She can't come." Bain sounded definite about that.

Murmur shrugged. "I don't think you have a say in it. She said she'd be there. You want to talk her out of it? Have at it."

Tirron made an impatient sound and stood. "I'll see you at seven." His expression said they were all incompetent imbeciles.

"Just a thought, but you might want to think of a way to get Ganymede's support without mentioning the exchange while Ivy's there tonight." Murmur watched the faery's shoulders tense.

"I'm not an idiot." He slammed the door on his way out.

"Could've fooled me." Murmur had a bad feeling about the faery, but this was Bain's party, so he'd deal.

Bain dropped onto the chair Tirron had abandoned. "Try not to drive him to a murder attempt. We need some semblance of teamwork here."

Murmur shrugged. "I don't trust faeries. Where did you find him?"

"An associate recommended him. And I needed someone who understood the faery mindset." Bain's frown said he wasn't as sure as he should be about Tirron. "I'll keep an eye on him."

Murmur didn't think anyone understood the faery mindset, not even a fellow faery. "We have another problem. Ivy's brother showed up this morning. He could be Mab's son, if her sons weren't all dead. My guess is that one of those sons spent some quality time with Ivy's great-grandmother. Both Ivy and Kellen can see through glamours. If they have any other powers, they haven't discovered them yet."

Bain's eyes started to glow. Not a good sign.

"And Ivy knows about the resemblance. That's why she wants to be at the meeting. She wants any information she can get that might help her protect her brother."

Bain closed his eyes. "Crap."

"Exactly." Murmur felt a stab of sympathy for Bain. "I'm sure Tirron saw the resemblance. I noticed that he didn't mention it to you."

"Did you find someone to take Ivy's place?" Bain kept his eyes closed.

"Yes."

The silence expanded as Bain waited for him to elaborate. He didn't.

Finally Bain opened his eyes. He stared at Murmur. "I'll trust you on this. Just make sure you have someone acceptable to the Sluagh Sidhe."

"She'll be everything they want." At least until she opened her mouth. Murmur sighed. Asima's music was back to profoundly boring. "Trust me." Or not. Murmur just hoped that Asima wouldn't do anything to ruin their plans.

Bain nodded. "You might want to hunt down Sparkle and see how the romance is going." He smiled. "And maybe throw a few bricks into the mix."

"Will do."

As he left Bain's room, he wished he was going in search of Ivy instead of Sparkle.

A short time later, a snarky Holgarth pointed him toward Sweet Indulgence, Sparkle's candy store.

Ivy stood waiting. Sparkle sat on a stool behind her candy counter. She waved her arms around, bracelets jingling and earrings swinging, as she ranted about Ganymede's sucky attitude.

"He says he cares, but has he lifted one finger from the TV remote to help with the extra work I have now because of the Big Boss? No. He says he cares, but has he taken his furry face out of the ice cream container long enough to have a meaningful conversation with me? No. He says he cares, but does he offer to go places with me? No."

Ivy tried to ignore the ongoing diatribe. She glanced at Braeden. He sat cross-legged on top of the candy counter looking bored—long dark hair shadowing his perfect face, his expression sensual and brooding, his finger tapping out an impatient rhythm on his knee. Nope. Didn't seem like sex would be happening anytime soon.

The door opened behind Ivy. She didn't turn to look. *Murmur*. She could sense him. And wasn't that freaky? He stopped behind her. She shivered, and not with the horror she should feel with a demon so close. Black and white had blended into a soft gray. She was starting to see him as he was, not the way his title said he should be.

He leaned close, and she could feel his warm breath against her neck.

"You smell of white sand and cool ocean breezes."

She smiled but didn't turn around. "Are you sure you're not smelling Sparkle's saltwater taffy?"

His soft laughter made her imagine the things they could do on that white sand.

"Obviously, I have to rethink my list of usually irresistible compliments." He slid one finger the length of her exposed neck.

Ivy sucked in her breath.

Sparkle glared at her. "He says we should be free to choose our own friends, but does he handle my perfectly innocent friendship with Braeden in a mature way? No."

Braeden narrowed his fae eyes. He obviously took issue with the "perfectly innocent" part of Sparkle's comment.

Ivy decided now would be a good time to interrupt, before she could no longer resist the urge to lean back against all that hard male flesh behind her. "Holgarth said you wanted to see me."

Sparkle paused and then nodded. "I want you to spy on Mede. I need to keep an eye on him. He doesn't handle rejection well. If Mede thinks he's lost me . . ." She shrugged. "He's the cosmic chaos bringer. Earth could end in a flash of light and a big boom."

Ivy did a few mental eye rolls. "I know he cares for you. Once he calms down, I'm sure he'll regret what he did." Or not. Who could tell with a cat? "But I don't think you have to worry about the earth." No one was *that* powerful.

"You are so young and naive." Sparkle looked sympathetic. "You haven't even begun to understand the power some of the beings in this castle wield. If you're lucky, you never will."

"She's telling the truth."

Ivy could feel Murmur's deep voice vibrating through her because, at some point, without her permission, her body had tipped back and was now snuggled into his. He was a magnetic force to be reckoned with.

"You want me to spy on Ganymede?" She couldn't believe what Sparkle was asking. "I thought you hired me to be your assistant." Normal personal assistants scheduled meetings, screened calls, set appointments, stuff like that. But when had anything about Sparkle been normal?

Sparkle smiled as though Ivy had finally gotten it. "Exactly. So assist me." Her expression said that everything was solved.

Ivy didn't know how to answer that kind of logic.

Murmur stepped into the conversational vacuum. "Feeling let down, Braeden? I bet you expected more from the queen of sex and sin?"

Braeden nodded. "I thought everything would be perfect. We're both sensual creatures. Equals." He thought about that. "No, I don't want to start our relationship off with a lie. No one is my sensual equal. But she's close."

Sparkle growled low in her throat. "Shut up, Braeden. And mind your own business, demon." She curled and uncurled her fingers, a cat flexing its claws before striking.

"That's the problem." Murmur walked over to Braeden and leaned against the counter beside him. "Sparkle is the cosmic troublemaker in charge of sexual chaos. No one can touch her when it comes to matching people who're completely wrong for each other. Did I say 'completely wrong'? Scratch that. They're incompatible except for the sexual attraction. The sex is always great for them."

He glanced at Ivy, and she had the feeling he was sending her a message. But the only words that registered were "sexual attraction."

Braeden looked intrigued. Sparkle just looked mad.

"But Sparkle's job isn't done just because she's identified her victims and gotten them together. She has to live up to her troublemaker reputation. So she manipulates them until they're in a sexual frenzy."

Braeden smiled. He seemed to think the words "sexual frenzy" were pretty special.

"When her victims are so crazy for each other that they're attached at the . . ." Murmur raised one brow. "Well, you can guess where they're attached. Once she has them where she wants them, she rips them apart." He cast Sparkle a glance filled with deep admiration.

Ivy knew she looked horrified. "She breaks their hearts? Destroys their lives?" *Takes away the great sex?* A few weeks ago she wouldn't have thought that was any big deal. A woman was better off without the drama of loving and losing, or at least finding out that the shiny veneer had started chipping off her man as soon as she fell for him. Too bad love didn't come with a long-term warranty.

Braeden smiled at Sparkle, and Ivy felt the power of that faery heat and beauty all the way across the room. But when Murmur returned to her, slipped his hand around her waist and pulled her close, all she felt came from him.

Murmur whispered against her ear. "He won't touch you." Implied was: *But I will.*

And Ivy believed him. When had she begun to trust a demon? Not only was she starting to find it hard to stay grounded, but she could almost feel herself floating away.

Braeden uncurled from his seat on the counter, dropped to the floor, and walked toward Sparkle. "We're alike, you and I. We both understand the power of sex, and we both care nothing for the emotionally weak who don't understand that we're not offering love. When you have no conscience, life is glorious."

"You've got it, Braeden. That's exactly why you're wrong for each other."

The dark faery turned to look at Murmur. "What?"

Suddenly, Ivy could hear soft music in her head. *Murmur.* The music should've felt soothing, but there was something about it . . . Each note seemed to prick her as it flowed through her mind. She winced at each tiny poke. The music irritated her, made her feel uneasy and annoyed with everyone here. She didn't want to be around them. Ivy shifted restlessly.

"You and Sparkle are too much alike. Her whole existence has been built around matching opposites, so it stands to reason she'd choose a man who was unlike her in every way. Where's the challenge if there's nothing about your mate that needs correcting?" Murmur glanced at Sparkle. "As much as I respect your talent, I think you bit off too much with Ganymede."

Sparkle seemed to realize what Murmur was doing at the same time Ivy did.

"Get your music out of my head, demon." Sparkle stood and walked around the end of the counter. "Did Ganymede send you?"

Ivy looked up at Murmur. His smile was slow and incredibly wicked. And the music kept playing.

"He might've mentioned that you could use some relationship advice."

Murmur sounded unworried, but Ivy could feel him tense.

Sparkle's eyes were amber slits. "Annoy me much longer, Murmur, and you'll be humming 'If I Die Young' on your way out the door."

Ivy couldn't believe she was trying to choke back laughter. Who would even think about laughing in the face of Sparkle's death glare? *You would, when you're with Murmur.* He made her feel safe, as if nothing bad could happen when he was near. *Demon, remember? He's the most dangerous thing in your personal universe.*

Braeden brightened. "Wait, I'd like to hear what the demon has to say. I haven't been this entertained outside of a woman's bed in centuries."

Strange. Braeden didn't seem to hear the music, or at least it wasn't affecting him. On the other hand, Ivy wanted to walk out the door, get away from all of them. Except for Murmur. She didn't want to leave him.

Murmur nodded as he stared at Sparkle. "You're fixated on manipulating the sexual lives of others, and Ganymede only cares about his personal comforts."

"We *both* enjoy using our powers." Sparkle's smile was simply a baring of her teeth. "For example, I'd get a huge rush from forcing you and Ivy onto the floor for sex hot enough to melt every chocolate in my store." She shrugged. "I won't do that here, though. I hate having to restock."

Murmur's expression said, *You can try*. He also didn't look as though he thought it would be a bad thing if he lost.

Ivy couldn't keep quiet. "You could do that, Sparkle?" She knew she must look all wide-eyed and . . . naive. She sighed. What did she really know about the nonhumans in the castle?

"Of course I could." Sparkle never took her attention from Murmur.

"You're only interested in how you look. Ganymede doesn't give a damn about his appearance."

Murmur tried to push Ivy behind him as Sparkle's anger exploded. "I have to look good. It's part of who I am. The queen of sex and sin can't look like"—she glanced at Ivy—"her. To do my job, I have to live the part. Mede can look like a slob and still destroy the world."

Can't look like *her*? What did that mean? Ivy caught a reflection of herself in the glass counter. There was nothing wrong with the way she looked. Then she stared at Sparkle. Okay, so no one would notice she was even in the room when Sparkle was around. She glanced at Murmur. His gaze was still fixed on Sparkle.

Murmur shrugged. "Just saying."

Sparkle took another step toward them. She seemed to be getting angrier by the moment. Ivy suspected the music was doing its thing on her too.

"What do you know about anything? You go around looking all hot and playing your damn music. You have nothing at stake, no one you could lose."

Ivy felt Murmur stiffen, but he didn't say anything. Still, she knew that Sparkle had scored. She didn't have a clue why, though.

"I almost lost Mede once. The Big Boss ordered Mede to give me up if he wanted to continue being a cosmic troublemaker."

Sparkle grew more agitated. Her hair was doing the floating thing again. Ivy backed up without Murmur's urging.

"Why would the Big Boss do that?" Ivy thought the Big Boss sounded like a petty tyrant.

"He said I was too shallow, that I wasn't good for Mede." Sparkle's voice was rising.

Ivy sensed power flowing from Sparkle. Suddenly, Ivy felt the first touch of lust. It was heat and need, a slide of phantom fingers stroking her body, heaviness building low in her stomach. She gasped and automatically looked at Murmur. His breathing had quickened. How could Sparkle do that?

"But he chose *you*, didn't he, Sparkle?" Murmur's voice was low, hypnotic.

"Yes." Her answer was a hiss of combined fury and satisfaction. "The Big Boss was just playing with him."

Murmur actually smiled in the face of all that anger. "He would always choose you. Never doubt it."

"I think we lost the point of this conversation somewhere along the way." Ivy was having a tough time concentrating. The music urged her to get away from everyone. They were annoying her, and if she could just be alone, everything would be fine. Meanwhile, lust was making demands. Do *something*. Correction. Do *someone*. And the someone was never in doubt. She clenched her hands into fists so she wouldn't grab some part of Murmur.

Murmur glanced at Ivy. "My point was that Sparkle is happiest when she's with someone who's the polar opposite of her. That would be Ganymede."

Sparkle tipped her head back and screamed. "Get out! All of you. Now!"

Ivy didn't wait for a second invitation. She fled the store with

Murmur and Braeden right behind her. Once on the sidewalk, they stopped.

Murmur looked at Braeden. "You're good. I'd never know the music was getting to you."

The faery shrugged. "I have my pride."

"What was that all about in there?" Ivy didn't have a clue. At least the music was gone. The lust? Not so much.

"It was about getting me away from Sparkle, and weakening her defenses so Ganymede could creep back into her good graces." Braeden smiled. "I was impressed, demon."

"You're not leaving, are you?" Murmur looked resigned.

"Not a chance. Before I came here, I was bored with my existence. Everything was so easy. Sparkle has energized me. She's magnificent, someone I finally have to exert myself to win."

His smile wiped away the coldness Ivy had associated with faeries. Of course, she only had Tirron to compare him with. Ivy could understand why Braeden drew women.

"I could make you leave." Murmur sounded as though the thought intrigued him.

Braeden kept smiling. "Eventually. But you saw how I resisted your music. I'm very old and very strong. Would it really be worth the effort? Besides, once Sparkle and I have satisfied each other, I'll move on and she can go back to Ganymede."

"He could destroy you." Murmur moved closer to Ivy and clasped her hand in his.

Braeden's expression turned sly. "And alienate Sparkle forever? I don't think so."

Murmur nodded. "I guess that's all there is to say, then." He turned and walked toward the castle, pulling Ivy with him.

The prickly music might be gone, but the lust had found a home. Ivy suspected it wasn't Sparkle driven. It had taken on a life of its own. She'd never known this kind of wanting before. It filled her, made her feel as though she'd burst with it. Could desire hurt? She'd never thought so. But she was rethinking a lot of things lately.

"What do you have planned for the rest of the day?"

Murmur made it sound like a casual question, but Ivy wondered. What if she said, "I have to sort a pile of complaints, and make love with you until we both collapse from exhaustion." What would he say? Did she have the guts to try? The old Ivy wouldn't, but the new and improved Ivy might just take the chance.

"I guess I have to spy on Ganymede." *Why don't you just say that you want him for the rest of the day?* She was such a wuss. "You know, if you told him what Sparkle asked me to do, my cover would be blown and Sparkle would have to pull me off the case." And she'd be free, free, free.

"Why would I want to do that?" He looked puzzled. "Watching you watch Ganymede will entertain me for hours. You may as well come with me while I make my report. It'll give you a chance to begin stalking him. He's probably in the kitchen now watching the chef and hoping for a handout."

She frowned. "By the way, why did you look at me when you were talking to Sparkle about her job?" They'd entered the castle by the side entrance that led past the kitchen.

"Because you and I *are* her job. You have to know she's been trying to get us together." He looked weary. "She wants us to have sex, and then she'll find a way to make you hate me."

Ivy pulled him to a stop in the dim hallway. "She can't do that if I won't let her."

"Oh, yes, she can. She'll dredge up something from my past that'll horrify you and you'll run." He looked away. "They always run."

Ivy felt as though someone had punched her. *They always run.*

Vulnerability? From Murmur? She almost forgot to breathe. Had he shown her the first crack in that hard, I-don't-give-a-damn shell surrounding him?

She had to choose her words carefully. No denial or sympathy. He'd never accept pity from her. She opened her mouth to reply.

"You're not making this easy for either of us, Murmur."

Startled, Ivy stared at the man standing in a shadowed curve of the hallway. Where had he come from?

"Not now, Klepoth." Murmur put his arm around her waist and pulled her against him.

"Now is the *best* time, old friend." The man's gaze touched Ivy. "When you have someone to share your experience with."

Ivy felt Murmur's anger, his *fear*. She looked closer at the man who could make Murmur afraid. He stepped out of the shadows, and she gasped.

He looked like a teenager—blue spiked hair, ratty T-shirt, ripped jeans, and lots of piercings. But his bright red eyes said he was something much more, something totally frightening. She shrank against Murmur.

"Klepoth is the demon of illusions, Ivy." Murmur's voice was tight.

Klepoth bowed to Ivy. "You're lovely, Ivy. And you must be very special to capture Murmur's interest."

"Leave her alone."

"Or?" Klepoth looked interested.

"Or I can promise your death will *not* be an illusion."

Klepoth widened his eyes in mock shock. "Threats, after all we've shared? I'm hurt." He smiled. "She'll be safe. But I do think she'd enjoy sharing an adventure with you."

"Don't."

Murmur's voice took on an urgency that scared Ivy. Something was about to happen, but she couldn't defend herself against what she didn't understand. Frantically, she swept the hallway, looking for someone to help or at least a weapon to use. Nothing.

Ivy didn't hear what brought Klepoth to his knees, his palms clamped over his ears, his face twisted in agony. But she could guess.

Murmur pushed her ahead of him. "Run. Don't look back. I can't hold him for long."

And leave him here to battle the other demon alone? Ivy might not have the physical or magical strength to help Murmur, but she had a scream that could shatter eardrums. She opened her mouth and let loose. "Help!"

Several things happened at once. Ganymede emerged from the kitchen with the chef right behind him brandishing a spatula. When the cat saw what was happening, he stopped, and the chef tripped over him . . . and plowed into her. Everyone went down in a tangle of arms, legs, and paws.

That was the moment that Murmur caught up. "Get up. Klepoth will have his head together in a moment."

"Actually, it's together right now. And every aching inch of it is pissed." Klepoth stalked toward them. "Look at the mess you've created, Murmur. Oh, what the hell, I'll take all of you."

That was her last thought before the hallway disappeared.

10

Murmur drew in a deep breath. Ah, the sweet smell of home—dirt, dust, and despair. He'd forgotten the joy of gazing across the vast . . . nothingness. Gray, rocky ground as far as the eye could see under a solid gray sky. He couldn't even spot where the horizon line was because sky and earth were the same color. Wow, how had he stayed away from this for so many centuries?

Damn, it was still as cold as Lucifer's ass here. He controlled his urge to shiver. *Never show weakness.* A lesson his master had physically hammered into him shortly after his creation.

He turned off Asima's music and whipped up something of his own, a sizzling song that crackled and popped in his mind, heating the air around him. He shared it with Ivy. She glanced up at him, surprised. He'd never told her that he could manipulate the environment with his music. Now she knew.

"Where are we?" Ivy moved close to him, her warmth reminding him of why he wanted to remain on the mortal plane.

"The Underworld. Klepoth's illusions are nothing if not accurate." Murmur glanced to where the other demon had found a boulder to sit on. Bastard.

Ganymede leaped up beside Klepoth. *"Crap. You mean this is hell? Where's the fire and brimstone? Where're the red guys with horns, tails, and pitchforks? Where's the big cheese?"*

"This is it, cat. I'd rather spend eternity in your version." Murmur didn't even turn to look at Ganymede. He stared into the distance—hating, *remembering.* "You might do lots of hurting in your hell, but you'd never be alone. This"—he swept his arm to encompass the vastness of it all—"is true torture. Aloneness—cold and complete—forever."

Chef George stared at Murmur, his mouth open and his eyes wide and staring. He'd dropped his spatula. He didn't seem about to say anything anytime soon.

"See, now this is a big-ass disappointment." Ganymede looked at Klepoth. *"Yo, explain this shit to me."*

Klepoth shrugged. "I'm the demon of illusions. The Master wants me to convince Murmur to spend some quality time in the loving arms of his demon family so he can rediscover his roots. Hey, just doing my job."

"Well, this sucks." Ganymede narrowed his eyes. *"Since you don't need anyone but Murmur, why don't you whip up an illusion of a sleazy dive with booze and lots of dancing girls? The rest of us will have a few drinks and wait this out. When you're done, you can pop us out of your illusion."*

"And if I don't?" Klepoth returned Ganymede's stare.

"Then I'd be bored just standing around. And when I'm bored, I cause trouble." Malice filled his feline eyes. *"You seem like a powerful guy, so I assume I'd have to break a sweat to escape your illusion. Hey, I'm lazy. I don't do hard. I'd just hang on the sidelines talking really loud and getting in the way while you tried to deliver your message to Murmur."*

Murmur felt anger thrumming through Klepoth, but he knew the other demon would have enough sense not to challenge the cat.

Klepoth nodded. Suddenly, a building popped up behind where he was seated. The sign above the door read FAT BUTT'S BAR.

"I figure that's not a slam at me, because if I thought it was, I'd have to tear out your throat." Ganymede hopped off the boulder and padded over to the still-speechless chef. *"Let's get out of this freaking cold for a while, George."* The chef obediently followed him through the door.

"Why didn't you just free them?" Ivy still pressed against Murmur.

Klepoth shrugged. "Once I've created an illusion, I can only maintain it if all the characters remain the same. I can change things within the illusion, but no one can leave once they're in."

Murmur pulled away and gave her a gentle shove. "Go with Ganymede and George. I'll come for you when we're finished."

"No. And don't try to talk me out of it. I'm not leaving you alone to face this. Whatever *this* is. So the faster we get it done, the sooner we can leave."

"Ivy, you can't—"

"I can."

Klepoth interrupted. "Let her witness what happens when a demon deserts his calling."

Well, hell. Murmur speared her with a hard stare he hoped would convince her to obey. "Don't try to interfere. This is all an illusion."

She nodded, but he saw the fear behind her eyes. "I know it isn't real."

He wished Ganymede had forced her to go with him, because knowing the illusion wasn't real didn't matter. Klepoth was a master. His illusions *felt* real. But Murmur had no more time to worry about Ivy.

The dead air moved. Not natural. It felt as though the entire Underworld gasped for air—in and out, in and out. A warning that *he* had come. The Master. First Murmur felt the dread, the animal instinct that said danger was near. Then came the vibration in the earth that signaled legions of demons on the move. And with them would come Ganymede's big cheese. Okay, maybe not *the* big cheese. The big cheese didn't bother himself with demon discipline unless it involved one of his arch demons.

They flowed across the barren landscape toward him, the thirty legions of demons he commanded—grotesque, powerful, deadly. They moved silently. Part of the horror of the Underworld was the absence of sound. Demons exchanged thoughts, so speech was unnecessary. Those trapped here who couldn't read thoughts existed in eternal silence. And there were just so many centuries you could spend talking to yourself. This was one of the reasons he clung to his music. If you'd never lived in total silence, you couldn't truly understand the beauty he found in melodies and rhythms.

Beside him, Ivy gasped. "There're so many of them."

"Those are my legions. The Master brought them along to remind me of my duty. I'm supposed to use them to visit destruction on earth." He laughed softly. "Instead of using my music to amuse myself."

Murmur felt her shudder. "Klepoth pulled up the most frightening demon images he could think of. We can take whatever form we choose. Personally, I don't like the clawed hands. It's tough to play a guitar with them." He didn't blame her for not laughing. It was pretty lame.

At a signal only the demons could hear, they stopped. The masses parted, opening a path. And something monstrous slithered toward them. Murmur glanced at Klepoth.

"Give me a break. The Master never took that form." Slimy and reptilian, it studied him from under hooded lids. Klepoth had nailed the Master's eyes. Even though Murmur knew the other demon was creating the image, it made him want to back up. He didn't. "Intimidating, though. Of course, anything more than ten feet tall would do that. But overall, a good job."

He started to hum in his mind. He'd keep it there. This was Klepoth's show, and he'd have to bear it to the bitter end without interfering. The Master had sent Klepoth, and the other demon wasn't about to shirk his duty when he knew what would happen to him if he failed. So even if Murmur tried to avoid him, Klepoth would just follow him around.

His master spoke.

"I am not pleased, Murmur." He spoke aloud in a wet hiss that revealed rows of sharp teeth. Drool dripped from his thick lips as he watched Murmur.

Murmur had been absent from the Underworld long enough to find his master's narrow red eyes with their slit pupils a little disturbing.

"I gave you power."

"Yes, Master." Not true. Murmur had gained his own power. His master gave no one power if he could help it, because that power could someday be used to overthrow him.

"I gifted you with legions of demons to do your bidding. How have you used them? I see no human deaths, no destruction on the mortal plane."

"I work alone, Master." He didn't think the kills he'd made with his music would impress anyone, certainly not someone who thought a death toll in the thousands was only a minimal success. So he didn't mention them.

Instead he called for his music—something strong, impenetrable—to form a barrier between himself and the pain. The music didn't come. Frantic, he tried again. The music had always flowed smoothly, an extension of himself. Now it was gone, as though it had never existed. For the first time in his long existence, he truly felt naked, *afraid*.

"You have failed. You don't deserve your music."

Each word cut at him in a very physical sense. Three deep slashes opened in his chest. Pain ripped at him. He gasped. Blood poured from the wounds and dripped onto the gray dirt.

"No!" Ivy's voice was a horrified whisper.

The Master wasn't finished. "You have killed less and less as the centuries passed. All of your talent wasted. This makes me angry."

Invisible claws raked at Murmur's back. He felt his shirt shred as agony burned through him. He clenched his hands into fists, digging his nails into his palms to counter the torture. Blood, warm and sticky, trailed down his chest and back. He would *not* scream.

"Stop it. *Now.*" Ivy's voice shook, but she stood strong.

He hadn't wanted her to see this. The pain in her voice hurt him as much as the Master's punishment. "It. Isn't. Real." He gasped between each word.

"The *pain* is real." Her voice no longer shook. Now anger hardened it.

He wanted to tell her to go inside with Ganymede, but it took all his strength just to stay on his feet.

"As I made you, I can destroy you." The Master rose to his full height, a scaly monster with clawed hands and feet along with a head that resembled a crocodile's. A long forked tongue darted out, testing the taste of his words. He found them good, because he almost smiled. "You will burn."

Murmur panicked for the first time. Not because of the Master's words, but because Ivy would see it. Real or not, he'd feel the searing agony of the flames, and he *would* scream.

He sucked in his breath as fire rose around him, closing off any escape. Heat blistered his skin, smoke choked him, and the first lick of flames touched him with the promise of unending torture.

Murmur tried to see Ivy through the rising flames, tried to speak words of comfort. But when he opened his mouth, he could only scream.

Ivy met his gaze, saw the agony in his eyes, and lost it. She forgot that Klepoth was the creator of the illusion, forgot that it was even an illusion. Murmur was suffering. That's all that mattered.

Stop! The word was in her mind. It swelled and grew until it filled her, until she knew it would explode from her, and that when it did nothing would ever be the same. *Because something else came with it.* She didn't understand the feeling, the *knowing.* Whatever *other* thing hid within her word, it pushed against her mind. Pushed and pushed until she opened her mouth and freed it.

"Stop!" The sound and power of her voice shocked her.

It was a silent explosion, silent like everything else in this damn place. She rocked with the pulse of expanding released energy. The sudden white flash of light blinded her. She flung her hand over her eyes.

And when she took her hand away, they were all back in the castle's hallway. She looked for Murmur first. He leaned against the wall, his breaths coming in quiet gasps. There were no wounds, no burns, not even any rips in his shirt. But his face looked drawn and strained.

Ganymede stood staring at her, a speculative look in his cat eyes. The chef sat on the floor wearing a glazed expression. His spatula rested on the floor beside him.

Finally, she looked at Klepoth. He lay on the floor, unmoving.

"You knocked him out when you tore through his illusion." Murmur sounded as weary as he looked.

Tore through his illusion? What was that about? She didn't have a clue what had happened.

"*Perfect timing, babe.*" Ganymede wasn't using subtle sarcasm. "*The dancing girls had just come onstage, and I had this giant dish of ice cream in front of me. The cute waitress even poured some Amaretto on it. The Amaretto was so that I could drown my sorrows over Sparkle and her freaking faery. I didn't even get a chance to taste it.*"

The old Ivy would've tried to keep the peace by apologizing. The new Ivy decided that Ganymede could suck it up. "That giant slimeball was hurting Murmur." She took a deep breath and asked the tough question. "What happened?"

"I think we just saw what Mab's side of your family tree can do." Murmur pushed away from the wall to walk over to her. He didn't touch her.

Ganymede sat down while he continued to offer her his unblinking cat stare. *"You've got magic, lady."*

Ivy shook her head as she started to back away from them. "No. I didn't do anything. All I did was yell."

"And that yell had faery magic attached. I could smell it." Ganymede shifted his attention away from her as George shuddered and then clambered to his feet.

"But why now?" It was all too much. She wasn't ready.

Ganymede stood and moved closer to the chef. *"Because this was the first time you called it."*

"No, no, I didn't." She was in full-throttle denial.

"You wanted something tonight, and you couldn't get it without help. So the help came." Ganymede seemed to feel he'd explained things sufficiently, because he turned his full attention to George.

Just in time. The chef took a frantic look around and then bolted.

"Shit. I have to catch him and erase his memory of this crap. If he quits, Sparkle will try to cook. She did it before. Food poisoning sort of sticks in your mind for a long time." Ganymede leaped after the chef.

"I don't think I've seen the cat move that fast since I've been here." Murmur sounded a little more normal.

Ivy's hand shook as she pushed strands of hair from her face. "What now?" *Someone tell me what's happening to me.*

"Now we get Klepoth out of the hallway." Murmur walked over to look down at the other demon.

Ivy couldn't work up any sympathy for Klepoth. "Why did he use that illusion? And how did he make it feel so real?"

"His job is to scare me back to the Underworld. Pain is a great motivator. He can make his illusions feel real because he can manipulate areas of the brain that perceive and control pain, just as he can control all of our senses. This is his power. I couldn't keep him out."

"He's evil."

Murmur looked pained. "We do what we were created to do. Klepoth wants to survive. We all have that instinct. So he does what needs doing."

Left unsaid was that he was no better than Klepoth. She didn't believe that. *Maybe you don't want to believe it.*

She had no chance to answer before Holgarth swept down the hallway—robe swirling, pointed hat tilting, snark cocked and ready to fire.

"We will never maintain our five-star rating if you insist on littering the castle with unconscious demons." He narrowed his eyes. "I'm not your friendly demon-removal service. I have other, more important duties."

"How did you know?" Ivy was learning to ignore Holgarth's rants.

"I felt the disturbance and correctly assumed you were responsible."

He was talking about "you" in the plural sense, because he swept both of them with an accusing glare.

"What will you do with him?" She glanced at Klepoth. He'd be ticked when he finally came to.

The wizard stared down his nose at the unconscious demon. "I do wish we had a garbage chute or an incinerator."

Ivy's horror must have showed, because Holgarth shrugged.

"Since we have neither, I suppose I'll have to shove him into a plastic bag and toss him into the trash bin. Tomorrow is trash day." He cast Murmur a calculating glance.

"No." Murmur scowled. "I won't do it."

"Why not?" Holgarth seemed sincerely puzzled. "He obviously did something to you. Your pain was strong enough to touch me."

Murmur kept his gaze on Holgarth. "He's not a thing to be thrown out. He did what he was created to do. We all do. He didn't give the order for my pain."

"We have to do something, and quickly. Guests who trip over bodies usually check out, and then they go home to tell their friends. It's bad for business."

The body in question groaned and opened his eyes. "Haven't had that bad a trip in centuries. I need a drink."

Murmur moved to Klepoth's side and crouched down beside him. "Go to my room. Order a drink. Wait for me. We'll talk."

Klepoth nodded as he looked past Murmur at Ivy. "You pack a punch."

"You deserved it." Ivy wasn't in the mood to back down from anybody.

Murmur helped haul Klepoth to his feet. Once upright, the other demon staggered toward the elevators. Holgarth sniffed before walking away, outrage in every stiff stride.

"Come to my room." Ivy didn't plant a question mark at the end. She headed for the stairs.

He hesitated before following her.

Once in front of her door, she unlocked it. "Lay on my bed. You still look a little shaky. I have to make sure my brother is okay." *I have to make sure I'm okay.*

She stood there until he closed the door behind him, then she went next door to talk to Kellen. He wasn't there. Panic was close to the surface as she pulled out her cell and called him.

Ivy didn't give her brother time to say anything. "Where are you?"

"I found someone to give me a tour of the castle." He sounded excited. "You won't believe it. I was sitting at the desk, and suddenly this cat appeared. She said her name was Asima and that she was a messenger of the goddess Bast. She freaking talked in my head."

Damn. Ivy didn't know what to do. She couldn't keep him isolated forever. "Put the cat on the phone."

"Huh?"

"Put the phone next to her ear." She waited impatiently for him to do it while she tried to figure out how to speak softly enough so that Kellen couldn't hear what she said.

She needn't have worried.

"I assume you have important information for me"—pregnant pause—*"or you just want to yell at me for being with your brother. Whichever it is, I'll speak with you mentally."*

A convenient skill. So, Ivy supposed, she just had to think what she wanted to say.

"Exactly." Asima purred her pleasure.

Okay, here went nothing. *"What do you want with Kellen?"*

"I don't have any friends in the castle, and your brother seems nice. I thought it would be fun to spend some time with him. Oh, and I know you must realize that he looks like Mab."

Hey, it worked. *"And you plan to do what with that information?"* She put all the coldness she could into her mental voice.

"I have no intention of harming your brother in any way. Consider my lips zipped."

Ivy didn't know how much she believed Asima, but she figured just this once she'd take the risk that he'd be safe. *"I don't mind if you show my brother the castle, but try to keep him away from the faeries. I don't trust them."* And I don't trust *you.*

Asima's purr got louder. *"And what will you do for me in return?"*

Ivy huffed her frustration. *"Name your price."* Maybe she should've worded that differently.

"I have tickets to a chamber music performance here in Galveston. Murmur will be with me. I'd like you to come too. This will be so much

fun." Her purr was a motor revving up before the big race. *"No one from the castle ever appreciates true culture."*

"*Fine. I'll go.*" Fun, fun, fun. She'd get more joy from poking herself in the eye. But being with Murmur would help. *"Bat the phone back to my brother."*

Kellen spoke. "No one said anything. What was that about?"

"We talked mentally." That sounded so cool.

"Wow. Do you think Asima could teach me to do that?"

"I don't know, Kellen. I really don't know." Right now she felt overwhelmed. "Look, I'll check in with you later. Have fun with Asima."

She needed advice. No, she needed more than just advice. She wanted the warmth of someone's touch, someone who'd listen and try to understand. Then she wanted to make love to that person, affirm that she was truly alive and human. Only one person would do. Murmur. A demon. Amazing. She returned to her room.

Ivy paused inside the door. Murmur lay on her bed watching her. He filled up her bed, big and so beautiful she felt like crying. Not the reaction she'd hoped for. "Feeling better?" She didn't think false cheer would fool anyone.

"I'm fine. Kick off your shoes and relax awhile." He patted the bed beside him.

She hesitated a moment too long.

He smiled, and she heard his music in her head. It was soft, sexy, and beckoned her with minor chords dipped in chocolate.

"We'll just talk." His smile widened. "For now."   *

She shouldn't go anywhere near that bed. He was too sensual, and she was too vulnerable. She wanted him, and that close he'd be able to feel the hunger vibes. Heck, they were strong enough to shake the bed. She should sit on one of the chairs. Definitely the chair.

Ivy walked over to the bed, kicked off her shoes, and lay down beside him. "I need someone to talk to."

"I'm listening."

His music slid over her body, trailing wisps of lust behind it. She shivered.

"Cold?"

"You know I'm not." She drew in a deep breath and tried to focus. "I'm worried about Kellen."

"You want to keep him safe."

Ivy turned on her side to face him. "I don't know what to do." She was going to tell him. "When I first got here, this place freaked me out. It still does."

"Understandable." He reached over and brushed a strand of hair from her face.

She waited a second before speaking to absorb the shock of that brief touch. *Focus, focus.* "I decided to leave. So I got another job."

He nodded, a slight widening of his eyes his only reaction.

"But the job wouldn't kick in for a few weeks." She sighed. "Now I'm not sure if I should leave here." *Leave you.* "Instinct tells me to take Kellen and run from all these people—dangerous people—who know what Kellen is."

"That might be the wisest course in the short term." He looked conflicted. "But as he gets older, he'll travel more by himself. One of the Sidhe will eventually see him." Murmur glanced away. "Or sense him. As he ages, his power will grow."

"But he's never shown that he has any power." *Neither did you until today.*

"He will. No one who looks so much like Mab could ever be powerless." He sounded certain of that.

"My father doesn't have power." She was grasping now.

"He does. But he's tried to suppress that part of himself. Would he admit he had unusual powers?"

Ivy closed her eyes. She thought about her mother's refusal to believe in his voices, *her* refusal to believe. "No, you're right. Dad never even told us he could see the fae."

"Kellen will need someone to guide him, someone who can prepare him to straddle two worlds." He paused to think. "He needs one of the Sidhe he can trust to help him."

Ivy knew her laughter reeked of bitterness. "Trustworthy? Do any exist?" She opened her eyes.

"There are good and bad in every race. Yes, this one you can trust."

That's all he said, and she believed him. She was finding it all too easy to believe everything he said and way too hard to remember what he was. A mistake? She didn't know.

He was silent for a moment, and when he finally spoke he said what she absolutely did *not* want to hear.

"You should explore your own power."

No. Not now. Not ever. "Maybe. Right now, though, I have other uses for the word 'explore.'"

His music wrapped around her, holding her tightly, warming her even as it shielded her from the worry, the fear, the *uncertainty*. He was everything. Maybe not forever, but at this moment he was all she wanted. She knew her eyes said what her words would probably botch. So she remained silent.

He turned on his side to face her and his music swelled. "Let's explore the outer limits, Ivy. And maybe when we get there we'll find there are no limits at all."

11

Coward. If she were braver, she'd reach out to touch him, allow him to see the neon-bright "yes" in her eyes. Instead, she glanced away before blurting out the first questions that popped into her mind.

"So, have you ever had a wife, children? How old are you anyway?" Her pillow talk needed a little polishing. Okay, so it needed some heavy buffing.

He remained silent for so long she thought he wouldn't answer. She took a chance and met his gaze. His smile said he understood exactly how she felt.

"I've lived thousands of years among humans and thousands more in the Underworld."

He *didn't* glance away. She guessed that proved which of the two in this bed was a giant wuss.

"I never stayed with one woman for more than a few weeks." He finally looked away. "Demons can't produce children."

"A few weeks?" That little tidbit shouldn't make her so happy.

After all, she wouldn't be with him any longer than that. *Do you want to be?* Ivy didn't know.

"Women don't love demons. They might lust after us for a while, but it doesn't take them long to sense what we are. Demons have nothing to offer humans except misery. And death. Can't forget death. No home, no family, no happiness, and then you die."

That "you" sounded sort of personal. A warning? "Wow, you fling a mean bucket of cold water." She rolled onto her back so he couldn't read her expression, but she watched him from the corner of her eye. "Would you change all of that if you could?"

"I never think about it. Wishing and hoping don't work for demons. So why bother?" His face was a blank slate.

"Well, I'm wishing and hoping for a lot right now." She wasn't doing a great job of keeping the tension from her voice.

He smiled. And Ivy decided that smile looked good enough to keep her here for well over two weeks.

"But there's a lot to be said for living in the moment." He propped himself up on his elbow and leaned over her. "In the end, that's all we remember anyway. It's never about the years, it's about those moments when magic happened." His smile faded. "Or didn't."

Crossroads alert. Ivy had always chosen the men in her life according to her mother's feet-on-the-ground rule. Mind over emotion. She'd taken careful steps so she wouldn't trip, always choosing well-lit roads—men with good jobs and no bad habits and who weren't prone to talking to themselves. Now was decision time. If she made love with Murmur, she'd be stumbling onto a side road— not paved and definitely not well-lit. Was the destination worth braving darkness and danger?

Murmur's music touched her. Not compelling her. *Seducing* her. The promise of pleasure and much more waited for her in that darkness. Ivy made her decision.

She reached up and slid her fingers along his jaw. "I'd hope this would last more than a moment. Interesting to see if the reality lives up to the music."

She felt his smile beneath her fingers.

"Oh, it definitely will." He glided his hand beneath her top and rested his palm against her stomach.

The warm pressure wasn't a light touch. It was firm, a claiming, but not in a bad way. "Arrogant male."

She absorbed his soft laughter, stored it away behind the door in her mind labeled Memories of Murmur. Ivy hoped she never ran out of storage space.

"Not arrogant, just honest." His hair trailed across her body as he lowered his head and covered her mouth in a long, drugging kiss.

Sensory overload exploded. His lips left her conflicted. Which to concentrate on—their firm pressure or the soft fullness of his lower lip? Which was it, firm or soft? She didn't know, so she shifted to the taste of him. Again that damn can't-decide thing. Was it hot male or dangerous delight? And his scent. It was all her dark fantasies rolled into one. Indescribable. All she needed to know, though, was that it was *his* scent and it would always take her back to this moment no matter where she wandered in the future.

He abandoned her lips to kiss a lingering path down the side of her neck before transferring his attention to the sensitive skin behind her ear. "It won't be long before I run out of uncovered spots to kiss. That would be an unfortunate thing."

"Unfortunate. Yes." Her breathing was doing weird things, making complete sentences difficult. "I have a problem too."

"Tell me."

His breath fanned her bare stomach where he'd already worked her top up to just beneath her breasts. Her shudder was all delicious anticipation.

"I have to peel the whole banana before I eat it. I mean, I know lots of people who peel as they go along. That's just not me." She raised herself a little so he could pull the top over her head. "I don't know how people get any kind of pleasure from a partial peel." Ivy lay back down as soon as he removed her bra. The cool air touching her nipples made them pebble. She yearned for . . . She knew what she yearned for, but first things first.

Her babbling about bananas died as she met his amused gaze. She swallowed hard as he yanked off his shirt.

He grinned. "I get it. We're both just half-peeled bananas. But not for long."

Ivy returned his smile as her tension faded. She reached for him.

Somewhere between the time she ran her fingers across the smooth, hard planes of his chest and the moment he moved in to trace her bottom lip with the tip of his tongue, they both lost their half-peeled status.

Ivy forgot exactly how she shed all her clothes as Murmur deepened the kiss. He wrapped his arms around her and pulled her close.

She accepted the invitation of his half-parted lips as she allowed her tongue complete freedom. No deep analysis went into his taste because the feel of his bare body pressed against the length of hers took her breath away. She closed her eyes and fought her need to crawl inside of him, to wrap herself around his pounding heart and become one with its beat.

Thump, thump, thumpthumpthump. She opened her eyes. Wait. Not *his* heartbeat. Not *hers*. What the . . . ? A *drum*?

He broke their kiss and rose above her, his eyes glowing red. She should be terrified. She wasn't. Because within those eyes she saw heat, desire, and need. For *her*.

And then his music broke over her, engulfed her, and the drumbeat went on. *Thump, thump, thumpthumpthump.* A melodic heartbeat growing, expanding, while the rest of the music throbbed with a sensuous rhythm that took form and color around her.

Fingertips of fire touched her nipples—teasing, warm lips licking at them until she arched her back at the pleasure-pain.

She couldn't see, couldn't think as the drumbeat soaked into her head, her body. Instruments she'd never heard before played an ascending scale of frenzied need, the notes flashing pinpoints of crimson along the length of her body. Touching, touching, always touching.

The sensations overwhelmed her. Ivy tried to focus, to see *him* beyond what his music was doing to her. She reached up, searching.

But a single voice broke from the sexual symphony. Not human. Deep, steeped in erotic purple, it spiraled around her reaching hands, wrapped her wrists in searing bands of sunset colors, and pulled her arms above her head. She was helpless, open to whatever the music chose to do with her body.

But where was *he*?

Ivy writhed, the heaviness low in her stomach demanding, screaming its need. She spread her legs, begging, wanting.

The music answered her, violins crying that they too needed, wanted. Notes—bright and fierce, muted and gentle—played counterpoint to the wash of melody drowning her body in a sea of sexual hunger. Starving. For his body and for . . . Not sure. Couldn't concentrate.

Those notes became warm lips covering her nipples, a teasing tongue flicking the hard nubs, teeth nibbling, driving her *crazy*.

Her heartbeat was now the deep booming of the kettledrum as the notes skipped down a descending scale, his tongue sliding across her stomach, his lips—no, no, not *his* lips, not *his* tongue—trailing a path up her inner thigh . . . And then . . . She closed her eyes, but the music lived on, building, clawing its way to a crescendo she knew would scatter her across the universe.

A single thread of melody—clear, haunting—*touched* her. It slid across the part of her that was already engorged, ready, and she screamed and fought and begged. Then it pushed into her and withdrew. In and out, in and out, it mimicked the rhythm of sex while the drumbeat became a drumroll.

Colors merged into black, and the black became his eyes. Black? Hadn't they been red or green . . . ? She couldn't remember, couldn't think, couldn't care. All she wanted was—

"Now. *Now.*" She had no other words, no breath to say them, even if she had more.

She stared up into those black eyes that were his, or not his, or maybe his, and felt her whole body clench around her silent cry. "I want you inside me *now!*"

The bed dipped beneath her, and she sensed that he was now straddling her. She felt him slip his hands beneath her bottom and lift her. The music was a solid wall of sound, and the sound was color.

The head of his cock pressed between her legs, pushing into her slowly, slowly.

"Faster, damn it." She was wet and clenching and almost insane with her wanting, her need to be filled. By *him.* But where was he? She couldn't maintain the thought, or anything at all except the sensations battering her, flinging her high and then dropping her only to toss her higher again and again and again.

He pushed harder, deeper, filling her in a way she knew she'd never be filled again. No empty spaces left. Anywhere. Inside or out.

He paused, and she could hear his breathing—harsh, rasping. Yes, that was the *real* him.

Then he began to move. He slowly withdrew until only the head of his cock remained in her. Pause. Plunge. Her whimpering cries punctuated the stretching, the thrusting.

The rhythm quickened. She grew greedy. She didn't wait for him to plunge into her now. She rose to meet each thrust, grunting with her effort, breathless, feeling it coming closer and closer. Reaching for it, reaching, reaching . . .

The world exploded. Her *body* exploded. All the colors flashed to blinding white. And the music . . . The music was Steven Tyler's primal scream in "Dream On." Dream on, dream on, dream . . .

She shuddered and cried out, a guttural scream of fulfillment. Spasms of unbearable pleasure shook her, and she knew bits of colored Ivy would be raining down for days.

And if his cry matched hers, she didn't know, didn't care. For this moment it was all about her, because he hadn't been there. She was alone with his music.

Ivy closed her eyes, savoring the weakening spasms, allowing her breathing to return to normal, her heart to beat to its own rhythm.

When she finally opened her eyes, he still knelt above her. His eyes were once again green. He watched her carefully. She allowed her gaze to wander the length of his body—sleek, muscular, sweat-sheened. Beautiful.

She felt a drop of her own sweat trickle between her breasts. "I've never known anything even close to what just happened." And she meant it. The dictionary definition of "orgasm" should read simply: "Murmur."

His gaze narrowed. He slipped off her and lay on his back beside her. "But . . . ?" He reached up to sweep strands of his hair from his face.

"Where were *you?* At the beginning I saw you, felt you, but then you were . . . gone." She rolled onto her side and walked her fingertips across his incredible chest. "I just experienced the most amazing event of my life, and *you* weren't there."

"I *am* my music. I thought you understood that." He didn't sound angry or disappointed or anything. His expression gave nothing away.

"No." Ivy didn't know how she could be so sure of this. "Your music is an extension of you, but I want the flesh and blood Murmur." God, she didn't want to hurt him. She tried for a lighter tone. "Not that I'd live through the real deal."

He didn't smile. "Perhaps you wouldn't."

He was kidding, right? She looked down. "I'm sorry. I'm ruining the moment." Where had this gone wrong?

Murmur drew in a deep breath and lay still, as though he was thinking. "My emotions ran too strong. The music was a buffer." He turned his head to capture her with his gaze. "It was safer that way."

"For who?"

He turned his head away without answering.

That went well. Way to mess up the most spectacular orgasm of her life. Ivy leaned over the side of the bed to retrieve her clothes. After slipping on her bra and top, she swung her feet to the floor and pulled on the rest of her clothes. Then she stood.

She didn't know what to say. *I never got to touch you.* It was reality TV at its best. She'd seen it, heard it, thought that she was sharing it, but when she'd touched the screen no one had been there. "I guess I'll see you at the meeting."

Ivy waited for him to say *something.* Had it meant anything to him? Should she even expect it of him? He was a demon, and he'd made it plain that his emotions didn't run on the same track as human emotions. That was the real problem. She kept forgetting the demon part. He'd become just Murmur to her; not a demon, merely a man. And she didn't know how to change that.

She walked to the door and pulled it open.

"Ivy."

She paused, but didn't turn to look at him.

"Sometimes we have to be happy with what we have and not wish for more."

She nodded before stepping into the hall and closing the door behind her. What if what she had wasn't enough?

Forcing aside thoughts that would lead nowhere right now, she headed for the stairs. She was supposed to be spying on Ganymede for Sparkle. So far she was doing a rotten job. Before catching up with Ganymede, though, she had to find out what Kellen was doing. She dug for her cell phone.

"Hey, Sis."

Kellen sounded cheerful, but something about his happy voice seemed false. Or maybe Ivy was growing more paranoid the longer she stayed in the castle. She tried to relax and accept what her brother said as truth. "So what're you doing?"

"I'm in my room. Doing research. Asima gave me a bunch of info about things."

Ivy just bet Asima had. "Great. I'll pick you up for dinner later, and then we can talk." Now who was sounding falsely cheerful?

"Sure. Oh, and I talked to Mom. She said it's okay for me to stay for a while as long as you don't mind. Dad didn't want me here, but he couldn't give any good reasons why I shouldn't stay, so Mom overruled him."

She controlled her sigh. Of course Dad couldn't reveal the real reason why he didn't want his son here. Could he? Maybe he should brave Mom's disbelief and tell her the truth. *Right, and I don't see you rushing to call Mom with all the gory details of life in the Castle of Dark Dreams.* But she'd have to lay out the facts for Mom when things settled down. Ivy would invite her mother for a visit, and then introduce her to the impossible.

Ivy wasn't sure where Kellen would be safer—here, where there were powerful beings to help protect him, or back home. What if she sent him home and one of the fae spotted him there? She couldn't follow him around for the rest of his life.

"We'll see about getting you into school tomorrow." That was one ordinary act she could perform amid all the extraordinary stuff going on.

And as much as she hated the thought, she hoped the faery Murmur had promised to send could teach Kellen ways to protect himself. Maybe she could learn something as well. Not that Ivy really believed she had any powers.

Ivy was still thinking about Murmur and Kellen when she walked into Sweet Indulgence. Sparkle was sitting on her stool behind the counter looking morose and working her way through an open box of chocolates in front of her. Braeden was nowhere in sight. Ivy breathed a sigh of relief.

"Where's Braeden?" She peered into the display case. Maybe she'd buy a bag of candy to share with her brother.

Sparkle made a face. "He said he wanted a challenge, but he really didn't. He's out hunting easier prey."

"Really?" Ivy studied Sparkle. Did she look as though she was having withdrawal symptoms?

"No. I said I needed time to cleanse my system of the Mede virus. He's amusing himself until I'm Mede-free." She bit into a chocolate. "Caramel. All gooey and sweet. Just like my Mede."

Sparkle closed her eyes and slowly slid her tongue across her lower lip—sexy, provocative. And she wasn't even trying. Ivy was impressed.

"If you say so."

Sparkle opened her eyes. She smiled at Ivy. "I could teach you how to do that."

"What?"

"Make men lust after you with just a few simple actions."

Ivy didn't think her shrug looked very convincing. "I don't care about men lusting after me." She was such a liar. She wanted Murmur to lust after her. And she was already thinking about ways she could use the chocolate and lip-licking thing.

Sparkle laughed. "Of course you do. Every woman does. But not every woman is lucky enough to have the queen of sex and sin as a boss. I'll teach you everything you need to know."

A scary but intriguing offer. Ivy tried to ignore her immediate surge of excitement. "Anyway, Ganymede's really worried that you won't forgive him."

Sparkle put on a militant expression. "As he should be. He has to realize, though, that he can't walk all over me."

Ivy bit her lip. She should probably keep her mouth shut, but all she could picture was Braeden out there somewhere seducing an innocent woman. "Whoever Braeden chooses, they'll die when he leaves."

Sparkle waved Ivy's worry away. "I sent him to Asima. I told him that she was an even greater challenge than I was. He was all motivated when he left." Her smile was spitefully malicious. "He'll keep the little bitch busy and out of my hair." She pushed the chocolates away. "Anything else to report?"

Ivy only hesitated a moment. Sparkle was her boss, so she owed her loyalty. "Ganymede wants to know why Murmur's music drew Braeden to the castle. Murmur set up a meeting at seven tonight in his room. Bain and Tirron will be there to talk with Ganymede. I'll be there too. I have to know what's going on so I can protect my brother."

"And no one told me?" Anger simmered and boiled as Sparkle tapped one perfect nail on the counter.

Ivy decided she didn't want to be anywhere near when Sparkle brought her hammer down.

"Hmm."

Sparkle could terrify with one word.

"You're going to bring a guest tonight, Ivy. Someone who will look out for your interests. Someone who *owns* this freaking castle, and damn well better be part of any *meetings*."

Without warning, the remaining chocolates in the box exploded into geysers of cream filling and marshmallow fluff. A sticky cherry plopped onto the counter in front of Ivy.

"Great." She was so not looking forward to this meeting.

"Now that we have that settled, let's talk about you."

Let's not. Ivy just wanted to get out of there.

"I assume the sex was spectacular."

"What?" Ivy widened her eyes. She had definitely not expected Sparkle to lead with that comment.

Sparkle's laughter was light and frightening. "I've been in the sexual chaos business for thousands of years. I recognize the signs of a woman coming down from an incredible orgasm. Of course, I expected nothing less from Murmur."

Ivy didn't know where to look or what to say. "Incredible. Very." Ugh. Had she actually said that?

"Tell me all the delicious details." Sparkle leaned forward.

Delicious details? "We made love. That's it." She might work for Sparkle, but once Ivy closed the bedroom door, her life was her own.

Sparkle frowned. She straightened. "Well, that's disappointing. At least tell me if you were completely satisfied."

Ivy hadn't intended to tell Sparkle anything. Really. It wasn't her business. But surprisingly, she found she wanted to tell her boss. Who else could she confide in? Who else would understand men well enough to figure out what was going on with Murmur?

"He took my breath away. It was the most amazing moment of my life." She clasped her hands in front of her and tried not to look too nervous.

"Yes?" Sparkle was leaning forward again.

"But he made love to me with his music." She exhaled. There. She'd said it.

Sparkle looked puzzled. "You mean his music was playing in the background while you touched each other's bodies with unspeakable, lust-filled, ecstatically joyous passion?"

Okay, she was going to have to give Sparkle a few details. "I mean that, except for the very beginning and the very end, the only thing that touched me was his music. It takes color and shape. It can physically . . . do things to you." Now she was embarrassed.

"Why? Why would he *do* such a thing? Not touch you with his hands, his mouth?" She sounded outraged.

Ivy shrugged. "He said something about it not being safe." She wished she hadn't said anything now. Sparkle looked way too horrified.

"Not safe?" Sparkle's expression turned thoughtful. "I'll have to look into this."

Please, please don't. Ivy would be mortified if Murmur found out that she'd blabbed to Sparkle. "I'm sure he had good reasons."

She didn't believe that, *couldn't* believe that she'd never feel his hands and mouth on her body. *Listen to yourself.* The last thing Ivy should want is any kind of relationship with a demon. But she kept forgetting *what* he was in the joy of discovering *who* he was.

"No, he didn't. There are *no* good excuses for not touching a woman. I won't allow him to hide behind his music." Sparkle narrowed her amber eyes.

Oh boy. Ivy had done it now. "Maybe I overstated—"

"Quiet. Let me think." Sparkle slipped from her stool and walked around the counter to join Ivy. "Come with me. We'll go to my apartment and begin your lessons."

"Lessons?" Did she just squeak?

Sparkle beckoned and Ivy followed. All the way into the castle and up to Sparkle and Ganymede's apartment, Ivy tried to make excuses for her wimpy attitude. Sparkle was her boss. Sparkle was a force of nature. Sparkle was totally scary. But the truth was that Ivy *wanted* those lessons, *wanted* to drive Murmur crazy until he was forced to lay hands on her. She smiled at the thought.

Ivy stepped into Sparkle's place and froze. Whoa. Sensual explosion alert. Erotic paintings lined the walls. Erotic sculptures rested on every surface. Coffee-table books dedicated to erotica were tastefully arranged on the, well, coffee table. Candles somehow managed to scent the air with lust. And finally, dim lighting set the mood for sex. At least Sparkle had the good sense not to have any sensual music playing.

"Welcome to my home." Sparkle frowned at the bowl of popcorn planted among the erotic books on the coffee table. "Mede is such a pig. He doesn't understand the importance of perception. You need to stage a sensual home, and a bowl of popcorn really doesn't send the right message." She whipped the bowl off the table and dumped it into the trash.

Ivy had the feeling Sparkle would get lots of chuckles if she could do that to all of Ganymede's things. "This is all so . . ."

"Overwhelming? Exactly. Now, let's get started on your lessons." Sparkle pointed to the couch. "Sit."

Ivy gingerly sat on the edge, ready to bolt.

Sparkle leaned over her. "Sit back. Relax. And learn."

The queen of sex and sin smiled.

Oh, crap.

12

Murmur lay on the bed staring at the closed door. She didn't understand. *He* didn't understand. Sex was always a physical release for him, nothing more. This had felt like a whole lot more. He'd had to take his hands off her before . . . Before what? Before he lost control and hurt her? Wouldn't have happened because he *never* lost control. Then *what*?

Maybe *she* wasn't the one in danger. He'd never wanted to touch a woman more than he'd wanted to slide his fingers the length of her bared body, had never needed to taste, to feel a woman's flesh beneath him more than he'd needed to do all those things with her. But he'd denied himself the pleasure. A survival instinct? No, that didn't make sense. He frowned. He hated things that didn't make sense, so he tried to stop thinking about it.

He got up and dressed, then headed for his room. Klepoth would be waiting for him. Murmur had to come to some sort of agreement with the other demon. Waiting for Klepoth to ambush him from every shadowed corner would get old fast.

Murmur opened his door, stepped inside, and then froze. What the hell? Klepoth had found a way to amuse himself while he waited. The demon was hopping and bopping to one of Murmur's CDs.

Murmur took a moment to really study Klepoth. When he was enjoying himself and not busy being a pain in the ass, Klepoth looked almost as young as Ivy's brother.

The other demon was smiling as he turned and saw Murmur watching him. He stopped dancing. Murmur could almost see him wrapping his evil-demon persona around him like a hooded monk's cloak.

Klepoth frowned. "About time you showed up." He flung himself onto a chair.

Murmur sat on the chair opposite him. "I had things to take care of."

Klepoth's expression turned sly. "Yeah, I get it. She's hot."

Jealousy slammed Murmur with enough force to make his virtual teeth rattle. He wanted to leap from his chair, wrap his fingers around the bastard's throat, and see how he enjoyed the illusion of dying. He took a deep breath and stayed seated. Wow, payback was a bitch. He'd felt superior when Ganymede had gone berserk over Braeden, but now Murmur knew exactly how the troublemaker had felt. And that was all kinds of scary.

Something in his expression must have alerted Klepoth, because he shut up. Smart demon.

Murmur leaned back and tried to look calm and detached. "Do you really think your illusions will convince me to return to the Underworld?"

Klepoth ran his fingers through his spiked hair. "I have to keep trying. You understand, Murmur. If I don't . . ." He shrugged.

"The Master will hurt you." Pain was the go-to solution for all of the Master's problems.

"Yeah."

When Klepoth wasn't working his illusions, his eyes were a bright blue. Right now, the rest of him might look like a teenager, but those eyes showed every one of his thousands of years of existence.

Something was forming in Murmur's mind. An idea. Crazy, but maybe possible. The emerging music in his mind was still faint but carried a hopeful backbeat with it. "You've gained lots of power since the first time I saw you." He narrowed his eyes, thinking. "I have too."

Klepoth looked puzzled. "So?"

Murmur paused. Once said, the words couldn't be recalled. "We're both almost as powerful as the Master now."

The silence seemed to drag on forever. He watched Klepoth's eyes widen, and then narrow. Finally, they just looked speculative. "Explain."

Murmur nodded. "If we both refused to return home, what would the Master do?"

Klepoth's laughter had a hysterical edge. "He's a fucking arch demon. What do you think he'd do?"

Murmur leaned forward. "Think about it, Klepoth. He couldn't just leave our punishment to his minions. We're too strong. He can't compel us to return. Once again, we're too strong. He'd have to come himself."

"Yeah, and he'd bring half of the Underworld with him."

"But if he came, it would be his first trip to the mortal plane in millennia. Think back to how weak we were when we first entered this world. We'd have the advantage because we've existed on this plane longer. And we each command legions of demons. Do you think he wants a very visible war, with humanity watching?"

For the first time, Klepoth seemed to be considering it. "We'd have to stick together."

"I think he'd cut his losses and forget about us." Here was the clincher. "Because if he came after us and lost, Lucifer would remove his ass from power. No one would respect an arch demon who couldn't defeat those he was supposed to command."

Klepoth looked uncertain. "Do you really think that's the way it would play out?"

"I can't be certain, but if I were the Master, I wouldn't think we were worth all that trouble." Now the decision was in Klepoth's hands. Did the other demon want to stay on the mortal plane badly enough to rebel?

"I like it here. I want to stay, but . . ." He bit his lip. "If I lost, I'd end up back in the Underworld. Not a great place to be with the Master pissed at me. I'll have to think about it."

"Take your time." Murmur couldn't believe what he'd just suggested. His music was still tentative but growing stronger by the minute. He'd added some bass to keep the beat of hope going.

When had he subconsciously decided he wasn't going back? *About a half hour ago in Ivy's bed.* Not that staying here would mean anything, because he didn't see Ivy settling into a long-term relationship with him. Did he want one? He didn't know, and he hated the not knowing.

Klepoth got up to leave. "Uh, could I borrow your CD?" His expression said he didn't expect Murmur to loan him anything.

Murmur saw himself in Klepoth. Old demons didn't expect kindness, let alone friendship, from others. That's why he valued what he had with Bain. "Take it."

"Thanks." The other demon grinned and grabbed the CD from the player. He headed for the door.

"Oh, and Klepoth, lay off the illusions. They're not working. They're just ticking me off."

Klepoth left without making a comment.

Murmur remained seated as he thought about tonight's meeting. He hoped Bain was practicing his groveling and begging. While he was at it, Bain had better come up with a few good reasons why Ganymede shouldn't chuck him out of the castle.

He gave up worrying about tonight and allowed his thoughts to return to Ivy. Murmur relived every moment of their lovemaking. He pictured her eyes glowing with heat and desire. For him.

That last thought made him feel . . . happy. He couldn't remember the last time he'd experienced that particular emotion. It felt damn good.

Ivy was nervous. She was getting ready to close herself in a room with a group of powerful nonhumans who weren't afraid to express their anger in terrifying ways.

And one of those nonhumans walked beside her. Okay, so Sparkle didn't walk. She swayed down the hallway to her own sensual rhythm while balanced on heels high enough to double as stilts. Awesome.

Ivy should back out of the meeting. No one would miss her. But she wouldn't. Because she needed to keep her brother safe. And also because of *him*. Murmur. Her obsession was pitiful. She wanted to be wherever he was. And it had nothing to do with her admittedly spectacular musical orgasm. Even when they were arguing, he made her feel good. Weird, but true.

They reached Murmur's door, and Sparkle knocked. Ivy stood behind her. Sparkle wore a shimmery black dress that molded to her bottom and stopped somewhere around the top of her thighs. It plunged in the back, and dipped even farther in the front. Long dangly earrings glittered in the hall lights, and her nails were long, scarlet, and should have been registered with the police as lethal weapons. Sparkle was ready for battle.

She felt like Sparkle's shadow, but a shiny shadow nonetheless. If Ivy had been one of the kick-butt heroines in the urban fantasies she read, she wouldn't worry about how she looked. Hey, kick-butt heroines didn't care about attracting men. They were totally focused on the next kill. And they were all so naturally gorgeous that they didn't need artificial enhancements. A little lip gloss to combat chapped lips, and they were good to go.

Ivy didn't fool herself. She might not be focused on the next kill, but she *was* waging her own brand of covert action. Call her shallow, but she wanted to look good when she walked into that room. For Murmur.

She'd allowed the cosmic troublemaker free rein, and Sparkle had created a minor miracle. When Ivy had looked into the mirror, she'd barely recognized herself. And her red dress hugged her bottom and plunged just as far as Sparkle's dress. If Murmur said he preferred the natural look, she'd know he was lying, because the mirror told the truth: Ivy had *never* looked better.

Still, Ivy felt jittery when Murmur opened the door.

Sparkle leaned past him to see who was in the room, and he looked past Sparkle to meet Ivy's gaze.

Murmur's eyes widened, and then his gaze slid slowly down her body, lingering on strategic spots. When he finished the return journey back to her face, he simply smiled.

That smile made sitting still for an hour so Sparkle could do her thing worth every minute. She returned his smile.

"Ganymede isn't here yet?" Sparkle sounded disappointed.

Murmur finally looked at her. "No. I suppose that will ruin your grand entrance. I didn't know you were coming." He glanced at Ivy, proving he had a good idea how Sparkle had found out about the meeting.

"I don't need a grand entrance." She swayed past him into the room. "And this is my castle, so I have every right to be here."

Murmur's gaze stayed on Ivy even though he was still speaking to Sparkle. "Where's Braeden?"

"He's attending some cultural event with Asima tonight." Her smile was a wicked twist of her lips. "I'm hoping that when he abandons her she'll go into a decline and disappear. Do you think I'm asking for too much?"

Sparkle didn't wait for an answer. She took a seat in the middle of the couch. She leaned back and crossed her long legs. She patted the seat beside her. "Sit here, Ivy. I might want you to take notes tonight."

Ivy joined her on the couch. She mentally scrolled through the actions Sparkle had tried to pound into her head while she'd worked on Ivy. Attempting to look casual, Ivy crossed her legs. Only an iron will kept her from trying to yank her dress down farther on her thighs. She barely remembered to dangle one stiletto from her toe. According to Sparkle, this drove men crazy. Go figure.

Murmur didn't look as though he'd need a mental health facility anytime soon, but he did watch her as he closed the door and then returned to his seat. When he met her gaze, she saw the hunger there. *Yes!*

"Why is *she* here?" Tirron sat on the end of Murmur's bed. He didn't try to hide his outrage that not only would he have to tolerate Ivy, but now Sparkle would be cluttering up their meeting as well.

"*She's* here because she wants to be." Sparkle's voice was a dangerous purr. "You look uncomfortable. Why don't you scoot back and lean against the headboard?" Her expression turned sly.

He scowled. "An *iron* headboard. Not exactly an enthusiastic welcome for your fae guests. And I still don't think you should be here."

Sparkle widened her eyes. "Oh, we have alternate headboards for those we *truly* welcome."

"Did you miss the part where she said she owned the freaking castle?" Bain sounded frustrated as he leaned forward in his chair.

Tirron seemed ready to quote the Privacy Act, but someone knocked on the door.

Sparkle still looked casually sexy, but Ivy sensed her tension. Ivy was feeling her own tension. She nervously twisted her ring. Loose stone. She'd have to get that fixed. She hoped everything went well, because if anything bad happened, she'd have to grab Kellen and run. Not something she wanted to contemplate right now.

Murmur didn't even get to the door before it swung open and Ganymede padded into the room, still in cat form. Someone else was with him.

The someone else was male. Tall and muscular with a tangle of dark hair and eyes a shade of blue so dark they almost looked black, he fit right in with the other men in the room. Crossing the room, he took the seat on the other side of Sparkle.

Ganymede leaped onto the coffee table and lay down with his back to Sparkle. His tail twitched, each twitch thumping against the glass top of the table. He didn't look happy.

"I brought Dacian with me. He's my bullshit meter for the night. That means if I think you're handing me crap, I'll confer with Dacian. If he agrees that you're bullshitting me, then the meeting is over, and you'll need to find a new home." He turned his unblinking cat stare on Bain. *"That means all of you."*

"Not so fast." Sparkle uncrossed her legs and leaned forward.

Every male gaze in the room except for Ganymede's snapped to Sparkle's plunging neckline. Ganymede didn't turn his head to look at Sparkle, but his twitching tail pounded out a furious rhythm on the table.

"As the castle's owner, I have the final say on who stays and who goes. Remember that." Satisfied that she'd asserted her authority, Sparkle leaned back and crossed her legs once again. Slowly.

Ganymede chose to ignore the interruption. *"Dacian, you know Bain and Murmur. The two new ones are Tirron—he's the faery who looks like he has a stick up his ass—and Ivy. She's sitting next to the freaking 'castle's owner.'"*

The temperature in the room dropped about ten degrees.

Ivy ignored Sparkle's hiss. Well, at least she'd finally gotten to meet Dacian the vampire. She offered him a smile and a small wave. He smiled back. Wow, Cinn hit the mother lode with this guy.

Ganymede indicated he was ready to get down to business by sitting up and wrapping his tail around himself. He scanned the others, skipping over Sparkle. *"Today a damn Gancanagh showed up at the castle."*

Dacian looked interested. "I thought there weren't any more of them."

"Yeah, well I wouldn't mind making them extinct."

Sparkle narrowed her eyes to amber slits, and Ivy decided that Ganymede needed to cut out those kinds of comments if he wanted her back. Ganymede seemed blissfully clueless, because he kept sticking his paw further into his mouth.

"Anyway, a bunch of dumbass women were all over him."

"Jerk." Sparkle didn't even try to lower her voice.

Ganymede flattened his ears but kept going. *"The faery calls himself Braeden. He claimed Murmur's music drew him to the castle. And since he was blasting Murmur's music all over the great hall, I sort of had to believe him."* He speared Murmur with a hard stare. *"I know you don't make those kinds of mistakes, demon. I want an explanation."*

"Guess that's my job." Bain sounded resigned. "I asked Murmur to use his music to draw the Sluagh Sidhe to the castle."

Sparkle clapped her hand over her mouth, her eyes wide and horror-filled. For the moment she was speechless.

Ganymede had no problem verbalizing his reaction. Ivy winced. She'd never heard so many curses strung together in one sentence.

"You're bringing the fucking faery host down on my castle?"

Ivy didn't for a minute believe the flash of lightning outside their

window, followed by a deafening clap of thunder, was Mother
Nature's idea.

She frowned. Faery host? What did that even mean? Sparkle
had removed her hand from her mouth and was glaring at Ganymede. Evidently the cat's "my castle" claim trumped the faery-host
news.

*"You have about two minutes to exist, so you'd better start talking
now."* Ganymede stood, ears pinned and a low growl warning of
bad things to come.

Jeez, could Bain be more freaking stupid? Didn't he know you
worked up to bad news gradually? You eased into it to avoid trig-
gering messy slaughters. It was called being subtle. Murmur raked
his fingers through his hair. Instinctively, he began building a tune,
one with the power of a heat-seeking missile. He'd have to disable
the chaos bringer before he could visit death and destruction on
them. Not that Murmur was feeling a deep need to save his fellow
plotters at the moment.

Murmur glanced at Tirron. The faery looked as though he was
mapping out the best escape route. Figured. Tirron was a runner
not a fighter—unless the odds were in his favor.

Murmur had to admit, though, that Bain made the best use of his
two minutes. He told his tale of woe with lots of extra embellishments.

The kidnapped woman had been the great love of his life, and
the Castle of Dark Dreams was the best place for his heroic last
stand against the evil faeries, because of the insanely powerful entities that lived there.

And those insanely powerful entities were also heroic beings
who would step up in defense of a helpless woman and her devoted
lover, because they were fierce defenders of what was right and just.

Murmur thought he would puke. Bain was absolutely driving
nails into their coffins with every word he spoke. Time to stop this
train wreck.

"What Bain is trying to say"—Murmur shot a shut-up glare Bain's way—"is that no one would be dumb enough to attack the Castle of Dark Dreams, because they know Ganymede would be here waiting for them."

He stared at the cat. Because as the cat went, so went the rest of the nonhumans. Edge was almost as powerful as Ganymede, but he wouldn't challenge the other troublemaker over castle business. The only problem Murmur foresaw was with Sparkle.

You'd think that a being who had existed for millennia would've learned something about women along the way, but Ganymede was a total dumbass when it came to Sparkle. And she was pissed at him. But right now Murmur couldn't worry about her. He had to concentrate on the most powerful one in the room.

"Of course, we all want a peaceful settlement." Not. Tirron would be doing everything he could to precipitate a battle so he could slaughter the Unseelie horde. Bain? Well, his friend just wanted the woman back, and he didn't much care if it involved a few hundred bodies along the way.

And Murmur? He gave lip service to the peaceful-settlement concept, but inside, where his demon lived, he wanted blood. Lots of it. He wanted to free his music to tear apart bodies, to destroy and destroy and destroy until nothing was left alive.

A red film slid across Murmur's vision, his heart beat faster, and music leaked from him. Poisonous and corrosive, it searched for a victim.

He heard Ivy's gasp at the same time Dacian's voice slammed into him.

"Shut it down, demon. *Now.*" The vampire curled his upper lip, exposing his fangs.

Murmur took a deep breath and shoved his music back into his mind. He shook his head to clear it. This was what it meant to be a demon, and he'd better always remember it. No matter how much he might seem human, he wasn't. He would always have to guard against moments like this, moments when he could lose control. Somewhere in the Underworld, his master was laughing.

And what had happened to his claim that he didn't want a war with the faeries? His bloodlust swept rational thought away.

He dared a quick glance at Ivy. She stared at him wide-eyed, and there was fear in those eyes. Shit. She'd heard the music.

He took a deep breath. "Sorry. Where was I? Oh yeah, the peaceful settlement. We all want it."

"*Some more than others.*" Ganymede's amber eyes said he knew exactly what Murmur hoped for.

"But if the faery host won't give Elizabeth back to Bain, we'll have to fight." He slipped Ganymede a sly glance. "I know your Big Boss has set limits on how much carnage you can create, but surely you have a right to protect what is yours. And if the faeries are the aggressors . . ." Ganymede could figure out the rest.

Everyone not named Murmur, Bain, or Tirron sat frozen. Murmur couldn't read their expressions.

The silence dragged on and on and on. Finally, Ganymede spoke.

"*Can't take a chance. Now that Sparkle is Big Boss in Training, he's keeping closer tabs on the castle. I'd be in deep shit if he turned up in the middle of things and caught me using . . . unnecessary force to flatten the faeries. So you probably need to go somewhere else. Hope you get your woman back, though, Bain.*"

Then Ganymede remembered his original mad. "*I think I'll still kick your butts down the stairs and out the door for sneaking behind my back and trying to draw me into your fight.*"

Murmur cursed. They were screwed.

"Not so fast."

Sparkle uncrossed her legs and stood. She did her sensuous

swing around the coffee table until she stood behind Bain. She
put her hands on his shoulders, and he tensed. Ganymede flattened
his ears.

"Bain's story touched me. It made me teary-eyed. I want to help
him recover his love." She met Ganymede's glare. "Besides, Murmur
can't leave yet. We have unfinished business." She smiled. "My
castle, my decision."

Murmur fought not to smile. Laughing at Ganymede never paid
future dividends.

*"What can you do against hundreds of faeries, compel them to have
sex with each other?"*

Ganymede had a convenient memory. Murmur remembered
Sparkle doing just that a few weeks ago. Okay, so most of those
involved had been human, but not all. Bain and Holgarth had fallen
to her compulsion. Sometimes the cat forgot that Sparkle had her
own brand of power. The Big Boss wouldn't choose anyone other
than a heavy hitter to take his place.

Sparkle's laughter taunted Ganymede. "I could, but when I'm
really ticked off, I simply take away their balls. Men seem incapa-
ble of thinking without them." She shrugged. "Women are more
reasonable. I could probably sit down with them and come to an
agreement."

"Really? Their balls?" Tirron sounded strangely fascinated.

"Really." Sparkle brightened. "Would you like a demonstration?"

Tirron tried for his usual cold and aloof expression, but Murmur
figured he was mentally clapping his hands over his endangered
body parts.

"That won't be necessary. I believe you."

"Good." She glanced around the room. "Anyone have problems
with my decision?"

No one spoke. Even Ganymede had enough sense to shut up.

With a furious hiss, the cat leaped from the coffee table and headed for the door. *"Let's get out of here, vampire."* He narrowed his feline eyes at Bain. *"Whatever happens when the Sluagh Sidhe gets here is on your head. I hope you have a big bank account, because I don't think the insurance covers faery attacks."* The door swung open ahead of him. He padded through, followed closely by Dacian, and the door slammed closed behind them so hard that Murmur was surprised the walls didn't shake.

"That went well." Sparkle's smile was triumphant. "I love bursting pompous bubbles." She glanced at Ivy. "Let's celebrate with a drink." Her attention shifted to Bain. "Keep me informed."

Bain nodded. "Will do. And thanks."

Murmur watched Sparkle and Ivy leave. Ivy didn't meet his gaze. He didn't blame her. His music had oozed evil, once again reminding her of exactly what he was. He tried to convince himself that he didn't care, but it wasn't working. He cared too much. And what the hell was he going to do about that?

"You scared the woman, demon. Be careful. Things will go smoother if she remains docile and ignorant." Tirron's stare said that Murmur was a clumsy idiot.

If Bain didn't need the faery, Murmur would show Tirron exactly how much power his music had. "The woman has a name. She's Ivy."

"She's a tool to secure the release of Bain's human toy. Don't forget that. And don't forget your part in our plan. Keep her happy and focused on you. Make her want you so much that she'll follow you anywhere. When it comes time to trade her for Bain's woman, we don't want her distrustful or unwilling to follow where you lead her."

Murmur had taken as much crap as he intended from this dickhead. It was time to clue him in about Asima. He opened his mouth to speak, but Tirron held up his hand.

"I hear something." The faery stood and stalked to the door.

Bain and Murmur remained seated. Murmur amused himself by

imagining how much he'd enjoy watching Tirron dance until his feet were nothing but bloody stubs.

Tirron paused in front of the door, and then suddenly yanked it open.

Ivy crouched on the other side, her hand frozen in the act of reaching for something sparkly on the rug. She looked past Tirron to Murmur.

Horror, fear, and soul-deep betrayal lived in her eyes. And even as he watched, disgust and fury joined the other emotions.

She'd heard.

She knew.

13

Ivy crouched in front of Tirron, the lost stone from her ring forgotten. He looked down at her—cold and not even close to human.

She'd known none of them were human, but for the first time she really understood what that meant. Not only had her rose-colored glasses hit the dirt, but Murmur and the faery staring at her now were grinding them into dust beneath their supernatural heels.

"Well, this is a complication." Tirron seemed mildly annoyed.

At the sound of his voice, whatever had held her frozen shattered. She came out of her crouch and ran.

Not the stairs. *Too easy for him to catch her.* The elevator doors were open. Was the elevator iron? Tirron wouldn't go near the iron headboard.

Maybe surprise would freeze him for a moment and give her a head start. *He didn't look surprised.*

Maybe some random person would come out of a room or up the stairs. *The hall was empty.*

If she could get inside the elevator, close the doors, and reach the hotel lobby before Tirron caught her, she'd be semi-safe. There'd be too many witnesses. *Human* witnesses. The human part was important. Of course, she didn't know how powerful he was. Maybe he could make them all forget what they'd seen.

Stop worrying about what-ifs. Think survival. She'd get to the lobby. Then she'd lie, make someone from the registration desk go with her to Kellen's room. She'd pay the person to stay with her while they packed and left. No, forget packing. *Just leave.*

Even as the disjointed thoughts flashed through her mind, the few rational brain cells still functioning screamed that she'd never get to the elevator in time, never get the doors closed. *Please, please, please.* The ragged plea was in sync with her rasping breaths.

Ivy didn't dare look behind her. She tried to scream, but all that came out was a hoarse croak. Panting from terror, she flung herself into the elevator and hit the ground-floor button.

She almost made it. The door was shutting when Tirron slipped into the elevator with her. The door closed completely and started down. Without pausing, he held his hand in front of the control panel and the elevator stopped its descent.

"There. Doors locked. No warning lights and bells signaling trouble. We can have our private little talk without irritating interruptions. It won't be a long talk, though. I don't do well in metal boxes."

Ivy didn't wait for him to do whatever he intended doing. She attacked—clawing, shrieking. Suddenly, whatever had happened during Klepoth's illusion kicked in again. Her power surge was an explosion of white light and a muffled boom. The force flung her back against the wall of the car. When her vision cleared, she saw Tirron scrambling to his feet on the other side of the elevator. His shocked expression would've been funny if the rage that immediately followed it didn't terrify her.

He didn't give her a chance to gather her strength before he was on her. No attempt at faery magic, just a straightforward need to hurt. He punched her in the face, knocking her head into the wall behind her. She fell. Pain washed over her and dizziness made her want to throw up. *Don't pass out.*

She tried to stand, but her body had decided that the prone position was more comfy. Ivy fought her body's weakness—concentrating, demanding that it move. But she hurt too much. Damn. Why couldn't she call up her faery power again?

Tirron leaned over her. He didn't say anything for a moment, just stared at her. Then he spoke. "You will obey me."

He was kidding, right? "Go to hell."

His anger seemed to have eased, replaced by a thoughtful expression. "Humans usually don't require threats. I merely compel. But I just tried to order your obedience. It didn't work. That coupled with your little demonstration of power shows an interesting level of strength for a mongrel."

What was he talking about? Murmur didn't have any trouble compelling her. Did that mean Tirron was less powerful than Murmur? The thought vanished as quickly as it came. Not important in the grand scheme of things. The faery in the elevator with her was her top priority.

He frowned. "I'm not going to allow you to ruin this for me, little bitch." His face hovered mere inches from hers. "You'll stay in the castle, and you'll do what you're told to do." He'd regained his cold calm. "Do we have an agreement?"

Had she ever thought he was beautiful? She wanted to cringe, curl up on herself, protect her body from his fists. No, she wouldn't be that person. She tried to ignore the trail of what must be blood trickling down the side of her face. She refused to speak. She glared up at him. Both hims. Ivy blinked. Still dizzy.

The common-sense part of her suggested it was easy to be defiant when he hadn't gotten to his threats yet.

"If you don't follow directions like a good little girl, here's what will happen: I'll kill your brother. Running won't help. I'm a hunter. That's why Bain chose me to track the faery host. I'm very good at what I do. I *will* find you." His smile promised that he'd enjoy watching her run, seeing her try to hide, feeling her terror. "You'll tell no one what we're planning—not Sparkle, not Ganymede, not your brother. Do you understand?"

Ivy didn't move. She was afraid to speak, afraid she'd scream at him and he'd kill her brother right now. Ivy would've defied him if he'd only threatened *her*, but she wouldn't take a chance with Kellen's life. So she choked back her words and nodded. Once she was out of the elevator, she'd think of some way to free them.

"Good." His smile was as icy as his words. "Now, we'll have to get you cleaned up before anyone sees you. I'll—"

Ivy had no idea what he would've said next because suddenly the car jerked as a heavy weight landed on the roof. She barely had time to register that fact before something peeled back the elevator's ceiling with a grinding and shrieking of ripping metal.

She looked up just as Murmur leaped through the opening.

This was a Murmur she didn't know. His eyes glowed red. His fingers ended in long, sharp claws. His lips curled back to expose pointed teeth. And he scared the hell out of her. But everyone was doing that right now. He may as well join the fun.

Everything seemed to move in slow motion now, or maybe that was just her general wooziness after getting Tirron's fist in her face.

Murmur landed in a crouch.

Tirron backed up, his eyes wary. "What's wrong with you, demon? She heard what we said about her. I had to stop her."

Murmur stared, his expression savage, as a sound seemed to take form and substance around him. It gave her an eerie, sick feeling. She shuddered. She couldn't hear it clearly, but it made her feel as though she were watching something terrifying drag itself from the primordial ooze—hideous and deadly.

"You hurt her. Your part in Bain's plan is finished. *You're* finished."

Tirron looked startled for a moment. He met Murmur's gaze. Suddenly he widened his eyes. "Well, well. Who would have thought. You've—"

The faery didn't get a chance to finish. Murmur leaped at him.

Ivy curled into the corner of the car and covered her head with her arms. Their kind of fighting might not kill *them*, but she had doubts about her survival.

Then . . . nothing. There was no music, no sounds of fists meeting flesh, no grunts and cries of pain, no magic whipping around the car. Only the sound of one person breathing. Not her. *She* was holding her breath.

She dared to look up.

Murmur stood in the middle of the car, his fists still clenched. But now his hands were just hands. No claws. He turned to look at her. Green eyes. He didn't smile, so she couldn't check out his teeth.

Wisely, he didn't try to touch her.

"Where'd he go?" She sat up, leaning her back against the wall.

"He dematerialized. He must be old if he managed it surrounded by all this metal. I sent my music after him. He'll keep running until he's back in Faery. That's the only place where he can escape it." He started to bend toward her.

She held up her hand. "Don't. Touch. Me." She took a deep breath. "Why didn't I hear your music?" Ivy needed a few minutes to gather herself together. Right now, bits of her were scattered all over the landscape, from I-hate-you to Please-hold-me.

"I blocked it. I sent my death music after him. Even though it wasn't aimed at you, hearing it wouldn't be something you'd forget."

"Nightmares?"

"Many." He took a step toward her. "Look, I know what you heard us say sounded bad . . ."

"You think?" Her face throbbed and her head hurt. She needed some industrial strength painkillers. "I won't believe anything you say, so don't bother trying to explain. But, hey, this is an easy fix for you. You can compel me to silence or make me forget. That's what you do, isn't it?" She was channeling her inner bitch, and she didn't care. She was aching inside and out.

She thought he'd continue to argue. He didn't. Without consulting her, he bent down and scooped her into his arms. Ivy thought about demanding that he put her down, but she was just too weary. Who knew that betrayal and disillusionment made you yearn for a nap?

A sound above them drew her attention. Bain balanced on what was left of the elevator's roof.

"What the hell is going on? Where's Tirron?"

Bain looked horrified when he saw her face. She must look like crap. Too bad. He needed to choose his evil cohorts more carefully.

"Ivy heard our discussion about her. She ran. Tirron caught her. He probably tried a compulsion on her, and it didn't work. So he beat her." He speared the other demon with a hard stare. "He won't be coming back." Murmur raised her toward Bain. "Take her to my room. I'll call Cinn to help her."

Bain leaned down and lifted her. Ivy wanted to complain that no one was asking what *she* wanted to do. She wanted to get Kellen and leave here. Leave her beautiful demon and his beautiful music and his ugly, ugly lies. She would go . . . Ivy couldn't remember where. She felt so tired, and everything hurt, and she couldn't seem to think. She closed her eyes.

Her first thought when she woke was that she *never* passed out. She remembered exactly what had happened up until Murmur handed her to Bain. Then, nothing. She kept her eyes closed, trying to get her bearings.

"She'll be fine, Murmur. A slight concussion. Just watch her for the rest of the night. I've left something for her pain. The eye won't look too bad by tomorrow. The cut bled a lot—head wounds do—but it wasn't bad."

"Thanks, Cinn."

Murmur sounded relieved, but of course he would. If anything happened to her, who would he trade to the Sluagh Sidhe for Bain's precious Elizabeth? But even as she thought her cynical thoughts, a small hopeful part of her wanted his worry to have nothing to do with his crazy plot.

"I have to get back in time for Holgarth's next fantasy. I'm playing the beautiful, clueless virgin for some old guy. Major eww. I really don't get it. I wouldn't fantasize about a gorgeous, stupid young stud." Long pause. "Okay, maybe I would if I were old and withered. If you need anything, just yell."

Ivy heard Cinn cross the room and then the opening and closing of the door. She was gone.

"She's awake, Murmur."

Sparkle? What was she doing here? In fact, where was *here*? Ivy opened her eyes. Ugh. She closed them again. Everything hurt.

"Where are the painkillers Cinn said she left?" Ivy didn't believe in stoic suffering when there were excellent drugs available to take it away. She managed to prop herself up against—she scanned the area—Murmur's pillow, with minimum wincing and only one "damn."

"Here." Sparkle handed her a glass that looked suspiciously cloudy.

Ivy hesitated. "What's in it?"

Sparkle laughed. "No poison. Cinn is a demigoddess. She's inherited some of Airmid's powers. Airmid is the goddess of healing plants. Cinn's drink will do more for you than any pill. Drink."

She did. For all of Sparkle's strangeness, Ivy realized she trusted her. Amazingly, even before she finished the drink, she could feel her pain fading.

Sparkle handed her a thick pad. "Put this over your eye. Cinn whipped up some plant thing that'll get rid of your shiner."

Ivy obediently pressed it to her eye. She was now coherent enough to notice Murmur. His long hair, which usually fell in a shining curtain down his back, was a mass of tangles around his face. His eyes were shadowed. He didn't approach the bed. He sat on a chair in the sitting area and watched her. His expression gave nothing away.

When he met her gaze, he nodded. "I just wanted to make sure you were okay. Stay here tonight. I've already told Kellen you'll be with me. He doesn't need to see you like this." He stood.

"You told him I'd be with *you*? He'll think—"

"He'll think we're doing exactly what we *did* do earlier today." He didn't smile. "He's a teenager. He understands the concept of sex between consenting adults."

She wouldn't think about what they'd done. "Fine. At least you're right about me not wanting him to see me like this." Besides, she had more important things to worry about. Tirron was gone, but would her brother be safe? *Will he ever be safe again?* "I should be near Kellen, though, in case—"

Murmur held up his hand to stop her. "I asked Ganymede to stay with him. I'll be in Bain's room if you need anything. He'll be busy with the fantasies for most of the night." Then he left.

"He didn't want to try to explain?" Lame question.

"He said you wouldn't want to hear it." Sparkle eyed her critically. "You look like shit."

"Gee, that makes me feel better." He could've at least *tried* to talk to her.

"He told me what happened." Sparkle looked as though she

wanted to whip out her makeup and hair products and go to work. "This is tough for me." She bit her bottom lip.

"I guess it would be hard listening to the kind of evil they were plotting." It was nice to have some sympathy.

"Evil plotting?" Sparkle sounded puzzled. "Oh no, I didn't mean that. I meant it's tough to sit here without making you look better. But if I touched your head, it would hurt."

"Right. Looks are important." She laced her words with all the sarcasm she could muster.

Sparkle smiled. "See, you understand. Not that you'll be joining the Sluagh Sidhe, but if you were, they'd value you a lot more if you looked gorgeous."

Ivy would have ground her teeth, but she didn't want to take a chance of bringing the pain back. "Tell me what the demon said." Yes, it was childish to refuse to say his name. But the old Murmur had been someone she cared about. Someone who she thought cared about her. This incarnation? Not so much.

"Bain planned all along to trade someone for Elizabeth. Without someone to offer in exchange, he'd have to battle the faeries. If it came to a fight, he wouldn't have a chance alone. That's why he chose to stay here. And he chose you because you were available and someone the faery host would accept."

"Bastard."

"Yes, well, we all do what works for us."

Ivy frowned. That didn't sound like a resounding condemnation of Bain. She didn't say anything, though, because she wanted Sparkle to get to Murmur's part.

"Murmur said he didn't want to trade you."

A little warmth crept into Ivy's cold heart.

"He said if they traded my shiny new assistant and I found out, I'd drag Mede into it. They didn't want to deal with Mede."

Warming trend over.

"So Murmur convinced Bain to trade someone else." Sparkle didn't seem able to help herself. She reached down and came up with her purse. She rooted around in it until she found her makeup bag.

"That's awful. You can't allow some other innocent to take my place. You have to—" She didn't get to voice her full outrage, because Sparkle had pulled her compact from her makeup bag and was poofing powder over Ivy's face.

"He didn't choose an innocent."

Sparkle carefully replaced the compact and then went to work with the blush. When she finally made eye contact with Ivy, malicious glee shone there.

Ivy opened her mouth to spout more outrage, but stopped to think. Who would put that expression in Sparkle's eyes?

"Ohmigod, he chose Asima." Ivy might not like the cat, but she didn't think she deserved to be kidnapped by faeries.

Sparkle handed her a lipstick and talked while Ivy put it on. "Asima is perfect. They won't keep her. She'll make their lives hell. And they can't kill her without making an enemy of the goddess Bast. So they'll end up dumping her, probably back in our laps." She frowned at the thought. "Anyway, she'll keep them happy until the trade is done. When they finally find out what they have, it'll be too late."

"That's mean."

Ivy's comment startled Sparkle into laying down the mascara wand. "This is making the best of a bad situation. Bain should never have come up with his crazy idea to free Elizabeth in the first place."

Ivy felt conflicted. "I think he should try to free her, but not this way."

Sparkle shrugged. "Well, it's done, so now we have to deal with it. If we don't offer something or someone in trade, Elizabeth will stay with the faeries."

Ivy was tired. She was glad that Murmur wouldn't have traded her, no matter what his reason. But she didn't like the idea of Asima taking her place. That was wrong. But she had no way to fix it that wouldn't end up in either a war with the faeries or Elizabeth remaining a prisoner.

"I think I need some sleep." A question nagged at the back of her mind.

"Sure." Sparkle dumped Ivy's makeup back into her purse. "At least now, if the fire alarm goes off in the middle of the night, you'll look awesome standing in the street in your nightgown. Oh, and before you panic, I'm the one who put it on you."

"Comforting thought." She must really be out of it. She hadn't even noticed the nightgown. Ivy watched Sparkle head toward the door.

"Someone will look in on you throughout the night."

"Not the de . . ." Oh, what the hell. "Not Murmur." Did she sound too wistful?

"Not Murmur."

Sparkle opened the door.

And Ivy remembered what had been nagging at her. "Murmur said that Tirron was old. How old is old for a faery?"

Sparkle paused. "Thousands of years."

She was almost afraid to ask the next question. "Do you think Kellen has enough faery blood to live that long?"

"He has Mab's face. I'd say there's a good chance." Sparkle stepped into the hallway and closed the door quietly behind her.

Ivy turned off the bedside lamp and lay in the dark. She wouldn't live long enough to protect Kellen. That meant she had to find someone to teach him how to protect himself, someone who knew what it meant to live for centuries. And no matter how betrayed she felt, there was only one person she'd trust with that job. Too bad she was never going to speak to him again. *Never.* She drifted off to the satisfying sound of that word in her mind.

She woke hours later—at least it felt that way—to the sureness that someone was in the room with her. Ivy lay still and cracked open one eye. Darkness. Her pounding heart eased a little as she remembered Sparkle saying someone would keep an eye on her during the night.

But there was a familiarity about the presence, a knowing. Murmur? She wanted to turn on the light and scream at him, make him tell her why he'd kept Bain's secret from her. But then they'd fight and he'd leave. And as stupid as it made her feel, his presence comforted her. So she closed her eyes and relaxed into the warmth of having him there.

Murmur sat in his room, in the dark, staring through the narrow castle window at the shimmering reflection of the moon on the Gulf of Mexico. That was him. A shaky reflection of the real thing.

During his long existence, Ivy was the closest he'd come to feeling *this*—the "this" as yet to be named and definitely not admitted. He'd fucked everything up, though. He would drink himself into oblivion, but a smashed demon woke up in the morning wondering what city he'd turned to ashes the night before.

At least Sparkle wasn't going to say anything to Ganymede. She had her reasons. For one thing, she was still pissed at the cat. And she was probably hoping to get another shot at working her personal magic with Ivy and him. Someone needed to tell her the game was over and she'd lost.

He turned his attention from the window to where Ivy lay sleeping. When Sparkle had told him that Zane would be watching Ivy from midnight until two, he exploded. So he was here now, torturing himself, and still seeing Sparkle's satisfied smirk in his mind.

What would Ivy do? Leave? Not smart. Tirron wouldn't stay in Faery, and when he emerged he'd be looking for revenge. If she did run, Murmur would make sure someone kept watch over her and Kellen. Not him, because she'd never want to see him again. He'd cancel the visit from the faery he'd asked to teach Kellen. Ivy wouldn't allow any of the fae within a mile of her brother now.

The knock on Murmur's door interrupted his brooding. He reached with his senses. Two people—Klepoth and . . . Kellen? Hell. With a muttered curse, he got to his feet and strode to the door. He yanked it open, stepped into the hallway, and closed the door softly behind him.

He glared at Kellen. "Your sister will lock you in your room forever if she finds out you were here with *him*." He nodded at Klepoth. "Luckily for you, she's sleeping. Where's Ganymede? He was supposed to stay with you."

Kellen's expression turned stubborn. "I'm not doing anything wrong." He glanced away. "Ganymede fell asleep with his face in the popcorn bowl."

The cat could forget about a career as a bodyguard. Murmur glared at Klepoth. "What do you think you're doing?"

Klepoth's grin turned to a scowl. "Who bit you in the ass? Kellen and I were just playing a few video games, talking about stuff, and . . ." For the first time the other demon seemed hesitant. "I was wondering what my chances were of getting into high school."

"What?" Murmur couldn't have been more surprised if Klepoth had said he wanted to sing with the heavenly choir. "You're ten freaking thousand years old." May as well make sure Kellen knew who he was dealing with. "Why would you want to go to high school?"

Klepoth looked away, but not before Murmur saw anger and embarrassment in his eyes. Klepoth didn't answer. He just shrugged.

"I think it's a great idea." Kellen jumped to Klepoth's defense. "We could start school together here. It's easier being the new guy if there's someone with you. Klepoth is staying at the hotel for a while, so we could hang after school." He shrugged. "You know, do things."

Murmur might be slow sometimes, but he finally got it. Klepoth didn't have a friend, had probably never had one. Like Murmur, he was beginning to want more than what his existence supplied. Kellen was his chance to fit in somewhere.

Murmur wanted to laugh at the image of Klepoth trying to blend in with the local teens, but he couldn't. It hit too close to home.

"It might work." Murmur put on his serious face. "If you need an adult with you when you register, let me know."

Klepoth looked offended. "Hey, I don't look that young."

Kellen laughed. "Yeah, you do."

Ivy would introduce Murmur to true hellfire and brimstone when she found out he'd approved her brother's friendship with the demon of illusions. After the last demonstration of Klepoth's power, he wasn't on her favorite-people list. But did it really matter? She couldn't hate Murmur more than she already did. Besides, he'd keep a close eye on Klepoth.

Kellen was immediately enthusiastic. "Great. Klepoth can help me find out if I have any powers." He glanced at the demon. "Can you do that?"

"Sure. No problem."

"Is that all?" Murmur wanted them to leave so he could concentrate on his bad temper, bad attitude, and his general crappy feeling of having lost something important.

"No, I wanted to speak to you." Klepoth raked his fingers through his spiked hair.

A rare nervous gesture from him. Murmur raised one brow, but didn't say anything.

"The answer is yes." He met Murmur's gaze. "You know, what we were talking about. I'm in."

"The answer is *no*." The door swung open behind Murmur, revealing Ivy doing a creditable imitation of a pissed off demoness. "Kellen, you will *not* go off with Klepoth. Do you know what he is?"

Kellen looked sullen. "He's the demon who creates illusions." He took a deep breath. "And he's my friend."

Something moved in Klepoth's eyes, an expression Murmur had never seen there before. Murmur found it tough to believe, but the other demon looked touched.

Ivy was clearly horrified. "You'll make new friends at school. You don't need—"

Klepoth interrupted her. "He *does* need me. I can keep him safe."

"Whoa, wait. I don't need anyone to keep me safe."

Like all human young, Kellen thought he was indestructible. Murmur could tell him that he was not, especially if the Sidhe came calling.

Klepoth smiled. "You do right now, but I'll teach you to defend yourself."

Kellen looked mollified.

Ivy did not.

But she didn't get a chance to voice her anger, because Kellen finally got a good look at her. "What the hell happened to you?" His shock quickly turned to anger. "Who hit you?"

Ivy hesitated. Murmur understood her reluctance to tell Kellen the truth. She wouldn't want to scare her brother. But Murmur had a little more belief in Kellen's ability to cope with the facts.

"Tirron hit your sister. She found out something that he wanted to keep secret. He thought hurting her would scare her into compliance." He glanced at her. "It didn't."

Kellen had already pushed to his sister's side to get a closer look, a closer look that only seemed to make him madder. "If I had powers, I'd make sure he never hit another woman." He clenched his hands into fists. "What was his secret?"

The moment of truth. Ivy would either tell him or she would lie. The Sidhe couldn't lie, but he didn't think she had enough of their blood to stop her from making something up.

Ivy bit her lip and avoided her brother's gaze.

"Tell me, Sis. I'm not a little kid anymore. I need to know." His voice broke. "Please."

She nodded and met his gaze. Then she told him.

Everything. Murmur would have liked her to have been just a little less truthful.

When she'd finished, Kellen didn't say anything for a moment. Klepoth looked surprised. Murmur knew it took a lot to put that expression on the other demon's face. But a visit from the Sluagh Sidhe had accomplished it. He wondered if Klepoth would bail on Kellen now. For that matter, he'd probably consider Murmur toxic too, an enemy of the faery host and his master.

Kellen finally found his voice. He stared at Murmur. "You sent your death music after him. Will it wait for him outside of Faery?"

"No. Once he escapes into Faery, the music will dissipate."

He nodded. "So Tirron can just wait until the music is gone and come after us again?"

"Yes."

Kellen grasped facts quickly. "We have to stay here, Sis. We have some protection in the castle."

Ivy suddenly looked exhausted. Murmur reached out to steady her. She tried to push him away, but he refused to be pushed. He wrapped his arm around her waist and held her steady.

"You should be in bed."

She ignored his advice. "Kellen, when the faery host reaches here, things will be dangerous. Things are dangerous *now*. I can't protect you against any of these people." She looked up at Murmur. "I don't know who to trust."

"I do." Kellen looked sure of himself. "I trust Klepoth, Murmur, and Asima."

Uh-oh. Murmur thought that last name was trouble.

Kellen met Murmur's gaze. "And I like Asima. She was kind to me, and"—his glance slid away—"she's lonely. She doesn't have any friends. Guess that makes her the same as a lot of us."

Murmur hated that Kellen was about to make him into the villain. "I won't let you do this to her." Kellen took a moment to think about what he wanted to say. "She wants to be needed. I bet if you asked for her help and treated her with respect, she'd try to help you."

Call him cynical, but Murmur didn't see Asima, the queen of what's-in-it-for-me doing anything out of the goodness of her tiny, feline heart.

"I'm going to warn her." His stare dared Murmur to stop him.

Ivy stilled, her eyes suddenly shadowed by fear.

Fear? She was afraid of him? She thought he'd haul out his drum solo and beat her little brother into the floor with it?

Klepoth understood the gauntlet Kellen had thrown down in front of Murmur, and its consequences. He shoved his new friend away from Mumur. "Let's get back to your room before Ganymede wakes up. He'll be pissed if he finds out we sneaked off."

Kellen nodded and reluctantly followed the other demon toward the stairs.

Instinct screamed that Murmur couldn't allow Kellen to blab to Asima. She'd make life miserable for all of them, and Bain's plans would be shot to hell. Murmur would have to find someone else to trade, and Ivy would hate and fear him even more for doing it.

Kellen paused at the top of the stairs.

Now. Erase his memory of everything. Erase *her* memory of everything. Problem solved. He was a demon. That's what demons did. *Do it, do it, do it.*

He felt her hand on his arm. No words, just her touch.

He turned away from Kellen and helped Ivy back into his room.

Probably the dumbest move of his entire existence.

14

Ivy stopped just inside the door. She was shaking. The way she was feeling, no way could she climb back into his bed.

He'd almost done it. He'd been ready to erase their memories. She'd seen the intention in his eyes. It would've been so easy for him. No more pesky complications. But he hadn't. She'd touched his arm, and then . . . he'd allowed Kellen and her to keep their memories, their very *damaging* memories.

Ivy wanted to believe he'd changed his mind because she touched him. But that would be assigning emotions to him that he might not be feeling. He confused her.

She couldn't concentrate around him, couldn't deal with her tangled feelings. And she needed to be clearheaded for Kellen. "I'm going back to my room for the rest of the night."

He raked his fingers through his hair. "Look, I can go to Bain's room. You don't have to leave."

"Yes, I do." How to make him understand? "Even if you leave, your scent is here, everything I look at reminds me of you. I need to be alone. I have to *think*."

She felt his need to argue; instead he nodded. "Fine. The clothes you were wearing had blood on them, so Sparkle left fresh ones for you." He walked to his closet and pulled out jeans and a top.

Ivy felt his gaze on her as she slipped into his bathroom and changed out of her nightgown. She put on her sandals and emerged from the bathroom to find him on his cell phone. He put it away as she approached.

"Sparkle will spend the rest of the night with you."

"I'm fine. I don't need anyone watching me."

"Cinn said that you did, and she knows best. Sparkle stays, or I stay." His expression said he knew which she'd choose.

And he was right. She didn't answer him, merely headed for the door.

He followed her. "I'll take you to your room."

She knew that wasn't negotiable, so she didn't waste energy arguing. Ivy said nothing as they walked to the elevator.

Her memories were too fresh, and she shuddered as the elevator doors opened. But she still felt too weak to take the stairs. She glanced at the car's ceiling. "It's fixed. That was fast."

"It helps to have a wizard and a sorcerer on the payroll."

Once inside the car, her muscles knotted, and her heart thudded loud enough to embarrass her. *Tirron's not here. He can't hurt you.* Too bad her mind couldn't convince the rest of her body not to go into fight-or-flight mode.

This time, Murmur was the one to touch *her*. He took her hand and held it in his warm grasp. "He's not here. He'll never be here again. I promise."

She wanted to yank her hand away from him. That's what she should do. She didn't. "Do you keep your promises?"

His lips tipped up in that breathtaking smile. "To you? Always."

"You lied to me." There. She'd said it. And it certainly had needed saying.

His smile faded. "I didn't lie. I just didn't tell you all the details."

"Lying by omission is still lying. Why?" She hadn't known how important that one word was until she realized she was holding her breath.

She exhaled and tried to relax. After all, there wasn't that much riding on his answer. They'd made love once. Big deal. It wasn't as though they had a relationship. He wasn't that important. *And you are such a liar.*

He remained silent until they were standing outside her door. "I knew I wasn't going to allow Bain to trade you to the faery host, so I didn't think it would hurt if you never found out about that part of Bain's plan."

"And?"

He looked away. "I didn't want you to leave."

"Why?" There was that word again.

"You were important to me even then." His expression said he'd explained as much as he intended. "I'll give you your space, Ivy. But I hope you won't decide to leave the castle until the danger from the faery host and Tirron are past. Even if you don't trust me to protect you, you can depend on Ganymede and Sparkle to make sure you and Kellen stay safe."

Without waiting for her response, he walked away.

"I trust you to protect me." She whispered her words to a man who was no longer there.

She *did* trust him to keep her safe. But she didn't know if that trust extended to other parts of her life.

Ivy was about to go into her room when she thought of her brother. It wasn't that she didn't trust Klepoth . . . Okay, honest? She *didn't* trust him. Walking to the next door, she rapped softly.

The door swung open and . . . no one.

"*Yo, cat level. Down here.*"

She dropped her gaze to Ganymede. "Good to see your nap time is over. Did Kellen get back?"

He narrowed his eyes. "*I was tired. I worked all day and then had to play bodyguard. A cat needs his naps. Your brother and the demon took advantage of my exhaustion.*"

"Work. Right." Ivy couldn't help her snarky attitude. She wasn't tuned in to her kind and gentle side right now. "So is my brother okay?"

"*He's tucked into bed all safe.*" Ganymede stared at her. "*Wow, you look like shit.*"

"That's what Sparkle said." She'd need some heavy duty concealer tomorrow.

At the sound of Sparkle's name, his ears pricked. "*Was she with that freaking faery?*"

"No, and she's right next door for the rest of the night. By herself. She's keeping an eye on me. Not that I need anyone."

His eyes gleamed. "*By herself? Maybe I'll visit for a few minutes later on.*" His tail whipped back and forth. "*Do you think she'd mind?*"

"She'd mind a lot less if you came armed with an apology for heaving Braeden out of the castle." Ivy didn't know why she was trying to help the cat when all she wanted to do was to fall into bed.

Ganymede seemed to consider this. "*Yeah, you might be right. Besides, even if she's still pissed, she won't do anything noisy that could wake you up.*"

Ivy nodded and walked back to her room. Once inside, she reached for the light switch. She squeaked her alarm as someone grabbed her wrist.

"Don't turn on the lights." Sparkle's voice.

Ivy gulped for air. "Don't ever do that again."

Sparkle didn't comment on the threat. "I'll lead you to your bed. Undress and slip into your nightgown. *Don't* turn on the lights."

"What's this all about?" She was almost too tired to care.

"I'm working on a surprise for you. It'll be ready in the morning."

"Great." Not really. She'd had enough surprises lately to last a lifetime. All she wanted now was sleep. Slipping into bed, she started to drift off immediately. *Please, no dreams.* Because they'd probably all revolve around a green-eyed demon who'd become way too important to her.

Murmur headed for Asima's room. Sparkle had whined about giving up a room to her, but if she hadn't, Asima would simply have made herself at home in some guest's room. Not good for business.

He allowed a melody to weave through his mind, something dark and solemn to fit his mood. If Ivy decided to leave, he wouldn't stop her. But he'd damn well make sure she was safe.

Make sure she knows how you feel about her too. She was better off without that little piece of information. Besides, he wasn't even certain what he could say to her. *I think I'm falling in love with you, but I'm not too sure because I've never loved anyone before.* He didn't think that would win any devotion points for him.

The music in his head gained strength and power. It was now a call to battle. He stopped in front of Asima's door. This was going to be bloody. But he needed to tell her before Kellen blurted out everything first. At least he could attempt damage control, try to put a positive spin on it. And if he thought hard enough, he'd find one.

To soften Asima up a little, he chose a musical piece from her playlist and allowed it to fill the space around him. Then he knocked.

The door swung open. No one was there. He stepped into the

room and closed the door behind him. Asima sat in the middle of her bed.

"I hope this is important, demon. I spent an exhilarating evening with Braeden, and now I need my rest." She leaped from the bed, padded over to one of the chairs, and jumped onto it. She sat again, curling her tail around her elegant body. She studied him from her slightly tilted blue eyes.

Before he got down to business, Murmur wanted to know something. "I assume you spent your time with Braeden in human form, so why take the shape of a cat just to sleep in your own room? I don't think Bast would notice."

"I find my feline form more relaxing. Besides, no one at the castle has seen my human form. What if I was called upon to save the castle in the middle of the night? Sparkle would see me. The slut queen would hate that I'm far more beautiful than she is. She's a vicious woman when she senses competition."

Murmur was sorry he'd asked. "Braeden's a Gancanagh. Legend says that once he leaves a woman, she dies from the withdrawal." He shrugged. "Just saying." There he went again, doing something kind. Somewhere, his master must be crying.

Asima made a dismissive feline sound. *"I'm not a mere mortal—weak, emotionally soft and squishy. I can handle Braeden."*

He dropped onto the chair across from Asima. Now for the tough stuff.

"Asima, the Sluagh Sidhe is on its way."

Her eyes widened. *"The faery host?"*

"Yes. Here's the deal." And he told her everything, including his decision to exchange Ivy for her as trade bait.

He waited stoically as she screamed, howled, hissed, and generally created the mother of all scenes. Finally, she began to run down.

"I'm a demon, Asima. We're cold, ruthless bastards. Betrayal is what we do. It's in our natures, so don't take it so personally. Now for the good news—you have friends in the castle."

That seemed to stall her next wave of feline fury. "*Who?*"

For the first time, Murmur really looked at the cat. And what he saw bothered him because, well, it *bothered* him. He shouldn't care about the shock and excitement in her eyes. No one should be that thrilled about having friends. *Except someone without any.*

"Kellen was pissed off when he heard what we were planning. He said he was going to warn you. And Ivy thought what we were doing to you was wrong."

If a cat could smile, Asima was smiling. "*They* like *me?*"

Murmur wouldn't exactly say that Ivy liked her, but he wasn't about to burst Asima's bubble of happiness. More kindness? When had he become capable of it? "Yes."

Asima seemed speechless for the moment. He took the opportunity to introduce his plan.

"I haven't spent my life believing in the goodness of others. If anyone did a favor for me, I expected to owe them. Nothing was free. Ivy told me once that maybe I should simply ask people for help instead of plotting and scheming. So I'm going to test her theory."

Asima still didn't say anything, but she was listening.

"Bain needs someone to trade to the faery host. I originally chose you because I knew they couldn't keep you." Wouldn't *want* to keep you. "You're too powerful. And even if you weren't, they wouldn't anger Bast by taking her messenger."

"*True.*"

She had to know where he was going with this, but she hadn't rejected him outright. Murmur was too cynical to believe she'd agree, though. Asima was like him in many ways. She lived by the a-favor-for-a-favor rule. But Ivy had wanted him to try, so he was trying.

"I'd like you to help us. Without someone to trade, the faery host won't release Elizabeth. And if Bain tries to take her by force, there'll be war."

"And I should care why?" Her question didn't have its usual bite.

"Because your friends care. And because I think others at the castle might think differently of you if you tried *being* a friend occasionally."

She hissed, and he hoped he hadn't gone too far. But then she began to clean her face with one paw while she looked thoughtful.

"Do you think they might sometimes go places with me?"

"They might if you'd stop criticizing their tastes in entertainment. Maybe you could even go somewhere with *them* once in a while, show them you have eclectic tastes."

Asima began to purr. She seemed to like the word "eclectic." She finally met his gaze. *"I'll do it."*

He widened his eyes.

She laughed. *"I shocked you, demon. You didn't think I was capable of changing."* Her laughter faded. *"But perhaps I'm tired of being alone."* She stared at him with those beautiful Siamese eyes. *"Perhaps you are too."*

He nodded and then stood. Murmur paused before leaving. "Thank you." He closed the door quietly behind him.

Klepoth was waiting for Murmur outside his room. "We need to talk."

Of course they had to talk. It was too much to hope that he could go into his room *alone*, lay on the bed that still held her scent, and spend some solitary time trying to figure out how he was going to untangle this mess Bain and he had created.

"Sure." He unlocked the door and stepped aside so Klepoth could enter. "What's happening?" Murmur experimented with a smooth wave of sound that should have eased his stress. It didn't work.

Klepoth didn't sit. He stood fidgeting. "Our master contacted me. He wanted to know how I was doing. I told him we weren't coming home."

Crap. Murmur's music shifted from smooth and calming to a rock anthem with lots of guitar riffs. "We probably should've given ourselves a little more planning time before breaking it to him." Like a year.

"Yes. Well, he's really pissed off." Klepoth avoided his gaze.

No kidding. "And?"

"He says he's sending his legions to drag our asses back to the Underworld where he'll personally oversee our torture for all eternity."

"Wonderful. Way to hold a grudge." Murmur wasn't surprised to hear that the Master was sending his demons. He and Klepoth would be okay, though, as long as the legions didn't show up on the same night as the Sluagh Sidhe. Things could be worse. At least the Master was staying tucked up in his comfy corner of the Underworld.

"Umm, he said he'll be coming with them." Klepoth finally met his gaze. Panic filled his eyes. "What'll we do?"

How the hell am I supposed to know? "Was he specific about when we could expect him?"

Klepoth shrugged. "It'll take him three or four days to gather his forces. He could show up anytime after that."

Murmur nodded. "I have to talk to Bain. Then we call up our own legions."

"The Master can only depend on his personal demons. Other arch demons won't help him. They'll be hoping for an overthrow so they can swoop down and claim his territory and forces." Klepoth brightened a little.

"We'll have to draw him away from the castle. We're already in deep shit because of the faery host. I don't want to know what would happen if a demon battle broke out in the courtyard. Find a sparsely populated spot in Galveston, and we'll figure out how to lure the Master there."

"I'll have the info for you by tomorrow." Klepoth was clearly relieved to have something to do. He started to leave.

"Oh, and Klepoth? Can I count on you to keep Kellen safe?"

Klepoth paused with his hand on the knob. "He's my friend."

Murmur watched the other demon leave. That was the most human thing he'd ever heard Klepoth say. Were the same changes happening to him? Sure they were. He was practically overflowing with kindness lately. The thought didn't horrify him as much as it should have.

As soon as Klepoth left, Murmur headed down to the great hall. He had to talk to Bain right now. The other demon wouldn't be happy about Murmur interrupting his fantasy, but tough shit. This was important.

He stopped in the dressing room to throw on a wicked-vampire costume and then joined Bain in a darkened corner of the hall where he'd cornered the fifty-something fair maiden.

The maiden was really getting into her part, screaming for the brave knight to save her while Bain hissed and showed fake fang.

Under cover of the fair maiden's terrified screeches, Murmur moved to Bain's side. "The Master is coming with his forces."

Bain's fake hisses morphed into very real growls. "Why the hell is he coming here?"

More shrieks from the fair maiden.

Murmur let a little red glow show in his eyes. "I've come to help my vampire buddy drain you dry, my lovely."

More squawks and screeches. Murmur did some head-humming to drown them out.

Bain snorted. "You don't call me your 'vampire buddy' in a historical setting. Now tell me about the Master."

"Klepoth and I have decided to stay on the mortal plane. Klepoth told the Master we weren't coming back. The Master's pissed."

The brave knight finally arrived. Dacian. Murmur wondered what the fair maiden would have to say if she knew her rescuer was the real deal. He almost smiled. Almost.

Bain flung his black cape aside and reached for his fake sword. "And?"

"And I'd like your support." He rushed on before Bain could reject him. "You don't have to openly side with us, but you're the Destroyer. You can do damage without tipping your hand." He added what he knew Bain would be waiting for. "I'll owe you a favor."

"Are you crazy? No. Keep me out of this." Bain snarled at Dacian, and the fair maiden screamed louder even as she copped a feel of the vampire's ass.

Dacian looked startled, but he didn't jump out of character. Murmur admired that, because he really wanted to shed his vampire persona and go all demonic on Bain.

Murmur didn't wait around to see the brave knight defeat the wicked vampire. Bain had said it all with one word. He and Klepoth would stand alone. Murmur returned to his room to put out the call for his legions of demons.

A while later, he lay on his bed absorbing Ivy's scent. He couldn't describe it, but it reminded him of warm, low notes flowing into a slow sensual melody. He slept with that melody wrapped around him, keeping all his other worries away for at least a few hours.

Ivy woke the next morning wondering if the ogre had returned and was practicing his clogging routine on her head. Ugh.

She groaned and flopped onto her back. Turning her head, she glanced at Whimsy. The plant looked green, bushy, and disgustingly calm. Ivy activated her brain and searched for any incipient panic. None. She recognized the storm clouds banked on her personal horizon, but they seemed safely distant from her present. "Thanks, Whimsy. I know everything will come crashing down once I move away from you, but I appreciate the peaceful sleep."

As Ivy climbed from the bed, she noticed her room for the first time. A big-screen TV that seemed to fill one whole wall was a new addition.

Sparkle sat on the couch, watching her from predatory eyes. "You're awake." Subtext: *It's about time.*

Ganymede lay on the coffee table, a bag of chocolate chip cookies open in front of him.

"I don't think I'm in the mood for whatever this is." Ivy dragged her aching body across the room to the coffeemaker. She'd hold thoughts of Murmur at bay until she had caffeine in her system.

"Of course you are. This will be epic, an effort for the ages. I've never attempted anything of this scope before." Sparkle's eyes were wide and excited.

Speaking of wide eyes . . . Ivy pried hers open enough to take in the total awesomeness of Sparkle's outfit. She wore skinny jeans with a glittery pattern snaking down her long legs, and a silky purple top that shimmered and shone in the room's light. Add in dangling purple earrings and sexy heels that looked obscene this early in the morning, and Ivy was officially impressed.

Caffeine. Now. Ivy concentrated on the brewing process and tried to ignore the cat and the queen of sex and sin behind her. She hummed to herself. Ivy was halfway through the tune before she realized it was one of *his* songs. Damn. She stopped humming.

"Well, aren't you even a little curious?" Sparkle sounded offended.

"Before my first cup of coffee?" She rolled her eyes to stare at the ceiling. "Thinking." Then she glanced back at Sparkle. "Nope."

Ganymede chuckled in her head. *"My sugarlump has outdone*

herself this time. She can't wait to show you. I added a few things here and there to give it that wow factor."

Ivy turned to look at him. "You made up?"

"I apologized. That's tough for a cat with pride. I admitted that she drove me crazy jealous with the freaking faery. Make up sex is the best." His purr was a contented rumble.

"Here? In my room?" *Eww.*

"Nah. We spent some quality time in the room behind Sweet Indulgence."

"Then who was watching me?" Not that she'd needed someone.

"Zane sat with you for about an hour. Nice guy. Hated him at first. Shows how first impressions aren't everything."

"Zane?" Ivy looked at Sparkle.

Sparkle smiled her sly smile and offered Ivy a finger wave. "I've already told Murmur. He didn't take it well. Other guests in the hotel complained about the marching band practicing in his room before nine in the morning." She glanced down and then looked up at Ivy from beneath her lashes. "Men are so predictable."

Ganymede flattened his ears.

"Not you, Mede. Never you."

Ivy had the feeling Sparkle was telling the truth. While the two of them whispered sweet whatevers to each other, Ivy got her coffee and moved to a chair. Couldn't put off whatever Sparkle had planned any longer. She settled back with a resigned sigh.

"Oh, good. You're ready." Sparkle almost clapped her hands in anticipation. "I created something amazing for you." She paused for effect. "I made a music video."

Ivy blinked. "What?"

"A music video. Of Murmur's life."

Ivy carefully set her mug on the coffee table. "I don't understand." She wasn't prepared, emotionally or otherwise, for this. "How do you even know about his life?"

Something in Sparkle's eyes shifted, and suddenly Ivy saw the ancient entity that was Sparkle Stardust shining in them.

"Mede and I are older than Murmur. I've been the cosmic troublemaker in charge of sexual chaos for millennia. You have no idea what I know." Then she smiled. "But you will."

Ivy couldn't help it: she shivered. Did she even know this woman? Then the old Sparkle was back. "I just want you to appreciate what you have." She glanced at Ganymede, who had his head buried in the cookie bag. "Isn't that right, Mede?"

"*Gssomm.*"

Ivy assumed that was a yes. "I don't have a clue what you hope to accomplish."

"More than you can imagine, Ivy." And Sparkle turned on the video.

Murmur's music filled the room—clashing chords, strident bursts of sound with no melody or rhythm. Just noise.

Ivy couldn't look away. She watched a creature crawling from the darkness, naked, covered in blood and filth. His gaze fixed on her, eyes glowing red, filled with savagery and a lust for death. He flexed curved claws, red with gore, his need to tear, to kill, obvious in that motion. Peeling his lips back, he exposed pointed teeth in a smile that was no smile at all. He was primal, evil, and he terrified her.

"That was Murmur right after he emerged from the Underworld. The blood was his own. His master believed that a demon was made, not born, that a demonic nature had to be beaten into his minions."

"No. *No.*" She shook her head, wishing she could bolt from this room and wipe the horrible image from her mind. But it was there. Forever.

"We move on." Sparkle's voice was a whisper promising more of the same.

The music gained intensity. A recognizable melody and beat

began to emerge. But it still spoke of a primitive need to destroy everything and everyone.

Ivy felt as though someone had taped her eyes open. She couldn't close them, couldn't escape the scenes rolling over her. Humans who died screaming, torn apart by teeth and claws. Destroyed villages, silent and empty, filled only with slaughtered bodies and flies drawn to the blood.

"Thousands of years passed, and Murmur slowly shed his savagery. His music became more important than the kill. And when he destroyed, he did it with his music. He was a surgeon, and his music was his scalpel." Sparkle's voice was a hypnotic chant.

The music became a smooth river of sound that separated into thin strands. Murmur used those strands to coldly and methodically cut his prey into nothing more than strips of bloody meat.

The images came faster, blurring into year after year after year of music and all the ways it could kill.

Ivy wanted to clap her hands over her ears, to shut out the music. The complex compositions had become so much more deadly than the raw sounds Murmur had cast out when he'd first crawled onto the mortal plane. They compelled you to dance and dance and never stop until you died. They wrapped fingers of sweet, sad notes around your throat and squeezed, and then . . .

Ivy frowned and stared at the screen. Something had changed. Murmur stood on a beach staring out at the water. His back was to her, but there was a familiarity to the scene.

Then the music shifted, became something softer, something . . .

She knew that music—the rhythm, the melody that tempted, seduced. She'd danced to it with him that first night.

And finally the last scene. Murmur lay in bed beside . . .

Fury washed over her. "How the hell did you get that picture? What right did you have to invade our privacy?"

"Forget the damn picture. Listen to the music, Ivy." Sparkle's voice had taken on an unaccustomed hardness.

Ivy opened her mouth to blast Sparkle some more, but then she heard it. *The music.* No violence lurked in the clear, pure notes. No deadly strands reached out to kill. Death no longer lived in it.

"When? I don't remember . . ."

"After he made love with you." Sparkle leaned forward, her eyes gleaming. "He didn't share it with you, probably didn't even realize what he was creating. This is important, Ivy. *You. Changed. Him.*"

Ivy merely stared. Sparkle had to be wrong.

"What he feels for you, the magic that happens when you're together, snapped the cord connecting him to his master. He has a chance for freedom now, if . . ." Sparkle frowned.

Ganymede was finally paying attention. *"If he can survive."*

"Survive what?" Ivy was frantic now.

"His master will come for him." Ganymede sounded matter-of-fact.

"Aren't you going to help him?"

Ganymede gave a feline snort. *"Hey, I have enough to do getting ready for the damn faery host. He'll deal."* He batted at the cookie bag. *"Or not."*

Ivy stared at the screen. It had faded to black, the music ended, the man gone. "Why did you do this?"

Sparkle shrugged. "You needed to know. So I showed you." She twirled a strand of hair around her finger and looked thoughtful. "We all change, even those of us who've existed beyond the few pitiful years humans have. *I've* changed. According to my job description, my only obligation was to bring you together, make sure you had incredible sex, and then insert some horrific detail that would keep you apart forever. Simple. Clean."

"Yes, well, that first scene from your music video qualified as a horrific detail."

Sparkle looked intrigued. "Did it work?"

Ivy didn't have to think about her answer. "No."

"I suppose I should've tried harder." She didn't sound upset. "Anyway, I felt a deep compulsion to make you understand what you'd given him. So I guess I was actually working against myself. It makes me wonder—about my evolution as a cosmic being, as a . . ." She glanced down. "How the hell did I get a scuff mark on my shoe?"

Ganymede finally abandoned the empty cookie bag. *"We'll leave you to think about things. Oh, and I got the shot of Murmur crawling onto the mortal plane. One of my best images."*

"How?" The question multiplied in overlapping layers of conflict, none of which had anything to do with Ganymede's statement. How had Murmur become so important to her in so short a time? How could she even consider a future with a demon? How did he feel about her for the long term? Wait, make that the short term, because her life was merely a blink compared to his. How, how, how into infinity, with no real answers.

"I was there. I saw. I remembered. And when my cuddlebug needed a money shot, I pulled it from my memory and laid it out on the screen." His voice was smug. *"Don't ask. It's a secret process."* He leaped from the table and headed for the door.

Sparkle uncrossed her long legs and stood. "I'd suggest you watch the video again once we're gone. The message will take a while to sink in."

Secret. All Ivy heard was that one word of Ganymede's. "Hold it right there, people."

They paused to stare at her.

"Who took the picture of Murmur and me? That was slimy and low and . . ." She couldn't think of a word that would live up to her fury. "You invaded our personal space." She glared at Sparkle.

Sparkle simply pointed at Ganymede.

Ganymede's laughter was a rumble of wicked enjoyment. *"I didn't have to be in the room with you. I'm the king of remote viewing. You can't hide from me. Ever. Remember that."* Then he was gone, tail waving a feline question mark.

She felt the virtual tape keeping her lids open ripped away. It hurt. She closed her eyes and breathed deeply. Then she opened them.

Ivy looked at the TV.

She reached for the remote.

15

Murmur stared at his watch and then scanned the hotel lobby. No Klepoth. It was already dark outside. He should have been home from school before this.

What the hell was a millennia-old demon doing sitting in a high school classroom anyway? Murmur hoped his teachers had enough sense not to fail him. Schools cost money to replace.

Just when Murmur had finally decided to call Klepoth, Ivy and Zane walked across the lobby. They didn't see him. She was looking up at the sorcerer and laughing. Murmur watched as they entered the restaurant.

He didn't even try to rein in his jealousy. His music stirred, and he took the mental image of him squashing Zane like a bug for a trial run.

What were they talking about? Was Zane teaching her how to keep nosy demons out of her mind while they shared a drink? Or was the sorcerer working his magic on her over a rib eye, baked potato, and salad? Murmur didn't dare think about dessert, or he'd lose it.

Thankfully, he spotted Klepoth heading his way. He strode to meet him. "Let's get out of here. I need a walk on the beach."

Klepoth looked puzzled, but didn't ask any questions.

Once they reached the edge of the water, Murmur relaxed the rigid control he'd held on his music. No sorcerers would die tonight. Or at least not for the next half hour. All bets were off after that.

"Where were you?" Murmur couldn't take his anger out on Zane, so Klepoth became his target. "I wouldn't want a mere life-or-eternal-torture battle with our master and his legions to get in the way of your extracurricular activities."

Klepoth shrugged off Murmur's shitty attitude. "After school, Kellen and I hung with some guys for a while. Shot some hoops."

"The Master could show up tonight, and you were playing basketball? You have to be kidding." Murmur felt as though he'd explode with his need to pound someone into dust. A nasty little tune featuring a banjo and a scratchy violin played in his head.

The other demon shrugged. "Who knows if we'll survive this? In case we don't, I want to go out with a few good memories."

Murmur had been readying another shot at Klepoth, but the demon's comment stopped him. He couldn't argue with Klepoth's logic.

Murmur *hadn't* been storing up good memories. After telling Ivy and Kellen about Asima's willingness to be part of Bain's plan, he'd purposely avoided Ivy for the last three days. She didn't need to be mixed up in their confrontation with the Master. Murmur couldn't take the chance that merely being with him might put her in danger.

Besides, she needed time away from him to decide if she could look past his devious and deceptive nature. Hey, even he didn't like himself very much right now. He hoped the old leopard-changing-its-spots thing wasn't true.

But the separation had turned him into a bad-tempered bastard.

Fine, so he hadn't been Mr. Sunshine before this happened. He thought of Ivy sitting in the restaurant with Zane and growled low in his throat.

His hair whipped in the wind blowing off the Gulf. Impatiently, Murmur pushed it away from his face. "Our legions are ready. They'll emerge from the portals as soon as the Master shows."

Klepoth had found a spot on the west end of Galveston Island that was almost remote enough for a demon battle.

Murmur glanced up at the dark clouds scudding across the evening sky. The surf churned as the wind whistled around them. Distant thunder rumbled. A storm was coming. "He'll be here tonight." The storm would cloak them from human eyes. "He'll wait until the storm breaks for maximum effect." Maybe he was even causing the storm. The Master's power was the big variable in the mix. Murmur *thought* he knew the extent of his strength, but he couldn't be one hundred percent positive. He just hoped that one unknown wouldn't destroy them.

"Yeah. I think you're right." Klepoth was doing a good job of hiding his fear. "Let's get moving."

The Master would sense where they were, and Murmur didn't want that to be at the castle.

Silently, they walked back to the castle's parking lot. No need to take anything with them. If they won, they'd be back. And if they lost? Well, the Master wouldn't allow them any mementoes from their past while he tortured them. Murmur did keep one thing, though. Even the Master couldn't touch the image of Ivy he carried in his mind.

Silently, they climbed into Murmur's car. And silently, they drove to what might be their last night on the mortal plane. Murmur hated the time it took to drive, but they had to conserve every bit of energy for the battle, hence the car.

All the way out to the west end of the island, Murmur thought about what he should have said to Ivy. It might not have mattered to her, but it would have made him feel a lot better.

What could he have said, though? "Let me take you away from everything you know, and I'll give you a life filled with demonic thrills?" Or maybe she'd fall for, "I love you. Let me light your fire." Okay, so she might be a little leery about lighting any fires around a demon. Humans tended to cling to their myths and stereotypes.

Love. He'd thought the word, but he didn't know if he believed in it. Demons didn't love. But this deep need, this *yearning*—jeez, that was a corny word—sure felt a lot like how humans had described the emotion. No one had told him how much it would hurt, though.

"We're here." Murmur pulled the car off the road and got out. Klepoth joined him. The storm was whipping itself into a frenzy. Jagged streaks of lightning lit the night sky. Perfect.

"We've done all we can. We've positioned our portals opposite each other." Murmur tried to think if they'd missed anything.

"He's in for a surprise." Klepoth's smile was a slash of white in the darkness. "He thinks only arch demons can open portals. No way will he believe how powerful we are until we kick his ass."

Murmur nodded. Kicking ass would be a good thing. "If we're really lucky, we'll trap him between us. While the legions are fighting, we'll take him down." Murmur only hoped they were as powerful as they believed they were. And that Klepoth had been right when he said the Master would be weakened for a while after crossing over onto the mortal plane. They needed all the breaks they could catch.

Klepoth cocked his head, listening. "The Master comes."

Murmur didn't doubt Klepoth's sensitivity to demonic vibrations. "Good luck." He paused, unwilling to say what needed saying. "Thanks for watching Kellen and for sticking with me on this."

Klepoth grinned. "No problem. Friends help friends."

Murmur frowned. Klepoth didn't have any problem saying the

"F" word. He forced a smile. "Yeah. Friends." Maybe the word would get easier with more use. Here was hoping he got a chance to test his theory.

He took a deep breath and released his true demon, not the weak-ass phony one he showed the human world. He called up his death music, felt it coil and writhe in him, clawing its way from the dark place he kept it prisoner most of the time. If Ivy saw him now, she'd run. Tonight he'd be the soulless killer all humans feared—merciless, savage, and a hell-spawn nightmare.

Finally, the storm broke. Lightning lit up the sky, and thunder crashed. Wind-driven rain lashed them. And the sound of pounding surf and howling wind made a fitting entrance for the Master.

A yawning black hole opened in the night sky, through which poured hundreds of demons mounted on grotesque creatures conceived in the depths of the Underworld. And at their head rode the Master.

Even as Murmur focused his power and ripped open his portal, he saw Klepoth doing the same. Within seconds, their legions burst through the openings to fling themselves at the enemy.

The demon battle blacked out the sky—deadly, vicious, and silent. No sound would wake the sleeping humans on the island. And more demons would spew through the portals to replace the fallen ones. The fight would continue until one of the leaders fell.

Murmur fixed his image of Ivy in his mind. He would return for *her*. Then he composed his weapon.

His death song was a musical scythe, given shape and form by its sharp notes and hard pounding beat. Power exploded in high screaming dissonance before dropping to a dark minor key. Voices emerged, chanting a requiem for the soon-to-be-deceased even as they destroyed with their horrific harmonies that slashed and maimed. Murmur swung the scythe in an arc of destruction. The music burned white hot as he left a trail of bloody demon parts behind him. Methodically, he fought his way toward the Master.

Ivy had blasted Zane for taking his petty revenge on Sparkle by answering all of her e-mails. He'd apologized by taking her to dinner. She'd enjoyed herself. He'd made her laugh with his stories about the castle. And he'd shown lots of patience as he went over the steps to keep unwanted visitors out of her head.

But now she was on her own for the rest of the night. Sparkle didn't have anything else for her to do, but Ivy didn't want to go back to her room. All she'd do there would be think about Murmur.

He'd been avoiding her, giving her space. That's what she'd said she wanted, wasn't it? Hey, with all of her Murmur-free time, she'd been able to finish reading the complaints. Holgarth had a lot to answer for. She was also finally doing some routine jobs for Sparkle. Normal stuff. But after three days without even seeing him, she was ready to admit that wasn't what she wanted at all.

She was considering ways to fix things as she wandered into the great hall. The fantasies were about to begin. Ivy stopped near where Holgarth stood. He was too busy ordering people around to pay any attention to her. *Thank you.* She didn't need his snark tonight.

Bain was walking across the hall, headed for the dressing room. She controlled her need to chase after him and ask where Murmur was.

Suddenly, Bain froze. He turned his head to stare at the far wall. Then he raced toward Holgarth, shoving people aside as he ran. What the . . . ? Curious, she moved closer so she could hear.

"Someone else will have to play the wicked vampire tonight." Bain raked his fingers through his hair.

Ivy frowned. Was he sick? He looked more upset than she'd ever seen him before, even more than when he was confessing his plans to Ganymede.

Holgarth drew himself up into a prickly column of outraged wizard. "That's not possible. It's too late to find a replacement." Then he spotted Ivy, and his gaze grew speculative. "A wicked vampire queen is not without precedent, though."

"Thanks. My master has entered the mortal plane on the west end of the island."

Holgarth looked alarmed. "An arch demon? In Galveston?"

"Murmur and Klepoth defied him. The Master will drag their dumb butts back to the Underworld. I'll do what I can." And then he was gone.

Ivy was left staring at the empty space where he'd stood a moment ago. She glanced around. None of the humans in the room seemed to have noticed that someone had just disappeared.

Holgarth looked worried, but that didn't stop him from turning toward her. "I seem to be short one wicked vampire. Do you think—?"

She didn't wait around for him to finish. Murmur was in danger. Ivy remembered Ganymede's words. *If he can survive.* She didn't even try for reason or common sense. No, she couldn't help him. No, it wouldn't be safe anywhere near a demon battle. Yes, he'd be furious if he knew what she was planning. None of that mattered.

Who could help her? There was only one person other than Murmur that she'd run to now. She raced out of the castle and into the storm, headed for Sweet Indulgence and Sparkle Stardust.

Panic had made her breathless by the time she reached the candy store. Ivy ignored Sparkle's startled expression as she leaned over the candy counter, dripping water and gasping for air. "Mumur's master has come for him. He and Klepoth are battling him some-where on the west end of the island." To her own ears her words sounded breathy and filled with terror.

Sparkle widened her eyes. "Now?"

Ivy could only nod.

Sparkle was already slapping the Closed sign in the window as Ivy straightened. "Let's go."

Ivy could've cried with relief that Sparkle wasn't going to try to leave her behind. She found enough breath to run the short distance to Sparkle's car.

"Aren't you going to call Ganymede to help?" She climbed into the passenger seat and held on as Sparkle peeled out of the parking lot.

"He's away trying to find out where the faery host is right now. Besides, he doesn't think Murmur needs any help. I'm not so sure."

Ivy *was* sure that Sparkle was breaking the sound barrier, but she wasn't about to tell her to slow down. "How will we find them?"

Sparkle never took her eye from the road. "Oh, we'll see them when we get close."

The rain was a solid sheet of water hitting the windshield. The *swish swish* of the wiper blades should've been a comforting sound, but it wasn't. Ivy couldn't see a thing past the front of the car.

Under any other circumstances, she would've demanded that Sparkle pull over. But not this time. What if the Master took him? What if she never saw him again?

When had Murmur decided to defy the arch demon? *You changed him.* Sparkle's words. No, this wasn't her fault. She wouldn't believe it. But still . . . She mentally urged Sparkle to go faster.

It seemed as though they'd been driving forever. How long did it take to get to the west end? Just as she opened her mouth to ask, Sparkle slowed the car.

"Look to your left."

Ivy obeyed. And gasped. Through the driving rain, she saw a massive roiling black cloud that not only filled the sky but covered the ground as well. Streaks of lightning tinged in red shot from the cloud. And beneath the car, she felt the ground shake. "What the . . . ?"

"The arch demon. We can only hope he doesn't rip the island apart." Sparkle sounded grim as she parked the car a safe distance from the cloud, which seemed to be expanding even as they watched.

"Why is it getting bigger?" What could she do against this kind of power? She mentally straightened her spine. It didn't matter. What mattered was that she was here for Murmur.

"More demons are coming through the open portals."

Sparkle sounded distracted as she stared fixedly at the rain-washed windshield.

Finally, she turned to Ivy. "I just called Mede home, but I don't think he'll get here in time. I couldn't reach the Big Boss." She pushed open her door and was immediately soaked. "Murmur and Klepoth owe me new shoes. Damn, why can't they do this crap on sunny days?" Sparkle stepped out of the car.

Ivy took a deep breath and got out too. She shivered in the cold rain. There might be thunder and lightning, but it was still February in Galveston. She followed Sparkle into the darkness.

They were trudging into the wind and rain. Ivy put her head down in a vain attempt to avoid the worst of it. Didn't work. Icy water trickled down her back and her wet shoes squished with each step.

Suddenly, Sparkle stopped. She crouched behind the remains of an old boat. Ivy did the same. For a moment, she felt a little relief from the weather. Then she looked up.

They were at the edge of the cloud, and Ivy got her first look at the battle.

The Master had brought his own brand of hell to earth. She didn't have any trouble spotting him. He had freaking horns—black, tipped in crimson, and the crimson was dripping blood. He'd rolled out his ugly face for the event. Probably wanted to scare the crap out of the enemy. Good choice.

He was a huge hulking man—okay, not a man, but he had male features—with the trademark red eyes of the ticked-off demon. His thick lips were drawn back in a snarl, made more terrifying by the bloodstained pointed teeth they exposed. Bloodstained? Did he use them to kill? Or maybe he sipped blood during the battle to keep up his strength. Ugh.

The thought made her feel like throwing up. Where was Murmur? Frantically she scanned the mass of fighting demons. They were covered in blood. How did they know friend from foe? Or maybe they just lashed out in a killing frenzy. The ground was covered with demon body parts, and those still battling stomped them into the blood-soaked earth as they fought to survive.

Ivy clamped her hand over her mouth. *Don't throw up, don't throw up.* She took deep breaths to push back the nausea. Too bad the coppery scent of blood filled the air. She dropped her hand. This was her reality. She'd deal with it.

"Are all the ones on the ground dead?" What did she know about demon mortality?

"Their physical bodies are." Sparkle was scanning the battlefield. "Their essence returns to the Underworld. They can't come back to the mortal plane for thousands of human years."

That meant that if the Master destroyed Murmur's body she'd never see him again. "Where's Murmur?" She blinked rapidly. *Absolutely not.* Crying wasn't an option. *Stay grounded.* Her mother's words. But her mother never had this scenario in mind when she'd said them.

"He's over there." Sparkle whispered close to her ear. She pointed.

Ivy looked. *There.* Even in the midst of a life-or-death struggle, he left her breathless. His long hair whipped around his face as he fought. His shirt was plastered to his torso, and he radiated deadly power.

"I'm giving you my magical earplugs."

"What?" She couldn't take her gaze from him. He was the only one not covered in blood. And he was alive. *Alive.*

"He's using his death music. It's not aimed at us, but even hearing a faint echo will put us on the ground. So my little spell will block his music as long as he doesn't get too close. The best part is that you'll be able to hear everything else fine." Sparkle looked smug. "It protects inside and outside the head. Many a night it saved me from listening to a cat who had a lot to say about nothing."

"Oh." Ivy was only half listening. She watched, mesmerized, as he swung what looked like a curved beam of glowing light. It almost looked like a giant . . . scythe? It cut down any demon it touched. Even the demons not touched, the ones who were just close to him, fell to the ground and convulsed. She shuddered.

Ivy followed his path of destruction as he fought his way toward the arch demon. Fear tore at her. The Master wasn't without his own skills. The earth moved around him, opening to engulf any enemies who drew close and then closing over them. Meanwhile he threw his hands out, sending tendrils of what looked like sizzling energy to cut apart Murmur and Klepoth's forces.

Sparkle poked her and leaned close. "See those demons fighting with themselves, and the ones banging their heads on the ground? That's Klepoth's work. He's spreading his illusions among the enemy." She laughed softly. "Go, Klepoth."

Before Ivy could reply, someone moved out of the shadows to crouch on her other side. Bain.

"What the hell are you doing here?" His disapproval included both women.

Sparkle glared at him. "We have a stake in Murmur and Klepoth staying alive and healthy."

Bain narrowed his gaze on Ivy. "You can't do anything to help either of them. Take the car and go back to the castle."

Not long ago, Ivy would've fled from the demon's anger. Not now. "No."

Bain widened his eyes. "No?"

"I can't help, but I care. So I'm staying." Ivy knew her stare dared him to do something about it. She only hoped he didn't take her up on the dare.

He made an impatient sound and turned his attention back to the fight. "The Master's legions are better trained, but I think the combined power of Murmur and Klepoth might be too much for him." He shook his head. "The silence creeps me out. Where're the shouts, the screams, the grunts and groans? You should be able to *hear* a war."

"Why aren't you out there fighting with them?"

Sparkle asked the question Ivy had been thinking.

Bain kept his gaze on the battle. "Murmur asked for my help. I turned him down. I couldn't take the chance that the Master would drag me back to the Underworld. Someone has to be here to free Elizabeth. She'll be trapped in Faery forever if I'm not there when the Sluagh Sidhe shows up."

Ivy wanted to call him a coward, to rant and ask what kind of friend he was, but she didn't. Instead she thought about Kellen, and what she'd do if he was in Elizabeth's place. "At least you're here now."

He nodded. "I'll help where I can without entering the fight."

"By the way, the Master doesn't seem worried about the music." That worried Ivy.

"He's an arch demon. He can resist the sound. But Murmur can kill him with the physical manifestation of it."

"Got it." Ivy decided she had a few more questions for Bain when this was all over. But she forgot about Bain when she heard Sparkle's gasp of alarm.

Klepoth was using his illusions to keep the Master's forces occupied while Murmur drew ever closer to the arch demon. But neither Murmur nor Klepoth noticed the fresh horde of demons pouring through the Master's portal.

"Fuck."

Ivy agreed with Bain's assessment.

Sparkle stood up, clearly visible if any of the demons were to look their way. They didn't. She clenched her hands into fists and thrust them into the air. Immediately, the new demons fell to the ground clutching themselves.

Ivy choked back a gasp. "What happened?" She barely remembered to keep her voice to a whisper.

Sparkle grinned. "I kicked each of them in the balls, magically speaking."

Bain snorted his appreciation.

There was no more time for celebrating, though, because the battle was ramped up to a new level. Murmur was only a short distance from his goal. The Master looked a little less confident than he had a short while ago. He pulled out the big guns.

Without warning, the earth opened between Murmur and the arch demon. Something slithered out of the chasm—a long snakelike something that wrapped around Murmur's ankle and yanked.

Ivy couldn't help it, she screamed and leaped to her feet. Bain stood beside her.

For the first time, Ivy saw Murmur stumble. He managed to control his music, but the thing dragging him toward oblivion wasn't reacting to his death song.

"The cursed snake is deaf. And it doesn't have a head to get into." Bain's voice was tight with worry.

Terror froze Ivy. What good was she? She couldn't even save the man she loved.

"Do something." Sparkle grabbed Bain's arm. "You're the damn Destroyer. Okay, destroy something."

Bain stilled. Ivy held her breath.

The snakelike creature had dragged Murmur almost to the edge of the fissure when the arch demon spoke for the first time.

"I'm torn, Murmur. How to destroy your mortal body? So many wonderful choices. You can fall to your death. Rather anticlimactic, though. Or I can tear your body apart. Much more dramatic, in addition to being a cautionary tale for any other demons who might think to defy me. Perhaps I'll combine the two. Yes, I like that." He smiled.

Ivy had never seen anything so horrible in her life.

"Do you have any final words?" The Master glanced over Murmur's head to where Klepoth still fought on. "The illusion maker won't last long once I've taken care of you."

"Go to hell." Murmur's voice was a rasp of defiance.

"Oh, I will. But you'll be going with me."

Ivy felt Bain tense a moment before he struck.

The tear in the earth snapped shut, cutting the thing wrapped around Murmur's ankle in half. It writhed in its death throes, releasing him.

Murmur didn't waste the opportunity. He struck at the arch demon.

The earth shook with the force of their coming together. They moved too quickly for Ivy to see more than the flash of Murmur's music or the sizzle from the Master's energy.

The demon armies stopped fighting and backed up. They clapped their clawed hands over their ears. Even with Sparkle's earplugs, Ivy caught the faint notes of something so terrifying that for a moment she couldn't breathe. Murmur's death song was growing louder, gaining power. How long could he keep it up?

This then would decide all of the demons' fates. Klepoth was trying to reach Murmur, to help with the fight, but he staggered and almost fell.

Ivy bit her lip. Klepoth was injured. Murmur would have to defeat his master by himself. She glanced at Bain.

"I can't help. They're moving too fast." Frustration lived in his voice.

Ivy's heart felt as though it would explode from her chest. Her breaths came in short gasps. Was it just her imagination, or were the flashes from his music growing dimmer, slower?

How could she help? She clenched her hands into fists, not even feeling the pain of her nails digging into her palms. *Do. Something.*

Her puny little puff of faery power wouldn't help. She had no physical way of saving Murmur. But . . . If he could get into *her* mind, would she be able to do get into *his*? Would he hear her if she concentrated on sending a message to him? Zane had explained a little of how it worked. She had to try. She wouldn't stand here and watch him die.

Closing her eyes, she pictured him, the way she'd first seen him— his long hair lifting in the breeze, his smile that had left her breathless, the strength and mystery of him. Once the image was fixed, she imagined sinking into him, reaching for his mind. She spoke to him.

"I'm here, Murmur. Keep fighting. You can't give up. If you lose, the demons will turn on me." Okay, so she was lying shamelessly. But if it revived his flagging energy, she'd lie like a rug. *"I love you. Come back to me."* Ivy would think about flinging the word "love" around later.

Ivy opened her eyes. She'd done all she could. But had it been enough?

"Yes!" Sparkle pumped her fist into the air.

Ivy held her breath and dared to hope. Murmur was beating the Master back. The arch demon stumbled, and that was his first and last mistake. Murmur swung his death music in a powerful arc and cut the Master in half.

Ivy turned from the carnage. Relief made her weak. She sank to the ground. The rest of the demons stood waiting. What did they expect to happen? She threw Bain a questioning glance.

"If Murmur chooses, he can take the Master's place. He'll add the arch demon's legions to his own. He'll be a force to be reckoned with in the Underworld."

And gone from the mortal plane forever. Ivy felt his words stab her in her all-too-vulnerable heart.

Bain looked intent for a moment, and then seemed to relax. "Murmur's shut down his death music." Bain turned and started to walk away.

"Wait. Where're you going?"

He looked back at Ivy. "I don't want him to know I was here."

"Why not, for heaven's sake? You saved him." Ivy couldn't hide her frustration.

Bain shrugged. "If he knows I helped him, he'll think he owes me a favor. It's a demon thing. But I didn't come for any damn favor. I came because . . ." He seemed lost for a moment. "Because he's my friend." He seemed amazed by the revelation. With a parting grin, he disappeared.

Sparkle laughed. "I like Bain a lot more now." She glanced down. "I think I'll hit up Murmur and Klepoth for two pairs of shoes." She studied her nails. "Hiding in the weeds didn't do my nails any good either. I'll add a manicure to my bill."

Ivy wasn't listening to her. She had remembered Klepoth. He was hurt. Now that the fighting was over, she ran to where he lay. The other demons looked startled, but when they moved toward her, Klepoth held up his hand to stop them. She leaned over him. "Are you okay?"

Klepoth shook his head. "Not right now, but I'll heal fast." He grinned up at her. "We kicked ass."

She smiled back at him. Somewhere during the battle, her distrust of him had vanished.

Ivy didn't get a chance to say anything, though, because suddenly someone grabbed her arm and spun her around. She looked up.

Murmur glared down at her. His eyes were still red, and fury gleamed in them. "What the hell are you doing here?"

He and Bain must have memorized the same lines.

"Don't you know better than to be anywhere near a demon battle?" He looked behind her. "I thought you had more sense, Sparkle."

Ivy had no idea what she would have said in reply, or even if she would have bothered answering him. She probably would have just flung herself into his arms. She didn't get the chance.

An unfamiliar voice spoke. "I hate to interrupt your justly earned celebration, but I really have a few things to discuss with Murmur."

They all turned. A new portal had opened, and a woman stood in the opening. She was the most beautiful woman Ivy had ever seen. Something inside Ivy shrank away, understanding without being told what she was.

Long black hair rippled down the woman's back. Her eyes were large and so blue they made Ivy's eyes seem like muddy water in comparison. Her lips were full and parted slightly in a smile no man would ignore. Ivy hated her.

He nodded. "Hello, Naamah."

16

"You were magnificent, Murmur."

"I didn't do it alone. Klepoth helped me." Murmur would have to thank him for saving his butt. He'd been inches away from a one-way ticket back to the Underworld when Klepoth had closed the earth. He glanced at his partner. The other demon was healing, but he wouldn't be much help if things got ugly.

Naamah didn't move from the portal opening; still, Murmur could feel her seductive power touching him. He remained unmoved. Coldly, he took stock of the demons behind her. Not enough for a full assault, but . . .

She laughed. It was a laugh meant to seduce, tempt, and conquer, right before she destroyed the object of her attention. "I only brought a few of my demons as bodyguards." Her smile hinted that he could guard her body in any way he chose.

He glanced at Ivy. She stared at Naamah with narrowed eyes and lips pressed tightly together. Something in her expression made

him smile. Jealousy. He recognized it in Ivy because he'd felt the
same emotion when he'd seen her with Zane.

He returned his attention to Naamah. "Why are you here? And
don't tell me it's just so you can congratulate me."

Naamah dropped her gaze to the scattered remains of the Master's physical body. She wrinkled her beautiful nose. Yes, he could
admit that everything about her was amazing. He felt nothing,
though, because he knew what lived inside her. But he was at ease
with her. He understood her, and he could use her.

She met his gaze. "We'll be neighbors. And I must admit to
looking forward to a few . . . neighborly visits."

She was trying for coy, but it wasn't working. He would respect
her more if she just acted like herself—vicious, gorgeous, and deadly.

"Aren't you going to introduce us, Murmur?" Sparkle had evidently reached her limit for silence.

"Sure. This is Naamah. She's the arch demon who controls the
territory beside the one that used to belong to my unlamented
master."

Naamah smiled at Sparkle. "I'm the demon of seduction."

She might have been smiling, but her eyes dismissed Sparkle as
being beneath her. Murmur thought she'd made her first mistake
on the mortal plane.

"A demon seductress?" Sparkle raised one brow. "If you're going
to stay on earth long, you'll need a complete makeover."

Naamah's smile died. "I'm perfect just as I am. Ask any man
here."

Sparkle shook her head. "How sad. You've obviously lived a
sheltered life. You'll have a lot more competition on the mortal
plane: women who understand how to create that certain look no
man can resist. You have a few problem areas, sister—wrong hair
style, wrong clothes, and definitely wrong shoes. Oops, no shoes.
My bad. Sweetie, the barefoot look is embarrassingly out of date.

And . . ." She widened her eyes. "Oh. My. God. No makeup. Never ever step outside without putting on your face." Sparkle brightened. "But anytime you want me to help you upgrade your look, stop by Sweet Indulgence, my candy store, and we'll see what we can do."

Naamah looked puzzled.

Murmur stepped into the silence before the demon realized Sparkle had insulted her. "We have things to talk about, Naamah. I'll contact you."

Naamah cast him a considering look before nodding. "I'll be waiting." Without another word, she turned and disappeared back into the portal. It closed behind her.

Klepoth released the breath he'd evidently been holding. "What're you going to do about her?"

"I don't know." He had a few options to consider. "I'll have to think about it."

Murmur chanced another glance at Ivy. The excitement in her eyes had dimmed since Naamah showed up. The arch demon's timing sucked. He was considering how to put the shine back in Ivy's eyes when Ganymede appeared.

"Yo, I'm here. Where's the battle? Point me toward the demon hordes and get out of the way." His ears were pinned back, and his claws were out.

Sparkle sighed. "The fight's over, sugarpudding. The good guys won."

Ganymede wilted. *"Well, crap. I was in the mood to kick ass, stomp heads, and crack ribs."*

"Maybe another day." At least the cat hadn't made the same mistake *he* had by demanding to know why Sparkle was here. Murmur had seen the look on Ivy's face when he'd gone all protective on her. "Give me a minute to dismiss the demons, and then we can get Klepoth back to the castle."

Murmur didn't wait to see if they agreed. He called Goloth, his

second in command, to him. Then he walked over to where Klepoth had managed to sit up. He made no comment when Ganymede,
Sparkle, and Ivy crowded around him. Let them hear if they wanted,
it wouldn't affect what he had to say.

He turned to Goloth. "You and Klepoth's second will be taking
all the legions back with you. The Master's demons are ours now.
Keep in touch with us. We're responsible for the defense of our new
territory. Report all abnormalities." He suspected there'd be a lot.
Demon legions were never a peaceful bunch. "Also monitor any
unrest among the souls we guard." The Master had ruled with a heavy
hand. The souls imprisoned in his territory would see anything less
as weakness. "Make sure you leave nothing here for the humans to
find." Translation: get rid of all body parts. He looked at Klepoth.
"Anything you want to add?"

Klepoth was still in obvious pain. He shook his head. "Sounds
good to me."

Goloth simply nodded and got to work.

By silent agreement, Sparkle and the others headed back to her
car. Ivy chose to ride in the passenger seat beside Sparkle. Murmur
helped Klepoth into the backseat with him. Ganymede plunked
his ample bottom between them.

The cat made a big deal of grooming himself. Murmur stared
out the window. The rain had stopped outside, but there was still
a storm brewing in the car. How could he explain to Ivy that he'd
avoided her for three days so she wouldn't be involved in the war
with his master? Not that it had done any good.

"The faery host is only two nights away."

Ganymede knew how to drop a bombshell. Murmur glared at
him. "Why didn't you say something before this?"

The cat paused in cleaning his paw to give Murmur an unblinking stare that said "dumbass" loud and clear. *"Because you were busy
doing other things."*

Ivy turned to look at Ganymede, alarm in her wide eyes. "What will we do?"

"*I'm on top of it.*" Now satisfied with his total awesomeness, Ganymede laid down on the seat. "*Holgarth and Zane will make sure the guardian gargoyles are ready. I've already called Edge and Passion back from Washington. We don't have many guests in the hotel at this time of year, but just to be safe, Zane will slap protective wards over the doors of all humans staying there. The faery host will show up around midnight. And then we'll kick butt. Did I miss anything?*" His self-satisfied expression said he knew he'd thought of everything.

Ivy shifted her gaze to Murmur, but he looked away. Now might be as good a time as any to reveal the little detail everyone had kept from Ganymede. "We have a plan to avoid a war with the faeries."

"*It better be good.*" The cat's tone said he hoped it was lousy so he could make up for what he hadn't done tonight.

"Bain figured that if we had someone acceptable to trade for Elizabeth, the Sluagh Sidhe might take her replacement and leave without a fight." Murmur decided to keep Sparkle out of this. She and Ganymede had just made up. The cat didn't need to know she'd kept this from him.

Ganymede speared him with an unblinking stare. "*Who?*"

"Asima has agreed to take Elizabeth's place." Murmur waited for the explosion.

"*You're freaking kidding me.*" Ganymede's response was an outraged hiss. "*The faeries aren't idiots. They'll recognize what she is as soon as they see her. And they'll know that if she doesn't manage to tear strips off them, Bast will do the job. Angry goddesses are a bitch. All I wanted was a friendly little skirmish, not a war with the faeries and a pissed off goddess.*" He batted at the back of Sparkle's seat. "*Have any candy in the glove compartment, cupcake? This crap is upsetting me.*"

"Nope." Sparkle didn't take her eyes off the road. "All I have is a pack of antacid tablets. Will that help?"

Murmur could feel his own temper stirring as Ganymede chewed the tablets. The music in his mind featured violins that sounded a whole lot like screeching cats. He wanted to reach into his head and tear the damn strings from them.

"This can work. Asima will be in human form. She'll play the part. She only has to fool them until Elizabeth is safe. Once the trade is made, the Sidhe will honor it. They're big on that kind of thing. Sure, they'll be furious, because they have to release her, but we can deal with that later. If it makes them go away, I'll promise them a favor." Not something Murmur wanted to do, but the fae valued a favor owed even more than demons did.

Ganymede snorted. *"What did you have to give her? Did she make you promise to go to operas, ballets, and other freaking 'cultural events' with her for the next thousand years?"*

Murmur's music was sounding a little violent. He tried to dial it back. "I talked to Asima. She doesn't want anything in return. She's lonely. She wants friends. I think we should give her the benefit of the doubt. People can change."

Ganymede's mumbled curses said he thought the whole idea sucked.

"I think it's a great idea." Sparkle almost hummed with happiness. "Maybe Asima will enjoy the company of the Sidhe. They share contempt for everyone that isn't as superior as they are. She'll fit right in."

"I think we all owe Asima big time." Ivy dared Sparkle or Ganymede to argue her point.

No one spoke up, so Ivy continued. "I want Kellen somewhere safe when the faery host arrives."

"That would be in the castle with us." Ganymede sounded definite. *"They're close now. Even if you took Kellen away and hid him somewhere else, their hunters would still be able to track him."*

No one seemed to want to comment on that, so silence settled over them for a few minutes. But Ganymede couldn't maintain the quiet for long.

"So, are you two going back to the Underworld? You'll be able to live the high life now." Ganymede thought about that for a moment. *"Or as high as you can get there. From what I saw in Klepoth's illusion, you'll have to do some major landscaping, build a big house, pipe in water for a waterfall and pond, stuff like that. But it's doable."*

"No." Klepoth's voice was weak, but he seemed sure of his answer. "I never want to see the Underworld again." He looked at Murmur. "Can we make that happen?"

Murmur didn't want to discuss his future now, in front of all of them. He wasn't going back, but he had to make certain no one would ever threaten his music, his freedom, or the safety of anyone he cared for.

Cared for. He was finally ready to admit how human many of his emotions had become. Surprisingly, he cared for quite a few people. But he *loved* Ivy. She'd said she loved him in his mind, but he had to hear it out loud, hear that she'd meant it and wasn't just trying to spur him to greater effort against the Master.

Naamah was his key. "We'll work on it." He refused to say any more.

Ganymede's amber eyes gleamed with avid curiosity, but he didn't press Murmur to elaborate. Smart cat.

For the rest of the drive, Murmur's mind churned with all he had to deal with. He had to make love with Ivy again. He had to come up with a plan that would allow him to stay on the mortal plane. He had to make love with Ivy again. He had to get ready for the arrival of the Sluagh Sidhe. He had to make love with Ivy again.

But as Sparkle parked the car and he climbed out, he knew he'd forgotten something. What the hell was it? He thought about it as he helped Klepoth into the castle. After getting the other demon settled in his room, he still hadn't remembered.

Murmur was about to leave Klepoth when he thought of something. He paused with his hand on the doorknob. "I owe you for closing that big-ass crater the Master created. You saved me."

Klepoth looked puzzled. "I didn't do that. I was busy staying alive." He grinned. "I'd say you have a faery godmother out there, but I know how you feel about faeries right now."

Wow, that was strange. Murmur closed the door and stood thinking for a moment. If not Klepoth, then who? Not Sparkle. She would've enjoyed bragging about how she'd plucked him from the jaws of death. Literally. Ivy didn't have that kind of power. Who else knew about the battle?

Then it hit him. It could only be one person. Murmur smiled. He'd thank his secret savior later.

As he walked back to the great hall in search of Ivy, Murmur returned to wracking his brain over the something important he'd forgotten. She wasn't there, but Asima was.

"I hope you haven't forgotten. You'll be accompanying me to the chamber music performance tomorrow night."

Well, crap. He'd been happier not remembering.

"Ivy will be coming. She owes me a favor as well."

Okay, maybe it wouldn't be so bad after all.

"Braeden will be my date." Asima's feline eyes turned sly. *"He does not owe me a favor."*

What did that mean? No, he didn't want to know. "Ganymede just broke the news. The Sluagh Sidhe will be here in two nights." A cat's face didn't show emotions, so he couldn't tell what her reaction was. "I'll meet you in the lobby. What time?"

"Seven." She started to pad away, but turned for one last comment. *"You have excellent taste in clothes, so I'll trust you to dress well."*

Murmur watched her leave. He thought about going to Ivy's room. They had a lot to discuss. *No, not tonight.* It was late, and she'd be tired. Besides, he had to secure his future first. He also had to compose the exact words and music to convince her to . . . to what? He was almost afraid to even think the words.

Holgarth and Zane stood next to the great hall door leading out to the courtyard. It looked as though they were arguing. Murmur felt some of his tension drain away. At least Ivy wasn't with Zane.

He didn't want to interrupt their fight, but he had to talk to Holgarth. And it had to be now, because he didn't know how long he could stay on his feet. He hadn't said anything, but his ex-master had tagged him a few times. Nothing that a good night's rest wouldn't cure, but he was hurting at the moment.

Murmur stopped in front of them. "Hate to interrupt a family discussion, but I need to talk to you, Holgarth."

Zane made a frustrated sound. "That's okay. I was leaving. I'm wasting my time here anyway." He looked at Murmur. "Maybe you can make him see reason. The castle needs more security. The gargoyles won't stop the Sluagh Sidhe. And Sparkle is overconfident. She thinks we'll be able to turn back the faeries. I've done my research. We have powerful supernaturals on our side, but the faeries have power *and* numbers. They'll be coming by the thousands." He cast his father one last impatient glance. "Good luck with that." Then he walked away.

"Thousands?" Wow. Murmur might not like Zane, but he respected his opinion.

Holgarth shrugged. "Perhaps. But many of those will be captured mortals. Zane is young and excitable. The castle will be fine."

Yeah, well, Murmur felt a little excitable too. The fae could simply overwhelm the castle with sheer numbers.

"You wanted something?" Holgarth was back to his pompous, lovable self. "My time is valuable. Oh, and congratulations on your big win. I assume you'll be returning to the demon realm?" His expression said that he'd help Murmur pack.

"For a short time. But first I need you to write up a contract for me."

Holgarth narrowed his eyes. "Sparkle has retained me to take care of her legal work. I don't freelance."

Murmur spun a soft melody promising Holgarth all kinds of good karma and surrounded the wizard with it. Holgarth frowned, but didn't seem to realize what was happening.

"I realize your job managing the fantasies and the general running of the park is a huge workload." *Don't lay it on too thick.* "But you also have a law degree. I'll pay you well for this contract."

Holgarth raised one brow. "And this contract would be for what?"

Murmur took a deep breath. "A secure future."

The wizard studied him for moments that seemed to last forever. Then he nodded. "We'll work out the details tomorrow."

Relief flooded Murmur. "Great. How much do you want—?"

Holgarth waved away Murmur's question. "You've helped save the castle and those in it several times. Consider this payment for services rendered." He started to turn away. "Oh, and you didn't need that rather insipid music to convince me. If you ever again feel the urge to ply me with music, try Metallica."

Metallica? Really? Who would've thought? Murmur smiled as he headed for his room and hopefully a peaceful night's sleep. And if he was lucky, the only thing that would interrupt it would be dreams of Ivy.

Ivy sat next to Murmur and listened to the small group of musicians. Asima and Braeden sat on Murmur's other side. The setting was beautiful: a large, airy room that ran almost the entire length of the huge beach house. A solid wall of glass faced the Gulf. The room's lights had been dimmed, and the outside spotlights showed waves rolling onto the beach. It gave the whole event an intimate feel.

But Ivy wasn't listening to the music. Her mind was busy untangling her impressions of the evening so far.

Ivy glanced across the men at Asima. Yes, she still had that unearthly beauty going on. The messenger of Bast was petite with long, shining white-blond hair and large, wickedly tilted eyes the same shade of blue as her Siamese alter ego. Her full lips tempted while her delicate features suggested fragility and vulnerability. Ivy thought that Asima was as fragile as a brick wall. Okay, so maybe that was a little jealousy showing.

Ivy decided that she was at least wearing a sexier outfit than Asima's. Her loaner dress from Sparkle was short, glittery, and swirly. It dipped in all the right places. Asima's dress could only be described as black and tasteful. It looked as though it cost a fortune, but Ivy liked Sparkle's sense of style better.

Braeden didn't seem to care what Asima was wearing. He spent more time staring at her face than at the musicians. Hard to believe, but it seemed as though the dark faery really cared for Asima.

Then Ivy forgot about the other two as she cast a sideways glance at Murmur. The expected breathless sensation hit her. He wore a suit tonight and made it look sexy and elegant. When he turned to meet her gaze, he smiled. And that smile was like a shot of emotional adrenaline. She wanted to reach out and touch him. Everywhere.

The day had been torture. He hadn't made any attempt to see her, and she wondered if her declaration of love had horrified his demonic soul. But it had taken only a few questions to find out that he'd closeted himself with Holgarth for the day. She was curious, but she wouldn't waste precious time with him on questions.

He leaned toward her. "We'll talk. Tonight. In your room." He shifted his body so that his thigh pressed against hers.

She absorbed the contact, even though too many layers of clothes separated them. His whisper was rife with hints about all the other things they'd do tonight. Ivy wanted to yell at the musicians to play faster, damn it. But he seemed to be enjoying the music, so she subsided.

A short time later, she heard him humming softly under his breath, something with lots of energy, a tune that *lived*. She wanted to tap her foot in time to it.

Suddenly, his music filled the room, intertwining with what the musicians were playing. It enhanced their melodies, made them richer, and dipped them in bright, warm colors.

The audience came alive. They leaned forward and tapped their fingers on the arms of their chairs. The musicians smiled and played harder.

A disembodied voice gave words to the music, and no one seemed to think that was strange. People in the audience sang along. Ivy winced when she heard Asima join in. No matter how beautiful she was in human form, she still sang like a cat, all high-pitched, screechy notes.

Suddenly, it was over. The audience applauded loudly and left talking about how they were going to pass the word to friends about how great this had been.

As they rose to leave, Murmur clasped Ivy's hand. She leaned into him. "Anyone who comes to another one of their concerts will be disappointed."

Murmur grinned down at her. "No, they won't. While I was creating the melody, I slipped it into the musicians' minds. They'll be able to play it again." He shrugged. "Not as brilliantly as I played it, but it'll satisfy the masses." He winked at her as he helped her with her jacket.

Ivy couldn't remember having seen him this happy, and she hugged the hope that she was at least a little responsible for it. Once outside, she glanced around. Asima and Braeden were right behind them, but the rest of the audience had somehow disappeared.

She frowned. Something about the silent emptiness struck her as creepy. She tightened her hold on Murmur's hand and walked faster. The demon battle had made her jumpy. She would have to get over it.

The night had taken on a thick quality that felt as though it clung to her. She wanted to wipe her hands on her jacket. Without warning, Murmur fell and lay still. Ivy screamed, but the sound seemed to be absorbed by the darkness.

Ivy dropped to her knees beside him even as she heard Braeden's curse and Asima's gasp. She looked up.

Tirron and eight others had stepped from the shadows. "I wouldn't move if I were you."

Ivy knew his warning was for Braeden and Asima. He didn't fear her puny power. Fierceness filled her. If they survived this, she'd learn to maximize any power she had. No more denials, no more excuses.

She placed her fingers on Murmur's neck. Ivy gasped. His skin was freezing. No pulse. Nothing. Fear almost made her lightheaded. "What do you want?" *Please wake up.*

Tirron smiled, that beautiful cold smile that terrified her.

"To kill you, of course."

While he spoke, his followers, five men and three women, circled them. Yes, the women had noticed Braeden, but they weren't giving in to his pull. Now, if he could only touch—

"Don't worry, I won't destroy Murmur's mortal body. I want him here to live and suffer. I don't care about the other two. But you . . ." His smile widened. "He cares about you. And you, after all, were the cause of all my trouble." He shrugged. "Although everything will work out anyway." His smile grew secretive. "The one who should die still will. That hasn't changed. I've just had to adjust my plans."

What the hell did he mean by that? Only someone very stupid would point out that he'd caused his own troubles, so she kept quiet. "What did you do to him?"

Tirron nodded toward one of the women. "Mielle quick-froze him. When he thaws out, he'll be fine. But he'll stay the way he is until I decide otherwise." Tirron shook his head in mock regret. "You weaken him. He was thinking of you instead of watching for his enemies."

Guilt gnawed at her. Tirron was right. She was a distraction. But since she didn't think she could give Murmur up now, she would just have to make herself strong. First, though, she had to survive the next few minutes.

The longer she could keep Tirron talking, the longer she'd stay alive and give Braeden or Asima time to act. She glanced at Braeden. He was backing up a few inches at a time. About a foot more, and he'd be able to touch Mielle. Asima hadn't moved.

And so Ivy babbled. "Are the others from the Seelie Court too? Why do you all sort of look the same? Are you related? Does each of you have a different power? How did you disappear from the elevator before Murmur could kick your butt?"

"Shut the fuck up!" Tirron had finally lost his cool.

Ivy flinched. Okay, maybe she shouldn't have asked that last question, but she'd been talking in a nonstop stream without even taking a breath. Her mouth had been way ahead of her mind. Funny, when she'd asked the question about the Seelie Court, Mielle had looked startled. Not that it mattered in the grand scheme of things. In a few minutes, Ivy would be dead, unless . . . Another glance showed that Braeden was within touching distance.

Holding her breath, Ivy watched him reach out and grasp Mielle's wrist. Then things happened almost too fast for her to follow.

Mielle tried to jerk her hand away, but Braeden had a firm grip. It took only a moment of contact for her face to go lax, her eyes to fill with mindless lust.

As Mielle went limp, she must have lost her hold on Murmur. His eyes opened. He took in the situation at a glance and leaped at Tirron.

Tirron's eyes widened. "Kill them." He stumbled back and the other faeries formed a protective shield in front of him.

Then Ivy got a demonstration of the enemy's power. She could hear the music forming in Murmur's mind. He wasn't being careful, but then, time was important. The beginning notes made her want to throw herself to the ground, dig a hole, and bury herself forever.

But before he could complete the melody, an unseen force flung him at least twenty feet through the air. He landed with a pained grunt against the side of the house. Where were the people inside? Didn't they know something was happening outside?

Braeden cried out in pain as a slash mark appeared across his chest. Blood poured from the wound, but he didn't drop Mielle's hand.

No one was paying attention to Ivy. She frantically looked around for a weapon. *Think.* What would hurt a faery? *Iron.* She needed something made of freaking iron. A heavy iron pipe would be great. No pipes, no pointy stakes, not even a dead branch. She was screwed.

But in the end, she needn't have bothered.

The attack on Braeden finally seemed to tear Asima from whatever trancelike state she'd been in. Throwing up her hands, she screamed into the malevolent night. "I call on the power of Bast. Hear me, beloved goddess."

Suddenly, Asima was gone. In her place was the largest lion Ivy had ever seen. Sure, she hadn't seen many, but this one was as large as a horse. And just in case someone stupid might mistake it for a normal lion, it was surrounded by shimmering power that extended outwards in rainbow waves.

The fight lasted about ten seconds more. That's how long it took

the lion to tear apart all the faeries except for Tirron. He'd disappeared at first sight of the lion. His followers had reacted a little too
slowly.

Ivy looked away. *Please, no more blood and body parts.*

"It's okay. They're gone." Murmur's voice warmed the side of her
neck.

Cautiously, she glanced at where the faeries had been. No bodies, nothing. "What . . . ?"

"Faery reclaims its own." Murmur looked worried. "I hope this
doesn't cause trouble with the Seelie Court. We already have our
hands full."

Hands full. *The lion.* Ivy frantically scanned the area. No lion,
but Asima was back. She was busy taking care of Braeden's wound.
Ivy allowed herself to relax.

"What did that all mean?" She placed her palm over his heart
just to assure herself that he lived. *She* certainly lived, because contact
with any part of his body made her heart leap and race. And he was
warm again. She could sink into his heat and stay there forever.

He pressed her hand against his chest for a moment before putting his arm across her shoulders and guiding her to where the others stood. As they walked, she noticed that the night had cleared
of whatever evil Tirron had whipped up. A cool breeze blew, and
she could see stars.

"You okay?" Murmur put his hand on Braeden's shoulder.

The faery nodded. He didn't even look at Murmur. His attention
never wandered from Asima.

Ivy silently applauded Murmur. She'd bet that a few weeks ago
he wouldn't have touched the faery willingly. "Thank you for what
you did. Both—"

Murmur put his hand over her mouth. "Never thank a faery.
They'll perceive it as a debt owed. And you don't want to owe any
faery a favor." He glanced at Braeden. "Sorry about that."

Braeden shrugged. "It's the truth." His expression turned sly. "Although, I can't say I wouldn't enjoy knowing you owed me a debt."

Ivy smiled weakly.

Murmur looked grim. "I'm damn glad both of you were here."

Without them, she'd be dead. She'd been useless during the fight. She tried to keep the knowledge from eating at her. She could do her self-loathing later.

Murmur focused his attention on Asima. "Thanks, Asima. But what took you so long?"

Asima smoothed down her dress, which didn't have a single wrinkle or stain. Most disturbing, her hair was still a shining curtain down her back, not one strand out of place. Ivy thought that was just sick.

Asima looked puzzled. "I thought it would be obvious. I could not take aggressive action against the faeries without gaining Bast's approval first. The goddess had to ponder the consequences of destroying them." Her gaze slid away from Murmur.

"I assume she gave her approval?"

Why was Murmur pressing? And Ivy would almost swear that she saw a flash of amusement in his eyes. What was that about? She could understand Bast's need for caution, because even a goddess wouldn't want to anger the entire Seelie Court.

The Seelie Court. Ivy frowned. Something pricked her memory, something important.

Asima fixed her attention on Braeden's chest even though his wound was gone. "She would have." She fussed with his shirt. "In a minute or two."

Braeden placed his hand over hers, stilling her nervous fussing. "Bast didn't give you permission?"

Asima looked away. "No. But they were hurting you. I couldn't allow them to do that. Bast will not mind."

Asima bit her bottom lip, and Ivy decided that Bast would mind very much. Asima made a giant leap upward in Ivy's estimation.

Braeden slid his fingers along her jaw, forcing Asima to look at him. "Your caring means a lot to me."

"If your goddess gives you any flack, let me know." Murmur smiled at Asima. "I'll compose a song for her that will repay her for your transgression."

Asima looked awed. Evidently a song created by Murmur as a gift was a precious commodity.

"Thank you." Asima smiled at Murmur. "That would go a long way toward placating her. And perhaps the queen of the Seelie Court will not be angry. Tirron and the others were not shining examples of that court."

They'd almost reached the car when Ivy finally put it together. "Wait. I have it."

Everyone paused.

"I don't think Tirron belongs to the Seelie Court."

17

"Doesn't belong to the Seelie Court? Explain." How could Bain have made that kind of mistake? Murmur searched his memory for clues that Tirron wasn't what he claimed.

Ivy raked her fingers through her hair as she met his gaze. "The first time Tirron spoke to me, he said something puzzling. He said we'd ride the night skies together."

"That would mean the Sluagh Sidhe. The Unseelie." Braeden sounded confused. "I didn't recognize Tirron or his buddies, but then, I'm a solitary faery." He glanced at Asima. "Until now."

Murmur shook his head. "Maybe you made a mistake. Maybe he didn't say exactly that."

Ivy's expression turned stubborn. "I have a great memory. No, I didn't mistake what he said. Besides, I didn't know anything about the Sluagh Sidhe at that point. Why would I imagine something that strange?"

Murmur knew he looked doubtful. "Bain knew this guy." But did he? "Or maybe not. I remember now. Bain said he didn't know him personally. Someone had recommended him." He shook his head. "But faeries can't lie. He told Bain he belonged to the Seelie Court."

Ivy looked a little deflated. "That's a problem. But other things fit. Tonight, when I asked if all of them were from the Seelie Court, Mielle looked startled." She glanced at Asima and Braeden. "And at the end, why did Tirron say that everything would work out anyway, that the one who should die still would? That sounds as though he's targeting one particular person."

"Smacks of a conspiracy to me. We don't need any added complications right now." Braeden looked worried.

We? Braeden seemed to be throwing his lot in with them. Murmur decided he wouldn't make a big deal of it. They could use the extra help.

"Faeries can't lie, but they can manipulate the truth by not answering or by only telling part of the truth." Asima slipped her arm around Braeden's waist.

"Who is the person who will die?" Murmur didn't like the thought that Tirron had used all of them to fulfill his own secret agenda. "I'll talk with Bain as soon as we get back to the castle. He'll still be working the fantasies."

No one spoke during the drive back to the castle. Murmur drove, and Ivy sat next to him. He made sure he didn't glance in the rearview mirror to see what Asima and Braeden were doing there.

As he parked the car, Murmur heard an imperious meow behind him. Asima was once again the cat Sparkle loved to hate. Braeden carried her into the castle while Murmur and Ivy followed behind them.

Ivy stopped and pulled out her phone. "Wait a minute while I check on Kellen."

Murmur stood nearby, trying not to listen in on her conversation with her brother.

"You're where? Don't you have homework?" She bit her lip as she listened. "Okay, but don't make it too late." She put her phone away and joined him. "He's in Klepoth's room. He says he finished his homework, and he and Klepoth are working on a project. I'm glad that he has a friend, but . . ."

Murmur felt a stab of resentment that he quickly squashed. Maybe she'd never get over her suspicion of demons. And that was a good thing. He tried to convince himself of that. "Klepoth is okay. Kellen is safe with him."

She turned wide eyes on him. "Oh, it's not that. I trust Klepoth. But I'm not being a great substitute parent. I don't have any idea how he's doing in school. I'm not making sure he gets enough sleep, or spending time talking with him. Once this faery thing is over, I'll have to do better."

Murmur hoped his relief didn't show. If she trusted Klepoth, it stood to reason she trusted him.

He expected her to begin walking again, but she didn't. She stood looking into the night. "Why did you avoid me for three days?"

A lie immediately popped into his head. It was a great lie. He was, after all, still a demon, and his instinct was always to lie if the truth made him uncomfortable. Well, now was as good a time as any to break that habit. "I didn't want you to find out about the battle with my master. And I wanted to make sure no one would associate you with me in case I lost. The Master would've taken great joy in hurting someone I cared for." He frowned. Truths were difficult. "I wanted to keep you safe." He hummed a calming melody in his head.

Her smile lit up every dark place in his sorry soul.

"Thank you." That's all. She started walking toward the door.

He grinned into the night. Okay, so sometimes telling the truth felt damn good.

Inside the castle, he gripped Ivy's hand just in case she had any ideas about escaping him. They waited until Bain had shed his vampire costume to approach him in the dressing room.

Bain pulled a shirt over his head before facing them. "A problem?"

"Tirron was waiting outside after the concert. He brought eight of his friends, all fae. Things happened. Asima saved our butts. Tirron escaped. His friends didn't. But the important thing is that Ivy put some clues together and came up with the theory that Tirron isn't Seelie."

Bain narrowed his eyes. "What clues?"

Ivy repeated what they'd discussed and then added, "Murmur said that you thought Tirron was Seelie. Are you sure?"

Bain remained silent for a moment. "Come to think of it, no one ever mentioned which court he belonged to." He made a disgusted sound. "How could I be so stupid? I just assumed he was Seelie because the recommendation came from someone I respected. He knew how I felt about the Unseelie."

"Did Tirron ever *say* he belonged to the Seelie Court?" Ivy stepped closer to him. "I understand faeries can't lie."

"He never came out and said it. He just allowed everyone to assume. Damn." He yanked out his false fangs. "He played all of us."

"In the morning, when everyone's rested, we'll have to work this out, because tomorrow night it's game on." Murmur glanced at Ivy, noting the strain in her eyes. They'd all had a rough couple of nights.

Bain nodded and started to leave.

"Bain."

The other demon stopped and looked back at him. "Thanks." Murmur still couldn't wrap his mind around the fact that Bain hadn't claimed a life-debt for saving him. Maybe, just maybe, the mortal plane changed everyone eventually.

Bain's eyes widened. He looked at Ivy.

So she must've known about it. Bain probably asked her to keep quiet. Murmur was okay with that.

Bain shrugged. "Just stay away from big holes from now on. I have other things to do besides hauling your sorry ass out of them."

"Yeah, well, thanks anyway." Okay, all this thanking business was embarrassing Murmur.

Finally, Bain smiled. "Hey, what're friends for?" And he walked away.

"Does it bother you that I kept quiet about Bain being there?"

"No. It was a good promise. Those are the kind that should be kept." He knew his smile was probably a little goofy. "Bain is really my friend." The tune buzzing in his brain was a little too fizzy, a little too happy.

She looked puzzled. "Of course he is. Why wouldn't he be?"

He shook his head. "You don't understand. In the Underworld, demons don't have friends. They form alliances. They do nothing without getting something in return. Bain and I have worked together before. He always wanted a favor in return for helping me. This time he doesn't." She had no idea how huge that was.

Her expression softened, and he didn't think he imagined the tenderness there. He looked away, unsure whether to feel embarrassed that he'd allowed his emotions to get away from him or to simply soak up what she offered.

"Everyone can change." She touched his chest with the tips of her fingers.

The pressure might be light, but it seared him just the same. "Even you?"

"Especially me. Before you, the word 'demon' only pulled up one response." She flattened her palm over his heart.

"Evil."

She nodded.

"And now?" He tried to look casual, unaffected.

Ivy laughed. "Shades of gray. Too many to count."

He could live with that.

Silently, they headed for Ivy's room. Once there, she flopped onto a chair, and he ordered them something from room service.

While they ate, he filled the quiet with small talk, carefully steering clear of discussing what might happen tomorrow night. He wanted tonight to be as worry free for her as possible.

Because, no matter what happened with the faeries, if his mortal body still lived after they left, he had to return to the Underworld. He'd gotten what he needed from Holgarth, and he already had Klepoth's agreement. Now everything hinged on whether or not he could convince Naamah.

But all that was in the future. Tonight was for them. She watched him as he pushed his plate aside, rose, and walked over to her bed. He pulled down the covers and then glanced at her. "I checked my music at the door tonight."

Her eyes widened. "Aren't you supposed to wait an hour after eating before exercising?"

He smiled. "I've always believed you should work off a meal."

Ivy didn't hesitate. She got up, grabbed her nightgown from the closet, and headed for the bathroom. "I'll take a shower while you create sexy rhythms in your head." She grinned. "Oops. I forgot. No music tonight."

Murmur kicked off his shoes and lay on top of the covers. While he listened to the sound of the water running, he called up a few of his own illusions that would've done Klepoth proud.

He wanted to go in and join her. Feel the hot water flowing down his back. Watch the drops sliding over her body. Then he'd smooth his fingers across her gleaming skin and . . . Murmur took a deep breath. He hoped she didn't spend much time in there.

About three years later, she came out of the bathroom. She brought with her the scent of whatever soap she'd used—something subtly sensual—and the moist heat of the shower. Her nightgown was silky and pink. It didn't cling to her, but it had its own sexy ripple as she moved.

She climbed into bed beside him and pulled the sheet up to her chin. "You can have the shower now."

Murmur didn't say anything, just got out of bed and went into the bathroom. He closed the door softly behind him.

Ivy mulled over her choices. She could leave the nightgown on, but then one of them would have to remove it. Pleasure interruptus. She could take it off now and wait for him naked. Would he think she was too eager? She smiled. Oh, what the hell. She stripped off the nightgown and dropped it beside the bed. Ivy didn't think there was such a thing as too eager when it came to how she felt about him.

She reached over to turn off her bedside light and noticed Whimsy. The plant looked a little droopy. "Feeling neglected, sweetie? Well, you get to do your thing tonight. I want only happy, sexy vibes floating around here." Ivy glanced across the bed. The lamp on Murmur's side was still lit. "The better to see you with," she whispered.

Ivy tensed as he turned off the shower. She waited . . . He opened the door and stepped into the room.

He was nude. And he was so beautiful it brought tears to her eyes. As he walked across the room to her bed, shadow and light played across the hard planes of his chest and his ridged stomach and curled around his sex. The shadows gave added definition to his muscular thighs as he moved.

Once he reached his side of the bed, he turned for a moment to fling his clothes across a chair. She sucked in her breath. His back was strong and smooth and tapered down to his waist, which drew her eyes down, down, down to the most perfect butt cheeks she'd ever seen. Tight and male, and she couldn't wait to—

He interrupted her thoughts of exactly what she'd do by grabbing the sheet and yanking it off her.

She gasped, but controlled her first instinct to cover herself. She met his gaze.

His eyes glowed red, and she understood what that meant now. He lay down and rolled onto his side. Then he slid his gaze the length of her body.

"You're the most beautiful woman in or out of the mortal world to me."

His voice was soft and laced with so much emotion and *truth* that she absolutely believed him. She swallowed her need to laugh nervously and deny she was anything close to what he believed. It was enough that *he* saw her as amazing.

She blinked away the sudden tears that had no part in her plans for the night. Before he could reach for her, she laid her hand flat against his chest and pushed. He rolled onto his back as she rose over him.

"I want to discover you tonight, touch all of you with nothing but silence between us." She lowered her head and slid the tip of her tongue across his lower lip.

"I wouldn't count on it being all that silent." His quiet laughter was filled with anticipation, *hunger*.

He reached up to run his hands over her arms, trailing his fingers across her collarbone and down to the swell of her breasts. "Who are you, Ivy Lowe?"

She shuddered. "I'm not sure." The path of his fingers left goose bumps behind. Ivy traced the shape of his face with one finger, and when she drew it across his mouth, he captured it with his lips. "I thought I was normal, ordinary, but I'm not. I'll never be that person again." She stared into his eyes as he swirled his tongue around the tip of her finger before nipping and releasing it. "I think we're a lot alike."

He raised one brow. "Let me guess. You've been on Google tracing your demonic ancestors. I never guessed."

"Nothing like that. We both started out thinking we were one thing, but now we find out we're something very different." Did she have the courage to say it? *Say it, say it.* "We both have jagged edges, but our edges fit together."

"Like a weird and wonderful jigsaw puzzle." He buried his fingers in her hair and drew her down to him. Then he covered her mouth with his.

It was a long, drugging kiss filled with discovery. She loved the way his lips moved against hers—slowly, sensually. His taste had changed. Tonight it was sweet with a touch of tentative. Why? But his scent was the same—warm, male, and distinctively his.

Gasping, she broke their kiss. She was drowning in sensation, allowing herself to sink into the magic of him. "I want to touch every inch of you." She heard his muffled laughter.

"Yes, well, measurements are changing rapidly. But have at it." He kissed a path along the side of her jaw and then whispered in her ear. "When I first reached the mortal plane, I was no more than a ravenous beast programmed to destroy. But one thing I remember—the scent of the cool breeze that night. I've never forgotten. *You* are my new memory, the one I'll never forget. You were the tipping point, and after you, I became something different."

Ivy smoothed her fingers over his pecs, rolling his male nipple between her thumb and forefinger. He moaned his appreciation. She would tell him with her mouth, her fingers, her whole body what she couldn't say now.

He'd taught her about shades of gray, and about being more than she thought she could be. Ivy circled his other nipple with her tongue and then drew it into her mouth. She flicked it with her tongue—teasing, tormenting—before nipping gently. His body shuddered beneath her.

"Let me—"

She placed her finger over his lips. "Shh. Allow *me*. You gave me all the pleasure the first time. I never got a chance to explore."

He didn't subside completely. While she licked a trail over his smoothly muscled chest and down over his stomach—she loved how his stomach clenched at the touch of her tongue—he rubbed circles on her back, each circle more urgent than the last.

When she came up for air, he speared her with a stare so hot, so erotic that she almost decided to cut her journey short, straddle him, and ride him into the sunset. Then she gathered her control, determined to finish her trip.

She bypassed her final destination for the moment to take a side trip along the inside of his muscled thigh. Ivy nibbled her way toward her goal, each taste of him tugging loose a strand of her control.

His breaths were coming in pained gasps. "You're a cruel woman. I've know kinder demons. Are you sure you're not . . . ?"

Laughter bubbled up and spilled over, relieving a little of her building tension. "No demons in my family tree, only faeries." She had to ask now. "Do your claws come out when you're . . . ?"

"Being sexually tortured by a heartless faery vixen? No, unsheathing my claws isn't instinctual. And please stop talking. I'm running low on control here." He emphasized how his control was teetering on the brink by spreading his legs and arching his back.

"Your music is, though, isn't it?"

Murmur clenched his teeth. "Doesn't matter. I gave the musicians the night off."

He bucked as she finally arrived at trip's end and celebrated by clasping his balls and squeezing gently. Thinking was growing tough, and speaking even tougher. Her heart pounded out a rhythm, and she realized that she missed the accompanying music.

She had no pity. Ivy licked a zigzag pattern up the side of his cock, then closed her lips over the head. Her magic tongue toyed with him—sucking, nipping, and licking until his guttural cry told her he was on the edge.

He wasn't the only one. She'd slipped from civilized everything into primitive grunts. With a moan, she flattened herself on top of him and felt his heat seeping into every inch of her body. She wiggled around to feel *more*. If she could only sink through his flesh and curl up inside him, life would be perfect.

With a muffled curse, Murmur's control snapped. He rolled with her until she was on the bottom, looking up at him. In a move too fast for her to follow, he was on his knees straddling her. He ran his hands over her body with fingers that shook, and when he leaned down to touch her nipple with his lips, she screamed. She freaking *screamed*.

She had only one working brain cell left. Ivy knew that because she'd counted. And since that one cell had to do the work of her entire brain because the rest of her brain was off partying somewhere south of her navel, it took a long time to think things through . . . *Instinct*. His music was instinctual. It was part of what he was. He was suppressing it now.

He lowered his head and touched her *there* with the tip of his tongue. She almost came off the bed as she whimpered her pleasure. She must've annoyed her lonely brain cell, because it was threatening to turn off the lights and head down to the party too.

Concentrate. It. Was. Hard. He'd slid his hands under her bottom and was clasping her cheeks—squeezing, squeezing. She blinked and forced one more thought out of her overworked brain cell. His music was part of him, and she missed it.

Ivy opened her mouth and said the last intelligible words she'd utter for a while. "I miss your music. Bring it with us."

And suddenly it was there—booming kettledrums, clashing cymbals, shrieking violins, and trumpeting horns. Yes!

Somewhere her brain cells were singing the melody while the rest of her warbled the chorus. A drunken chorus, because she couldn't think, couldn't talk, couldn't do anything except *feel*. And it was almost too much.

He whispered words she couldn't understand as he lifted her to meet his thrust. She was absolutely *not* whispering as he pushed into her—slowly, slowly, excruciatingly and unbearably slowly. She shouted her joy as he finally filled her, stretching every inch of her body around him.

And then he drew out. She moaned. He plunged in. She moaned louder. In, out, in, out until the friction became a chain reaction. Friction, spark, ignition, lift off!

The music was a thundering crescendo as she arched to meet his final thrust. This time she heard his cry a moment after hers, his explosion joined hers, and the musical notes hung in the air, raining down bits of melody as the spasms grew weaker and weaker until she lay exhausted.

He lay beside her and simply held her. She could feel the *thud, thud, thud* of his heart, still racing, and his rasping breaths slowly evening out and slowing. Finally, they both lay still.

It was quiet. The moment was right. "You know I meant it when I said I loved you."

He didn't move. For once his music was still. "I thought you might've said that just so I'd fight harder."

She knew her laughter sounded nervous. "Well, that too. But I do love you." She waited.

"I love you too."

The silence had color and texture. It was the quiet right before laughter, the soundless footsteps of happiness, the . . . Oh, shit, she was crying.

He let her cry. And when she was finished, he handed her a tissue without commenting. She smiled. He was a guy. Tears tended to leave males speechless no matter what their origins.

"In case you were wondering, those were tears of joy."

"Good. I don't always understand human emotions, and tears make me nervous." He smiled as he brushed back a few strands of hair from her face. "We need to discuss things."

Uh-oh. Nothing good ever began with those words. "Why?"

"Because everything has changed now. We have to face what's coming."

No, no, no. *Please don't bring me down from this high.* She was soaring—out of the galaxy, past the Milky Way. All the way to the edge of the universe. *She* was the Big Bang. A serious discussion would send her tumbling back to earth.

"Your family."

She sighed. "Right. My family." Ivy hit earth with a dull *thud.* "I guess introducing you to Mom as my demon lover might cause a few cracks in our family structure." What could she possibly say to her always-grounded mother? How could she shield Kellen from the consequences of Mom finding out he had faery blood?

"My connection to the Underworld."

Now *that* really scared her. He didn't want to return, did he? "Your master doesn't have power over you anymore. Won't they leave you alone now?"

"Not necessarily. It's complicated."

"*How* complicated?" Lord, please let him stay with her.

He glanced away. "I had Holgarth draw up a contract. Right after the faery thing is settled, I'll return to the Underworld and try to hammer out an agreement with Naamah. If she goes for it, we'll be able to live here without fear."

"And if she doesn't agree?" Panic rode her. She took a deep breath, trying for calm, trying for confidence.

He shrugged. "I don't know."

Ivy didn't even have to think about her next words. "If you have to live in the Underworld, I'll go with you."

Murmur looked as close to shocked as she'd ever seen him. "You'd do that?"

"Believe it."

Sadness moved in his eyes before wonder replaced it.

The sadness tore at her heart. He didn't say it, and she refused to ask, but for a moment the truth had been there for her to see. She wouldn't be able to follow him.

He drew her to him. His heart was a trip-hammer, and she gloried in this proof of his feelings as her head rested against his chest.

"You're the only one who has ever loved me unconditionally." His laughter was soft, with a catch in it. "You're the only who's ever even *liked* me unconditionally. I'm not particularly likeable. I have a snarky sense of humor, and I can be a real pain in the ass. Do you think you can live with that? Forever?"

She wouldn't think about the forever part, because her forever wouldn't be forever at all. What she couldn't face, she'd put aside for later.

"Absolutely."

The silence curled around them, warm and comforting. But Ivy knew it wouldn't last, that the real world would eventually intrude.

Finally, he rolled onto his back and said the words she'd dreaded. "First, we have to survive the faeries."

18

Waiting was the hardest part. Murmur stood in the castle courtyard looking up at the midnight sky. Ivy stood beside him. He didn't want her there. They'd fought about it. He'd ordered her to stay in Kellen's room with her brother behind a warded door. That hadn't ended well. She'd said she would stand beside him to face the faery host.

He loved her, and he feared for her. But he silently promised Ivy that no faery evil would touch her tonight, even if he had to wrap the entire castle in his death music.

Sparkle joined them. Ganymede wound around her ankles. She wore her own version of battle dress—black leather pants, black leather bustier, and black knee high boots. She carried a black whip that she snapped against the side of her boot. She'd allowed her long red hair to fly free tonight.

Ganymede chuckled. *"Dominatrix Sparkle is in the house. She wanted me to wear a spiked collar. Not going to happen."*

Sparkle sniffed. "Perception is everything. I intend to project the image of a confident, sexy, powerful woman. The Sidhe appreciate presentation."

Ivy watched the sky anxiously. "When do you think they'll get here?"

"Anytime now." Sparkle shrugged. "Relax. We have lookouts on the walkway at the top of the wall. They'll warn us. Holgarth and Zane activated all the gargoyles throughout the park. They'll make the faeries think twice."

Murmur glanced behind him at the giant gargoyles guarding the great hall doors. Their eyes glowed yellow. He didn't know how much he trusted them. They hadn't given Archangel Ted much trouble. He hoped Holgarth had done a major tune-up on them since that battle.

Wind whipped through the courtyard, and high above them thin clouds scudded across a full moon. "A good night for a faery hunt." Murmur half closed his eyes, searching the part of him that *knew* things. The faeries were so close now that he could feel his music returning to him, bringing the Sluagh Sidhe with it. He only hoped everyone at the castle hadn't made a deadly mistake.

The sound of a collective indrawn breath drew Murmur's attention back to the present. He turned toward the great hall doors.

Asima stood there. Braeden stood beside her.

Murmur smiled. Asima had managed to suck all the air from the courtyard.

Ivy spoke first. "You look like a faery princess, Asima. They won't be able to resist you."

Murmur had to agree with Ivy. Asima wore a gown that practically floated in the breeze. White and beautiful, it contrasted with her long black hair and spectacular blue eyes.

"*That's Asima?*" Ganymede's voice held awe. "*Looking good, babe.*"

Murmur had forgotten that none of the others had seen Asima out of her cat form. He allowed himself to enjoy the moment.

"Asima?" Sparkle didn't try to hide her shock and disbelief.

"You look amazing tonight, Sparkle." Asima swayed toward them, every step graceful and confident.

Murmur silently cheered. Asima had taken his advice and was trying to reach out to others. He hoped Sparkle didn't shoot her down.

Sparkle blinked. "Amazing? Are you sure you're Asima?"

Asima smiled. "Of course." Her smile faded. "Do you think the faeries will like me?"

Braeden spoke up. "They'll love you." He cast a warning glance at Sparkle. "Won't they?"

Sparkle had moved closer to inventory Asima's outfit. Ganymede padded along beside her. She evidently couldn't find fault, because a reluctant smile tipped up the corners of her mouth. "That's exactly the dress I would've chosen to impress the Sidhe. They don't have adventurous taste in clothes."

Murmur didn't know if Asima would think that was an insult. He never got to hear her response because suddenly one of the lookouts shouted.

"They're coming!"

The defenders of the castle poured into the courtyard—Edge and Passion, Dacian and Cinn, Holgarth and Zane. Klepoth and Bain came out last. The two demons joined Murmur and Ivy.

Klepoth glanced around. "I have a bad feeling about this."

Murmur nodded his agreement. Everyone except Dacian had met during the day and talked defense and offense until he wanted to tell them to shut up. There was no defense against the faery host. You were either more powerful than them or you weren't. And considering their numbers, he was coming down on the side of "we're screwed."

"None of them have ever seen the faery host. I have." He clasped Ivy's hand and held on tight. He speared her with his gaze. "If things start to go south, stay with me. I'll make sure you get out of here."

"You're scaring me." She looked uncertain.

He didn't want to frighten her, but she had to understand how dangerous the faery hunt was. "You'll be safe as long as you stay with me." She would've been safer if she were in Kellen's damn room.

Through all of this, Bain said nothing. He just stared into the sky.

And then it was too late to worry.

Next to him, Klepoth whispered. "Holy hell."

The Sluagh Sidhe came.

A roiling black cloud filled the sky, darker than the night as it swept toward the castle from the west. It blocked out the moon, and as it grew closer Murmur could make out shapes and faces. Terrible and terrifying, the cloud that was no cloud drew near enough for everyone in the courtyard to realize that thousands raced through the air toward them.

"*Oh, shit.*" Zane said it for all of them.

Sidhe knights—tall, slender, with their cold faces and long, silvery hair—rode through the sky mounted on faery horses. Beside them raced their hunting hounds—huge black beasts with glowing eyes and slavering jaws. Hundreds of the fae filled the sky above the castle. And flying with them were humans, their bodies lost in the swirling cloud. But Murmur could see their faces—screaming, crying, horrified faces.

The gargoyles roared their challenge into the sky. Without warning, the gargoyles beside the great hall doors disintegrated, leaving nothing more than a pile of rock dust.

Zane glanced at Holgarth. "That can't be good. If we survive, you might consider replacing them with missiles."

It was a testament to how upset Holgarth was that he didn't even come up with a sarcastic reply.

A voice emerged from the mass of faeries converging above the castle. "We followed your music, demon. You desire something. State your wish, and then we'll dance." Pregnant pause. "Or perhaps you'll die."

Everyone in the courtyard looked at Murmur.

Bain moved closer. "Do you want me to speak?" His face had grown pale.

Murmur could only imagine what his friend felt now that he was so close to Elizabeth. Before Ivy, he wouldn't have understood. "No, they want to speak with me." Ivy squeezed his hand.

He shouted into the sky. "We propose a trade before the dance begins. You have a human named Elizabeth. We would like to trade one of ours for her."

The faery laughed. "Why would we do that? What is to stop us from keeping the one we already have and also taking the one you offer?"

Now began the game of chicken. "Ganymede, Edge, and Sparkle Stardust stand with me." Murmur knew the Sidhe would recognize the cosmic troublemakers' names and know how deadly they would be in a fight. "Two demons, a vampire, a wizard, a sorcerer, and a demigoddess also are ready to defend the castle." He didn't mention Passion because he still wasn't sure what to call her.

Braeden looked at him, and Murmur mouthed, "Not yet." The faery was one of their own, and his words might carry weight as a last resort.

"Impressive." The faery's voice sounded as though he meant it. "Show us the one you wish to trade."

"This is Asima." Murmur nodded for her to make her entrance.

Asima glided into the moonlight. She was light and air, and Murmur would have bet she was using some of her power to glamour them all. Not that she needed to. He couldn't imagine the faeries turning her down.

"We accept the trade."

"Well, hell, that was too easy. They could've at least shown a little fight." Ganymede sounded disgruntled.

Suddenly, Asima was gone, and another woman stood in her place. Young, with long dark hair that fell around her shoulders and wide brown eyes, she wore a gown from another time. She looked terrified.

Bain gave a choked cry and stumbled toward her. "Elizabeth!"

She froze. "Bain?"

He reached her and drew her into his arms. "You're safe now."

Eyes wide and staring, she jerked away from him. She covered her mouth with her hand and backed away.

Uh-oh. This didn't look good. Murmur glanced skyward. He couldn't see Asima. Braeden looked agitated. An agitated Gancanagh was not a good thing.

"What's wrong?" Bain didn't move.

"I want to go back to them." She glanced toward the faery host. "I don't belong here anymore." Tears spilled from her eyes. "I'll never belong here again." She brushed at the tears with her hand. "I have someone I care . . ." Elizabeth seemed to remember who she was speaking to—a demon with immense power and a sometimes-uncertain temper. "I'm sorry, Bain. I'm so, so sorry."

Bain's face was marked by the centuries he'd searched for her, all that he'd sacrificed for this moment. Everything he felt lived in his eyes—fury, sorrow, and in the end, no expression at all. "Go. Return to your faery lover."

Murmur really didn't want to break this to the guy in the sky. "Elizabeth doesn't wish to stay here. Take her back and return Asima. The trade is canceled."

Laughter filtered down from above. "But we are happy with the trade. We'll keep Asima."

Braeden leaped into view, his fist raised toward the faeries. "She is mine. Return her."

"Braeden?" The faery sounded shocked. "We thought all Gancanaghs were lost. Mab will want to know."

At the same moment, the sound of feline frenzy broke over everyone. It was the high scream of an angry cat interspersed with howls and growls. Along with the furious hissing and yowling came shouts of pain.

Ivy grabbed Murmur's arm. "She's returned to cat form to try to escape. We have to help her."

"I'm coming, Asima." And Braeden simply winked out.

A few seconds later, more angry shouts and the sounds of fighting echoed down to the courtyard.

"We'll have to save Asima, our beloved friend." Ganymede sounded gleeful.

"Beloved friend?" Sparkle sounded incredulous.

"Crap, we can't fight all of them." Zane just sounded horrified.

Ivy pulled Murmur's head down so he could hear her above the shouts, yowls, and other assorted sounds of chaos. "Tell them who Asima is."

Murmur nodded. He shouted at the faeries. "Hey, listen up. Asima is the messenger of Bast. The goddess is the protector of cats. I don't think you want a pissed-off lion in your lap."

Silence fell for a moment.

"Bast?"

"Right."

"You tricked us."

The faery sounded more outraged than angry. But then, not many would dare mess with the Sluagh Sidhe.

"We'll consider your request."

It was said with such venom that Murmur knew there would be payback, not something he wanted to dwell on.

"No." Ivy's voice was filled with horror.

It took a moment for Murmur to realize Ivy wasn't commenting on his negotiation with the faery. He turned to follow her gaze. "Great. Just freaking great."

Kellen had almost reached them. His expression said he knew he was in deep shit, but he didn't care.

Ivy pulled away from Murmur and grabbed Kellen's arms. "What do you think you're doing? It's dangerous out here. Go back to your room. Now." Her voice shook with fear for her brother.

His expression turned stubborn. "No. I deserve to be here. I can help."

Murmur didn't need one more thing to complicate his really crappy night, but he got it anyway.

Thousands of voices rose from the faery host. Shocked, everyone in the courtyard stared into the sky.

"She comes, she comes!" The cries rose, voices filled with fear, awe, wonder.

"Who the hell is coming?" Dacian looked as though he wanted to rip someone's throat out.

Murmur couldn't blame him. "I only know one person who'd cause that reaction." He closed his eyes, took a deep, calming breath, and opened them again. "Mab."

The faery leader's voice announced what Murmur had already guessed.

"Mab—Queen of Air and Darkness, the Winter Queen, and Queen of the Unseelie Court honors us with her presence. Kneel."

Murmur glanced around the courtyard. Nope, no one was kneeling. Way to tick off the queen. Of course, he wasn't kneeling either.

He was too busy trying to shove Kellen back into the castle where Mab couldn't see him.

"Stop, demon."

Too late. Mab stood on the walkway at the top of the wall. And even though Murmur had seen her once, thousands of years ago, the sight of her still weakened him.

The queen of the Unseelie Court was icy beauty so perfect that one look told you she was not of earth. Large eyes as dark as the coldest winter night; full, red lips that would smile even as she killed; and hair so black that Murmur almost suspected she'd absorbed the darkness around her.

Her dress was made of icy ripples that sparkled and gleamed. And even as he stared, ice crept over the castle. Icicles hung from ledges and roof, sheets of ice spread across the courtyard, and ice wrapped everything not flesh and blood in a shimmering cocoon.

Murmur shivered. He grabbed Ivy's hand and held it tightly. She still had her hand on Kellen's arm. He leaned close. "No matter what you do, don't touch her. Let me protect Kellen." Mab could deal out instant death too quickly for him to save Ivy. Too quickly for him to save himself either, but he wouldn't pass that info on to her.

Mab's gaze focused on Kellen. Emotion touched her eyes. Murmur doubted that happened very often. She floated effortlessly down to the courtyard.

"Come here, child." She beckoned.

Kellen didn't react to being called a child. He moved away from Ivy's hand and started toward Mab.

"No." Ivy reached for him.

Murmur grabbed her, pulled her back, and whispered his warning: "You can't fight Mab. She'll destroy you, and then what good will you be to Kellen? She won't hurt him, and we'll find a way to stop her."

He felt Ivy shudder. She clenched her hands into fists, and Murmur knew she was only a heartbeat away from ignoring what he'd said and racing after her brother. He wrapped his arm around her waist and hung on.

Kellen stood in front of Mab, and only a fool wouldn't see the resemblance. She reached out and touched his cheek. Murmur could see the tiny ice crystal that remained there.

"Tirron told me of you, but I couldn't believe him. I had to see for myself." Her expression softened. "You look exactly like my son. You'll return with me to Faery and take your rightful place as a faery prince. You'll learn about your true heritage and soon forget your life here."

Murmur clamped his hand over Ivy's mouth to stop her shout. She bit him. He grimaced but didn't take his hand away.

"I'm afraid that neither of you will be returning to Faery, my queen. Oh, wait, you are no longer my queen."

Murmur knew that voice. With a growl, he released Ivy and swung to confront the new threat. Tirron stood behind him. But that's not what had caught Murmur's immediate attention. From the east, across the Gulf, swept an army of faeries. They weren't dressed as knights, and along with them came what looked like hundreds of the darkest fae dredged from the depths of the faery realm. Murmur stepped from between Mab and Tirron. He dragged Ivy with him.

"You would rebel against *me*? You would attempt to overthrow *me*?" With every word, the night grew darker, colder. Snow began to fall.

Tirron's laughter had a hysterical note to it. "I first planned to create a war between the Sluagh Sidhe and those in this castle. I knew it would draw you from Faery, here to the mortal plane, where you would be most vulnerable. That did not go as planned. But as soon as I saw the boy, I knew I could use him. You would leave Faery to see the one who wore your son's face. That sentimental mistake means someone else will rule the Unseelie Court by morning."

Defining moments don't come often, but Ivy recognized one when it slapped her in the face. She was at exactly the right angle to see what Tirron held cupped in his hand. She didn't have to know what it was to understand it was meant to kill Mab. For a split second, Mab's gaze touched Kellen, her arm outstretched to push him from harm's way. Everyone else's attention was on the queen, waiting to see what she'd do.

Tirron raised his hand.

There was no time for questions—Whose survival would keep those she loved safe? Which one was a lesser evil? Did she want to be responsible for someone's death?

No thinking time, only reaction time.

"Watch out!" Even as she shouted, she flung her puny puff of faery power at Tirron. As it had before, it did little more than knock him down.

He never got up.

Mab took in the situation at a glance. She smiled. She didn't even raise her hand, but between one moment and the next, she encased Tirron in ice. His horrified expression was frozen forever behind his ice wall. "Foolish one. You were not the first to challenge me. I'll simply add you to the ice sculptures in my garden. You'll fit right in among all the others who thought to overthrow me."

Then Mab stared at Ivy.

Ivy knew she looked stricken. Tirron had terrified her, and she'd wanted him gone from her life, but violent death still sickened her. Especially when she was directly responsible for said death.

Mab spoke. "I owe you a life-debt." The queen frowned as she stared more closely at Ivy. "You also bear my son's blood."

"Kellen is my brother." A life-debt? Hope flickered in Ivy. The queen owed her a favor.

There was no more time for conversation. Tirron's ragtag group of rebels had to know their leader was dead and that their only hope for survival lay in completing Tirron's bungled job. They swept from the sky in a rush of frigid air and rage-filled cries.

Mab held out her arms and spread her fingers. Crystal shards of ice formed at the end of each one. "Attack!" And her knights streamed down from above. The snow fell harder, faster until it became a blizzard.

Murmur shouted above the sounds of battle. "Faery war! Everyone into the castle." He looked at Ivy. "I'm going after Kellen. Stay safe."

Without giving Ivy a chance to say that she wanted to go with him, Murmur pointed her toward a door she could no longer see through the driving snow, and then disappeared into the white wall of the blizzard. Damn, she was turned around. Panicked, she stood still trying to get her bearings.

Sparkle appeared beside her. She held a grumbling Ganymede in her arms. "It's colder than the devil's tits out here. Let's get inside."

"Fighting all around me, and I can't do anything. I want to tear something apart, knock something down, blow something up."

"I'm sure you do, sweetie." Sparkle patted his head. "I'll get you all comfy inside with a big bowl of ice cream and the remote. You can watch a violent, gory movie."

The cat's hiss told Ivy what he thought of Sparkle's idea.

Ivy peered into the driven snow. "I can't go in. Murmur's out there searching for Kellen." She wrapped her arms around her body and tried to stop shivering.

Sparkle grabbed her arm and pulled. "Then there's nothing to worry about. Murmur will bring him back."

Before any of them could move, about a dozen of Mab's knights stumbled into view. They held a large sack made of some kind of faery cloth. Screams of feline rage came from inside the bag. And from the way the sack was bouncing and heaving, Ivy understood why it took all of them to hang on to it.

"You belong to us now, little bitch. You'll fly with the Sluagh Sidhe until we say you can leave." The knight spoke through gritted teeth. Livid scratches covered his face and hands.

Ivy gasped. "They have Asima. We have to help."

Sparkle looked puzzled. "Why would we want to do that?"

"She's our friend." Ivy took a look at Sparkle's expression. "Okay, so she's my friend. *Do something.*"

Sparkle glanced around as though she might spot someone else who'd ride to Asima's rescue. She stared down at Ganymede.

He glared up at her. *"Forget it. I'm depressed. I don't do good deeds when I'm depressed. Besides, those faeries look a bloody mess. Asima's winning the fight. I bet they're afraid to let her out of the bag."* He closed his eyes.

Then Sparkle looked back at Ivy. She heaved a huge exaggerated sigh. "I can't believe I'm agreeing to this." She moved closer to the faeries. "You only desire one thing"—Sparkle glanced around—"to get naked and seduce that tree." She pointed to a small tree barely visible through the driving snow. "Oh, and you might want to lose the cat. The tree is a jealous lover."

Without even blinking, the faeries dropped the sack and ripped off their clothes. Asima crawled from the bag and launched herself at Ivy. She put up her hands just in time to catch the cat.

"I'd love to stick around and watch." Sparkle seemed serious. "But I'm freezing."

Ivy's final view of the faeries was of them naked and pushing each other aside for a chance to stroke the tree. Nope, didn't want to see any more. She stumbled after Sparkle with Asima in her arms. "Will they stop?"

Sparkle shrugged. "When I release them." She leaned into the wind as she stumbled toward the door. "Which will be right about now. It's too freaking cold to concentrate."

Once inside the great hall, Ivy set Asima on the floor. They were both still shivering. Ivy ran back to the door. "I have to find Murmur and Kellen."

"*Where is Braeden? He was trying to protect me. I think the faeries might have hurt him.*" Asima's cry sounded strangely like a human baby.

Ganymede leaped from Sparkle's arms. "*Hell, can't anyone get a quiet moment around here? If I can't kill something, then I want a nap.*"

Ivy crouched in front of Ganymede. "Please. Find them."

Ganymede offered her his I'm-a-cat-so-I-don't-care stare.

Ivy resorted to a weapon she rarely used. She allowed a few tears to slide down her cheek. *Not* fake tears.

"*Oh, jeez, don't do that.*" With a few colorful words of protest, he padded back out into the snow.

Everyone milled aimlessly around the great hall, listening to the battle going on outside, watching the wind-whipped snow through the few windows and waiting.

Ivy and Asima were just about ready to brave the faeries and the snow when the door was flung open. Murmur and Kellen staggered in, supporting Braeden between them. Ganymede padded behind them. The cat looked a lot perkier.

"*I got to lay a beat-down on some fae creatures. Think they belonged to Tirron. Don't know what they were, but now they're dead. I feel all energized.*"

Murmur and Kellen laid Braeden on the floor. Asima curled up beside him and made soft mewling noises.

"Will he be okay?" Ivy wanted to wrap her arms around Murmur and never let go again. Gradually, she stopped shaking.

Murmur nodded. He watched as Dacian and Zane picked Braeden

up and carried him toward his room. Asima padded beside them. He bit his lip in a seemingly vain attempt not to smile. "Braeden is suffering from exhaustion more than anything else. When we got to him, he'd collected his own army of devoted fans. He'd touched as many of Mab's faeries as he could. You can guess what happened."

Everyone stared at Murmur. "Hey, I'm not knocking it. We each use the weapons given us." He moved to where Ivy stood.

Ignoring his wet clothes, Ivy reached up and tangled her fingers in his hair. She drew his head down and covered his cold lips with hers. She deepened the kiss, warming him in her unique way. Then she buried her head against his chest. They stood that way for a few minutes. She sighed and looked at Kellen. "Are you okay?"

Kellen nodded. He glanced at Klepoth. "When Mab killed Tirron and everything exploded, Klepoth got me away from Mab. Then we got separated. Murmur found me. We stumbled across Braeden on the way back." He stared at Ganymede. "Then the cat showed up. He was all happy because he'd killed some faeries." Kellen's expression said that he didn't know how he felt about Ganymede's glee.

Only when Kellen stopped talking did Ivy realize that the sounds of battle had ended. She glanced at Murmur. He stepped to the door and opened it carefully. Ivy peered past him. Outside, the night was once again clear. Faery bodies littered the courtyard. And in the middle of the carnage, Mab stood.

"Bring the boy to me." It wasn't a request.

"No." Ivy's response was automatic. She reached for her brother.

"I have to go, Sis." Kellen moved away from her grasp and tried to squeeze past her into the courtyard.

Murmur turned to watch them.

"Don't go out there, Kellen. She'll try to take you to Faery." Desperation pounded at Ivy.

Murmur met her gaze. "Do you want me to stop him?"

Kellen glared at him. "This is my decision to make. Stopping me now won't change anything in the end. It might just mean some of you will die. Mab won't give up on me."

Murmur raked his fingers through his hair. "Damn, why isn't anything ever simple?" He cast her an apologetic glance. "He's right, Ivy. You can't run from Mab forever. Let Kellen talk to her. I'll go with him."

Panic and fear lived in Ivy. What could she do? She didn't have the power to keep him safe. Finally, she nodded. But when Kellen and Murmur walked out into the courtyard, Ivy went with them.

She tried not to look at the blood, the bodies, the body parts. Ivy avoided looking at faces, expressions frozen in horror as they died. She tried not to throw up when she passed the ice sculpture that was now Tirron.

They stopped in front of Mab. She gave them a tight smile. "Is this a one-night sale? Do I get three for the price of one? I want only Kellen at this time." She looked at Ivy. "I might wish to speak to you and the rest of your family at another time."

The thought of the Queen of Air and Darkness descending on her family terrified Ivy. But never let it be said that she was wise in her choice of battles. "You can't have Kellen."

Mab raised one brow, as though the idea that someone would speak to her without an invitation amazed her. "Of course I can." She seemed to mull the situation for a moment. "I realize that he is your brother, so I'll allow you to visit him in Faery."

How kind of you. "Kellen should have some say in this. It's his life." *Please, please make the right decision, baby brother.*

"I don't want to live in Faery." Kellen's eyes were clear and fearless.

Ivy had never been prouder of her brother.

Mab frowned. "Why ever not?" She looked sincerely puzzled.

"My family is here, my friends, my home." He hurried on as he saw Mab's expression darken. "This is all I've ever known. But I'd like to get to know you. I'd like to visit Faery, maybe during summer vacation." He looked at Ivy for support.

"Impossible. You belong with your kind." Mab reached for him.

Kellen stepped back and suddenly a wall of ice rose between him and the queen. "No."

Ivy hissed at him. "Where did you learn that?"

He never took his gaze from Mab. "I wasn't messing around all those times I was with Klepoth. He was teaching me to use my power."

Shock filled Mab's eyes, followed closely by satisfaction. "My son would have been proud of his descendent."

Ivy decided now was the best time to intervene, before the confrontation escalated and Mab remembered her anger. "Queen Mab, you said that you owed me a life-debt. I'd like to collect now."

Surprised, Mab turned to stare at her. "What?"

"I want you to allow Kellen to live his life here and visit you during his summer vacation, if that's what he chooses to do. This is what I ask for saving your life." She glanced at Murmur. Would Mab make her into a matching ice sculpture with Tirron?

But Murmur was smiling, his eyes filled with pride. For *her*. Ivy returned his smile. And she hoped he saw the "I love you" in it.

Mab narrowed her eyes and tried to glare Ivy into submission. Ivy ignored her glare.

Finally, the queen nodded. "So be it." She turned to Murmur. "My knights tell me that you owe them a dance, demon."

Murmur bowed. "Of course." He nodded at Kellen.

And Ivy watched her brother link arms with the Winter Queen and lead her into the Castle of Dark Dreams.

The faeries danced away the rest of the night—some in the great hall, some in the courtyard; some chose to dance in the air. Before the dancing began, all the faery bodies disappeared, including Mab's newest ice sculpture. The ice melted from the castle and ground.

Before the Sluagh Sidhe disappeared at dawn, Mab used her vast power to ensure that none of the humans on Galveston Island would remember anything strange. Personally, Ivy wouldn't have minded if she never saw the faery host again.

And while Murmur created music for the faery host, Ivy waited in her room. Kellen was long asleep, exhausted. She had no one to talk to. Only time to think. She knew what Murmur would do when he finished with the faeries. He would leave. She closed her eyes against the pain of knowing that. It seemed that her future rested in the scary hands of Naamah.

The sun was rising over the Gulf when he came to her. He kissed her, drew her into his arms, promised to come back to her, and left.

She waited through the day and into the night, staring at nothing, seeing only her memories. And wondered how she would survive if he never returned.

Ivy showered and changed into her nightgown. She climbed into bed, pulled the covers up, and prepared to act as though she'd actually be able to sleep. She looked at the clock. Midnight.

Then she heard the *snick* of the lock, and the door swung open. She lay frozen, her eyes fixed on the doorway and the man who filled it.

Murmur smiled at her as he strode into the room.

She started to leap from the bed, but he motioned her back into it. "You're exactly where I want you to be."

Tears streamed down her face, and she didn't give a damn if he saw them. She swiped at them as he quickly undressed and climbed in beside her. He wrapped his arms around her.

"Naamah accepted Holgarth's contract. She gets to use the Master's territory and legions along with the legions belonging to Klepoth and me as long as she protects our safety on the mortal plane. No one from the Underworld will ever bother us, because she's now one of the most powerful arch demons there."

"Can she be trusted?" It was almost too good to be true.

"Naamah is greedy, and contracts are binding to a demon. She'll keep her end of the agreement."

"And now?" She felt breathless. He had always done this to her.

"Now we can make love forever." He stripped off her nightgown and ran his fingers the length of her body.

And if forever wasn't really forever, Ivy didn't care. She'd settle for right now.

She turned off the light.

Epilogue

What a difference two weeks had made. Ivy held Murmur's hand as they headed toward the lobby doors. She needed a walk on the beach to get away from her family. She loved them, but she wanted time alone with the man she loved.

Sparkle intercepted them just outside the doors. Asima padded along beside her. When Asima wandered off for a moment to check out a new guest arriving at the hotel, Sparkle watched her go. She sighed. "I saved her from the faeries, ergo we're best friends forever. Just kill me now." But she didn't look totally unhappy with her new friend. "We have made a little progress, though. She took me with her to shop for new clothes." Sparkle's smile was filled with sly triumph.

But her smile faded when she finally looked back at them. "Bain disappeared right after the Sluagh Sidhe left. I can assume he isn't coming back."

Ivy watched sadness fill Murmur's eyes.

"I wish he'd talked to me. Maybe I could've helped him." He

rubbed a spot between his eyes. "His search for Elizabeth was his reason for existing."

"Maybe he returned to the Underworld." Ivy wished she could do something.

He shrugged. "I don't have a clue. I just hope he'll get in touch with me someday."

"As much as I regret his leaving, we need someone to take his place." Sparkle watched Murmur like a spider ready to pounce on a particularly tasty bug.

Murmur raised one brow. "And?"

"Ganymede and I think you'd be perfect. You're smart enough to step right into a managerial spot with Dacian and Edge. And as an added bonus, we get someone who can supply music once in a while. I mean, if that's what you'd like to do." She quickly turned to Ivy. "And of course, you'd still be my assistant. Kellen could keep the room he has now and stay at the same school. I think Klepoth wants to join the staff, so he wouldn't be losing a friend."

Murmur glanced at Ivy.

Relief flooded her. They could stay here. She knew her smile stretched from ear to ear. "Perfect. I get to trade snark with Holgarth every day. I'd miss that if we had to move."

He looked at Sparkle. "I'd say that's a yes."

Sparkle nodded her satisfaction and clicked away on her mile-high stilettos. Asima fell into step beside her.

They continued down to the darkened beach.

"How're things going with your family?" He squeezed her hand.

"Dad is more relaxed than I've ever seen him, and Mom . . . Mom is amazing." Ivy would never have believed her mother's reaction to proof that the whole paranormal world really did exist. "You know what she told me? She said that staying grounded means that when the ground shifts beneath your feet, you simply keep your balance and adapt."

"Your mother is a wise woman." He stopped walking.

"What?"

"Do you recognize where we are?"

She looked around. Suddenly, she knew. "This is where we danced on the night I met you."

He smiled at her. "And now we're back with 'forever together' in front of us."

Ivy tried to push aside the stab of pain she felt every time he mentioned "forever." She glanced away, watching the Gulf. The water was calm, just as it had been that first night.

He put his fingers under her chin and turned her face until she met his gaze. "We *can* have forever, Ivy."

She knew her laugh sounded false. "No, I refuse to ask Dacian to bite me. Fangs aren't my fashion statement of choice."

He merely smiled. "Dance with me."

Ivy gazed up at him. He was as he'd been then. His shining blond hair still fell in a smooth curtain down his back. And his thick lashes still framed the most beautiful eyes she'd ever seen. But he was no longer a tall, elegant stranger.

She moved into his arms, and they danced. Nothing had changed. Dancing with him still felt like floating. Once again, she kicked off her shoes. The water sparkled, and stars filled the skies. And Ivy felt young again as the music lifted and carried her, a magical melody that would always play in her heart. She threw back her head and laughed as her hair swung in the soft breeze.

He leaned close to whisper in her ear. "Demons have powers connected to their special talent."

"Fascinating." She smiled up at him.

"And one of my demonic talents is gifting immortality in my own special way."

She simply stared at him, for the moment robbed of her ability to talk.

"You will never grow old if you dance with me each day." His breath moved warm against her ear.

Happiness flooded her and spilled over in stupid tears. "Really?"

"Really."

"Then I guess I'll have to dance with you for the next thousand years."

"It sounds like a plan."

Laughing, they danced on the dark beach. And for Ivy, as it would always be, only the man and the music mattered.